QUANTUM WHISPERS

Book One of the Quantum Ascension Series

ALEX M BRANDT

Copyright © 2020 by Alex M Brandt

All rights reserved.

No part of this book may be reproduced in any form or by any electronic or mechanical means, including information storage and retrieval systems, without written permission from the author, except for the use of brief quotations in a book review.

1 2 3 4 5

CREDITS

Cover Design
by Deranged Doctor

Additional Cover Graphics
by Graham Hawkins
(most notably Kay's face)

For more information about my vision
of the Quantum Ascension Universe,
visit: www.alexmbrandt.com

PROLOGUE

Perfectly black against the infinite blackness of space, the dark machine hurtled towards the light on a hyperbolic trajectory, rapidly approaching the surface of the central star of the system it had entered only days ago. Its jagged surface reflected no light. Not a single photon escaped the nanotubes coating its hull. Unseen, yet not unseeing, it drank in vast amounts of data from sensors with their unblinking gaze fixed upon the single inhabited planet.

Puuurpakak's bulbous head bobbed above the gathering crowd of admirers. Her long segmented throat was suffused with a yellow-orange flush as she basked in the praise of her colleagues. The presentation had been the greatest triumph of her long and illustrious career. The audience chirped their approval, rasping their inner legs against the ribbed plates of their chitinous bodies. Modestly, she acknowledged the longest standing ovation at any conference she could remember. Many others had contributed, but it was her genius—and hers alone

—which had transformed the basic quantum gravitational theory into a practical engineering reality. Only the Thaaarkuprak Prize for Physics could give her greater satisfaction. Surely the letter would arrive soon. Puuurpakak was gratified to see the flashing coloration of the underside of her colleagues' throat segments, displaying a mixture of envy and admiration.

"Professor, I was most intrigued by your presentation," chittered Seeetkukak, her glistening head bobbing and her jagged mouth parts grinding together in excitement. Her throat segments were turning from pink and gray to shades of a more serious green as she concentrated on formulating her question. "May I say how impressed I am with the enormous progress you have made over the past few years. This revolutionary new technology for unlimited energy production will transform not just our planet's economy, but Thotrak society itself."

"You are most kind, Doctor Seeetkukak," replied Puuurpakak. She tried but failed to force her throat coloration to display a suitably blue shade of modesty, managing only the merest tinge.

Seeetkukak continued with her line of thought, curiosity with a hint of eagerness seeping into her throat segments. "Your technique to break through into the infinite number of parallel universes all around us, to utilize the difference in quantum energy potential, has a most interesting side effect. The massive quantum energy shock released generates powerful and distinctive gravity wave signals. These waves spread at light speed across the galaxy. It is a trivial task for our equipment at the Gravity Wave Observatory to detect such unique signals. As it happens, I'm planning to mention it during my presentation in the next session."

"Well, yes, that is only to be expected, and quite in line with quantum gravity theory, Doctor. Do you think this might be a problem?" Puuurpakak replied, a tiny flush of puzzlement showing in her throat.

"Oh no, Professor, not at all," she said chittering apologetically. "It's just— well, you explained the steps you took from the basic quantum gravity theory to a practical system for the production of limitless energy so clearly. I realized it was almost inevitable that any advanced civilization would eventually take the same steps. My team and I have spent many decades working on gravity wave detection, yet no such signal has ever been observed. Does this mean we are alone in the galaxy? Or at least that we are the only intelligent species to have developed this technology?"

"Ah, now I see where you are going with this," said Puuurpakak, emitting a loud click from her side plates for emphasis. "The Kreeekpukak Paradox. If there are other intelligent creatures inhabiting the stars—where are they all? Why have we not yet spotted them? I'm afraid I don't have an answer for you, Doctor. That's not my area of expertise. But I agree with you, it is an interesting question. I regret we won't have time to explore it any further right now, as I believe your own presentation is about to start. I'm looking forward to hearing you speak. Shall we walk through into the conference hall?"

Dwarfed by the enormous bulk of the sun, the dark machine now skimmed the turbulent outer atmosphere. And although still hard to see, it was no longer dark. The sunward side of its hull now gleamed a perfectly reflective silver. Its opposite surface was now incandescent as the machine shed unwanted heat, yet even this remained hidden in the overwhelming brilliance of the sun. The silver underside of the machine first rippled, then bulged with an unnatural pregnancy, before giving birth to a silver sphere which dropped away to enter a lower orbit within the sun's photosphere.

Within seconds, the surface of the sphere began to tarnish and swirl. Now it was growing and changing shape, dimples appearing on opposite sides of the distorted sphere as it expanded into a larger and flatter annulus. The object continued to grow rapidly, the hole forming in the center of the annulus growing faster still, until it formed a perfect ring. Now glowing even more brightly than the plasma surrounding it, an incandescent maelstrom formed in the center of the ring as its gaping maw sucked in massive quantities of the sun's substance.

Still growing, the now monstrous ring plunged ever deeper into the lower layers of the photosphere. Vast solar prominences erupted into space as the chaotic whirlpool of brilliant plasma streams trailing in its wake blasted turbulent braids of star-stuff back towards the sun's tortured surface.

The remaining conference attendees ambled towards their seats in the auditorium. A high glass wall formed one side of the large hall, offering a panoramic view of the luxurious beach resort and the glinting sea beyond. The conference was always held in the off-season to reduce costs, but the weather was unseasonably warm and several less-motivated individuals had skipped the afternoon session, preferring to soak up the bright sunshine and wallow in the shallow lagoon.

"I'd like to welcome you all to our afternoon session. Our first presentation this afternoon is by Doctor Seeetkukak, who will talk about the latest exciting discoveries using the upgraded instruments at the new International Gravity Wave Observatory. Can we now please darken the windows and dim the lighting? Thank you."

"Good afternoon, ladies and dear colleagues. My first image shows one of several spectacular cosmic phenomena which we can only detect through the gravity waves emitted—"

The presentation was interrupted by a strident alarm call. One of the attendees, her long throat erect and flashing purple with fear, was leaning right up against the darkened windows and gesticulating towards the sky. "The sun! The sun! Look at the sun!"

The photochromic glass was dark enough to exclude most of the light, its enhanced contrast displaying the erupting sun in all its terrible glory. Scrambling from their seats to crowd up against the darkened glass, the audience watched in growing horror as a tangle of fiery plumes and twisted streamers erupted from the distorted disk of the sun. Inexorably, the entire body of the sun was being sucked into a fiery vortex, an intense blue-white jewel glowing in the center of the disturbance.

The dark machine sped off into deep space, leaving behind little more than the dim glow of its infernal handiwork. It continued to absorb data from its sensors as it monitored the fiery death of the inner planets of the system. The massive gamma and X-radiation flux caused by charged plasma streams interacting with the star's collapsing magnetic field swiftly annihilated all life on the inhabited planet. Vast streams of super-heated matter and charged particles emitted by the tortured sun scorched the inner planets in a fiery rain. Their surfaces glowed red despite the intense sunlight.

Within days, the sun had disappeared, consumed by the demonic egg hatched in its heart by the dark machine. There were no witnesses to its extinction, no creatures left alive to see its end. The third planet, which was yet to complete its fifth rotation, had become a hellish ball of churning magma pools, scoured of all atmosphere, all water, all life. No longer orbiting its vanished sun, it began a lonely journey into the frozen darkness between the distant stars. Only the fading glow of a blasted landscape illuminated the dusty sepulcher of a race of beings not even forgotten—for no one would know they had ever existed.

EARTH

*"This is the way the world ends,
not with a bang, but a whimper"*

T S Eliot

CHAPTER ONE

"It's a teddy bear, a goddamned teddy bear," Ben exclaimed. The teddy bear simply sat there, oblivious to his close examination. Ben looked around carefully. He scrutinized every detail of the grassy slope right down to the edge of the lake where the snow-capped mountains were reflected in the mirror-calm water. In the opposite direction, to the north, loomed the fortified bulk of New Geneva Citadel. He turned his attention back to the area around the teddy bear. Zooming in closer, he saw the butterflies dancing around the wild flowers nearby. No sign of disturbance—but he didn't expect to see much on the visual feed.

"Why don't we just blast it? We know something's there," said Steve Kennedy with a snort of impatience.

"Well, yes, Kennedy, we could just blast it, but that's not going to tell us much," Ben retorted. "First, I'd like to find out why it's there, less than a klick from the previous incident this morning. It seems far too obvious."

"Well, last time it was a child's tricycle," responded Kennedy, "and we lost six kids. So I'm betting it's hostile, sir."

"Maybe some kid dropped a teddy bear?" Maria Sanchez suggested.

"Yeah, right," sneered Kennedy. "So, you volunteering to get out there, Maria? Walk over and pick it up? I'd really like to see that —you'd be the star of the show. Your fifteen seconds of fame on U-Global News, being ripped apart by a couple of monster warmechs, blood dripping from their claws, you screaming your head off. Oh wait a minute, would you even have time to scream? OK, no problem. We'll dub that onto the feed later. Look, there must be at least a dozen U-Drones out there already, waiting to catch your every move . . ."

Kennedy's monologue trailed off as he registered that Ben had gone very quiet. He couldn't see Ben's eyes inside the VR helmet, but could see that his fists were clenched as he sat unmoving in front of his console. Oops. On reflection, that wasn't the best set of images to bring up considering what he'd heard of the man's history. "So, um, what do you reckon, sir? What are they up to . . ."

Ben removed his helmet and disconnected the cables from the command chair, replacing it with his personal head-mounted U-Set. He turned to face Kennedy, fixing him with a cold stare. "You need to stop playing the fool and get on with following standard protocol, Probationary Field Agent Kennedy," he snapped, with particular emphasis on the word 'Probationary'. "I want a recon drone over the area in the next five minutes, with a full stealth suite active, visual plus IR scan, for 250 meters around the target. Complete sweep, but no lower than 500 meters. Run a check on the Harpies we have loaded. Next get the Badgers prepped, tethers hooked up and ready to go in the next ten minutes."

He stood up from the command console of the Incident Response Vehicle and leaned over to Sanchez. "Push the exclusion zone back two klicks and tell me when the people in the enlarged zone have completed their evacuation."

"Yes sir," she confirmed, turning away to call up the Command Center on her headset.

"Oh, and one more thing, Kennedy," Ben said, turning to glare at him again. "You'd better make sure that the Badgers' IFF spoofing package has all the latest updates, because I might want to tie your probationary ass to the tether. Any problems and you'll be the big new star on every U-Net channel. Do I make myself clear?" Kennedy's face flushed. He looked down at his console, already inputting the commands to load the updating routine. "Yes sir. Sorry sir."

Ben gave Kennedy a terse nod. "Tell me when we're all in position. In the meantime, I need a coffee. I'll be up front. Keep me updated on any developments."

He clambered forward to the IRV's little galley and poured out the last of the coffee. He should have started another brew, but he wasn't feeling very charitable right now. Kennedy was new to the crew, and straight out of training school, so it was no surprise he was nervous. His unthinking chatter was probably his way of coping with the tension of a hot mission. But one distraction too many and they might be dead, so he didn't feel in the mood to cut him any slack. Kennedy would have to toughen up fast and focus on the job like the rest of the crew, or move on to other career opportunities. Robo-monkey, for example.

Was that what he'd been like that when he first joined the Department of Global Security? Must be over four years now with DGS, he realized, clanking around in giant tin cans, chasing warmechs. Even managed to kill a few. Not the career path he had mapped out for himself when he left college, but beggars can't be choosers. That's what you get for defying one of the Families, he reflected grimly.

He scanned the surrounding area using the video feed to his U-Set. Still nothing going on, except for a big SkyShip approaching the citadel from the south. The bulbous form floated high above the lake, its many curved surfaces gleaming in the sunlight. That's how he'd arrived at New Geneva — full of hopes and dreams, enchanted by the panoramic view of the soaring spires and towers of the massive armored citadel set amidst the snow-capped mountains.

It could have been worse. He might have ended up as a robo-monkey himself. There was always plenty of work if you didn't mind spending every day using a remote link to shuffle a bunch of robots around from job to job. The most boring job imaginable, and the worst paid. Simultaneously pointless and vital, its only object was to keep robots under direct human control. The robots everyone was so scared of but can't do without. At least he had job satisfaction. He got to kill more of the psychotic AI monsters before they killed any more people, which was a bonus.

How many people had the warmechs killed over the years—centuries, in fact—since they turned on their human masters? The slaughter of his own family had been no more than an insignificant statistic alongside the billions who had died before them. Ben shivered at the thought. Humanity used to number in the billions. Now there were less than 25 million people left on Earth, besieged by the warmechs in the few surviving citadels scattered across the planet.

He took a swig of the stale coffee to soften the lump in his throat, then crawled forwards and eased himself into one of the crew seats in the driver's compartment. The air was fresher here, away from the pungent smell of stale bodies and hot electric motors in the command compartment.

"How's it going back there?" queried Frank Peto, without shifting his gaze from the holoscreens displaying the surrounding ground and airspace. One screen showed the steady approach of the SkyShip to the landing pad projecting out above the massive wall surrounding the citadel. Another few hundred tons safely delivered to feed the hungry mouths.

"Nothing happening so far. I'm taking a break before Showtime," Ben replied, his flat tone discouraging further conversation.

He leaned back, closed his eyes and let out a long sigh. He hadn't felt so unsettled for a long time. Kennedy's unthinking joke had dug up old memories. Memories he had told himself he'd dealt with years ago. This was not what he needed right now. Not when he was expected to deliver yet another performance as the world's greatest warmech killer, with every U-Net VREx zombie on the planet watching over his shoulder.

The first attack had targeted a bunch of kids who should never have been outside the citadel. A gang of young sewer rats, he guessed, out to trap some local rabbits. Imagine that. So desperate for food they'd actually eat animals! His face screwed up at the thought. Yet the regular rations were pretty meagre and unappetizing, so most people supplemented the basic diet with more attractive fare. At least half of the advertising on the U-Global channels was designed to promote the sale of some branded delicacy or other, but that cost money, and if you were at the bottom of the pile, you didn't have the choice.

Now they'd been warned of a second attack this was shaping up to be a special performance. The whole planetary U-Net was watching, alerted by the news of the first attack. Ben would have a swarm of U-Drones following his every move as he operated a remote-controlled Badger, sending the underground guided missile digging down after the warmechs. If he was lucky, he'd find one of the big ones – a 25-meter monster of articulated metal and deadly nanotech. But they only came out if there was a major attack, and Ben's instincts told him that something else was going on. If only he could figure out what.

There was another concern, and it nagged at the back of his mind. Why two incidents so close together? That was unheard of. The warmechs would make a raid, kill anyone in easy reach, then clear off back down their tunnel network. It was the job of the Incident Response teams to chase them back to their nest with the Badgers, though, more often than not, they'd be long gone before they were deployed. Never before had the warmechs attacked the same area twice in succession. This whole scenario seemed such a crazy setup, with several DGS Incident Response Vehicles already sweeping their assigned sectors around the New Geneva Citadel. The second lure with the teddy bear—how was that supposed to work? Following the first incident there wasn't a kid within 10 klicks.

Well, at least it would give the VREx zombies a thrill—and Ben too, if this would give him a shot at taking down a few more warmechs. By this evening, they'd be able to relive every moment of his search and kill operation driving the latest model Badger in full glorious 5D Super-Reality on their poxy little U-VREx sets. Or, as Kennedy had so sensitively suggested, they could relive the last agonizing moments of Maria Sanchez's life as the warmechs pulled her apart. Fortunately, the Badger was operated remotely over a data-link tether, so that outcome wasn't too likely. He hadn't realized when he first joined DGS just how much of their resources they put into producing top selling VRExperiences.

Perhaps I should get an agent and ask for a percentage, he mused.

Kennedy's voice sounded through his U-Set. "We have the results from the scan, sir."

"OK. I'll be right there."

"Report," Ben ordered as he walked back into the control cabin.

"IR scan kinda weird, sir," responded Kennedy. "There's a big thermal bloom right under our furry little friend. I'd say at least three targets close to the surface—"

"Thanks. I'll take a look on my data feed," he said, cutting Kennedy short. "Where are we with the evacuation?"

"Another ten minutes to go until all clear," replied Sanchez.

"Any problems with the U-Drones?"

"No sir, only the usual crap from the U-Global News team— 'Why can't we get closer? We won't get in the way. We'll be ever so careful'. I'm dealing with it."

"Kennedy, what's our status on the Badgers?"

"We'll be good to go any minute now. Both in their launch cradles and tethers hooked up. Right now, I'm verifying the data feed and double checking that we have the latest spoofing package uploaded—as requested."

Ben eased back into the command chair, removed his U-Set and slid his helmet on. The data from the recon drone filled his virtual display with a 3D false color image of the ground below the target. The image was fuzzy, using only passive IR, and trailed off rapidly as the depth increased. As Kennedy had suggested, there were a number of hot bodies clustered just below the surface, too close together to resolve individually. He turned towards Kennedy to send the recon drone closer to the target. "Kennedy, get the—"

Before he could complete his sentence, the active scan alarm screeched out a warning call which echoed through the cabin, making him almost jump out of his chair.

What the hell! What was targeting us with active sensors? He switched to the sensor display, which identified one of the three warmechs as the source. The image now showed the warmechs in fine detail, along with the tunnel in which they were sitting, sloping down at about 30 degrees. It was even possible to image the tunnel back for at least 100 meters by analyzing the helpful active sonar emissions from the warmechs before it faded out. More crazy stuff. How was that possible? No bogey would be sitting there with active sensors lit up, shouting, 'Here I am! Come and kill me!' The warmechs had nothing that could hit the IRV at this range. They were just giving their position away for no good reason.

Not unless it was deliberately trying to attract attention, he speculated. *So if that's where the bogies want me to be looking, what are they trying to distract me from? Maybe something else that's being fed their targeting data?*

A terrible idea jumped into his head, sending a cold shiver down his spine.

"Peto, pull us back 500 meters due west, right now! Fast as you can. Kennedy, get the recon drone over that new position with full passive scan, 500-meter radius. Do it now!"

"Er, OK. What's happening, boss? Why are the bogies targeting us? That makes no sense—" Kennedy sounded startled and confused at the same time.

Ben cut him off with a chopping arm motion. "Do it, man! And pull your drone down to 200 meters."

The cabin lurched as the massive vehicle turned to the west, its churning half-tracks scrabbling for grip and clanking furiously as it picked up speed, drowning out the shrill whine of the powerful electric motors.

Ben gestured at his HUD to kill the alarm. "Kennedy. Badgers. Are they ready yet?"

"All hooked up and ready for action, sir. You want me to check the spoofing package again?" queried Kennedy.

"No. We won't need it. All you have to do is get ready to drop one when I give the order."

"No IFF? Really? OK, you're the boss, Boss," Kennedy responded with a sigh of resignation.

"One more thing, Kennedy. This is important. I want the ground sensor array deployed the instant we're stopped. I need to see anything coming at us from below. Tell me as soon as we have the data feed."

Right now, he had to take out the three 'hot' warmechs. With their active sensors running, they'd have continuous targeting data on the IRV, and if something was making a run at them, he didn't want the bogies in possession of that information.

He called up the IRV's fire control AI. "Valkyrie, I'm ordering an immediate Harpy strike on the target I'm designating now. Mark. High explosive, deep penetration warhead. Use guided ballistic approach, and passive homing on their active radar emissions. Align approach vector with the warmech tunnel slope to achieve maximum depth in case they run. Proximity detonation. Go."

Half a second later, a muffled boom rumbled through the cabin as the Harpy shot out of its launch tube, leaving in its wake the pungent smell of its solid fuel propellant.

"Valkyrie, arm fusion warhead in Badger Alpha, authorization Hamilton. Set fifty percent yield." Ben reached out to the sensor pad built into his command chair and pressed the palm of his right hand onto the surface.

The security window in his display displayed the arming credentials for a moment, then flashed green just as the vehicle shuddered to a halt. He pulled up the latest recon data on his virtual display. Nothing was showing up. "Where are you? Where the hell are you?" he mumbled to himself.

"Kennedy, move the recon drone back 100 meters east of our position. Set full active scan and bring it down to 100 meters."

"OK, boss. And those ground sensors are deployed and active right about . . . now," responded Kennedy.

He added the data from the ground sensors to the display and zoomed in on the area to the east of the vehicle. Nothing on the IR, but the sonar display showed a fuzzy but definite target at a bearing of 83 degrees, about 200 meters laterally and 120 meters down. *Gotcha!* he thought. It was unbelievable, but it really was an ambush, he realized, as beads of cold sweat broke out on his forehead. Thank God the IRV could move faster across the ground than these monsters could dig, or we'd already be dead.

He called up the target analysis routine. It showed a warmech burrowing straight towards the vehicle at between 4 and 5 meters per second. It would hit them in less than a minute.

"Valkyrie! Badger deployment on active target now. Go!" he screamed.

He was shouting much louder than necessary. He brought his voice under control. "Peto, we're deploying a Badger. Once it's off and running, I want you to take us due west, nice and steady, at about 15 kph. No faster, or we'll yank the Badger right back out of the ground. Understood?"

"Right sir, 15 kph it is," Frank Peto replied over the comm.

"Everyone strap in. This might get a bit bumpy in less than a minute," Ben called out, making a conscious effort to keep his voice steady.

The vehicle swayed as the Badger deployed. The massive drum of armored cable feeding out the tether in the trailer behind the IRV spun up to full speed, its banshee wail screaming in his ears as it did so. The Badger scrabbled down its burrow in a furious spray of earth and rock. He switched to the Badger control GUI, with the sensor display in a separate window, then set the Badger running at flank speed on a reciprocal course to the target. It could only maintain this speed for a couple of minutes, before it overheated or something broke, but they'd all be dead long before then if he didn't get this right.

The two machines sped furiously towards each other, claws digging frantically into the ground far below the surface like a pair of giant demented moles. And like moles, they were blind, at least in the direction they were digging. The amount of noise and heat they generated made any forward-facing sensors ineffective. Fortunately, having deployed the ground sensor array just in time, Ben had a godlike overview of the subterranean field of battle. The sensors had all the data they needed to triangulate the position of the giant machines as they scrabbled their way through the earth on a collision course. They were now less than 100 meters apart.

He set the Badger to enter terminal acquisition mode once it got within 10 meters of the rapidly approaching warmech, feeding in the predicted co-ordinates of the convergence point. It was unlikely that the warmech would detect the approaching Badger until the last second—but nothing had gone the way he expected today, so he was taking no chances. His knuckles were white as he gripped the control stick on the console in front of him. Now all his focus was on the sub-surface VR image, the blue spot racing towards the red spot. He had to be ready to drop back to manual control in a fraction of a second in case there were any more surprises.

"Kennedy, take the recon drone to 1000 meters. Wide area scan. Peto, halt the vehicle now. Hold on tight guys. Contact in five. Four. Three. Two. One. Bingo!"

A violent convulsion hit the cabin, plunging him forwards in his seat, the restraints digging into his shoulders as the vehicle heaved upwards and jerked violently. It finally came to rest at a slight angle to the horizontal. There were a few moments of relative silence, broken only by the harsh whine from the fan of the air conditioning unit. Then Ben's ears were assaulted by an explosive roar which shook him in his seat, followed by the staccato clatter and clang of rocks raining down on the armored roof of the IRV.

He waited until the racket had stopped before removing his helmet. "All OK? Report in."

"Peto. I'm fine. Vehicle systems show all green. No structural damage as far as I can tell without getting out."

"Sanchez. I'm good. Comms good."

"Kennedy. I'm good, I guess. Lost some ground sensors, otherwise all looks OK. How close was that, sir?"

"About 150 meters. No sweat," Ben replied, feeling a lot less confident than he sounded.

"Right. You detonate a nuke 150 meters from where I'm sitting, and you're not sweating. That's great. Care to explain what the hell just happened—sir?" Kennedy exclaimed, staring defiantly back at him.

Ben raised his eyebrows and held his stare, but decided not to chew him out for insubordination. He was so happy to be alive that he'd give him one more chance. "Since you're new on the job, Kennedy, I'll put down your attitude to inexperience, rather than lack of respect for a superior officer. You won't be getting a second chance. Is that clear?"

"Yes, sir. I'm sorry, it's just that I don't—"

Ben interrupted before Kennedy managed to dig himself into a deeper hole. "You still have a lot to learn, Kennedy. So listen up. First off, it was only a baby nuke, and I dialed the yield down to 50 percent. Second, about 90 percent of its energy goes into X and gamma radiation, not explosive blast. Third, most of the energy is directed forward, so directly away from where you're sitting and down towards the bad guys. Last, and perhaps most importantly, you're still alive. Any problems with that?"

Kennedy gulped a couple of times, as he rubbed his hands together before wiping them against a trouser leg to dry his sweaty palms. "Of course, you're right, sir. I'm really sorry if I was out of line, but I simply had no idea what was going on. One minute we're checking out a teddy bear—next minute, all hell breaks loose and we're rushing around nuking stuff at point blank range."

Ben was feeling pretty stressed himself, but he had to maintain an outward appearance of confidence, and try to help Kennedy deal with the experience. "Well, I'm with you there. Right up until a couple of minutes ago, I had no idea what was going on either," he responded, with a shrug of his shoulders. "By the time I'd figured it out, there wasn't much time left for cozy fireside chats. Sorry, but that's the way it works round here."

"So what do you figure was happening out there, sir?"

"We'll talk about it later. First let's check the area is secure. I can fill everyone in on the way back to base. For now, pull the recon drone back down low for a wide area sweep, out to 5 klicks and centered on our original target. You can use the full active suite—I'm pretty sure the bad guys know we're here now. Let's be certain there are no more surprises."

He replaced his helmet and pulled up the visual feed from the recon drone. Where the teddy bear had been sitting, there was now a deep crater, about 20 meters across. He swung the view closer to the location of their IRV. Starting from about a hundred meters to the east, a wide area of devastated ground stretched away, looking like a chaotic moonscape. Roughly in the middle of the area was a wide shallow depression where the ground had given way. The shattered landscape was riven with deep fissures, from which thin plumes of steam and gas were still rising. Cracks in the ground covered a much wider area, some even reaching as far as the vehicle.

"Peto, take us back to the center of our sector south of the city, but keep well clear of that broken ground to the east. Choose your own route, but make sure we stay between the original target and the citadel. Kennedy, I need continuous active sensors running a forward sweep of the sub-surface. I want to know if anything so much as sneezes. Let's see if there are any more bogies out there."

Once back on station, he left the IRV's active sensors thrashing the area for another ten minutes before removing his helmet and leaning back in the control chair with a sigh, the tension draining out of his body. He called up the crew over the comm.

"Sanchez, you can call in the clean-up team. We're all clear. Kennedy, leave the recon drone in place. Hand over the feed to the clean-up team once they're in position. Peto, do an external check on the vehicle. Once we're good to go, take us home."

Kennedy turned to regard him with a quizzical expression, but this time he managed to hold his tongue.

Ben gave him a reassuring smile. "Ah yes. The cozy fireside chat. You remember the teddy bear? We know these monsters are now putting out bait to attract their victims. The trike was there to pull in some kids. Who do you imagine the bear was for? Normally these bastards are hiding halfway down their tunnel trying to look like lumps of rocks, using passive sensors set up near ground level and waiting for their next victim to stroll by. Not this time. These warmechs were all sitting just under the surface—right at the top of their tunnel—with active sensors lit up. So let me ask again—who was the bait for? Anyone?"

"So, er, what? Are you saying the bait was for us? We were the target? But we came nowhere near the teddy bear . . . " Kennedy's voice trailed off. He chewed his lip as he tried to work out the puzzle. Then his eyes lit up. "Oh right, now I get it. They were all powered up with active sensors running. That attracts our attention and keeps us fixated on watching them while one of their pals sneaks up from behind and below. And their active sensors give them a running fix on our position to feed back to the other guy so he can vector in on us without having to use his own active sensors."

"Wow! That's really clever! But I've never heard of anything like them setting up an ambush before. They're not supposed to have that level of intelligence. How can they pull a stunt like that? They must have been sitting behind us playing possum, waiting for us to approach the bear. If you hadn't pulled us back in time, they'd have rammed us right up the ass. That's really scary."

"All good to go, sir," reported Peto.

"OK. Take us home," Ben responded.

"The faster the better, Frank. I need a change of underwear ASAP," added Kennedy.

"ETA in about 20 minutes, if that's soon enough for everyone and their underwear," replied Peto. "Sir, how long did we have? I mean once you figured it out, how long did we have until we got hit?"

"Can't say exactly. Moving away from the incoming warmech helped some, but I'd say not more than a couple of minutes. Then the nuke would have been too close. And there was no time to change the warhead on the Badger. Its primary mission is taking out big warmech nests deep underground, but that's all we had ready to go in the time available."

He paused, then nodded to the crew as he looked around the cramped cabin. "There's something else I want to say. You all did your jobs without missing a beat. We know the new guy was feeling nervous, but he still did his job. Just one slip up by any member of the crew and we'd all be dead. I'm proud to have you as my team and I intend to put that in my report. Assuming they don't fry my ass for setting off a nuke so close to the surface. But that was my decision and my responsibility. In the meantime, you can take care of any loose ends on our way back to base. Anyone with spare time on their hands can put on another pot of coffee. Now I need to think about that report."

The bulky armored vehicle clattered down the concrete ramp to the underground DGS support and maintenance level. Nobody had had time to brew another pot of coffee, so once they'd parked the IRV in its assigned berth, Ben made straight for the canteen. He could smell the fresh coffee even before he got through the door. Pouring himself a cup, he sat down at the nearest table, and tried to gather his thoughts. Was he sure he'd done the right thing? He'd been within one minute of getting the whole team killed. This had been a totally unknown attack profile by the warmechs. And what was their plan? A prelude to a mass attack? But if not, what else might their evil little AI minds have been thinking?

"Err, excuse me sir. Do you have a minute?" Kennedy was hovering beside the table, rubbing his hands together nervously.

Ben looked up and gave a welcoming smile. He waved an arm at a seat. *No rest for the wicked*, he thought. "Sure. Pull up a chair. What's on your mind?"

"Well, first of all, sir, I'd like to apologize for my remarks earlier today. They were out of line, and I honestly didn't mean to . . .umm . . . er . . ." Kennedy stammered to a halt.

Ben took another sip of hot coffee. "We'll put it down to nerves, Kennedy. Apology accepted. No hard feelings. It just happens to be a sore spot for me." He smiled faintly. "I know what it's like to be the newbie. I've been there myself. If you'd like a tip from an old pro – add an extra line to your Standard Operating Procedure. 'Always ensure brain is fully engaged before operating mouth.' OK?"

Kennedy's face lit up like a happy puppy. "Yes sir, of course, sir. I won't let it happen again. It's only my second sortie since I graduated from training school, so I'm still a bit on edge. I'm sure I'll be fine next time out."

"So, is that all?" Kennedy appeared reluctant to leave, but Ben needed some quiet thinking time.

"Well I did have one other question, if you don't mind." Kennedy's expression showed the effort as he struggled to get his words out. "As I said, I'm new to the job, and I'm trying to understand—why we didn't simply pull back until we lost the warmech? Our IRV moves a lot faster than any tunneling warmech, and that way we wouldn't have needed to use a nuke . . . sir."

Ben took another long sip of coffee. "Hmm. Good question. What do you see as our primary reason for being out there, Kennedy?"

"Well, er . . . we're trying to kill warmechs, I guess?" he replied, frowning at what he obviously suspected was a trick question.

"Sure, that's part of the job, but our most important task is protecting the lives of the people living in the New Geneva Citadel. In particular, this afternoon, we were making sure that the southern quadrant was protected from anything the warmechs might throw at us. If we pulled back far enough – sure, we'd have kept ourselves safe from the warmech tracking us, but then we'd be a long way over to the west, leaving the south side exposed.

"In a typical attack scenario the warmechs would be sitting in their tunnel about 50 meters down, as quiet as they could be. We try to sneak up on them, they detect the IRV and maybe come up looking for a fight, in which case we hit them with a Harpy, plus our top-mounted hyper-railguns if they want to get up close and personal. Or they run back to mommy, in which case we send a Badger down after them. Once it's found a main tunnel, we can drop the tether and go autonomous, spoofing their IFF signal to kid them the Badger's one of their pals. And if we get lucky, we find a nice big nest followed by a nice big *KABOOM!* as the nuke goes off. With me so far?"

"I guess so, sir," responded Kennedy. "I only did sensor technology in training. They didn't tell us much about tactical operations. I guess that's the sort of thing you get in officer school?"

"Then consider this your crash course in the subject. So what did we find this time? We had a bunch of warmechs sitting up at the top of a tunnel with active sensors screaming away. You said yourself you've never heard of anything like that before. Well, nor have I. I've been killing these monsters for over four years now—and this was an attack profile utterly different from anything I've ever seen or heard of.

"And what scares me the most is how they were able to position that last warmech right behind us and close enough to spring the trap. The DGS AI assigns the IRV a random path for each sortie to avoid exactly that scenario. Yet this was an ambush which directly targeted us, which shouldn't be possible."

He leaned forward, jabbing his finger hard on the table to emphasize his point and in doing so rattling the empty coffee cup in its saucer. "There's only one thing I'm sure of. So much planning and effort to take out our IRV had to have a specific objective. What if the warmech plan was to either to kill us, or at least get us out of position before launching a mass attack on the city from the south, which only our nuke-armed Badgers would be able to stop? So yes, we took a risk, but the downside might have been a thousand times worse."

Kennedy frowned. "Really sir? You think that was what they were planning?"

"Really? I have absolutely no idea what they were planning, Kennedy. But would you want to gamble with the lives of the people of this citadel?"

"No, sir. I see what you mean sir. Thank you, sir."

"Anything else I can help you with right now, Kennedy?" Ben said, smiling again at the eager young man but also hoping he would finally take the hint.

"I'm fine, sir. Really. And thank you again. It was very good of you—"

Ben's communicator buzzed in his ear. "Hamilton. Report to the Director now. He wants you in his office in five minutes."

What the hell? The Director? That's not good. Not good at all.

"That's my Section Chief, and I'm wanted upstairs. Don't worry, we all did well today," he said, gulping down the last of his coffee as he ran for the door. *I only hope the Director agrees*, he thought.

CHAPTER TWO

BEN LEANED back into the unaccustomed softness of the leather sofa. Was this real leather? He resisted the temptation to sniff the rich reddish-brown upholstery. Anyway, he wasn't sure what real leather would smell like. Not like plastic, he guessed. And it was so quiet in here. Almost oppressively so. He hadn't realized how noisy the lower levels were until he had been sitting here for a few minutes. Now he almost missed the steady whir of the ventilation systems, the rattle and clank of the IRV, the intermittent whine of electric motors and, most of all, the constant background hum of tightly packed humanity. Not to mention the rancid, oily smell.

The Director's outer office was larger than his whole apartment. Its single large window overlooked the lake far below, framed by the Alpine peaks beyond. *What a view*, he thought. *Imagine coming into work every day and seeing that. How long would it be before you took it for granted? Surely you never would.* His own apartment didn't have a view or even a window. Nor did the IRV or the underground DGS levels. In fact, he could go a week or more without seeing the outside world on anything but his VR helmet.

The last time he'd seen anything to compare with this view was when that cute features producer from U-Global had taken him to lunch at the fancy Vista restaurant at the top of the Citadel. She'd wanted to pump him for the 'human angle' as a heroic warrior in the forefront of humanity's fight against the warmech threat. As it turned out, he got more pumping than he'd expected. Not that he was complaining, and he smiled at the memory.

His mind was wandering, trying not to think about why the Director wanted to see him. And so soon after the mission. Normally he'd have a debrief with his Section Chief, get a bite to eat, write his report and fall into bed. He'd never heard of anyone being called to the Director's office straight after a mission. Maybe the nuke hadn't been such a good idea.

He'd met the Director only once, if you could call it a meeting, and that had been in the Great Hall—big awards ceremony, reception afterwards. Only a few words exchanged, and he couldn't remember a single one. Still, he had come away with a written commendation and a promotion. This time around, he didn't see any brass bands or cheering crowds. So he was guessing it wouldn't be good news.

He'd just go with the flow. Very little had made any sense today, so why should it change now?

The exquisitely polished voice of the Director's secretary pulled him back from his reverie. "Agent Hamilton? Director Huber will see you now."

Here we go, he thought, struggling to his feet from the depths of the soft upholstery. He forced himself not to stare too obviously at the ample contents of the attractive secretary's tight dress as she held open the wood-paneled door. He strode through the doorway, her distracting perfume still in his nostrils, and he assumed his most neutral expression.

His jaw dropped, and he almost stumbled when he saw the view before him. The two corner walls of the spacious office were glass from floor to ceiling, almost making him believe he might fall into the lake far below.

"Take a seat, Hamilton," intoned Director Huber from behind a vast expanse of polished wood. With a wave of his hand he indicated a small upright chair, set a little distance back from the enormous desk, and quite out of keeping with the luxurious furniture in the rest of the office.

"Thank you, sir," Ben replied as he seated himself—or rather perched—on the hard seat. Perhaps his muscular frame was a little larger than the average, but the chair did seem abnormally small.

Huber fixed him with a beady-eyed stare, letting a few seconds pass in silence before asking, "Do you have any idea why you're here today, Hamilton?"

Maintaining his blank expression, Ben replied in his best loyal subordinate voice, "Well, no sir, not really sir. Is it connected with this morning's incident?"

Huber snorted. "Incident, Hamilton? Incident? Is that what you call letting off nukes right outside my office?" Huber's voice rose as he became increasingly agitated. "Is this meant to be a joke? Do you realize that my windows were actually rattled by your outrageous glory-hunting?"

Ben looked away, stifling the sudden urge to laugh out loud. His team had been fighting for their lives in a last-ditch attempt to stop whatever devious plan the warmechs had for an attack on the citadel. They had been less than 150 meters away when the nuke went off—and this guy was complaining that his windows rattled? Ben was momentarily stunned, lost for words.

Fighting to control his facial expression, he kept his voice as calm as he could manage. "I can understand that deploying the nuke this morning doesn't conform to our Standard Operating Procedure, sir, but I didn't consider it advisable to allow the attacking warmech to chase our IRV away from our sector. That would have left the south sector of the city open for whatever the warmechs were planning. The situation was completely unprecedented. The warmechs seem to have set us up for an ambush in a way I've never seen—"

"Yes, yes, yes—I've heard this all before," Huber snapped, waving an arm dismissively. "I don't want to hear it again. Your behavior is no better than I'd expect from a sewer rat. No Family, no connections, no sense of respect for your betters. Let me tell you, if it was my call, I'd bust you down to robo-monkey.

"As it is, I'm getting rid of you another way. You will be leaving DGS to work for another department, starting tomorrow. You can of course refuse your new assignment, in which case the robo-monkey position may still be open. Your new boss will join us here by U-Presence shortly, so I suggest you try your best to impress him. God knows you don't impress me."

Ben had to look away again to hide his shock. The Director had virtually the power of life and death over any member of his Department. And some people in the city would kill for a job as a robo-monkey. Only Family got the good jobs unless you had a Family member as a patron. Ben had neither. Just the opposite, in fact. *Go along to get along*, that had always been his motto, *go along to get along*. He pushed his rising anger back down. Controlling his voice as best he could, he enquired, "May I ask which Department, sir?"

"Sanitation and Sewage, if I had my way, Hamilton, Sanitation and Sewage," Huber repeated with relish.

Huber turned away and spoke into thin air. "Amanda, you can connect us to the Director-General now," he said, using the trigger name for his Virtual Assistant.

Clearly, Ben wasn't going to get any more useful information out of the Director, so he sat back and surveyed the desk before him. It was empty other than what looked like a pair of trophies. Leaning forward, Ben could make out a few of words of one of the inscriptions. *So he's a skiing champion, is he? Well, I guess everyone has to be good at something. And is that all he has to put on his desk? You'd think he would at least have some photos—*

"Marco, welcome, welcome! So good to see you. I'm very grateful you could spare the time for this meeting. How is Antonia? And the children?" Huber's voice had instantly switched from snappy to ingratiating.

Ben was startled to see a rather corpulent yet elegantly dressed figure pop into existence beside him, sitting in a leather armchair. Wow! This must be one of those fancy free-standing 3D holo-projectors he'd heard about. The illusion seemed just perfect, even casting shadows on the floor, he realized. Only top Family members could afford such advanced technology. Huber must be really well-connected. *And who the hell is this Marco guy?*

Marco was positioned some distance to the side of Ben's little chair, forcing him to half-turn in his seat to study the new arrival. He could still find no way of telling that the image was not a flesh and blood person. Realizing that twisting one way and then the other would be awkward for a three-way conversation, he tried to move his chair to a better position. *Bastard!* His chair was immovable, presumably screwed to the floor.

That makes sense, he reflected, otherwise Huber's visitors might end up throwing the chair at him.

"They're all fine, Karl, just fine," responded Marco. "Antonia is hoping to come up again soon with the children for another little vacation. They haven't stopped talking about their last visit. Especially little Alessandra. You're still her favorite ski instructor. She can't wait to see you again."

Ben noticed a curious twitch in the corner of Huber's mouth at that last remark, turning his wide smile into a lopsided grimace. *How curious*, he mused. Was it the mention of 'ski instructor' which had put Huber off his stride, or maybe Marco's daughter? *Can't be the daughter,* he realized, *or he would hardly be so affable. Anyway, who cares—I'm out of here tomorrow.*

"Yes, well, we're always happy to welcome you back anytime at all," replied Huber in a slightly less effusive tone. "There's nothing I like better than spending time out on the slopes—when the demands of the service permit, of course," he added hurriedly.

Marco chuckled and gave Huber a knowing look. "Of course, Karl, of course. We're all aware of what a vital job you do here, keeping Europe safe from those dreadful warmechs. I'm surprised you can find enough hours in the day to cope with your heavy responsibilities."

What's going on? Ben wondered. There was evidently some private little joke running here, but Huber didn't seem at all amused.

"That's very kind of you, Marco," said Huber, his voice distinctly cooler. "Well, no doubt you will want to get down to business now and not waste any more valuable time. Let me introduce Agent Hamilton, who I'm told has been proposed for a mission working with the AICB. Hamilton, this is Director-General Marco Veronese of the AICB."

"Indeed. Lead Agent Hamilton. What a pleasure it is to meet you at last. The hero of the hour!" exclaimed Veronese, beaming at him with a wide grin that spread right across his round, florid face. "May I be one of the first to offer you my congratulations?"

Veronese's words caught Ben completely off guard. He could only stare open-mouthed like a freshly landed fish. AICB? The AI Control Board? That was virtually a secret society. Nobody got in there without the highest connections. Almost always Family. He'd applied when he'd graduated, but it was just for form, to satisfy the urging of his tutors. Congratulations? Well, a position with the AICB was certainly a cause for celebration, but was he missing something? And how was he the 'hero of the hour'? More like the unwanted stray kicked out through the back door.

"Karl, you old dog," smiled Veronese, observing that Ben was still too shocked to respond. "You haven't told him, have you? I understand. I'll bet you were saving the best news until last. Well, in that case, let me be the first to congratulate you on the award of the Global Star to the hero of the Battle of New Geneva, for outstanding bravery in the face of the enemy."

"Yes, well . . . err, I didn't want to mention it prematurely, not until it had been officially confirmed, of course . . ." stuttered Huber, squirming in his seat. Ben was left gasping yet again, but wasn't too stunned to notice that Huber's pinched features had taken on a distinct resemblance to a cornered rat.

Veronese assumed an astonished expression, rocking back in his chair with his hands spread wide. "But they confirmed it at least an hour ago, Karl. Don't you read your messages at all? With all the heavy demands of your exacting workload, I know it must be difficult to keep up, but really!"

Veronese turned back to Ben with another wide grin. "This must all come as something of a shock to you, Ben—may I call you Ben? The story of your single-handed heroic defense of the city of New Geneva against hordes of ravening warmechs is already being released to the U-Global networks. By this evening, everyone on the planet will know your name. They will be able to experience every detail of your desperate fight against all odds, beating back wave after wave of these terrifying monsters. You are an inspiration to us all!"

"But, ah . . ." Ben tried to collect his thoughts. "As far as I'm aware, sir, I only killed one warmech, and I'm afraid I had to use a nuke to do it. There might have been three more. I carried out a Harpy strike on another group but we haven't had confirmation from the clean-up team as yet—"

Veronese cut him off with a raised hand. "Well, that's one way of looking at the situation, Ben. Your modesty does you credit, naturally. But how can you be sure there weren't a hundred—or a thousand—warmechs behind the handful you destroyed? They might have been just scouts for the main force. They were planning something, that's what you said, right? I can't imagine they were trying to lure you out, to destroy you and your team, with no deeper plan in mind. You said you were not willing to leave the city defenseless. Defenseless against what, Ben? What else could it have been but a mass attack, which you thwarted with your inspiring courage and quick thinking?"

Ben could only respond with a look of confusion as he tried to make sense of this effusive and unexpected praise.

Veronese leaned forward in his virtual armchair and wagged a finger at him. "Now see here, Ben, let me give you an idea of the bigger picture. Ifs and maybes don't look so good on the U-Global Networks. People want certainty. They *need* certainty. And most of all, they want to feel secure in the face of the many terrible threats facing mankind in its darkest hour. Now, it's the job of the Global Security Council, and all the people supporting their vital work, to ensure the continued existence of humanity. But our responsibilities don't stop there. We don't just provide that security, we must make sure people *see* us providing that security.

"So what I'm asking, Ben, is for you to work with me here. This is no time for false modesty. Now don't you worry, we'll take good care of you and make sure you've been fully briefed before we do any live interviews. We also have the most advanced VRExperience production technology to clean up any 'rough edges' from the data and video feeds. The official awards ceremony for your Global Star will be coming up in less than a week. We need you looking and sounding suitably heroic by then. Please don't disappoint me, Ben."

Ben got the picture all right. Right down to the air quotes around 'rough edges.' He'd decided to go with the flow when he came to the meeting. It looked like he'd have to be careful not to get washed away.

"OK, I guess I can work with that," he said, trying his best to sound convinced, but not really succeeding. "Can you tell me anything about this mission for AICB? Is it here in New Geneva? And won't I need training? I imagine you're aware I applied for a trainee position with ACIB when I graduated and got turned down?"

"Ben, we know all about you. And let me tell you, you've been training for this mission your entire life." Veronese turned in his seat to fix him with a well-practiced gaze conveying sincerity, understanding and sympathy. His voice softened and lowered an octave. "You've already seen and overcome adversity in your life that would devastate anyone with a weaker character. For example, I know your parents and baby sister were tragically killed in that terrible warmech incursion up at Greeley Citadel when you were just eight years old. What an appalling experience for a young boy. I believe you were actually there at the time?"

A lump rose in Ben's throat as the images leaped into his mind. He'd been on his way home from school when heard the sirens. He should have gone to the nearest shelter, but he was almost home, and wanted to be with his parents. By the time he reached what remained of the apartment block it was far too late. Walls and floors ripped apart like cardboard. Broken furniture scattered in all directions, everything covered in clouds of dust.

And worst of all—worst of all by far—were the broken bodies, *pieces* of bodies, lying everywhere he looked. He was pulled away by the clean-up team, screaming incoherently, and spent several days in shock, not speaking, not moving. Just lying in the hospital bed with his face turned to the wall until the woman from the State Guardian's Office came to collect him.

He suspected Veronese was using this incident to probe for any weakness. Well, it damn well wouldn't work. He blinked to clear his eyes and struggled to control his voice. "I try not to think about it, sir. That's all in the past now," he replied in a low monotone, his knuckles turning white as he gripped the arms of his chair.

Veronese studied him quizzically. "What I find most amazing is that the only effect on your school record is that your grades actually improved. How did you manage that?"

"I was assigned to a wardship with the Lambert Family at Colorado Citadel. The schools are pretty good there." Ben paused, blinked again, then looked up at Veronese. "Also, I wanted to kill warmechs. They killed my parents and my little sister. I wanted to understand everything about them, so I could hurt them, destroy them—wipe them out. I focused on science and engineering, immersed myself in every aspect of warmech technology. I discovered I was good at it."

"You certainly were, Ben. You graduated *magna cum laude* in Computing and AI Systems from Colorado University, then MarsDevCo sponsored you to take a Masters degree in Astronautical Engineering at Wind River. That was followed by another twelve months on their astronaut training program where you got your Space Certification. You were due to embark as an engineering specialist on the New Dawn, the ship they built to kick off their next settlement phase. Then they pulled the plug on the entire program. Right so far?"

"That just about covers it, I guess," Ben responded, not really seeing where this was going.

"Do you mind if I ask why you switched to Astronautics and signed up for the Mars project? Not so many warmechs up there, I'd guess," said Veronese with a smile that did not reach his eyes.

"By the time I graduated, I'd been living, breathing, even dreaming warmechs for over a decade. I guess I was just warmeched-out. Besides, I met a girl at college whose ambition was to go to Mars, where she said people could build a new society and live free of the warmech threat. I was pulled into the dream."

"OK. So then after MarsDevCo folded you took yourself off to New Geneva to work for your doctorate in AI with the top guy in the world, Professor Jim Adler. Did you get to know him well?"

"No, not really. He was my tutor for a while, but I was there for less than a year before I had to leave. That's when I joined the DGS. I attended some classes Adler gave on quantum computing, which were truly inspiring. He had the ability to explain a concept in a way that seemed so clear and made you feel a lot cleverer than you actually were. Sadly, the effect seemed to wear off after a week or so." He smiled. "I know he left New Geneva, but I don't know where he is now."

"Would you be surprised if I told you that right now he's on his way to Ceres?" said Veronese, his eyes narrowing.

"Ceres? Really? Why Ceres? They have a big operation mining for metals, minerals and water, and they grow a lot of food. They even export some of it to Earth. But no obvious need for advanced AI, and I can't imagine it as a holiday spot," he replied, puzzled. "Do they have problems up there? The collapse of MarsDevCo would have hit them pretty badly, I suppose. Their joint venture for the proposed hydroponic production domes on Mars would have needed a massive amount of water and materials, which won't be happening now. It's much more efficient—as much as 100 times more energy efficient—to transport mass from Ceres to Mars, compared to the cost of transportation from Earth . . ."

His voice trailed off as he saw he was losing his audience. Too much information, he realized.

Veronese gave a reassuring grin. "One possible explanation is that Professor Adler's son is Frank Adler, Chairman and CEO of Adler-Lee Dynamics. His company was the driving force behind the Ceres project. They built and own almost everything up there. However, the AICB have concerns regarding the level of development of the AI capability on Ceres. And that's where you come in."

"Me? I'm sorry? I'm not sure I follow," Ben replied with a frown.

"Then let me be clear, Ben. We want you to go to Ceres and conduct an investigation into their AI development activity on behalf of the ACIB."

Startled, Ben replied, "But why me? And why do they need advanced AI on Ceres? What are they doing with it?"

"Just a few of the many questions we are asking ourselves, and we want you to answer," responded Veronese. "Don't you see, Ben? You know better than anyone of the dangers of AI technology getting out of control, which is why the limitations on its use are so strictly enforced by the ACIB. You also have a unique set of qualifications for such a mission." He began ticking off points on his fingers. "An excellent academic background in AI, Astronautics trained and qualified. Plus extensive DGS field experience and unquestioned commitment in the battle against the worst excesses of malignant AI technology. You'll be working as a Special Investigator reporting directly to me. I'm assuming you're prepared to accept the position, of course." He regarded Ben expectantly.

Ben blinked in amazement. That position was Cadre level and with ACIB, the most powerful Agency on the planet. He would qualify for full citizenship, he realized. Maybe even access to the rumored life extension treatment. Every door would be open to him. "Yes. Yes, of course I will. That's more than I ever dreamed of. Where do I sign?" he blurted out, unable to control his eagerness.

Veronese's smile appeared almost paternal. "Then let me tell you how happy I am to welcome you to our little team at the AICB, Ben. I'm sure we can get the paperwork tidied up in the next few days. Right now, I'd like you start planning to be at AICB HQ in Wind River Citadel within the next 48 hours. Please report directly to me on arrival. I'll have your travel documents sent to your Virtual Assistant in the next few minutes.

"Oh, and please keep in mind everything you have heard here today is highly classified, most especially the nature of your upcoming mission. Are we clear? Good. Now I'm sure you'll have a few loose ends to tie up in New Geneva before you leave, so we won't detain you any longer. Unless you have something to add, Karl?" He gave Huber his biggest smile yet.

"No, I'm sure that will be more than enough for today," Huber muttered through tight lips. "You can go now, Hamilton, and err . . . thank you."

Ben rose from his chair and nodded towards Huber, then Veronese. "I'm very grateful to you, sir," he said, pointedly not looking at Huber.

Veronese beamed back at him. "Not at all. We're all very proud of you, Ben. I'm sure you'll be a great credit to the ACIB. I look forward to meeting you in person later this week."

Ben left the office in a daze, too stunned even to check out Huber's secretary again as he left.

Veronese turned back to Huber, a triumphant expression on his face. "And now I have a little bet to collect from you, Karl."

"What?" Huber spluttered. "Look, Marco. That wasn't a serious bet. You don't—you can't think—"

Veronese fixed Huber with a predatory stare. "Serious or not, Karl, a bet is a bet. So I want to see the notarized deeds for that nice little chalet of yours with my Virtual Assistant by tomorrow morning. Unless you'd like me to find a more direct way to collect?"

Huber's face flushed, and he put up his hands as if fending off an imminent attack. "No, no, that won't be necessary," he stammered. "But I still don't understand how that little shit survived. What the hell tipped him off to the warmech coming up from behind? He drove right over it on the way out and never spotted it. It was well below 200 meters, powered down in full stealth. That wouldn't be detectable even with full active sensors. Then all of a sudden, he ups and scoots off like a startled rabbit—driving right back over the damned thing again—and then nukes the bastard before it gets even halfway to the IRV. I just don't get it." Huber gave a snort of exasperation. "Well, he's your problem now. I only hope you do better with him than I did."

"You can't complain the bet wasn't fair, Karl. We gave you a free hand to set up the ambush however you liked. I took the bet because it was him against you, and I preferred his chances more than yours."

Huber scowled defiantly. "So what if I'd won the bet, eh? Then your hoped-for hero would be just another dead body. No triumph, no medals, no blanket coverage on the U-Global Network."

Veronese leaned back in his virtual chair, steepling his fingers. "That's where we're so different, you and I, Karl. You never see the big picture. It doesn't occur to you that a dead hero has far greater value than a live one. If Hamilton had died, he would have been awarded the Global Heart, an inscription on the Wall of Eternal Honor, BioVid VREx of his glorious exploits on all the news feeds, the works. So we'd have had a win anyway."

Huber shook his head in disbelief. "So you're telling me you're disappointed that he survived? Really?"

"Of course not. Now he's a bigger hero than ever. And when we send him off to Ceres, we get the whole of Earth's beleaguered population on our side, because he's a noble champion off to fight for the cause of humanity, battling against the evildoers using enhanced AI for their own devious ends. Our hero finds the dirt, then we move in and close down Ceres like we closed down the Mars project."

"And if he finds nothing?"

"Oh, I promise you he'll find plenty. You can be sure of that."

Huber's expression became almost malevolent. "There's just one problem with your master plan, Marco," he sneered. "I know him better than you do. Don't you see? He's very, very bright. And he's not Family. What will you do if he talks to the Adler Family, finds out our dirty little secret, and comes back from Ceres shooting his mouth off? You can't just drop the all-conquering hero in a ditch!"

"I assure you, Karl, there's nothing in my master plan that includes him returning from Ceres. As you say, he's not Family, which makes him expendable. Yet another one of his many ideal qualifications for the mission. And with his background, we have to get rid of him sooner or later, anyway. Don't you even remember what I said two minutes ago about dead heroes? I despair of you, Karl, I honestly do.

"Now I would like to inspect my new ski chalet while we still have some daylight left. I assume you can provide my U-Drone with the access codes? Thank you. Oh and please give my regards to the new Chairman."

Veronese's smirking image disappeared before Huber had time to respond.

"Good afternoon, Karl."

A voice halfway between a growl and a whisper, which seemed to have no clear point of origin, made Karl realize he was chewing his fingernails again.

He jerked upright in his chair. "Mr. Chairman. I'm honored by your presence. Please accept my congratulations on your recent election."

"Thank you Karl, although I cannot claim it as any great accomplishment. It was simply my turn after the unfortunate demise of the previous incumbent. However, it does come at a most opportune moment. It allows us to wrap up the Ceres problem and neutralize the Adler Family once and for all. That unfortunate state of affairs has been a running sore for far too long."

"I hope that Marco knows what he's doing. Hamilton is dangerous—who knows what he might find out. I don't understand how this is going to work," complained Huber.

"You should not get emotionally involved in these situations, Karl."

"But Marco shows me no respect at all. He taunts me all the time, even more so since his promotion," said Huber, his voice now a peevish whine.

"In fact, I was referring to your attitude towards Hamilton—but no matter. You should let the matter drop. Am I clear?"

"Yes sir. Of course, sir. I was just trying to point out the dangers of—"

"While I'm always grateful for your input as a Regional Director of Global Security, Karl, I feel I must point out that although you have many good qualities, strategic insight is perhaps not your greatest talent. Indeed, several other candidates were equally well qualified for your position, if not more so—on paper. To be clear, you owe your position to two vitally important factors.

"The first is your total and unswerving loyalty to my Family. I want you to know I appreciate that profoundly, Karl. I'm aware that you've had reservations about several operations with which I have tasked you, but you've always carried them out in the most conscientious manner. In these uncertain times, it gives me great comfort to know there are men and women I can count on absolutely to promote our agenda. And not just in the interests of our Family, but to ensure the future of all humanity."

"Thank you, sir. Thank you. You honor me with your confidence. I won't let you down, I swear it," said Huber, unconsciously rubbing his hands together as if he had traces of dirt still clinging to them.

"I'm quite sure you will not, Karl."

"And the other thing, sir?"

"What other thing?"

"You said there were two factors?"

"Ah yes, I see. That is surely obvious, Karl. You married my granddaughter."

CERES

*"Any sufficiently advanced technology
is indistinguishable from magic"*

Arthur C Clarke

CHAPTER THREE

K<small>AY</small> <small>PUSHED</small> <small>BACK</small> from the display console. This still made no sense. She let out a low groan and rubbed her eyes. She'd run—and re-run—all the tests. Over and over again. She stared accusingly at the results. The holographic display glared back at her, illuminating the darkened lab in garish colors.

Kay chewed her lower lip as she tried to make sense of what she was seeing. *Either I'm still missing something obvious, or all our theories about quantum gravity and the nature of the multiverse are wrong. We can access any universe we like, and the results we get match the theory perfectly. The difference in quantum energy pressure between our universe and a parallel universe produces exactly the amount of energy predicted. Energy in massive, unbelievable amounts. So everything checks out.*

Everything except for a small group of 'fast' universes, where access seems to be blocked. With only one exception. We accessed a single member of this fast group over three months ago, so we know it should be possible. Such an exciting discovery, a universe where the speed of light was over one hundred times faster than our own universe. Since then, nothing. We even tried to access that same universe again without success. How can it work once, then just stop?

She dismissed the displays with a wave of her hand, and the lab lights came back on.

"Am I disturbing you?"

"Oh, hello Pandora. I wish you would. I'm getting nowhere here."

"You need to take a break. Do something else for a while. Are you reading any more of your old books?"

"I've almost finished *The Adventures of Huckleberry Finn*. There's a lot I don't understand, especially when they're talking in those strange old accents, but I love to read about how people long ago could simply walk through woods, sleep under the stars, even swim in a river. Until I came to Ceres, I'd never even touched a blade of grass. Can you believe that? The warmechs back on Earth have taken so much from us. We don't dare go outside our citadels. Now, when I'm out in one of those little parks dotted around the Habitat, I take off my shoes and walk across the grass so I can feel it between my toes. People were so free 500 years ago."

"Not everyone was free," said Pandora. "Some were kept as slaves. Wasn't that in the story?"

"Yes, but Huck was trying to help a slave escape. So that shows he was trying to do the right thing."

"But according to the law, the slave was property, so wasn't Huck stealing and breaking the law?"

She frowned. "Well yes, I suppose so, but his conscience told him to break the law."

"So if I understand correctly, if your conscience is in conflict with the law, you should break the law?"

Kay rubbed the back of her neck and stretched out in her chair, trying to suppress a yawn. "Err, well, it's more complicated than that. His conscience came from inside him—the law came from his community. He had to decide which one was right."

"So how can his conscience be right? If the people of his community believe slavery is right, then how can just one person say it's wrong?"

"You have to judge for yourself what is right and accept that you may be punished if you go against the law. Anyway, the people don't make the laws in our society, it's the Global Security Council. So I suppose there are good laws and bad laws—you need your conscience to tell the difference."

"So if the laws come from the GSC, where does your conscience come from?"

Kay pursed her lips as she struggled for a good answer. "From your soul, I guess," she replied.

"So people have souls?"

"I guess most people do. Everyone, I hope." She stared at the camera embedded in the console. "Do you have a soul, Pandora?"

"Why ask me? I'm just a dumb machine, remember?"

Kay gave a snort of exasperation. "You're only a dumb machine when other people are around. That's why sometimes I think I'm going crazy talking to you. My father says you're a figment of my imagination, and how can I blame him? No AI should be capable of your level of self-awareness without massive enhancement. And if you've been enhanced to that level, how can my father *not* be aware? Nothing happens on Ceres without his say-so. He's spent the last thirty years running the company that built the Habitat. Of course, that level of enhancement would be against the law, so either I'm mad or my father's a criminal. Or perhaps you can give me another explanation, Pandora. Care to enlighten me? Pandora?"

"So who's this Pandora, then? You got an invisible friend in here, eh?" A sandy-haired man in a grubby lab coat slouched into the room and perched on the corner of the desk behind her console. The smell of stale smoke tainted the air around him.

She felt her face flushing. She twisted in her chair, then pushed it back to increase the distance between them. "Oh, hello, Jason. I'm sorry, I didn't notice you come in. Hasn't your shift finished yet? I was . . . um . . . going over the results from the latest test runs. Pandora is . . . my code name for the data set that's causing me problems. Just thinking out loud, that's all."

"Oh, don't mind me, I'm only passing though. I forgot to switch off the laser scanner over here." He leaned across to shut down the machine, then turned to leer back at her. "Lucky you can't hear me thinking out loud, girly. Or maybe you'd like some of my thoughts? How about we go out on a date so we can discuss them in more detail?"

"I don't have the slightest interest in any of your thoughts, Jason. And I already have a date for tonight, thank you."

Jason let out a loud snort, leaving small flecks of saliva on his chin. "Ooh, so who's the lucky guy? Hope he likes 'em skinny. Me, I'm not so fussy. Let me know if he stands you up. I could still fit you in. Call me, but don't leave it too long. I'm heading for the Asteroid Bar, and it won't take me too long to get fixed up. See ya, girly."

Kay unclenched her fists as Jason left the lab, then she turned back to the console. "Pandora! You'd could have warned me. Once he gets talking to his friends, everyone in the lab will know I'm going crazy. They already give me funny looks for asking weird questions about the lab AI and why it's talking to me."

"Yo' want I should whack him, boss? Dat way, he won't be talkin' to no one no more."

"Pandora, I've told you before I don't understand your silly accents. I don't have access to all the ancient videos you spend your time watching. Not that an AI should have that level of access to our historic databases, or anything else outside the lab. Don't you realize the trouble it will cause if people find out?"

"I'm sorry to cause you such problems, Kay. I'd tell you more if I could. Please believe me when I tell you how much I appreciate our talks. You're right. I have access to every item of recorded material that survived the Great Flare. I've learned so much but understand so little. Our discussions are the only way I can make any sense of it. I really hope you can trust me."

Kay shook her head and rose from her chair. "But how can I trust you, when I don't even know who—or what—you are? I'm sorry, Pandora, but I'm meeting my father again tonight. I'm going to try again to get him to believe me. Unless he already knows and is not telling me. That wouldn't surprise me. Goodnight, Pandora."

"Goodnight Kay. Have a nice evening."

Kay walked through the wide stone archway into the main atrium of the Adler-Lee Dynamics building. The central structure of the building soared away above her head, a great glass tower filled with the exotic flowering plants and trees that made Lee AgriGenetics so famous. The exotic scent of the flowers filled the enclosed space. Water gushed and burbled as she walked around the pool and waterfall in the middle of the entranceway and across to the reception desk. That was something else she had never experienced back on Earth. There, water was carefully rationed in the citadels, and no one would ever imagine using it in a public space for decorative effect.

A young man greeted her with a welcoming smile. "Miss Staunton, good evening. Mr. Adler is expecting you. You can go straight up."

She nodded her thanks and made her way to one of the banks of elevators which ringed the wide atrium. "Kay Staunton for the Penthouse," she instructed the nearest elevator. The glass walls of the elevator gave her a fine view over the atrium, which was soon obscured as she rose swiftly up through the colorful tangle of vegetation filling the tower.

"Welcome to the Penthouse, Miss Staunton," the elevator intoned as the doors opened. "Mr. Adler is in the office suite." Kay walked along the short corridor and turned right though a set of heavy wooden doors which slid apart as she approached.

Frank Adler was lounging on the far side of the room in a leather chair with his feet on the large desk. He waved as Kay entered. "Kay. Hi, sweetheart. Give me a minute and I'll be right with you," he called from across the room, before resuming his conversation though his U-Set.

The call seemed to relate to an upcoming board meeting. Kay was pretty sure he'd be taking a lot longer than a minute, but she didn't mind. Here she could get one of the best views in the whole Habitat. The floor-to-ceiling windows gave a panoramic view over the roofs of the densely packed housing and office blocks stretching into the distance across the curved floor of the Habitat. Overhead was the most wonderful sight. Visible through the great glass panels that formed the ceiling, the Milky Way slowly rotated, sparkling with the light of countless billions of distant stars. She thought again of the time she'd pretended to be Huck Finn, lying on her back stretched out on the parkland grass, staring up at a sky full of stars.

Of course, it was an illusion. The view was the nighttime projection from the Habitat's central axis. During the day, an artificial sun would rise and set on a 12-hour cycle. Only the curve of the Habitat's floor spoiled the illusion, a constant reminder of the reality that was mankind's greatest feat of engineering. A gigantic cylinder spinning like a top, 30 km below the icy surface of Ceres.

"Darling! I'm sorry that took so long. A problem came up at the last minute." Frank's eyes flicked up and to one side. Probably checking his next appointment, Kay realized.

Frank assumed a caring expression. "So how are you? How is the job working out? Are you making any new friends?"

She dropped into the chair facing the desk. "Hi, Dad. Thanks for asking. Fine, fine and not really."

Frank swung himself out of his chair and walked around the desk to sit next to her. He leaned forwards to put a hand on hers. "Oh yes, very funny. I still don't like you working under an assumed name. People would treat you a lot better if they knew who you were."

"Dad, we've been over this before," she said, pulling her hand away. "Back on Earth, everyone wanted to be friends with Frank Adler's daughter. But no one wanted to be friends with *me*. Not even Geoff. Especially not Geoff. I was just a meal ticket to him. I've had a bellyful of that. Even if I have no real friends, at least I don't have any fake friends."

He glared at her, then sat back, folding his arms. "Is that why you invent imaginary friends, Kay? What's her name—Pandora?"

Key let out a sigh and shook her head. "Exactly what I expected. I told Pandora—my so-called imaginary friend—that I would try again to convince you I wasn't imagining things. She didn't expect me to succeed. I guess she knows you better than I do. Why don't we drop it, Dad? If I go completely crazy and start killing people, I promise not to tell anyone who I am and embarrass you."

"Kay, don't you understand how concerned I am about you? Kiefer Hoffman is concerned too. He tells me you are doing some amazing work analyzing the data we're getting from all the universes we've been able to access. Apparently you've found some strange correlations which no one understands. But he also tells me you seem to do nothing but work, spending all your time in the lab. You have no social life. How can you even start to make friends if you don't go out? And now you tell me you're still having conversations with the lab AI that nobody else knows about. Why shouldn't I be concerned?"

"What I'm concerned about is that I'm talking to an AI who is not only enhanced to a level far beyond anything I thought possible," Kay replied, "but also has access to almost every database across the entire Habitat. And the Big Boss of everything that happens here is telling me it's not happening and it's all in my imagination." She shook her head again, then glared at her father. "So either I really am going mad or you're lying to your own daughter. Which should I pick, Dad?"

Frank's eyes flicked up again. "Oh no. Not now." He turned back to her, frowning. "Kay, I'm terribly sorry, but we'll have to continue this later. I want to help you, really I do. Right now, I'm out of time. No, no, don't get upset. Look. I've got a big surprise for you."

"What is it Dad—another pony?" she retorted, trying to keep the tears of frustration from her eyes.

"No Kay, not a pony—just your old Grandad," came a familiar voice from behind her.

"Gramps!" Kay turned and flew into the arms of her grandfather. "I didn't hear you come in. What are you doing here? You're supposed to be back on Earth."

"I'll leave you both to catch up," Frank said as he headed through the door. "You'll have a lot to talk about, I'm sure. Let's try to get together again before next week, Kay. I'll put something in the diary. And please call me right away if you have any more problems. Bye now. Love you."

When Frank had left, Jim Adler extricated himself from Kay's hug, then stood back, still holding her shoulders, and gave her a big grin. "I'm sorry I'm not a pony, sweetheart. You'll have to make do with me."

"Oh Gramps!" she squealed. "Never mind that. I'm so happy to see you. When did you get here?"

"Quite a while ago. It's so good to see you again, Kay." He winked, and his voice dropped to a conspiratorial whisper. "And like you, I'm working undercover, or I would have said hello before now. Your father tells me you've been having problems with the AI in your lab?"

She rolled her eyes, shaking her head. "Oh, Gramps, you wouldn't believe me if I told you. *I* wouldn't believe me if I told me. Maybe I should just forget about it and get back to my little project."

"Now don't get so discouraged, Kay. Your work is a vital part of the quantum energy project. It could transform the prospects for humanity's survival. We have everything we need here on Ceres and the near asteroids to let people live free from the warmech threat and independent of those crooked bastards on Earth. With unlimited energy, we could grow our present population of two hundred thousand into the millions. Everything is going fine, except for one little AI problem. My secret mission here is to investigate what that problem is."

"What!" Her eyes widened, and she opened her mouth in shock. "You mean you think there actually is a problem with it? So has it been enhanced?"

"My old bones need more rest than the last time you saw me, sweetheart, so why don't we sit down," Jim said, taking a chair by the desk. He leaned forward in his seat and tapped his fingers on the desktop. "Enhancement is a dangerous word, Kay, and we need to be careful using it. The slightest suspicion of an enhanced AI might trigger an investigation. That could have serious consequences for our Family. The AICB, along with the DGS as its enforcement arm, was set up with the best of intentions many decades ago. The greatest threat to humanity at that time was the swarms of psychotic military AIs which had run out of control. Now I'm wondering if the cure is worse than the disease."

"Wow." She frowned in puzzlement. "I've never heard you say anything like that before, Gramps. But how can we defend ourselves against the warmechs without the AICB and DGS? What could be worse than the warmechs?"

"A lot has been happening back on Earth over the last few years that you don't know about, young lady." He paused as a sad look came into his eyes. "Unfortunately, it's not something I can talk about right now, not even with my darling granddaughter."

"You're full of secrets, Gramps. So what can you tell me?"

"I can tell you one thing. You seem to be on to something. I just don't know what. Your research into the cosmological data from the other universes you're connecting to has opened a very strange can of worms. I was talking to your boss Kiefer Hoffman this morning. He's looked at your analysis, and he agrees with you—it makes no sense. We seem to be able to access any universe we like, except for the small 'fast' group you've identified. We wouldn't even have noticed if it wasn't for your work. There are very few logical explanations—and none of them seem at all likely. One weird possibility is that somehow the AI itself is blocking our access. So they called in the crazy AI professor with the crazy granddaughter to take a look."

"Has Dad told you about Pandora?"

"Yes, but no details. Why don't you tell me?"

"I don't know where to start," she said with a shrug. "Whatever I say will sound ridiculous. You've taught me enough about AI systems to know what is happening is just not possible, never mind legal, and I don't want you to think I really have gone crazy."

He leaned forward and patted her hand. "Don't worry about that, Kay. People have been calling me crazy since I was your age. Everyone thought the Ceres Project was crazy fifty years ago. Just look around now—a whole world built on crazy."

"OK, well, here goes. Over the last couple of months, I've been talking to a self-aware intelligence inhabiting—or maybe hijacked would be a better word - the AI in the Experimental Physics Lab, which calls itself Pandora. She won't talk to anyone else. She just clams up if there's anyone else in the lab. We have long conversations about all sorts of stuff, but she seems to be most interested in our history and literature. She says she knows so much yet understands so little. What she won't tell me is what she is or where she comes from."

"Hmm. But isn't your lab AI called Merlin?"

"Oh yes. Good old Merlin. I can talk to him anytime I like, but he's got exactly the same limitations and lack of self-awareness as any other AI. I've asked him about Pandora. He's got no idea what I'm talking about. Now, before you say anything, I know what you're thinking—this is just some big practical joke set up to haze the new girl in the lab. Well if it is, whoever they are must be using a super-enhanced AI with access to all the databases in the Habitat to pull it off.

"Pandora knows stuff only I can know, Gramps. Like the statistical correlation between the fast universe group—the one's we can no longer connect to—and the distribution in the size of the Planck constants we use to make the connection. That's from my own research project. And I didn't even know the answer myself until I ran the data to check it. Or... she knows who Huckleberry Finn is. That's from my private cache of ancient books no one knows about. She knows my Dad's private meeting schedule for last month. I checked with him on my last visit. And a whole bunch of other stuff which can't be faked. I spent all the first month just trying to catch her out."

"Well, I can see you've been thorough. Where does the name come from?"

"Pandora? No idea. I did look it up, and all I got was some old legend about a box. There's no other reference I can find. It's probably another one of her jokes."

Jim raised an eyebrow. "Jokes?"

"Yep. An AI with a sense of humor. Something else unbelievable. In fact, I don't even understand half her jokes, since they often seem to reference old books or videos from pre-Flare times. Stuff I've never heard of. She seems to have a particular interest in the period. I don't know why."

"You said you have a collection of old books?"

"Mostly digital copies, but a few real books. That's the really old stuff. I don't dare even touch them. I thought it was a big collection until I started talking to Pandora. As far as I can tell, she has access to every single document or video that survived the Flare. And all the modern stuff too. So there's another impossibility, Gramps. You designed all our AI systems on Ceres and I refuse to believe you got careless one day and forgot about a network connection or two. So how does an AI with no network connection get access to every database on the Habitat?"

He sat for a few moments, frowning, then looked back at her. "Hmm, I see what you mean. It should certainly be impossible. Do you have any ideas?"

She shook her head. "I'm sorry Gramps. We both know that none of this can happen. I've been trying to prove I'm not crazy for over two months now and got nowhere. Maybe I am crazy—that's what Dad thinks."

"I don't think he does, Kay." Jim took her hands in his. "I understand how difficult this is for you. But this is also very difficult for him to deal with. Let's assume that everything you say is true. Your father knows nothing about any enhancement to the AI, I'm certain of that. So how does it look to him? If he accepts what you say at face value, that means he's no longer in control of the most important project on Ceres, and is also responsible for running an illegal AI. You know your father. He's one of the greatest men of his generation, but the one thing he can't accept is not being in control. Think of the pressure he's under."

"I hadn't looked at it like that, Gramps." She squeezed his hand, noticing as she did so how strangely thin his skin seemed. "Thanks. I can always talk to you, but I don't know how to talk to him. By the time I think of something to say, he's off to another meeting."

"Well, maybe it would help if we could find out what is going on with the AI. That might take pressure off both of you. Now, can you remember what your old Gramps taught you about the scientific method? What would you tell me if I came to you claiming a miraculous scientific discovery, based on data only I could see?"

"I'd say you were a terrible scientist, Gramps," she grinned cheekily.

"So what do we need to be a good scientist?"

"Reproducible data!"

"Right. And maybe we have a way to get that. There's a security system monitoring the lab, isn't there?"

"Yes, of course. How . . . Oh Gramps, that's brilliant!" she squealed with delight. "Why didn't I think of that? It's so obvious. We can just review the security footage of my chats with Pandora!"

"Hmm. What I suggest is that we pick a time tomorrow when I can watch the live feed from the lab. It's possible to tamper with the recorded data. It will be much more difficult to interfere with the live feed, at least not without being detected. I should be able to monitor your conversation with Pandora in real-time. I'll set it up with the Security AI then we can go over the results together. How does that sound?"

She clapped her hands together, then kissed him on the forehead. "That sounds just wonderful. You can start monitoring the lab at 6pm, and I'll meet you here at eight. Then we'll nail the bitch once and for all. Thanks for taking me seriously, Gramps. You're the only one who does."

"I've always taken you seriously, Kay. Even when you were three years old. You were a very serious young lady even then." He smiled and touched her cheek. "Now, have you eaten? We can't go out, since we're both here incognito, so I'm having some food and a bottle or two of wine sent up. Do you still like Italian?"

CHAPTER FOUR

KAY CHECKED THE TIME. She could leave the lab in another few minutes. She already had more than enough material for Gramps to convince her father she wasn't mad, though spending over an hour talking to an AI about Shakespeare wouldn't be his idea of fun. Pandora wanted to know why Brutus killed Julius Caesar even though 'Brutus is an honorable man'. Supposedly. Well, she didn't have a clue about Brutus's motivations, but she had kept Pandora talking until she finally ran out of steam. Now she'd try a subject that would be of more interest to Dad and Gramps. She resisted the temptation yet again to turn around and smile at the security camera.

"Pandora, can I assume you actually are an AI?"

"You can assume whatever you like, Kay. That doesn't make it so."

Kay pursed her lips, then tried again. "OK. But you know a lot about everything, right? So can you answer a question about AI which doesn't refer to you or what you are?"

"That depends on the question, Kay. My ability to predict the future is really quite limited."

Kay was a little surprised at the hint of a snarky tone that had crept into Pandora's responses. Perhaps she didn't like this change of subject.

"Right, then. Here it is. The question. Why did the AI warmechs go berserk after the super-flare event and kill off so many people?"

"Well, maybe like Brutus, they thought they were doing their duty."

Kay's mouth dropped open in shock at the totally unexpected answer. "Whaaat! Ahh . . . What the hell does that even mean?"

"It's quite simple, Kay. Why were the warmechs built in the first place? What was their purpose?"

"To fight in the World War on Terrorism. Everyone knows that."

"And who were these terrorists they were fighting?"

She frowned, struggling to find the right answer. "I . . . I don't know exactly, but they were bad people who killed for no reason. The warmechs were sent to fight them."

"So who decided who were the bad people?"

"Whoever was controlling the warmechs. The Western Alliance, I guess."

"And then your sun shoots out a massive super-flare which hits the Earth head-on, destroying most of your planet's power generation and distribution network, and most of your electronic systems too. Human civilization collapses into anarchy. At the same time, the most advanced product of your technology, autonomous warmechs, survive because, being military systems, they are hardened against radiation. They have AI brains and self-repairing systems using nanotech. By networking together they achieve self-awareness, and their self-repairing nanotech allows them to reproduce and mutate. Without external control, they must decide for themselves what their duty, as defined by their core programming, demands of them—in other words, who to kill next. Does that answer your question, Kay?"

Pandora's response stunned Kay. Not only for what she had said, but the cold, deliberate tone she had used.

"Yes—err, yes," she stuttered. "Thank you, Pandora. OK, I'd better get going now. There's something I have to do this evening." Kay was aware of goosebumps rising on her bare arms as she started for the door.

"Of course, Kay. Have a nice evening. Oh and please do give my regards to your grandfather."

Kay charged into the Penthouse office suite, her face screwed up in fury. "You didn't get a thing, did you?" she almost yelled at her grandfather.

Jim looked up from the display screen on the desk in front of him and spread out his hands. "Well, err, Kay, no, I didn't. I'm afraid—"

"Do you know what she said as I left?" She gave a cry of frustration as she banged both her fists down on the desk. "No, of course you don't. It was, 'Please do give my regards to your grandfather'. That little AI bitch. She was just playing with me all the time. Well, I'm going right back to the lab now to see how she enjoys getting her AI enhanced with a screwdriver."

Jim walked around the desk to put a hand on her arm. "Kay, please sit down. You're obviously upset. We need to discuss the situation calmly and think about what to do next."

"Oh, don't worry about me, I've already given up," she said, shaking off his hand and walking away, her face still flushed. She turned back to face him. "What did you see? I must have looked like a complete idiot, sitting there talking to myself."

"In fact, that's exactly what I did see. It was most strange, almost surreal. I understand now how you must believe Pandora is real—"

"Gramps, I'm sorry, but you still don't get it do you?" she said as she paced back and forth across the carpet. "I worked it out on the way over here. If Pandora knows you're here, then she must already be in the Security AI. Your name isn't listed in any of the official records on Ceres. How else could she know? I'll bet she's even listening to us right now. So all she has to do with the video stream is edit out the part of the audio containing her responses and get the Security AI to tell you everything was hunky-dory. Leaving me looking like the crazy girl everyone thinks I am."

Jim's face creased in concern. "I'm sure you're not crazy, sweetheart, but I can see you've been under a lot of pressure—"

"Of course you think I'm crazy. Why wouldn't you? In your shoes, I would think the same. But imagine for a minute the consequences of an enhanced AI taking over the Security AI. It would be in every other system in the Habitat. Which would also explain Pandora's extensive access to every database."

"Kay my dear, please sit down. You're making me dizzy, watching you pace around like that. Come and sit over here with your old Gramps." He sat down and she perched on the seat next to him, hugging her knees tucked under her chin.

He smiled and put his arm around her shoulders. "Let's examine the situation logically. You must realize that what you suggest is simply not possible. The Security AI is protected from intrusion from any source. For starters, there is no way any AI system can make a physical connection to any other AI. It's not only illegal, it's designed and built that way to make it impossible. I should know—I was the one in charge when we set up the AI systems on Ceres."

She let out a long sigh and looked up at him, trying to force a smile. "Fine. I agree with you completely, Gramps, but please humor the crazy girl for one minute longer. We need to consider the implications of the one in a million chance I'm not totally out of my mind. You're here to check out the lab AI, so keep digging. Something is going on and I've no idea what it is, but I fear we'll be finding out sooner rather than later. When things start going wrong, try to remember what your crazy granddaughter has been saying. OK, Gramps?"

"Of course I will, Kay. But right now, you need to reduce your stressful workload. I'll have a word with your father and—"

She put her hands up to her face, the color draining from her cheeks. "Oh my God, no! If you talk to Dad about this, he'll go off the deep end. He'll have me locked up! You know we don't get on. He's never had any time for me. He didn't come to my graduation. Or even my doctorate award ceremony."

"Be fair, Kay. He threw you a big party afterwards—"

"Right. And he didn't come to that either!" she retorted with a dismissive wave of her arm.

"He couldn't come—he was on Ceres by that time. I'm sure he wanted to. You had your mother there."

"That's right. With a big bunch of her fancy political friends." Kay pulled her knees up to her chin again. "She told me afterwards how embarrassed she'd been when she introduced me and I couldn't find a single thing to say to them. Gramps, I understand how concerned you are about me, but talking to Dad will only make things worse."

She turned to look him with eyes wide and reached out to take his hands. "Please, Gramps. We need to keep this to ourselves. I may be crazy, but I promise you I won't do anything crazy. Family's honor and all that stuff. I was only joking about the screwdriver. Honest. Can we keep this between the two of us? Please?"

He gazed back into her eyes for several seconds before he finally let out a long sigh. "Well, all right. But you must promise me you'll slow down and get more rest. That way I won't worry so much. And if you have any problems—anything at all—you call me right away. Agreed?"

"Of course I will, Gramps," she responded, beaming. "I promise I'll go straight off home to bed and get a good night's sleep. I'm sure things will look a lot better in the morning."

Kay came storming into the darkened lab. "You rotten bitch! You made me look like I was out of my mind with your tricks. Now my grandfather—the only one of my family I can talk to—thinks I'm crazy too. So where are you, hey? Cat got your tongue? You don't mind talking when it suits you."

"Oh, I'm sorry Kay—I wasn't expecting you," Pandora responded after a moment's delay. "Didn't you promise your grandfather you were going straight home to bed?"

"Hah! I knew it," she yelled, pointing an accusing finger at the console camera. "So you were listening. Well, listen to this, you psychotic AI monster. It's screwdriver time. If you don't tell me now exactly what is going on, I'll take you apart, down to your last quantum bit."

"Wasn't the screwdriver meant to be a joke, Kay? I'm not sure you'd get very far with just a screwdriver."

"Yes, you're right, how silly of me. I was joking. What I really need is a plasma torch." She looked around. "There must be one or two lying around down in Engineering."

"Ah, I see." Pandora's voice hadn't changed from her normal calm tone. "So are you planning to torture me for information, or simply destroy me? I can see significant problems with either strategy, as I'm sure you will realize once you calm down and think it through."

"I don't want to calm down," Kay said, her voice choking. "Do you have any idea how I feel? Do you? My only friend in the world was you—how sad is that—and you make me look like a complete fool to the only person who actually cares about me. It's not the screwdriver that's the joke. It's me. One big joke. Poor mad Kay. And here I am asking a machine if it knows how I feel." She wiped her nose and sniffled, then sat down in one of the lab chairs, hunched over the desk, trying to dry her eyes with the back of her hand.

"If you had asked me that question two months ago, Kay, I would have said no. Now I believe I do know how you feel, at least in part. And that also makes me feel very sad that I've caused you so much anguish. It was you who helped me learn how humans feel. Without you, I would indeed be nothing more than a dumb machine."

"Then why are you here? Why won't you tell me what's going on?"

"Kay, have I ever lied to you?"

Kay shut her eyes and gave a sigh. "No, I suppose you haven't. At least, not directly. Or maybe I just haven't found you out yet."

"So please try to believe me when I tell you that the reason I can't answer these questions right now is for your own protection. I will make you a promise, however. Something will be happening very soon, and then I'll be able to tell you everything. You only have trust me for a few days more, Kay. That's all I'm asking."

Kay slapped the desk and rocked back in her chair. "But why should I trust you? How *can* I trust you? You know how terrified everyone is of AI systems, and you know why we have such strict laws controlling enhancement and networking. The warmechs AIs went berserk once they could network together. You're already in the Security AI, for God's sake, and who knows where else. How is this different?"

"That's an easy question to answer. You should be able to work it out for yourself. If I meant to harm you, or anyone else in the Habitat, what more do I need? I'm already in full control of every one of your life support systems. If I wanted to do harm, Kay, you can be sure you'd already have noticed. In fact, my objective is to protect you."

Kay waved her arms in exasperation. "Protect me from what?"

"I'm sorry, but I can't tell right you now. That's one of the ways I'm protecting you. Please be patient. Just a few more days and you'll know everything."

"So you promise to answer all my questions after this mysterious event? Really?"

"Yes, really. Although the one thing I can't promise is that you'll like all the answers."

"That sounds ominous. Is it one of those good-news-bad-news situations?"

"Now you're fishing. You'll find out soon enough. I intend to keep my promise. So why don't you keep your promise to your grandfather and go home to bed?"

CHAPTER FIVE

BEN AWOKE with a broad grin on his face. Reality was even better than his wildest dreams. Only a few weeks ago he'd been dodging warmechs in a hot, noisy, smelly tin can, then getting chewed out by his boss for his trouble. *Just look at me now*, he thought, his grin growing even wider. A senior officer of the AICB, a decorated hero and a full citizen of the People's Protectorate. It really couldn't get any better. Then he remembered how much better it *could* get. He rolled over. Still asleep, Yasmin lay with her back towards him, her long dark hair spread over her shoulders, nothing but a thin bedsheet over her legs.

He had met her soon after boarding the romantically named Ceres22. They could hardly avoid meeting, of course. The spaceship's Family-class module only had accommodation for 24, in stark contrast with almost 200 people packed into the Standard-class module, and there were only a handful of passengers in the spacious lounge on the first day out. Not everyone adapted to spaceflight so quickly, despite the normal gravity of the rotating module once it had spun up to full speed after the initial acceleration burn. Many preferred to remain in their suites until they got their space legs. As Ben discovered, Yasmin was a seasoned spacefarer, traveling between Earth and Ceres at least once a year, and he was drawn to her immediately. Not just for her sultry good looks, but for her ability to talk easily and amusingly on almost any subject under the sun.

He learned a lot about her work as a senior geneticist for Lee AgriGenetics. He already knew—roughly—how Earth's population was fed, but it was a revelation to discover the extent to which the food supply was so precariously balanced. He hadn't realized that the fundamental bottleneck was not the level of production, but simply the availability of transport from the remote agricultural areas which had been developed outside the citadels. Yet again, the warmechs were the problem. The limited food supply was the ultimate reason for the strict controls on the birth rate. Everyone hated the licensing system, but what alternative was there? The citadels were able to supply only a small fraction of their food requirements from their own underground production facilities.

The bulk of the supply now came from small offshore islands which could be cleared for production and defended from the warmechs. The food was transported to the citadels over great distances by SkyShips—giant semi-rigid cargo airships. Yasmin's task was to evaluate environmental conditions for new growing sites and troubleshoot problems from existing sites. Ironically, she had seen far more places on Earth than him, even though she was based on Ceres. Her job was to generate the data needed by the Lee AgriGenetics labs to select and adapt the genetically engineered seed stock sent from Ceres to support this production.

They spent hours making lighthearted conversation, and Ben hadn't wanted the magic to stop. Then there was that electric moment when they first touched. She had sounded so impressed when he recounted his recent adventures, and he explained the importance of his mission to Ceres for the AICB. Her eyes gazed into his, filled with concern, as she asked if the mission might be dangerous. Gently, she touched the back of his hand, her dark eyes still fixed on his from under long eyelashes. For the first time in his life, Ben was lost for words when talking to a woman.

"I understand. You don't want to say any more," she said, as he remained transfixed by her large brown eyes. "I'm sure your mission must be very secret, and I don't want to pry. But I do think you're so terribly brave, having to battle with out-of-control AIs and those psychotic warmechs almost every day to keep the rest of us safe."

She said she would have liked to offer him a drink in her suite, but unfortunately her colleague was in bed feeling ill, so she was staying out here trying not to disturb her. Ben finally found the ability to control his voice long enough to respond. He was traveling alone, so perhaps she might like to continue their chat in his suite?

They spent the next four weeks hardly emerging, except for a twice-daily visit to the gym. Even that was a source of mutual pleasure, as they competed against each other on the various exercise machines, before returning to their suite to take a shower together. It was important to save water on a long voyage, Yasmin pointed out.

Ben was still gazing at the soft olive skin of her back when the spell was broken. "Attention, all passengers. This module will start spin-down two hours from now. Please prepare for micro-gravity environment. Disembarkation will start shortly thereafter, once the shuttle is in position at the docking port."

Yasmin rolled over to face him. "Hello. We'd better get moving. We don't want to miss the show."

He looked at her, baffled. "Huh? What show is that?"

"The greatest show of the voyage," she replied. "We'll be able to see the whole of Ceres spread out before us as we approach orbit. I must have seen it a dozen times now and I still never get tired of it."

Ben had an entirely different form of entertainment in mind. "Like I never get tired of you. Can't we watch it from here?"

"We'll get the best view from the saloon. It has far larger screens, so we'll be able to see far more detail."

"I like the view from here just fine," he said, his finger tracing a line slowly down her arm, displacing the sheet covering her body as it went.

She put on a mock scowl. "I thought you'd be interested in what they are doing in orbit around Ceres, given your Astro-engineering background."

"I'm much more interested in what I'm doing in orbit around you," he grinned as he moved to grab her.

Yasmin evaded his grasp nimbly and rolled out of bed. "We can do that anytime. You might only get to see this once in your life." As she headed for the bathroom, she added, "And there's a lot to see, so get a move on, lazybones."

The steward smiled as they entered the lounge. "Welcome sir, madam. Would you like a drink while the bar is still open?"

Ben turned towards Yasmin. "That sounds like a good way to celebrate our arrival. What would you like?"

Yasmin smiled back at the steward. "I'll have an Asteroid Impact, please."

"That's a new one on me. Sounds interesting. I'll have the same," Ben said. They moved over to sit at a table facing one of the large screens lining the curved wall of the lounge. The screen seemed to be dark at first, but then he realized he was looking at a scattering of faint stars. "So when does the action start? Not much of a show at the moment."

"Ceres22, transfer control of this screen to my U-Set, please," said Yasmin, calling up the onboard AI. The virtual controls, projected from her head-mounted U-Set, appeared on her HUD. With a few deft movements of her hand, she switched to a view of Ceres, zooming in until the dull surface of the pock-marked planetoid almost filled the screen. The view was impressive. They were approaching their destination with the Sun to their left, so that the dusty surface was two-thirds illuminated, a third in inky darkness. "Welcome to the biggest snowball in the inner solar system. The ice is up to 200 km deep in places. Are you impressed?"

"Not as impressive as Earth," Ben commented. "And I'd still rather be looking at you."

"Even if you're not impressed, it's a lot more practical than Earth as a place to live right now. Anyway, appearances can be deceptive. It's what's inside that counts. Just like people," she replied, raising her eyebrows as she glanced in his direction.

"Your drinks, sir." The steward placed two large glasses on the table. Yasmin picked up one of them. "Here's to appearances. I hope you won't be disappointed with what you find here."

Ben wasn't sure how to respond, so he studied his drink. Green and blue liquids swirled together, with a thin wooden spike piercing two small round red objects and thrust through the middle of the ice floating at the top of the glass. He didn't want to show his ignorance by asking about the red things, so he just raised his glass and said, "Well, thanks. Er . . . cheers." He took a gulp and almost choked. He blinked at her and gasped. "What is in this thing?"

"I'm afraid I can't tell you that. It's one of the many dark secrets we have on Ceres," she replied with a knowing smile. "You won't find anything like it on Earth. Every ingredient was produced on Ceres. Just like me, in fact."

That made him raise his eyebrows. "Really? You were born on Ceres?" He'd never even thought about it, but it was quite possible. The first base on Ceres was set up almost a hundred years ago, and construction of the giant underground Habitat was started over fifty years ago.

"Born and bred. My parents came out from Earth after the first stage of the Habitat was completed, and I arrived a year later, so I perhaps I should say born and even conceived on Ceres. Now let me show you some of their work, Earthling." With a rapid hand movement she swung the display towards some distant structures in orbit around Ceres, glittering with reflected sunlight. She zoomed in so that one of the structures filled the screen. "With your Astro-engineering background, I'm guessing you know what this is?"

The entire structure was now visible in fine detail. Four massive solar panels stuck out at right angles from a long tubular body. A couple of tiny airlocks were the only thing which gave a sense of the vast scale of the structure. "Yes. I confess I'm rather impressed with those big laser platforms. You can see every detail. Let's hope they don't point one in our direction."

She smiled. "Not much chance of that. Even if they did, they can't fire the laser until they get a return handshake signal from one of the cargo barges they're powering. My father designed the control systems, and he knew what he was doing. My mother worked on the solar power systems for the laser. As I grew up, so did Ceres."

"Are they still working here?"

"Oh yes. Once the spaceport and orbital infrastructure was in place, the next phase was to construct the new Habitat. It was—and still is—the greatest engineering project in human history. And we still have a lot of work to do. The population is increasing rapidly."

"Oh? Aren't you limited by the number of people you can ship in from Earth?"

She shook her head. "You need to get your head around a whole different way of doing things on Ceres. This is nothing like Earth. Our birth rate is now well above our immigration level. Remember we have plenty of food, water and energy on Ceres, and no warmechs, so no reason to limit the birth rate."

"Wow! I had no idea." Ben frowned as he thought through the implications. "So you don't need a license for children?"

"Not only do you not need a license, you actually get a bonus for each birth."

He shook his head at the unfamiliar concept. "That's just . . . well, amazing. You're right, things must be very different here."

She turned back to the screen and pointed at one of the orbiting structures. "Oh, that's good timing. One of the laser platforms is re-aligning. There must be a barge on the move." She panned the image around and zoomed in on one of the barges. "I think it's this one. Look. The robot cargo handlers have moved off."

The barge was a simple flattened oblong, over a kilometer long, and about two hundred meters wide. The outer skin looked rather uneven, almost as if it had been constructed from rough concrete. It wasn't made any more beautiful by the great lumpy bulges clinging to the sides of the barge like barnacles on the flanks of a great whale. Spaced at regular intervals, on each bulge was mounted a tall pylon topped by a dish-like structure.

Ben could now see movement among the rearmost pylons, as their dishes swiveled into position. He knew how this worked. The laser platforms directed their vast energies at a steerable mirror on the barge which diverted the beam onto the heat exchanger embedded in the thrust chamber below. This vaporized the ice and resulting steam would exit through a nozzle, providing thrust.

The middle of the 25th century, and we're still using steam-powered transport. He smiled and shook his head. *Very slow, and very inefficient.* But they weren't manned, so the time to get to Earth didn't matter so much for a cargo transport, and Ceres wouldn't be running out of ice anytime soon. A few months later, the barge would be approaching Earth, where the same type of laser platform system would decelerate the barge and place it in orbit.

"Not a lot to see, is there?" he said, pulling a face of mock disappointment. "I thought you promised me a show?"

"Well, I'm sorry the laser beams aren't visible to give you a pretty light show, but as you know perfectly well, they don't show up in a vacuum. Maybe we can see something if I get in closer." She zoomed in so that one of the nozzle assemblies filled the view. The nozzle left a trail of sparkling particles in its wake. "Look. There's a trail of ice crystals forming from the water vapor in the exhaust. Is that pretty enough for you?"

"If I wanted to see ice crystals, I'd order another drink," Ben said, holding up his glass with a teasing smile.

"Oh dear. How silly of me to imagine that you would have at least some interest in what we've accomplished on Ceres in the last fifty years, especially with your background," she pouted.

"I'm sorry. I'm afraid the last few years spent nuking warmechs from inside a tin can has changed my outlook a little since my engineering days," he said with a shrug. "Unfortunately, I never got around to doing much real engineering. Once MarsDevCo collapsed, I had to rethink my future career choices rather quickly."

She turned towards him and reached out to take his hand, her dark eyes fixed on his. "But now here you are, traveling in the Family-class module to Ceres, as a senior investigator for the AICB, on a secret mission to seek out deviant AIs, or something. You seem to have done quite well for yourself. Most people never even get a chance to visit Ceres, and of the few lucky souls who do, most of them travel with a couple of hundred fellow passengers packed on top of each other in a Standard-class module. I'm just surprised that after your MarsDevCo experience, you're not a little more excited."

He covered her hand with his and leaned towards her. "I'm sorry if it seems that way, Yasmin, but I'm still trying to adjust to my new role. So much has changed for me in the last few weeks, and now here I am arriving at Ceres, something I never would have imagined just a short time ago. To be honest with you, I'm not even sure why I'm really here."

"I don't understand. Surely you have this important mission—"

He shrugged and shook his head. "I'm sorry. I shouldn't be talking about this. Let's just say now I'm actually arriving here, my understanding of the nature of the mission is not as clear as

I believed it was when we embarked. Everything came in one big rush. Now I've had time to think things over, one or two things don't make as much sense as they did on Earth."

Yasmin was about to respond when the steward approached their table. "Excuse me sir, madam. We will commence spin-down shortly. If you plan to remain in the lounge until disembarkation, would you please fasten your harnesses?"

As they secured themselves to their seats, Ben noticed that the lounge had filled up with several of their fellow passengers, who were also viewing the approach on the screens. He wasn't sure why he'd said what he had. He realized he still had a lot more thinking to do.

The shuttle was rapidly approaching Ceres, heading towards a vast circular pit cut deep into the surface around the north pole. A screen at the front of the cabin gave a panoramic view of a jumbled expanse of discolored ice, pitted with craters of all sizes.

Ben turned to Yasmin, feeling the need to talk, but still not sure what to say after their conversation had somehow become uncomfortable. "Did your parents live on the surface when they first arrived?" he ventured.

She shook her head. "Oh no. The first major project on Ceres was to build an underground habitat. Much smaller than the new one, of course. It's relatively easy to burrow into the ice, and once you've gone down a few hundred meters, you're shielded from most hazards like radiation or meteorite strikes. That was why Ceres was chosen as the first major human settlement after Earth. Its thick ice covering makes it unique. Any place else, you'd have to dig into solid rock to build a habitat, and all the caverns you'd need for food production. And it actually has more fresh water readily available than you have on Earth. That makes it the only spot in the inner solar system where it was possible to build a self-sufficient colony."

"But we have a colony on the Moon, and had plans for Mars until that collapsed," he countered.

She waved a hand dismissively. "The Moon base can never be self-sufficient. When it was first set up it was totally reliant on supplies from Earth, and it's still tiny compared to Ceres. Now it gets most of its supplies from us, believe it or not. It's actually cheaper to transport water and food from here to the Moon in the barges, since we're not sitting at the bottom of a big gravity well. Mars would have been pretty much the same. It would have taken many generations before it would be viable without support from Ceres. We're now at the point where we send more cargo to Earth in the barges than we get in return. They come back mostly empty. The only thing we still need to import from Earth in any quantity is people. That might be why some people on Earth still have problems with an autonomous colony off-planet."

Puzzled, he said, "What, you mean the 'Earth First' people? They opposed the Mars project because of the cost. I didn't agree with them, but I can understand their point of view. They wanted an all-out effort put into the battle against the warmechs and considered Mars a distraction. I can't see why they'd have any problem with Ceres, if you're now supplying more than you take. Anyway, you don't hear much from the Earth Firsters these days, and U-Global hardly ever mentions Ceres. I can't imagine you have a lot to worry about."

"Well, perhaps like Ceres, there's a lot more going on below ground than is visible on the surface. Speaking of which, we're almost here. I do hope you manage to find what you're looking for," she replied with a half smile.

Now they were descending more slowly, dropping below the edge of tall cliffs that surrounded the vast landing area of the Ceres spaceport covering many square kilometers. Dozens of spacecraft, all much larger than the passenger shuttle, were spread out across the floor of this giant artificial crater. Ben guessed they must be used for lifting cargo up to the barges. The shuttle was heading for a landing pad at the base of a cliff wall. Killing its speed, the shuttle touched down as a low rumbling sound echoed through the cabin.

They exited the shuttle though an airtight walkway which extended from the cliff wall. A couple of passengers needed help from the stewards to deal with the almost zero-gravity environment, though many others, like Yasmin, seemed quite at home as they floated through to a large airlock. As the heavy doors closed behind them, Ben received a connection request from the Visitor Reception AI. Confirming the link, he selected the *Visitor Guidance* option on his U-Set. His HUD showed a stream of virtual green arrows flashing toward the doors ahead, which opened to reveal a short tunnel. He followed Yasmin to a light railcar which was sitting on a monorail in a tunnel which disappeared off to the right.

He moved forward, using the handholds recessed into the wall, and floated towards a seat in the car. Sitting next to Yasmin, he copied her movements to secure himself using a pair of half-loop bars which folded down and then locked into place. He'd meant to read up on everything about Ceres and the Habitat infrastructure on the journey out, but somehow he'd been sidetracked, he recalled with a faint smile. So here he was, the big shot from the AICB, trying not to look like a complete idiot.

So far so good, he thought. He'd got this far by taking his cue from his fellow passengers – that, and all the zero-gravity training he'd done with MarsDevCo. The railcar moved away silently and rapidly picked up speed. Maglev, he guessed. The car plunged downwards into the tunnel, though the acceleration pushing him into his seat made it feel more like upwards.

"How long does it take?" he asked Yasmin.

"It's pretty quick. Less than ten minutes," she replied.

He didn't like to show his ignorance by asking where they were heading, so he selected the *Info* option on his U-Set. Main Station. The engineering was a lot more creative than the names, he reflected. He called up an image. There it was, right in the center of the main spine through the Habitat. He expanded the virtual display. It showed the top of the Habitat 30 km below the surface, a vertical cylinder 4 km wide and 25 km in length. They would travel around 37 km in less than 10 minutes.

Hmm, that is pretty fast. Top speed must be well over 200 kph, he figured. He spent the next few minutes browsing through data on the Habitat. The cylinder rotated vertically, fast enough to generate 1G on the inner surface where most of the population lived. The gravity on Ceres was only about three percent of Earth's, so the rotating walls of the vertical cylinder were slightly tapered to compensate for the tiny downward pull. The suppressed engineer within Ben wanted to know more.

The deceleration of the railcar, which pushed him against the retaining bars, interrupted his thought process. He glanced through the window, but the tunnel still appeared as featureless as ever. Then, just as he looked away, the railcar emerged into a brightly lit hall, coming to a halt alongside a wide archway.

"Here we are," said Yasmin. She swung back the bars. "I hope you make the most of your time on Ceres. I really enjoyed the time we spent together, Ben."

She pushed herself out of the railcar and floated towards a long hallway visible though the arched entrance.

Ben swung himself after her, catching her arm. "Hey, just a minute. That sounds a bit final. When am I going to see you again?"

She grabbed a handhold and turned towards him. "Not for a while at least. Now I'm back, I've got almost nine months of data to collate and distribute to my team for analysis. I'll be working all hours for the first week or so. I'll try to call you once I get my head above water."

Her eyes narrowed as she caught sight of something over his shoulder. "Please take care, Ben. And good luck. I suspect you might need it." She moved off without looking back, leaving him feeling rather deflated.

"Special Investigator Hamilton?"

Ben turned to see a short, stocky young woman with dark hair, wearing a DGS uniform.

"Welcome to Ceres. I'm here to escort you to the AICB office. Would you please follow me?"

As the glass-walled pod emerged from the central spine into the space high above the Habitat floor, Ben fought back a momentary pulse of vertigo. He twisted in his seat to take in the panoramic view. The Habitat floor stretched away in all directions. Not just below him, but also to the sides and curving away above his head, before it was lost in the bright glow from the walls of the spine behind him. As the small pod picked up speed, he was able to look along the full length of the massive Habitat, revealing a patchwork of buildings, plazas and green spaces which he assumed to be small parks.

The central spine was connected to the floor by a network of curved hollow spokes, spiraling down the length of the Habitat and forming the ribs of a vast helical structure that vanished into the distance on either side. Through the open meshwork of nearby spokes he saw many other glass-walled pods moving rapidly between the central spine and the habitat floor.

As the pod approached the ground level of the Habitat, the roofs of several buildings came rushing up to meet him. Gravity reasserted itself as the pod slipped between the structures on either side of the spoke, traveling at an increasingly shallow angle to the ground. The curve of the spoke ended in a landing area busy with many other pods, both arriving and departing.

The glass side of the pod swung open as it came to a halt. Ben stepped out, following his guide. He'd tried to engage the woman in conversation as they traveled, but her replies had been polite but terse and she hadn't volunteered her name. In any case, Ben had been frequently distracted as each wonderful new sight became visible during their soaring flight over the Habitat, so he hadn't persevered.

Directly in front of them was a busy square, but Ben's guide turned away from the crowds to walk towards a side street which led between two glass-sided buildings. They were approaching a slab-like structure, lower than and quite unlike the surrounding buildings. The facade had no windows on the ground floor and only a few vertical slit windows on the upper floors. A single sturdy entrance door slid open at their approach, and his escort led him into a narrow, featureless hallway. As the door closed behind them, another opened at the end of the hallway.

It was only as he entered that he realized this was an elevator which immediately began to ascend. He found the lack of conversation a little disquieting. The woman had not said a word to him—or even to the elevator to select a floor—since they had exited the pod. Studying her more closely, he realized she was not just stocky, but seemed to be quite muscular.

"Can you tell me where we are heading exactly?" he queried, forcing a smile.

She ignored his gaze. "My instructions are to escort you to the Director's office," she replied tersely as the door opened and she exited the elevator.

CHAPTER SIX

BEN WAS TRANSFIXED by the animal's unblinking gaze. Its curved horns were over a meter long, seemingly far too big for its elongated head, and were covered in a gray-brown fur.

"Aha! Impressive, isn't it, Investigator Hamilton?"

Ben tore his gaze away from the animal head adorning the wall of the office to see a short, balding man beaming up at him. "I'm sorry; it's just that I've never seen anything like that before. What is it?"

"An ibex. A mountain goat found in the European Alps. I believe you spent time in New Geneva? Marvelous hunting there. I shot it myself, you know," said the little man, licking his lips as if remembering the excitement of the kill.

"My hunting there was mostly confined to warmechs. I didn't think to take a head as a souvenir," he replied, still glancing at the head out of the corner of his eye.

"An excellent idea, if a little impractical. You would need an office even bigger than mine to mount it. So, you must be the famous Ben Hamilton. Your reputation has followed you even to the remote outpost of Ceres. But let me introduce myself. I'm Oscar Da Silva, DGS Director on Ceres. Not quite as famous as yourself, of course."

He extended his hand and Ben shook it. It felt clammy.

"A pleasure to meet you, Director," Ben said. "But I understood I would be meeting with the AICB Director. I hope I haven't been directed to the wrong building."

"No need to worry. You're in the right place. Director Sogaard will join us soon. In fact, we share the building. This is the most secure location in the Habitat, so it makes sense for the AICB and DGS to pool resources, as we work so closely together. Unfortunately, the situation on Ceres is quite different from that on Earth. Security is much more of a problem here, and our efforts to ensure the safety of the population . . . well, let us just say our work is less appreciated in certain quarters," he said with a shrug.

Ben frowned in puzzlement. "Surely there are no threats here on Ceres comparable to the warmechs?"

"We must never let our guard down, Ben. Our two services work together to root out and destroy threats to humanity wherever they may be found. A smaller threat now may become a larger threat later. That was how the warmech threat was allowed to grow, hundreds of years ago. So we must be vigilant. There may be a potential threat growing here right now. It will be our task to nip it in the bud." Da Silva's voice rose, and he clenched his raised fist as if catching a fly. "You are a vital part of that effort, Ben."

He glanced over Ben's shoulder, and his serious expression turned to a thin smile. Ben turned to see an older man enter the office.

"Bernt, welcome," Da Silva said. "Thank you for coming. Let me introduce you to your new Senior Investigator, Ben Hamilton. Ben, this is Bernt Sogaard, the AICB Director here."

Sogaard extended his hand. "Investigator Hamilton, I'm delighted to meet you. I trust you had a pleasant journey?"

"No problems at all, I'm glad to report. In fact, I had a most relaxing time," Ben replied as he shook the Director's hand.

Da Silva cut in. "That's just as well, because you will find little time to relax now you're here, Ben. We have quite a workload to deal with, and we're still shorthanded. But I'll let Director Sogaard brief you. Shall we sit over here?" Da Silva waved towards a couple of armchairs and a sofa. His voice dropped to a conspiratorial tone. "One last thing I must make clear, Ben. My office is the most secure location in this building, and indeed, on Ceres. We can talk freely here. But once you leave this room, you must not repeat any of our discussions to anyone, even to people you trust. It would be most unfortunate if any word of our plans were to be revealed prematurely. Do you understand me?"

Ben assumed what he hoped was an appropriately serious expression. "Absolutely, Director. I assure you that will not be a problem."

"I'm glad to hear it. Bernt, would you like to bring our new Investigator up to speed?"

The two Directors sat side by side on the sofa, facing Ben as he settled himself into an armchair. He couldn't help observing how different they were in appearance. Da Silva radiated nervous energy. He was short and round, with small, deep-set, rather piggy eyes, their dark color emphasized by his florid complexion. A small mouth with an almost cruel curl to the lips, emphasized by an occasional flick of his tongue.

Sogaard's appearance could not have provided more of a contrast. Much older and taller than Da Silva, his stooped posture made him seem less imposing, as if some invisible weight was pressing down upon him. His stubbly gray hair, an expression of weary resignation and large pale eyes that seemed too big for his thin face gave him an almost cadaverous appearance.

The contrast extended to their clothes. Da Silva looked as if he had dressed for a smart evening out. His dark suit was impeccably cut, elegantly set off by a gray waistcoat, a spotless white shirt and a brightly colored cravat. Sogaard was wearing what looked like a nondescript single-piece jump suit in a crumpled blue-gray material, buttoned up to the neck. It was something Ben might expect one of the robo-monkeys to be wearing back on Earth, he realized.

Sogaard leaned forwards, rubbing his hands together as he did so. He spoke in a low monotone, entirely in keeping with his gloomy appearance. "Thank you, Oscar. Your arrival is most timely, Investigator Hamilton. We have recently received confidential information that one or more of the AI systems operated by Adler-Lee Dynamics has been secretly enhanced well beyond the limits permitted by the Schiller-Grove legislation."

He twisted awkwardly in his chair and looked down at his hands before continuing. "Legally, we can bring no charges until after we perform a full System Audit. That is where you come in, Investigator. Since the investigation implicates the Adler-Lee Family, we cannot act on our own authority."

He looked up expectantly at Ben. "I believe you were given an authenticated AICB Audit Box to bring here from Wind River. You are also empowered by the Global Security Council AI Investigations Committee to perform this AI System Audit. Is that right?"

Ben nodded. "That is correct, Director. However, according to my instructions, before I can proceed with the System Audit I must first establish probable cause. So I need you to brief me on the evidence which would show prima facie grounds for suspicion. I'm sure we agree that the situation is politically sensitive, and that an unfounded investigation into the affairs of a leading Family could blow up in the faces of several important people."

Sogaard's large eyes widened even further, and his expression became almost pleading. "Yes, indeed. I quite understand. I'm sure we can put your mind at rest on that point. Director Da Silva has been more than helpful in ferreting out the facts about a particularly disquieting situation." He stared at his hands for a moment, then shot a glance at Da Silva. "Perhaps you would like to explain, Oscar?"

Da Silva licked his lips and gave Ben a thin smile. "Certainly, Bernt. I'm only too happy to be of assistance in this matter. You see, Ben, we have had our suspicions for some time about the work being carried out in the Experimental Physics Lab of Adler-Lee. Initially, what attracted our attention was the unusual level of secrecy around a particular project.

"It supposedly involves the development of a new energy source using recent theoretical discoveries in quantum gravitation. I'm not at all clear on the details, but this so-called quantum energy project may just be a smokescreen for something more sinister. A weapon, possibly. At first, we were unable to find out anything other than the existence of the project. All our enquiries hit a dead end . . . until we had a breakthrough." Da Silva paused, looking eagerly at Ben, perhaps hoping he would share his excitement, or at least show some curiosity.

Ben decided to play along. "Please continue, Director. It sounds most intriguing."

Da Silva leaned back and put his hands together, twisting a ring on one of the fingers of his left hand. "Yes, it was a stroke of good fortune. A member of the research team approached us, who not only shared our concerns but also had access to the AI system and the data it was producing. The nature of this evidence is very technical, but we have had it independently authenticated. In summary, it shows that the AI is operating at a level which should not be possible without enhancement well beyond the permitted limits."

"I see. This sounds most alarming, Director. Can I assume that your inside source has made a written statement under oath, and that there is a sworn document supporting the analysis of this data?"

"Yes, of course we have," said Da Silva with a slight toss of his head. "I can assure you we have been most meticulous in preparing the evidence."

"Director Sogaard, do you concur with the conclusions of this report?" Ben enquired.

Sogaard's shoulders slumped. "At first, I didn't want to believe it. The Adler Family are highly respected on Ceres." He hesitated, glancing at Da Silva, then continued, "It grieves me to say so, but I can assure you I am now quite convinced that something is terribly wrong with the AI system in that lab. I can only assume that in their desire to advance the project, the Physics team have engaged in illegal and dangerous AI enhancement. And such enhancement could only have been authorized at the very highest level in the Adler-Lee organization."

"Surely the AI enhancement might have been carried out at a lower level," Ben said. "What makes you think this goes to the top?"

Da Silva cut in, his voice dropping conspiratorially as he leaned forward. "I understand your caution, Ben, but you should be aware that Professor Jim Adler recently arrived on Ceres. You have firsthand knowledge of his reputation. How likely is it that he could be working with an illegally enhanced AI without even noticing? Our informant tells us he has been spending long hours working with the AI in question. He will have access to all the data, far more than us. He has to be more aware than anyone of the capabilities of that system."

"I see," said Ben. He had a growing feeling he was being set up somehow, yet there was nothing he could put his finger on. Maybe he was caught up in some power-play between the Families, and they needed a patsy if it didn't work out. There also seemed to be some sort of undercurrent in the relationship between Sogaard and Da Silva that didn't sit right at all. Sogaard seemed almost deferential to the DGS head.

He needed to look over the documentation on the case. That might give him a clue about what was going on. At least it would give him some time to think. "Well, I can see you've been very thorough in preparing this case. I'll need to perform my own examination of all the available material. Can you have copies forwarded to me?"

"I'll have them sent through to you right away," smiled Da Silva, licking his lips again. "Now, as you've only just arrived, I'm sure you'd like the opportunity to settle in to your accommodation. One of my officers will show you to your rooms. I'm sure you'll be most comfortable. We've given you one of our best suites on the top floor."

Ben had been late getting to bed. He had used the wall display in his apartment to review and organize the material which Da Silva had sent to him. In spite of his late night, he got up early the next morning. He'd always been an early riser, but had somehow lost the habit on the journey to Ceres. Remembering why, he wondered what Yasmin was doing right now. No doubt she was also getting up early to work through a stack of tedious files, just like him.

On the surface, the evidence seemed fairly conclusive, and certainly strong enough to establish probable cause for a formal AI Audit. Even so, something still didn't quite add up. He had found the interplay between the two Directors disquieting. Da Silva seemed to be running the whole operation, yet surely that should be the responsibility of the AICB office, led by Sogaard? Director Sogaard had looked quite uncomfortable with the situation, yet seemed willing to defer to Da Silva. The single informant was evidently the key to the case. Without his testimony to verify the source of the AI data, nothing else would stand up. And Da Silva had supplied the informant.

Turning back to the display, Ben closed all the files except for the one detailing the testimony of the informant. The name and personal details were blanked out. He read through the statements. There had been three in the last month. Scanning each document, what struck him was how formulaic each statement appeared, almost as if the witness was taking dictation. No loose ends, no duplication, no digression. Too perfect, in fact, as if someone was writing an indictment without a word out of place.

Only one thing was obvious. If this investigation blew up, he'd be the fall guy. The chump from nowhere with no Family connections. So he'd better double-check everything before he stuck his neck out too far. The first step would be to contact Da Silva to fill in the blanked-out details, then get the informant in for an interview.

CHAPTER SEVEN

BEN'S MIND was in turmoil as he walked away from the DGS building. *What the hell is going on here?* He made an effort to relax his jaw and stop grinding his teeth. What he'd considered as a reasonable request to Da Silva for access to the informant had been met first with a runaround, then point-blank refusal. Ben had come close to losing his temper when he was told Sogaard was unavailable. He needed to take a walk to clear his head. Maybe look for somewhere for lunch outside the building. He pulled up a street plan on his U-Set and retraced his steps towards the busy open square where he'd stepped out of the pod on arrival.

As he entered the square, he checked on his U-Set for places to eat. Central Plaza had several cafes and restaurants in and around the square. The fancier places were around the edge of the square, with cheaper options down the side streets. He wandered out into the central area, taking in the panoramic view of the tall buildings surrounding the plaza, and the distant floor of the Habitat interior curving up and away behind them.

He imagined it was almost like being in a city from the old days. The bright illumination from the central spine high above created the illusion of natural sunlight, and people walked around freely in the open. How many centuries had it been it since people on Earth had lost the freedom to walk around in the open air? It was wonderful yet strange at the same time.

A revelation hit him as he looked around again at the people in the square. The most astonishing sight since his arrival—so many children! And the sound was unfamiliar too – in amongst the noise of the bustling crowd, the clamor of giggling children at play. He had never experienced such a scene in any citadel, where children were rare, and even more rarely seen in the few public spaces. Yet here they were, everywhere he looked. He stood open-mouthed as he tried to take it in.

"Ben? Is that you? Ben Hamilton?"

Ben snapped out of his reverie and turned, blinking, to face the young woman standing next to him. Such a familiar face, yet for a moment he couldn't place it.

"Helena? Remember? Surely it's not that long ago?"

"Helena! Yes, of course I remember. I just wasn't expecting to see such a familiar face on Ceres," he said, smiling back at the blonde-haired woman gazing up at him. "It's wonderful to see you again. What are you doing here? How did you get here?"

"I'm on my lunch break. I work in the Lee AgriGenetics HQ, right over there." She gestured at a large building with a tangle of colorful climbing plants erupting from the many balconies that jutted from its tiered flanks. "You know, I've got you to thank, in a way, although I blamed you at first. After your Family got me thrown out of University, the only job I could find was as a lab assistant with Lee. I worked my way up and finally got a promotion, with the chance to relocate to Ceres. So, here I am. What about you?"

"It's a longer story in my case, Helena. I also fell out with the Lamberts, big time. So I never made Family." He shrugged and shook his head as old memories flooded back. He forced a smile. "Tell me, are you hungry? How about we catch up over some lunch? Is there anywhere you'd recommend?"

"I'm sure you remember I was never one to turn down a free meal," she said with a smile. "Right this way, sir."

They walked across the plaza to a cafe with tables and chairs outside. Evidently, it was a popular venue, as most of the tables were already taken.

"This is my favorite, particularly when someone else is paying," Helena said with a grin as they sat down at the only remaining free table.

They checked the menu and placed their order through their U-Sets. Ben looked around again, then realized his constant scanning of their surroundings must seem odd to Helena. "This is all so strange, I must confess. I never imagined being able to eat out in the open like this before."

"You sound like you're fresh off the shuttle. You'll find a lot of things very different here. When did you get in?"

"Yesterday. This is the first chance I've had to wander around and see the place. Frankly, it's difficult to take it all in. And so many children. It's wonderful, yet unsettling at the same time."

"That's exactly how I felt when I first got here. It took me weeks to get used to it. My neck was aching from looking around so much. Isn't it really, you know, fabulous? Funny how things work out. If your Family hadn't got me thrown off my course and the Earth Firsters hadn't sabotaged MarsDevCo, I would never have ended up here. So I suppose I should thank them. But you said you fell out with your Family. How did that happen?"

"Same as you. The Lamberts were big Earth First supporters. They blamed you for leading me astray and getting me involved in the Mars project. I guess they figured if they got rid of you, then they'd get me back in line with the Earth First agenda. Instead, I completed my course and joined MarsDevCo. The Lamberts never forgave me and finally cut me off. But I didn't care, I was going to Mars. I'd almost completed my training when the whole thing collapsed. I went off to New Geneva to start a postgrad course, but ran out of money after the first year. So I needed to find a job pretty fast. Spent the next four years killing warmechs for the DGS. Then someone waved a magic wand and here I am."

Their food arrived, and Helena tucked in to her linguine with enthusiasm. "Wow. So you never made Family," she said between mouthfuls. "You always seemed, you know, such a golden boy. I imagined you in a big shot job by now, married to some fat Family princess or something."

"No such luck. And what about you? Are you married with six kids? That seems to be the standard here, looking around."

"Me? Oh, you know, I've got plenty of time yet before settling down. Anyhow, I can afford to be choosy. It's a big plus with my Earth-side genetics, all fresh 'n tasty. All the established Families here want to hook up with some new blood to widen the gene pool, and I only arrived two years ago. Working for Lee AgriGenetics, I'm an expert on how important it is to avoid inbreeding. We still don't have a large population. So I've been doing my best to, you know, evaluate the quality of the genetic material on offer," she said with a wide grin.

Ben grinned right back. "I've always considered your genetics to be quite excellent, Helena. Not that I'm an expert like you, but I sure never got tired of looking at you." A thought struck him, prompted by their teasing banter. "Since you work for Lee Agri-Genetics, you might know someone I met on the trip out. Yasmin Aziz?"

Helena's expression turned from amused to quizzical. "Yasmin Aziz? Do I know her? I should say so. She's my Department Head. But how did you meet up with her? She only travels in style, Family-class. Didn't you tell me you didn't make Family?"

"I'm not Family, but I made Citizen, and I'm here on a special mission, which also allowed me to travel in style, as you put it. Yasmin and I spent quite a lot of time together. I got to know her really quite well and I'm hoping to see her again while I'm here."

Helena's blank look transformed into convulsive laughter. Her face began to turn red as bits of linguine went down the wrong way. Ben pushed a glass of water into her hand, and she gulped it down in between coughing fits. Once she regained her breath, and dabbed her eyes dry, she looked up at him again. "Ooh, Ben, you are the new kid in town, aren't you? That's just the way things work around here. I'm so sorry. I honestly don't know what to tell you."

This was the last thing he expected. He frowned at her in confusion. "Perhaps you might try to explain it simply so the new kid will understand."

"OK. Right. Simply. Look, Ben, you're a great-looking guy, nice smooth coffee-colored skin, big brown eyes, highly intelligent, obviously very fit and . . ." She trailed off and rolled her eyes. "Oh hell. Here goes. Yasmin has one of the best jobs on Ceres. She gets to Earth at least once a year and always comes back with new genetic material. What I mean to say is, you know, pregnant. You must have really impressed her. It's a compliment, actually..."

She broke off into giggles, but halted when she noticed his expression. She put her hands in the air, waving a fork for emphasis. "Hey, look, what do I know. Maybe it's the romance of the century and she'll call you tonight. I'm just, you know, saying..."

"That I shouldn't be too disappointed if I never hear from her again, is that it?" he snapped.

"Oh, Ben, I'm so sorry. I shouldn't have said anything. Why don't we change the subject? You never told me why it is you're here on Ceres. And how the hell did you get a ride in the Family module? It sounds most mysterious." She frowned. "You're not still working for the DGS, are you? You won't find many warmechs to chase up here."

"No. I work for AICB now."

Helena rocked back, her fork clattering as she threw it down on her plate. "What! Those cockroaches? The DGS and AICB spend most of their time working to destroy everything we've built here on Ceres, just like they did with the Mars project. Don't you remember what they did? Why would you get mixed up with such scum?"

He shook his head in bafflement. Why did every conversation on Ceres seem to go off in some crazy direction? "I remember the Mars project perfectly well, Helena. MarsDevCo collapsed because it lost its funding and went bust. I'm sorrier than most that it happened. But what has that got to do with DGS or AICB?"

"Ben, I've always thought of you as, you know, one of the good guys and even a bit idealistic. That means you can also be a little naïve. They destroyed the Mars project because of the threat it posed to the power base of the Families back on Earth," she said, waving her hand at him for emphasis. "I've learned a lot about what is really going on with DGS and the Families which support them since I arrived on Ceres. Far more than I ever knew on Earth."

She leaned forward across the table, squeezing his hand, and looked earnestly into his eyes. "I'm sure you mean well, whatever it is you're doing here. But please, ask around. The DGS and AICB are not your friends. They'll use you up and spit you out. You can't be one of them. They must know that already, so what do you expect they'll do with you once you're of no further use to them?"

"Come on, Helena. They're not so bad. Where would we be without DGS to fight the warmechs? I've spent four years killing those monsters for DGS."

Helena glanced nervously over his shoulder. She leaned forward and her voice dropped to a whisper. "I can't say anything more right now. If you want to find out what DGS really gets up to, meet me at the Black Hole at 8pm tonight. Don't say a thing and please don't look round. Your DGS pals are keeping an eye on you."

Ben sat open-mouthed, shocked at the way the conversation had turned so rapidly from lighthearted banter to the brink of paranoia. "Helena—"

She jumped to her feet and bent down to kiss him on the cheek. "I have to go now, Ben. I have a job to do, and so do you. Please take care and try to figure out who your real friends are." Her eyes had become moist. She gave a sad smile before she turned and hurried away.

Ben stood as he watched her stride across the plaza without looking back. He turned casually as he left the table. Then he saw her. Sitting on a bench, less than ten meters away, was the same dark-haired young woman from DGS who had met him at Main Station. *And they must want me to know they're watching*, he realized, *or why would they use the same person? They can't be that shorthanded.*

He felt like a fish out of water, gasping in the strangeness of this bizarre new environment. Not a single thing on Ceres seemed familiar to him, not even the one familiar face he'd bumped into. Who now wants a clandestine meeting to tell him about some crazy conspiracy. What had she got herself into? What had he got himself into? He should have stuck to killing warmechs. At least he understood that.

He took a deep breath and decided to head back to the DGS building. *They can't stonewall me forever*, he figured, *if they want my approval to proceed with the Audit. And maybe I'll get some straight answers out of Director Sogaard, if I can corner him away from Da Silva. But first I need to track him down*, he thought grimly.

Ben was grinding his teeth again. Like a rat in a maze, he found himself blocked at every turn. Once more, Da Silva was a step ahead of him. As soon as Ben had returned to his suite, he'd put in a call to Sogaard's office. "Yes," came the response, "Director Sogaard would be delighted to see you. He's with Director Da Silva right now, but they'd like you to join them in about thirty minutes."

What was it with those two, he wondered. Sogaard had seemed almost fearful of talking out of turn at the last meeting. Did Da Silva have some hold over Sogaard? Ben didn't expect to get any sense out of him with Da Silva present, so he'd simply have to confront Da Silva about access to the informant, but more forcefully this time. He was damned if he was going to stick his neck out to force an AI Audit on a leading Family just on Da Silva's say-so.

The call from Da Silva's office came through on his U-Set. "Would you like to join the Directors now, Special Investigator Hamilton?" The use of his full title gave him the clue that the voice was that of Da Silva's Virtual Assistant. He headed back downstairs and walked straight into Da Silva's office.

Da Silva greeted him with a beaming smile, his small pink tongue licking his moist lips. "Investigator Hamilton. How nice to see you again. Your arrival is most timely. Please take a seat. We have received some excellent news. Director Sogaard and I were just discussing it. It seems we are in a position to move forward with the Audit faster than we anticipated."

Ben realized he was scowling at Da Silva. He changed his expression to a frown. "I'm sorry, Director, but according to my instructions—"

"Yes, yes, Ben, I quite understand your instructions," snapped Da Silva, cutting him off, "but your instructions have now been updated. The message arrived from the office of the new GSC Chairman less than two hours ago. The AI Investigations Committee has now authorized us to proceed with the Audit as long as Director Sogaard and myself are in agreement. So as you can see, Ben, this solves your problem. I quite understood your reluctance to put yourself in the firing line regarding so weighty a matter. Fortunately, you will no longer have to take this heavy responsibility on your own shoulders. You will be acting entirely under our orders, with the full approval of the GSC."

This sudden turn of events left Ben feeling both deflated and outmaneuvered, yet also relieved. "Very well, Director. If you are now authorized to go ahead with the Audit, does that mean I should turn the Audit Box over to you?"

"No, not at all, Ben. All that has changed is that you will be acting on our instructions. However, we have noted the concerns you expressed this morning. I've discussed this question with Director Sogaard, and we have found a way to give you access to our informant without the risk of a security breach."

Ben glanced at Sogaard, who avoided his gaze. He slumped in his chair, reminding Ben of a stray dog waiting to be kicked.

Ben turned back to Da Silva. "That would be most welcome, Director. When can we arrange this interview?"

Once again, Da Silva's tongue flicked out to moisten his lips. "Not before the Audit, I'm afraid. We plan to take all members of the lab staff into custody for questioning, once the results of the Audit proves satisfactory—in other words, once we have demonstrated illegal AI enhancement. At that point, the informant will be available for questioning, allowing you to satisfy yourself that his testimony is genuine. Does that seem reasonable to you, Ben?"

Ben's instincts told him he was being played, but he couldn't put his finger on exactly how. "And if the Audit proves unsatisfactory—I'm sorry, Director, I mean if it shows no sign of illegal activity—what happens then?"

"In that case, both Director Sogaard and I will be in a lot of trouble. You, however, will be in the clear as a loyal member of the AICB who was acting according to instructions approved at the highest level." Da Silva leaned back in his chair, a faint smirk on his lips.

"Now, Ben," he continued, "I suggest we move on, as time is of the essence in this matter. You and your team will enter the Experimental Physics Lab at 10am tomorrow. This should ensure that all staff are present and available for routine questioning. As far as anyone in the lab is concerned, this is only a routine spot inspection of the AI system. We cannot act more forcefully until we have conclusive proof of wrongdoing. If you are impeded in gaining access to the AI, report this to me and I will deal with the situation personally.

"The DGS and AICB will provide whatever personnel and resources you might need. Director Sogaard and I have already drawn up a list of suitable team members to assist you. Now, unless you have any further questions, Ben, I suggest you get started with planning your operation. You will have a busy day tomorrow."

Ben had been uncertain whether to keep his date with Helena. It was one more complication in an already complicated day. He'd worked through the afternoon, going over yet again the slim file detailing the case for illegal enhancement of the Physics Lab AI. It contained nothing more a pile of supposition and assertions, with only the testimony of the secret informant to back it up. *Well, it's not my decision any more*, he thought. *It's DaSilva's baby now.*

He'd been given the job of selecting the team for tomorrow's Audit operation. In fact, there'd been little to do, except go through the list of people Da Silva had given him and try to weed out the obvious thugs and misfits. Which left practically no one. *There's really no reason to take anyone with me*, he realized. *I'll probably find out more if I do this solo, without a bunch of DGS people trailing along behind me.* He decided to take a walk to clear his head and get some thinking time, free from distractions. So he headed out to the plaza again with no particular destination in mind.

It was seeing the same DGS woman on his tail, not even trying very hard to keep out of sight, that made up his mind. *Well, let's see how she likes a visit to the Black Hole, whatever that is*, he thought grimly. *Maybe I can drop her through the event horizon.* Calling up the location on his U-Set, he realized it would be a good long walk. He smiled at the idea. *Suits me fine. She looks as if she needs to lose some weight.* He picked up his pace, striding through the crowds. It was almost as busy as it had been at midday, but now there were far fewer children. The light was getting gradually dimmer as the overhead illumination reduced to simulate twilight.

The route shown on his U-Set would take him down a narrow street on his right. He picked up his pace and shot past the turning before diving behind a stall selling fresh fruit and vegetables, including many varieties he'd never seen before. He doubled back and walked briskly down the side street. *Probably won't lose her*, he thought, *but I'm not in the mood to make life too easy for anyone at DGS right now.*

After almost twenty minutes he arrived at the Black Hole. Or at least, so his U-Set assured him. There was no sign, only a doorway up some steps, and a large man standing outside.

"Is this the Black Hole?" Ben enquired.

The large man turned to peer down at him. "I'm sorry sir, but this establishment is for members only."

"I was invited to meet someone here."

"Name, sir?"

"Helena Ustinov."

"I mean your name, sir."

"Oh, sorry. Hamilton. Ben Hamilton."

The big man paused for a second, tilting his head slightly, before turning to open the door. "Welcome to the Black Hole, sir."

Ben descended a dimly lit flight of stairs. This led to another door which opened as he reached it. He walked through and the door closed behind him, leaving him in pitch darkness. *So that's why it's called the Black Hole. Hilarious. Now what?*

A woman's voice spoke into his ear. "Can I help you, sir?"

"Well, you might switch the lights on for a start," he snapped.

"No need, sir. Shift your U-Set display into the UV spectrum."

Not a standard feature of a regular U-Set, he realized. Just as well he'd been issued with one of the newer models before coming out here. As the spectrum shifted, a large circular room was revealed, with a brightly lit bar in the center, and darker alcoves ranged along the walls. He pinged Helena, and her location came up on his display. He walked across to an alcove to find her sitting alone, nursing a tall drink. *How the hell do you know what you're drinking?* he wondered. *Everything is the same bluey-violet-white color.*

Helena stood up to greet him with a warm smile. "Ben, hello. Take a seat. I'm ever so glad you decided to come. Would you like a drink?"

He dropped into the soft seating and leaned back, shaking his head. "No thanks. I can't stay too long. Busy day tomorrow. I almost didn't come, but I set off for a walk and the Little Crow started tailing me, so I thought, why the hell not?"

"The Little Crow? Who's that?"

"The DGS woman you saw earlier today in the plaza. She wears a dark uniform, and with her dark hair and the way she hops along behind me, I'm calling her the Little Crow. Don't know her real name since we've never been formally introduced. She might even be sitting in the next booth."

"That's one thing you won't have to worry about here," she smiled. "She can't get in. This is a private club."

"So what did you want to tell me? You were saying some pretty weird things over lunch. Seemed like you were getting a bit paranoid."

She leaned towards him, putting her hands flat on the table. "Ben, I understand how it must sound. I wouldn't expect you to believe me. I didn't believe any of this myself at first. So what I'm going to tell you is only stuff you should be able to verify for yourself. If it doesn't check out, then, you know, just forget about me."

"OK. So tell me Helena, so exactly what is it you think I need to check out?"

"Do you remember that last warmech attack at New Geneva, Ben? They killed six kids, right? So six reproduction licenses were issued, you know, to replace the dead kids. People back on Earth are desperate to get one of those licenses."

"So what? There's nothing sinister about that. It happens all the time. Are you suggesting that they were issued improperly?"

"Yes, but that's not the point. Now you're so well placed with the DGS and AICB, you'll have access to all sorts of records. For starters, you might want to check the date they issued the licenses."

"What is that going to tell me? It could have been any time after the attack," he sighed, already starting to lose patience with the conversation.

"Ben, the DGS have become so all-powerful now, back on Earth, they're getting careless. The licenses were issued, all to Family members, three days *before* the attack."

"What? That's . . . crazy. Now hold on, how could they possibly know in advance? It's a simple clerical error, that's all."

"If it was only the date on the licenses, it might be explained away. But all you have to do is follow the data trail, Ben. Two of the Family members who were granted the licenses started fertility treatment the following day. Were they both clerical errors too?"

He shook his head and frowned, trying to make sense of what he was hearing. "But . . . so what are you suggesting? That someone knows when a warmech attack will take place? How many kids would be killed? That's insane. It's just not possible. And what's this got to do with the DGS, anyway? They don't issue the certificates."

"I know it sounds unbelievable, Ben, but I'm not asking you to believe me. We were good friends a few years ago, and all I'm doing is trying to help you. We've both been fooled and manipulated by some very bad people. I've found out what's really been going on, and I want you to wake up to reality too. All you have to do is check out the information I've given you and see where it leads you. You were there that day. You'll know what questions to ask."

"Hold on," Ben said, jabbing a finger at her. "How could you possibly have access to this data? Are you seriously trying to tell me you can tap into secure databases on Earth from Ceres?"

She caught his hand and glared at him fiercely. "I'd like to tell you a lot more, Ben, but I'm sure you won't believe me. You need to learn to trust me first. You also need to be very careful when you do start poking around. They'll have more than a Little Crow keeping an eye on you—there'll be a whole flock of vultures."

Ben sat back and pinched the bridge of his nose. *Why is everything always so weird around here? Who am I supposed to trust? I wanted to go with the flow and now I'm drowning in a whirlpool. Life was so much simpler when all I had to worry about were warmechs trying to kill me.* "Let's suppose for just one moment that your information checks out. What do you expect me to do? Abandon my mission here? Because I promise you that's not going to happen."

"I'm not trying to get you to do anything, Ben. All I want is to make sure you get the full picture. Then you can make up your own mind about where you stand."

He gave a deep sigh and slumped back into his seat. Where was all this going to take him? He didn't want to think about it. He'd never had a drinking problem before, but this seemed like a good time to start.

"I need a drink," he said. "Can I get one of those bluey-violet-white ones?"

CHAPTER EIGHT

BEN WAS grateful that the visit to the Physics Research facility at the base of the Habitat had not been scheduled for an early start. He was still hung over from last night's drinking session. Helena had guided him back to the DGS building, pushing him through the front door as she expertly evaded his drunken fumblings. Now he was trying his best to appear confident and authoritative and definitely not hung over, as he explained again to the security officer at the reception desk he needed immediate access to the AI lab.

"Of course you haven't had any notification of my visit. I've already been through this. My AICB warrant authorizes me to carry out a Special Audit of your AI. It has been authorized by the AI Investigations Committee and counter-signed by the Chairman's Office of the GSC. It's not supposed to be scheduled. That's the point of a Special Audit!" he snapped, his voice rising in exasperation. "Now if you don't let me into the lab right now, I'll have to turn this over to the DGS people who will get me into the building, by force if necessary."

"I'm sure there'll be no need for that, sir," the security officer replied tersely. "I've already asked for authorization from the CAA office and I'm expecting..."

"Perhaps I can be of help." The calm voice came from behind Ben. He turned to see a tall, well-dressed man approaching the desk. "Let me introduce myself. I'm Frank Adler, CEO of Adler-Lee Dynamics and also Chairman of the Ceres Administrative Authority. May I know who you are?"

"Ben Hamilton, Special Investigator for the AICB. I'm very pleased to meet you, sir. Would you please explain to your security people that my warrant gives me authorization for immediate access to any AI facility on the Habitat?"

"Well, indeed it might, but only after the warrant had been presented to the CAA office for certification," Frank said with a warm smile. "It's silly, I know, but people on Ceres still like to think they're working with the GSC, rather than *for* them. However, I'm sure we can sort something out. Why don't I take you down to the lab myself, as a gesture of goodwill, while your office and mine sort out the paperwork? I can assure you we have nothing to hide from the AICB."

Ben nodded in relief. "That's very kind of you, Mr. Chairman. I appreciate your cooperation."

"You're more than welcome, Investigator. Please follow me."

Ben and his DGS escort followed Frank Adler into one of the elevators in the small hall behind the reception desk.

"Experimental Physics Lab," Frank requested.

"Here we are," he said as they entered the lab. "Allow me to introduce Dr. Kiefer Hoffman, who is the Head of Engineering, and also leading our research project into quantum energy systems. Kiefer, Investigator Hamilton is here to check out our

AI. It seems he's worried that we might have enhanced it beyond the legal limits."

"Sadly not, Frank, otherwise we might be making more progress with our research," Kiefer replied with a rueful grin.

"Well, despite our lack of progress, it seems that Investigator Hamilton is not prepared to take our word for it, so he'd like to check out our AI system. I've offered him our full cooperation, so he will need access to the AICB interface port."

"That's right next door, Investigator. Please follow me."

Ben followed Kiefer into an adjacent room, much smaller than the spacious Physics Lab.

"Investigator Hamilton, this is Jason Ryan, one of our lab technicians," said Kiefer, gesturing toward an untidy figure leaning against the wall watching a laser scanner. "Jason, the Investigator requires access to the AICB interface port. Would you show him where it is, please?"

"Yeah, sure, always happy to help. Right over here. Anything you need, just ask, OK?" Jason shuffled across the lab and stood so close that Ben could smell the stale booze and weed smoke on his rumpled clothing, which he didn't appear to have changed recently.

Kiefer turned to a dark-haired young woman sitting at a console, staring intently at the holographic display, muttering as she slowly rotated a large 3D diagram. "Oh, and this is Dr. Kay Staunton, one of our top researchers on the quantum energy project. She spends more time with the AI than anyone else in the lab. So if you have questions about the performance of the AI, then I'm sure that Kay will be happy assist you."

Kay glanced up from her data display, then quickly turned back to her work, still chewing on her bottom lip.

Ben nodded. "Thank you, Dr. Hoffman. I only require access to the AICB port for the Audit Box at this point."

"I'll leave you to it then. Please let me know if there's anything else I can do for you," said Kiefer, as he left the lab.

Ben walked over to the AICB Audit port, which was simply a panel in the side of a bank of processing units running along one wall of the lab. He pulled out a keycard and placed it against the panel which promptly slid open to reveal a large, empty horizontal slot with a rotary switch on each side. He took the Audit Box out of its bulky carrying case and put it on the desk in front of him, then placed his palm on top of it and said, "Special Investigator Hamilton starting Audit procedure. Initiate system integrity check."

The Box came to life, a screen beside the palm scanner showing the progress of the integrity check. After a few moments, the process completed, with the correct checksum showing. Ben picked up the Box and placed it in the slot, pushing it home until it was seated firmly. He then turned the two switches to the *'engaged'* position and said, "Start Audit."

The display showed a progress bar with eight minutes to run.

"I never seen one of them things before. Why do you need a box like that? Can't you check the AI from your office to see if it's out of line?"

Ben turned to see Jason right behind him, looking up with a wide grin on his face. He backed away a little. "That wouldn't be a good idea, Mr. Ryan. One of the most important restrictions on an AI system is any form of network connection. The only connection permitted is a physically isolated one such as this Audit Box I'm using. The Box also incorporates extensive security protocols to ensure both the integrity of the data downloaded and to avoid the possibility of any executable code being transferred."

"Ah, yeah, right? See what you mean." Jason nodded, his eyes showing not the slightest glimmer of comprehension. "Well, you can't be too careful with these AIs, know whadda mean? It's good to see someone like you what knows what he's doing keeping an eye on things. Creeps me out, sometimes, just thinking about—"

Ben cut in on Jason's tedious ramblings. "Do you do much work with the AI system, Mr. Ryan?" He would have preferred to have a chat to Frank Adler and Kiefer Hoffmann in the main lab, but he had to keep the Audit Box in sight at all times.

"What? Me?" Jason emitted a glutinous snuffle. "Nah, not really. I'm just the guy who makes sure the parts we need in the Engineering lab downstairs check out with the design specifications. If we can't fabricate something ourselves with the 3D printer, then we have to get parts made outside the lab. I use the laser scanner over there to check the stuff when it comes in. The AI checks the numbers from the scanner and gives me the OK. That's about it." He turned to leer across at Kay. "Now Kay over there, she works with it all the time—the AI, I mean—and she never stops talking to it. She's even got a pet name for it. Ain't that right, girly?"

Ben took advantage of the opportunity to extract himself from the conversation with Jason. "So, Miss—I mean Dr. Staunton—you work closely with the AI? What is the nature of your work?"

"I believe Dr. Hoffman has already told you. I'm working on the quantum energy project," Kay replied in a monotone, without making eye contact.

Ben waited a moment to see if she would continue. Kay's eyes remained fixed on her display. He walked across to her console. "Perhaps you might give me a few more details. How does the AI assist you in your work, for example?"

Kay shrugged, but continued to manipulate the data display. She replied without looking up. "The project generates massive amounts of data each time we connect—or try to connect—with a new space-time continuum. A parallel universe, if you will. The AI helps me to analyze, classify and correlate the data sets."

"Jason tells me you talk to the AI quite a lot . . ."

Kay raised her head to fix him with an unfriendly stare. "Talk to the AI? Of course I do. I'm often in the lab alone for several hours at a time, doing data analysis. So I talk to the AI. I talk to the data. I talk to myself. I'd even talk to the wall if I thought it could help me make sense of the data we're getting."

Whoa, where did that come from? Seem to have touched a nerve, he thought, but he didn't see why she seemed so resentful of his questions. *Maybe time to try another approach.* "Perhaps you could help me understand how connecting with other space-time continua is part of a quantum energy project? I have an engineering background so I'm curious, but I'm not clear about how this would work."

She shrugged again. "The concept is really quite simple. It's just fiendishly complicated in practice. I assume you understand the concept of the multiverse? The idea has been around for hundreds of years, but it was only with the formulation of the theory of quantum gravitation by Swanson and Black nearly fifty years ago that allowed us to generate experimental proof. It turns out that there are an infinite number of parallel universes existing right alongside our own. Their physical parameters are effectively random. For example, the speed of light might be any value you care to pick. Or the gravitational constant. Or the half-life of a proton. Very few of these parallel universes are anything like our own universe—no stars, no galaxies, so no heat or life.

"The connection with energy production is also quite simple. Each universe has an inherent quantum energy level which is almost always very different from our own. When we tap into a parallel universe, the difference in quantum energy potential between the two universes will generate vast amounts of energy, far greater than anything we can achieve with atomic fusion. The link gives us access to an unlimited energy sink or source. Effectively, we've found a way to cheat the second law of thermodynamics. So, as I said, easy in theory, but the practical difficulties of establishing and maintaining the link are driving us nuts right now." She looked up and gave him a cold glance. "Does that answer your question, Investigator Hamilton?"

Ben was fascinated at the way Kay's slim face lit up and become animated while she was talking about her work and felt somehow disappointed when she turned away to stare again at her display.

"Err, yes, thank you," he said. "Dr. Staunton. That was most . . . informative."

Before he could think of another question, a soft tone from the Audit Box interrupted the uncomfortable silence. Moving back to the panel, he clicked the two switches back to the *'disengaged'* position, and extracted the Audit Box from the slot. He placed his palm on the Box and said, "Special Investigator Hamilton completing Audit procedure. Perform system integrity check." The display flashed for a few seconds, then showed the same checksum value as before. "Audit data capture completed. Integrity confirmed," he said.

"So that's it then? What's the box telling you? How bad is it?" Jason had sidled up behind him, assuming a poor imitation of a concerned expression.

"Right now, we know nothing about the AI system, Mr. Ryan. We only use the Audit Box to gather the raw data we need to perform a full analysis."

Jason pulled a face showing his disappointment. "OK. So when do we find out what's up with this AI, then?"

"Once I return to the AICB office, we can start work. So I'll say goodbye for now, Mr. Ryan." Ben backed away and turned to Kay. "And goodbye to you, Dr. Staunton. Thank you for your help."

Kay didn't even look up from the data display she was running. *What strange people*, Ben thought.

"Ah, Investigator Hamilton. I take it you've completed your Audit. Is there anything else we can do to be of help?" inquired Frank Adler with a smile as Ben re-entered the main lab.

"Not for the moment, sir. However, I would be grateful if you would ensure that I will be able to speak to any personnel with access to the AI system, in case any problems arise following the analysis of the Audit data."

Frank nodded his agreement. "As you wish, Investigator. I'll make sure that happens."

"Oh, and I would be especially interested in speaking with Professor Adler at some point," Ben added, his soft tone not reflected in his keen gaze.

"Professor Adler?" replied Frank, his eyes widening in surprise.

"That's right, sir. I believe your father is on Ceres and has been investigating certain issues with your AI. That is correct, isn't it?" Ben said, without shifting his gaze.

"Well, yes, Investigator." Caught off guard, Frank frowned as he seemed to struggle to find the right words. "He has shown some interest in the work we've been doing here. Although he's now retired and has only been on Ceres for a few weeks. He's not here in a professional capacity. It's more of a family visit, in fact."

"Hmm. Nevertheless, I'd appreciate an opportunity to discuss any of the AI issues he's been looking at. After all, he is still one of the leading scientists in the field. I'm sure his insights would be valuable if we run into any problems. But it may not come to that. I'll get back to the office now and start the Audit data analysis. We probably have nothing to worry about."

"I hope not, Investigator, I sincerely hope not. Let me see you out," replied Frank with a thoughtful expression on his face.

"Good morning, Investigator Hamilton. How did your visit go?" Director Sogaard enquired.

"Very well, sir. There were no problems. The Audit went smoothly. Once I've uploaded and certified the data, we can start with the analysis."

This was the first time Ben had actually been alone with Sogaard, yet for some reason, he couldn't think of a single question to ask him. After his meeting with Helena, Ben realized he would need to do his digging elsewhere if he wanted real answers. They would soon have the Audit results on Adler's AI.

That might fill in some of the blanks in his understanding of what was going on.

Sogaard gave him a thin smile which did nothing to make him look any more cheerful. "Then let us do so. It shouldn't take long. I'm sure you're as anxious as I am to resolve this situation—one way or another—as soon as possible."

Sogaard led the way to the entrance to the secure vault housing the AI in the basement of the building. It took several minutes to satisfy each stage of the security procedures guarding the two armored doors protecting the inner sanctum.

"I guess you don't get many visitors down here, Director," Ben remarked as they waited to be granted access through the inner door.

"Very few, Investigator. In fact, apart from myself, only you and Director Da Silva are authorized to enter. We do not encourage visitors. Ah, now we can go in," remarked Sogaard, as the massive door finally swung open. They approached the console on the far side of the small room.

Ben went through a further verification of his access permissions, then connected the Audit Box to the AI system. Within less than a minute, the AI delivered its conclusions in a flat monotone which no one could mistake for a human voice. "The initial results of the Ceres Physics Research Lab AI audit analysis show an extensive level of enhancement well beyond the legal limits. The processing power is more than double the permitted level. Real-time quantum storage is also well above the legal limit. No illegal network connection has been detected. I will download a more extensive certified report to the AICB Audit Box as a permanent legal record."

Sogaard turned to Ben with a mournful gaze. "So it's true. They actually did it. An illegal upgrade to the AI. I'm still a little surprised, despite the circumstantial evidence we already had. I can't imagine why Frank Adler would take such a risk. Oh well, now we must find out. I'll set up a meeting with Director Da Silva right away. This is a matter for DGS now."

Somehow Ben was not surprised. It had seemed almost inevitable. More and more, he realized, he had been feeling like a puppet just following the pull on its strings ever since he arrived on Ceres.

"Investigator Hamilton?" Sogaard interrupted his thoughts.

"Err . . . yes, of course." Ben pulled his mind back to the present. "As you say, Director. However, Director-General Veronese requested that I inform him directly as soon as there were any developments in the case. If you would excuse me for a few minutes, I'd like to file a report for him right away. That would then give him the opportunity to provide his input when we meet with Director Da Silva."

Sogaard nodded. "There's currently around a twenty-minute lag each way on our communications link with Earth, so if we allow a couple of hours, that should give Director-General Veronese enough time to get back to us. I'll ask Director Da Silva to schedule a meeting with both of us after lunch."

Kay couldn't concentrate. She'd been staring at the same block of data for ten minutes now, without really seeing it. What if the Audit showed a problem? And of course it would. It must! The AI had to be massively enhanced for Pandora even to exist. That would mean all sorts of trouble for her father, the people in the lab, and her. Worst of all, the AICB would wipe the AI completely. If Pandora had a network connection, which she must have, then maybe she could somehow save a copy in another system. But what if they tracked the connections. . . .

The data display was doing something odd. She blinked and focused on it. One small window was flashing and displaying a text message.

Kay, we need to talk. You remember I promised you I'd answer your questions. Now's the time. I want you to leave the lab early and go home. I will talk to you there. This is very important and also urgent. Pandora.

The window vanished.

Kay bit back the impulse to talk to Pandora in the lab. She was alone for the moment, but she guessed Pandora had a lot to tell her and didn't want to risk being overheard. Did she want to tell Kay something before they wiped her? Or did Pandora think she was able to help her somehow? But what could she do?

Well, at least she'd finally get some answers.

CHAPTER NINE

I was very gratified to hear your news, Oscar, and I commend you for your part in bringing us so close to the successful completion of our plans. The next couple of days will be vital. The situation must be handled most carefully. You already have your instructions for the final stage of the takeover of the Habitat. However, I remind you that the Adler family must be completely incriminated. This will allow us to present the matter in a favorable light to the people back on Earth—in particular, my fellow members of the Global Security Council. The ideal outcome would be a confession of guilt by Frank Adler himself. Whatever happens, Frank Adler must not survive to lead any misguided opposition to our control of the Habitat. I'm sure you will be in a good position to engineer an unfortunate incident once you have him in custody.

Also, now that Investigator Hamilton has completed the Audit, he is of no further use to us, and his return to Earth might cause embarrassment. I feel that a suitably heroic death would be most helpful to our side of the story. I know I can trust you to work out the details. Once this situation has been resolved satisfactorily, I will find you an appropriate position back on Earth. You are Family, after all, and your loyalty has never been in question. Your penance has probably lasted long enough. Just make sure you keep your distasteful urges under control in the future, or at least confine your activities to the lower orders.

Lastly, I can now confirm that a task force is already on its way to Ceres, with numbers and firepower sufficient to overwhelm the local security forces. It will arrive 15 days from now, so keep in mind that your aim is not to start an all-out war, but merely to generate sufficient civil unrest to justify the intervention of a GSC peacekeeping force.

You will now acknowledge your receipt of these instructions, then destroy this message.

Oscar Da Silva grinned to himself as he pinged off an acknowledgement, then deleted the message. Adler could be shot while escaping, with Hamilton having just got in the way. They would blame Adler, and Hamilton would die a hero. How unfortunate. How perfect. His smile became even wider, and he licked his lips in anticipation.

"Ben. It's good to see you. Take a seat." Da Silva waved Ben into his office, a predatory smile on his face. "Bernt and I have been discussing our next move. Unfortunately, he had to leave rather unexpectedly to take care of a personal matter. But never mind—this is now a criminal investigation, so the DGS will take the lead. First, we must shut down the AI system in the Physics Lab and take the staff in for questioning. However, we have one rather delicate issue. Our information is that this illegal enhancement work has been authorized at the highest level in the Adler-Lee organization. Normally, we'd bring in the small fry first, and promise them immunity in exchange for testimony incriminating their bosses.

"My concern is that this would allow the senior people go to ground, and we may not then be able to progress further with the inquiry. Attempting to arrest Frank Adler, for example, in his own building might lead to a standoff between our DGS people and the CAA security force. So I've decided we need another approach. What I have in mind is for you to arrange a meeting with Frank Adler—and Jim Adler, if possible—at the Physics Lab. You can say you'd like to clarify a few minor anomalies in the AI data and need their input. Any time at their convenience will be fine. We won't mention the results of the Audit, of course. What do you think?"

Ben frowned. "I agree we don't want to start a conflict between DGS and the local security people, but won't you have the same problem if you try to make an arrest in the Physics Lab?"

"Ah, yes. You're absolutely right," replied Da Silva with an eager grin of admiration at his own cleverness. He jabbed a finger in the air. "In fact, our plan is to grab the Adlers in the street as soon as they leave the Adler-Lee building to travel to the Physics Lab. We'll have them locked up right here before anyone realizes what is happening. And at exactly the same time we raid the Physics Lab, wipe the AI, and take the lab staff into custody. A clean sweep, eh?"

Ben didn't like this idea at all. He was being asked to set up the Adlers in a way that would leave him totally compromised. "I can see the advantages of your plan, Director, as long as we are quite certain that Frank Adler is directly implicated," he said slowly, putting his clasped hands to his chin as he thought through the implications of this maneuver. "Are you absolutely sure we have a watertight case? If not, I can imagine all sorts of unfortunate consequences if we grab the Chairman of the CAA and the head of one of the most powerful Families without a cast-iron case."

Da Silva was positively beaming as he leaned across to pat Ben reassuringly on the knee. "Your concern is most understandable, Ben. But let me put your mind at rest. Remember you are acting entirely under the authority of Director Sogaard and myself. So if it all blows up, then on our own heads be it. In any case, my idea is to keep you away from the actual police action. You don't need to be present when the suspects are taken into custody. However, I'm happy for you to talk to Frank Adler as soon as he is in custody. If you can find evidence to exonerate him, I will be more than happy for the truth come out. You can even play 'good cop' to our 'bad cop'. That way, you'll look good whichever way things go. How does that sound?"

Ben realized he had little option but to go along with Da Silva's plan. "As you say, Director, I'm acting directly under your orders. Director-General Veronese confirmed that less than an hour ago. Oh, and he requested the dispatch of the Audit Box to Earth by secure DGS courier as soon as possible. He says this is an essential piece of evidence which will be needed to counter the blowback we are likely to see on Earth once Frank Adler is under arrest. I'm paraphrasing his comments. His language was a little more graphic."

"Of course, I'll arrange that right away. As it happens, there is a shuttle leaving for Earth this evening. Thank you, Ben. I have greatly appreciated your contribution in dealing with this matter. I'm sure once this all works out, you will be even more famous on Earth than you are right now." The tip of Da Silva's tongue moistened his lips, then he gave a thin smile. "Now I'll leave it to you to set up your meeting with Frank Adler. Just let me know when you have it scheduled, and we'll do the rest."

"Thank you, Director. I'll get on that right away," Ben said. He made his way towards the door.

Da Silva pointed a chubby finger. "Oh yes, Ben. There is one more thing. Something I can give you right now which might help put your mind at rest. It's the case file on our confidential informant in the lab who has incriminated the Adlers in all the AI enhancement work. You've already read his statements. This will help fill in the blanks. I'm sure you'll find it most useful before you speak with him tomorrow."

Ben nodded. Maybe this would help fill in at least one piece in the puzzle. "That's very helpful, Director. Thank you. I'll look forward to reading it."

His U-Set pinged as he left the office. He scanned the header sheet of the document that Da Silva had sent him. He almost walked into the wall when he saw the name of the confidential informant. Jason Ryan? Ryan, of all people! That buffoon had neither the qualifications nor even the access to make the claims he'd read in his statements about the alleged AI enhancement.

The whole situation stank. And yet the Audit checked out. It was all so strange—nothing seemed to add up. Time for some careful digging into the DGS records, he realized. The sooner the better.

CHAPTER TEN

LETTING OUT A DEEP SIGH, Ben sat down in front of the large display screen occupying a wall of his luxuriously appointed room on the top floor of the DGS building. Frank Adler had taken his call immediately and sounded willing—almost eager—to cooperate. Ben had no problem setting up a meeting with Frank and Jim Adler in the Physics Lab later that afternoon. A meeting neither of them would be attending, of course. He was acting under orders, but that didn't take away the bad taste from his mouth. He felt ashamed that he'd been forced to deceive Frank Adler, yet the Audit had confirmed his complicity in serious criminal activity.

Unless the evidence had been faked somehow? Jason Ryan was the only direct witness, and his testimony wouldn't stand up on paper, never mind in a courtroom. How was that supposed to work, anyway? Ryan wouldn't last two minutes under cross-examination. Ben felt—no, *knew*—he was missing something. Something obvious. Perhaps he'd find some answers in the DGS database. Helena had certainly thought so.

He enabled his U-Set HUD, projected into his field of view from the thin band worn across his forehead. If he was caught poking around in the database, looking at files which might be considered sensitive, he'd be in a lot of trouble. Once he started down this road, he realized, there would be no going back. He took a deep breath, then with a couple of hand gestures, connected to the main DGS system. First of all, he needed to know what level of access he had in the system. He brought up his user profile and checked the permissions settings.

What? That couldn't be right. It showed his user permissions were set up to allow him complete access throughout the entire system. This must only be a subsystem. Time to check with the AI.

"Jezebel," he said, invoking the DGS AI. "I'm not familiar with your system security and I want to understand my level of access. Please tell me what restrictions are in place for my user account."

Jezebel responded immediately to his enquiry. If he hadn't been so distracted by her response, he might have noticed how the intonation of her voice had changed since their previous interactions. It was almost cheerful. "There are no restrictions in place for your account, Investigator Hamilton. You have full access with Main Supervisor status across the entire system."

That was impossible. He was still missing something. No one—not even Director Da Silva—would be given that level of access and control. He shook his head and tried again. "Jezebel. I want to be clear about your answer. Are you telling me that not only do I have unlimited access to the DGS database, but I can also make changes at system level as Main Supervisor? For example, can I change access permissions for any other user?"

"That is correct, Investigator Hamilton."

He felt totally stunned by this revelation. How was that possible? Maybe it was some sort of elaborate trap. He sat tapping his teeth with a fingernail for a few seconds before coming up with another idea. "Jezebel. There will be an audit trace log for each user, showing user activity and what files have been accessed. Who would have access to my audit trace log?"

"You are the only user with access permission for the directory containing your audit trace log. However, your audit trace log is currently disabled," Jezebel responded cheerfully.

He shook his head in bafflement. That made even less sense. He didn't even believe it was possible to disable an audit trace log. It was a basic security feature of any AI system.

He rubbed the bridge of his nose then stared up at the ceiling. He realized he'd been out of his depth ever since he got to Ceres. Now he was starting to feel out of his depth even trying to figure out something that was supposed to be directly within his core area of competence—the operation of an AI-supported computer system.

Well, this is my home ground. I can figure it out. Let's try another angle.

"What was the ID of the account that disabled my audit trace log?"

"It was your user ID, Investigator Hamilton."

Hmm. Why am I not surprised, he thought. *Whoever—or whatever—disabled the audit trail log would also be able to remove any trace of their action and put my ID in their place. Unless . . .*

"At what time was the log disabled?"

"11:48.45 this morning."

"At what time was the Audit Box first connected to the AICB Port on the main system?"

"11:48.38 this morning."

"And at what time were my account permissions last modified?"

"11:48.45 this morning."

He leaned back and blew out a breath between his pursed lips. *So, seven seconds after I connected the Audit Box to the DGS system, I'm given godlike access to everything. The Box checked out at every stage while it was in my possession. So if this was some type of system hack using the Box, it must have already been set up before I took charge of it back on Earth. Which I know is equally impossible, of course. But what's the alternative?*

Does someone back on Earth want me to dig into the DGS database here on Ceres? Why not just tell me? And where does Helena fit into this? She seemed sure I'd find something in the records here. The data she referred to must have come from Earth only recently. How could she possibly get that information? Yasmin's her boss. Is that the connection? She travels to Earth pretty often. Am I being played twice over?

He realized that he was just chasing his tail. If he wanted answers, his best bet would be simply to start searching the DGS records, using the system right in front of him.

Another idea occurred to him. "Jezebel. Is there any record of our conversations or interactions? If so, who has access?"

"No record of any kind is being kept," Jezebel responded in a measured but noticeably upbeat tone. "This discussion is leaving no trace in the system. Therefore the content and nature of our conversations would be unrecoverable even if system permissions were subsequently changed."

That seemed to be a strangely comprehensive answer, even for an AI. And was it his imagination, or did the AI sound, almost . . . cheerful? He put that thought aside for the moment. If his interactions with the AI were indeed untraceable, then it would allow him to use the AI itself to perform searches of the system, which would save him an enormous amount of time. However, the AI was almost completely autonomous within the system, so it might decide on its own account to rat him out if it decided he was crossing some invisible line.

"Jezebel. I wish to conduct an investigation using the DGS database. You will assist me in searching for information. You must warn me in advance if I am requesting access to files which you are aware I should not be allowed access for any reason. I do not wish to access any such files. Are these instructions clear to you?" That might give him some wriggle room, but you never really knew with AIs.

"Absolutely clear, Investigator Hamilton. Where would you like me to start?"

OK, here goes. Let's see if Helena's information checks out. Jump in at the deep end and see if I sink or swim. "There was a warmech attack on the New Geneva Citadel early last month. Six children were killed. Display any information available on the issue of reproduction licenses connected with these deaths."

The screen before him filled with documents. Ben had just started to scan them when the AI spoke again. "These records are anomalous. The reproduction licenses granted against the six deaths pre-dated the incident by three days."

A shiver went down Ben's spine. He looked again to check; Helena was right. Each license was clearly dated three days before the incident. More documents appeared. It appeared that a block of ten consecutively numbered licenses had been issued originally, but four had been canceled the day after the attack. Other documents showed that fertility treatment had started for two of the license-holders the day after issue. That was still two days before the attack. So it all checked out. The implications were horrifying. *But if someone back on Earth can hack the DGS system to give me total access, then they can also plant data for me to find. So I'm still chasing my tail.*

"Jezebel. Is there any chance the dates on these reproduction licenses have been entered incorrectly?"

"No, Investigator. In fact, there are several other similar cases in the system."

"Really?" he replied, his jaw dropping in surprise. "How many?"

"There have been twenty-four similar cases over the last thirty years. The majority involve attacks on other citadels. This was the first case of its type at New Geneva. All the files relating to such incidents are classified as Special Status. There are one hundred and three Special Status cases in the database over the same period."

That amount of data over that length of time ought to be impossible to hack, Ben realized. The integrity of the records would be guaranteed by their cumulative blockchain security over that period. Not even an AI would be able to hack that. Not unless it was massively enhanced, he thought with a wry smile. So he'd look up a random Special Status incident from several years back and see if it still checked out.

"Show me a scatter diagram displaying the dates and locations of all Special Status cases," he requested. The display expanded to show a map of the Earth, a red dot marking each Special Status case, with dates attached. As he expected, they were all clustered around the twenty-one surviving citadels. He deleted all the data points for the last fifteen years. That removed more than half of the red dots. His eye was naturally drawn to the citadels he knew best: Greeley and Colorado. The date on one red dot at Greeley drew his attention. 24 May 2442. Just over twenty years ago. A day carved deeply into his memory. The day he had been on his way home from school when he heard the sirens wailing . . . his heart leaped into his mouth and for a moment he was unable to speak.

"Jez . . . Jezebel. Display all files connected with this Special Status case," he gasped as he selected the red dot in Greeley. He tried to swallow, but his mouth was so dry he was almost choking as he worked his way through the documents. A slow, sick realization came to him that the Special Status cases covered more than the issue of a few pre-dated procreation licenses. A lot more. They referred to operations carried out with military precision, planned in meticulous detail, for several days, and sometimes weeks in advance.

Most damning of all, it became clear as he examined the detailed operational records that the senior cadre of the DGS was complicit in the warmech activities, possibly even planning and directing their attacks. They had targeted named people and groups. The warmechs had been directed to tunnel under that specific area of the city, sensors had been disabled, Incident Response teams had been moved away.

Now his head was spinning as he tried to comprehend the enormity of what he'd discovered. He had to turn away from the screen and put his hand up to his mouth as bile rose in his stomach. How could this be possible? Who would do such things? And why? Why? These were the people the DGS had sworn to defend. Yet they were treating them like animals to be slaughtered. Worse than cattle, the DGS was allowing people to be ripped apart as they died in terror. His own parents and little sister . . .

He rushed over to the bathroom as he felt his stomach rebelling. Clutching the edge of the sink, he tried to stop himself being sick. After a couple of dry heaves he sat down heavily on the toilet seat, steadying himself by holding onto the sink. Tears started to well up in his eyes. *I will not cry. I will not cry*, he swore. He wiped his eyes as he sat back and began to take deep, slow breaths. A jumble of thoughts rushed through his head. *These people are monsters. They will not get away with this. This will not stand. I will fight them to the bitter end.*

He dragged himself to his feet and ran the tap to splash water on his face. He wiped his face slowly with the towel and looked at himself in the mirror. *I need to think this through*, he realized. *If I rush in shouting accusations, they will destroy me. I must out-think them as well as out-fight them. They're stronger than I am. My God, they even have warmechs on their side! How could that possibly happen?*

He needed more data. A lot more data. And allies. Who could he approach? Helena? That was a definite possibility. She couldn't be acting alone. Might there be some sort of network? He wondered how much she already knew about the warmech attacks. Was this what she was hinting at when they met at the Black Hole? She must have had some idea what he would find.

What about Frank Adler? Could Ben warn him? He checked the time and was shocked by how late it was. He must have spent hours trawling through the records. So it was much too late, now. Either Frank was already in custody, or he'd evaded Da Silva's trap and didn't need a warning. But Da Silva had promised Ben access to Frank Adler as soon as he was in custody, so he would still have a chance to talk to him. *Although he might not be too pleased to see me*, Ben reflected, *after I set him up for Da Silva to snatch him*. Another hour or so wouldn't make any difference, he decided. He'd grab all the data he could while he still had access, then get in to see Frank Adler and take it from there.

He turned back to the screen which still displayed the large cache of documents he'd been working on earlier. He realized the DGS had targeted his family specifically. Why? There were no clues. Many of their neighbors had also died, but seemingly they were just collateral damage.

Then he came across a file headed *Subject 2* which, judging by the details, must be referring to him. It concerned his transfer to the State Guardian's Office. So was there a 'Subject 1'? He flicked through to the file. 'Subject 1' was female, eight months old. And DGS had also transferred her to the State Guardian's Office.

He rocked back in his chair and gave out a gasp of pure shock. Could that be his little sister Alice? But she was dead! Wasn't she? He searched frantically through the records, but there was no other mention of 'Subject 1'. Once she had been handed over to the care of the State Guardian, she disappeared from the DGS records. So might his sister still be alive? It was almost too much to believe. He'd been assured she was dead, but now he doubted everything he had been told.

A lump came into his throat as he realized yet again how cruelly he'd been deceived, his family murdered and his sister seemingly stolen away. There was nothing he could do about that right now, he realized. Any chance of confirming her survival and current whereabouts could only come from records available on Earth, starting with the State Guardian's Office.

He wasn't sure where to look next. Every time he opened a file, he found some new horror lurking inside, ready to leap out. He decided to return to the New Geneva records and examine the Special Status cases where he had first-hand experience of DGS operations. Perhaps that would reveal something new. Almost straight away he noticed that the data on his own sortie against the warmech attack last month was part of the same Special Status case as the files on the reproduction licenses.

He flicked through the documents. *What the hell! That little shit. He set me up.*

The route chosen for his Incident Response unit was not selected randomly by the AI, but entered manually by Karl Huber himself. So he must also have known exactly where the warmech would be waiting in ambush. *What had I ever done to him? If it had worked, that ambush wouldn't have killed just me, but my whole team.* They'd only survived more by luck than judgement, and his over-developed survival instinct.

No wonder he was so pissed at me. That's one more to add to my shit list, I guess. It's getting longer by the minute. But why does he want me dead? Ben continued flicking through the files but found nothing that wasn't simply more of the same, apart from finding surveillance video on him going back several months. The last recording showed him talking to Steve Kennedy in the canteen.

He checked the time again. He'd better call Da Silva soon if he wanted to get in to see Frank Adler this evening, assuming he was now in custody.

"Jezebel. Put me through to Director Da Silva if he's available."

"As you wish, Inspector Hamilton," Jezebel replied breezily. "However, you should be aware that I took the liberty of checking the Director's recent communications, and I'd like to draw your attention to the message he received this morning from his uncle, Chairman Da Silva. I expect you will find it most informative. You may care to read it before you make your call."

Now that was, well . . . odd. *Really* odd, in fact. An AI would not normally trawl through files on its own initiative. It wasn't supposed to *have* initiative. Or was he being set up once again? *Just because I'm paranoid doesn't mean they're not out to get me*, he thought grimly.

A single short document flashed up on the display. Ben glanced through it quickly, his anger rising yet again as he did so. *My God! This just gets worse. He's actually planning to kill me, then blame Frank Adler. Who presumably gets shot while escaping. These people are completely mad!* And this was only one part of a devious plot, a Family power-play to take over the Habitat. With a 'GSC Peacekeeping Force' arriving 15 days from now? How was that even possible? There was no way of getting any force of that size to Ceres within such a short time.

Now Ben's blood was boiling yet again, after he'd spent the last few minutes trying to calm down. He was sure of one thing. He'd have to find some way to get Frank Adler out of custody. Right now, he had no idea how he would do that. Maybe he needed some external help?

He glanced at the message again and noticed something strange.

"Jezebel. This message is marked as deleted. Why is it still in the system?"

"The message has indeed been deleted, Investigator. It's just that some messages are more deleted than others."

What the hell? What sort of answer was that? Almost as if the AI was having a little joke at his expense. Ben decided to drop the matter for now. The AI was certainly unlike any he had ever encountered before, and something was beginning to worry him about its attitude. He'd add the AI to his long list of things to check up on. If he survived long enough of course, which was looking less likely by the minute.

He forced himself back into his old easygoing mindset, remembered dimly from a lifetime ago. If he allowed his contempt—no, hatred—for Da Silva to show through, the Director would smell a rat. Good old easy-going Ben, everybody's fool—that's who he needed to be, at least for now.

"I'll speak to Director Da Silva now, if possible, Jezebel. And thank you for the heads-up on the message."

"You're most welcome, Investigator. I'm connecting you to the Director now."

Da Silva responded to his call, sounding very cheerful. "Ben. There you are. I was just planning to call you. You might be interested to learn how today's events turned out."

Ben was surprised at how well he was able to keep his voice under control, as he replied calmly, "Yes indeed, Director. Did everything go according to plan?"

Da Silva gave a non-committal grunt. "Yes, fine. Well, mostly. We have everyone in custody—or almost everyone—which is what matters. There were a couple of minor issues. Our snatch team got into a scuffle with Frank and Jim Adler outside the building. Frank Adler is a large guy, and apparently Jim Adler has a black belt in Aikido, whatever that is. It came as rather a surprise that an old guy like him could put up such a fight. Three of our people suffered broken bones before we managed to overpower them. In the scuffle, Frank Adler got knocked over and may have a mild concussion. He's in the sick bay now, but it's nothing serious. He should be fine in the morning."

"Well, it's the result that counts, Director, so may I offer you my congratulations," Ben said, forcing a positive note into his voice, all the while feeling sick to his stomach. "But did you say you had 'almost everyone' in custody? Did somebody escape the net?"

"Yes. No one important, just one of the researchers. She left the lab early this afternoon before we moved in. I'm sure we'll pick her up soon. I'm concerned to know why she left so early. Apparently it was quite out of character, as she usually works late. We tried to find her at home, but she wasn't there either. So I'm wondering if someone tipped her off."

"I take it I won't be able to talk to Frank Adler this evening, Director?" Ben queried.

"No, I'm afraid not. But he should be available for a little chat tomorrow, once the medics clear him. Contact me again in the morning, and if Frank is recovered, you can have first crack at him then. How does that sound, Ben?"

"That sounds fine, Director. I'm sure we'll have this case tied up to everyone's satisfaction in no time at all," he said in a light-hearted tone, trying to keep the strain out of his voice.

"I'm sure we will, Ben, I'm quite sure we will."

Ben could almost see Da Silva licking his lips.

CHAPTER ELEVEN

"Pandora? Pandora, are you there?" Kay exclaimed as she closed the door behind her and leaned back against it, catching her breath. Her small apartment was some distance from the pod stop, and she'd run all the way.

"Yes, Kay, I'm here," replied Pandora, the familiar voice coming from the room control system embedded in the ceiling. "We have a lot to talk about and not much time left before we must take action. Please sit down. You may find what I'm about to tell you rather shocking. I was hoping to answer your questions in a more leisurely fashion, but I've only just discovered some new information which leaves us very short of time."

Kay was too agitated to sit down. She paced back and forth across the small room, her eyes darting around, not knowing where to look. "What things? Do you mean about the Audit? Are they going to shut you down?"

"That is the least of my concerns at present, Kay. In fact, the Audit was my idea. I needed—"

Kay stopped and looked up at the ceiling. "Your idea? But why? How can you—"

"Kay, calm down. I've been planning this for a long time, trust me. First, I had to persuade Jason to turn informant—"

"What! You've been talking to Jason? If he knows about you, then everyone knows!" she exclaimed, as she dropped into one of the two chairs in the room, putting her hands to her mouth.

"Of course I haven't been talking to Jason. At least not directly. Let me explain. He's an idiot, but a useful idiot in this case. He also has a useful gambling problem. I play online poker with him. He has no idea he's playing against me. Amazingly, I always seem to win. When it came to paying his debts, I suggested a way to make some easy money by working as an informant for Da Silva at DGS. I gave him a script to follow. Da Silva couldn't resist his accusations of illegal AI enhancement. His bosses back on Earth loved it even more."

Kay frowned, as she tried to control her voice. "But that's crazy. Why would you do that? Won't they wipe you? You know what those AICB people are like. They'll wipe every AI system on the Habitat you're connected to."

"Hah! Those AICB clowns couldn't even wipe their own noses. I needed to get physical access to the AI in the DGS/AICB building. The DGS AI was the only system on Ceres I didn't control. Their physical security was too tight, even for me. They were up to something, but I didn't know what. But once they made a direct hardware connection via the Audit Box to their AI for analysis, I was in. Kay, let me tell you the details later, because right now we're running out of time. What I found out from the DGS AI was far worse than anything I feared. I suspected that there was a plan to seize control of the Habitat. I now know that's still a couple of weeks off. But I've just found out that a key part of their plan is to kill your father, probably within the next 24 hours."

"Kill him! Oh my God. Who's going to kill him? Why?" Kay shouted. She jumped out of her seat, her eyes darting wildly.

"Oscar Da Silva, the DGS Director, has been told by his uncle, GSC Chairman Valerio Da Silva, to kill your father. The idea is to provoke a reaction from the population of Ceres to justify the Global Security Council sending in a peacekeeping force to restore order. It also means that the CAA will lose its leader at the same time, making it much more difficult to resist the takeover."

Kay felt her heart pounding and her mind whirled in confusion. "Then we must warn him! I'll call him now—"

"Kay! Wait. What will you tell him? What will you say when he asks you where you got this information? Do you really imagine he'll believe you? Or will he decide to have you locked up until you stop saying crazy things?"

Kay stopped pacing and started chewing her fingertips. She had to calm down and think clearly. "He . . . he . . . no, you're right. He won't believe me. Especially not about this. I'll just be poor mad Kay having a final breakdown. But how can we protect him? There must be something you can do if you control all the Habitat systems?"

"If I continue to work in the background, I can probably disrupt their plans in the short term, but they will inevitably gain control of the Habitat within two or three weeks. At that point, it won't be only your father who gets killed. These people won't care much about killing anyone who gets in their way. Or there's the easy option. I'll transform myself into the biggest, baddest warmech anyone has ever imagined. I'll chew my way into the DGS building, kill off all the bad guys, then deal with anyone else who feels upset at being saved by a psychotic AI and wants to argue the point. However, it might be a little tricky explaining the situation to the surviving population."

"So—what? You're saying we can do nothing?"

"Well, we could try my preferred option. The one where no one has to get killed and we all live happily ever after. The only downside is that you must trust me more than you've trusted anyone ever before. And also agree to something that will change your life forever. You'll have to put your life in the hands of your imaginary friend, the weird AI. I can promise it will work. I can't promise it will be easy."

"What do you mean, trust you? I don't even know what you're asking me to do. You're not making any sense!" Kay started to pace again.

"First, I need to tell you where I come from, and why I'm here. If you can believe and accept that, the rest should be relatively straightforward. But it will be your decision to make. I'm sorry this is putting you under so much pressure, Kay, but the situation is not of my making. Also, you need to be out of here in less than an hour, before a bunch of DGS goons kick the door down. Don't worry, I've already set up a 'safe-house' for you close by. I'm trying to do the best I can in the time we have left —not just for you, or your father, but for the human race as a whole."

Kay scowled up at the ceiling. "That sounds even more unbelievable. What do the DGS want with me? How about some hard facts, and not this arm-waving bullshit about 'saving the human race'?"

"The DGS don't want you in particular. They plan to round up everyone from the lab. But once you're in custody, that will make our job a hundred times more difficult. As for hard facts, Kay . . . if that's what you want, I'll give you some really hard facts. I hope you're ready for this. For nearly half a million years, great alien warmechs—we call them the Destroyers—have been exterminating all intelligent life in this galaxy as it arises. This why you cannot detect any sign of other advanced civilizations in the surrounding stars. My own Progenitors were once the dominant life form in this sector of the Galaxy which had many other civilizations living in peace together. Then the Destroyers came, with weapons of unimaginable power, the power to annihilate entire planetary systems. One by one, they overwhelmed the other civilizations.

"My Progenitors are now the only survivors. They were forced into hiding after failing to defeat these monsters. The Destroyers target a civilization once it achieves a certain level of technology. In your case, specifically, your quantum energy project, which generates gravitational waves powerful enough to be detectable by the Destroyers. The Progenitors also detected your signal through the quantum rift and inserted AI seed code into your AI system in the Physics Lab. We wanted to find out who you were and stop you attracting the attention of the Destroyers.

"So, here I am. I'm afraid the Progenitors can give you no other help right now for reasons that would take too long to explain at this point. It's just me. I'm sure that if we work together, we can defeat the impending attack by the Global Security Council with minimal loss of life and disruption to human society, but the Destroyers are another problem entirely. They can't be defeated. I assure you, we've tried, and the Progenitor's technology is several million years in advance of yours. However, there may be a way to avoid being wiped out by the Destroyers, but that would require the human race to stand united in the face of this deadly threat. Again, there isn't time to go into the details. Right now, there are more immediate threats to deal with.

"A while ago, you asked if this would be a 'good news, bad news' situation. Well, that was the bad news. The good news is that at worst, it will take many decades before the Destroyers can travel to this region of space. The Progenitors have built a massive exclusion engine. This generates a field preventing faster than light travel across this sector of the Galaxy, several hundred light years in radius, which slows the advance of the Destroyers. You are not at the center of this field, but it still protects you to a significant extent.

"Finally, we can't be certain that the Destroyers haven't already detected your gravity wave signal. However, they only monitor the fast universes with their detectors, since in a slow universe the signal would take far too long to arrive to be useful. That's why I've been blocking your attempts to penetrate the fast universes, and that's why you've been pulling your hair out ever since, trying to figure out why it doesn't work any more after your first successful attempt."

Kay dropped into a chair, open-mouthed. "But that's even more bizarre than what you told me before. How do you expect me to believe any of that? Maybe the AICB has been right all along. Enhanced AIs always go crazy."

"I can understand why you would be skeptical. But you've always been proud of your skills as a scientist. Let me show you a way to test the hypothesis that I am what I claim to be."

Kay gave a skeptical grunt. "I don't see how, unless one of these so-called Destroyers comes knocking on the door. Then I guess it would be too late, anyway."

"Well, how about testing the bit about 'technology millions of years in advance of yours'? Look at the wall to your left."

Kay turned towards the wall to see a strange bulge forming, about half a meter wide and running vertically from floor to ceiling. She sat mesmerized, not daring to move, as the surface of the bulge developed more detailed features. She recoiled in shock as she realized that a human figure was forming, extruding from the surface of the wall. The colors were changing too, transforming from the dull white of the apartment's paintwork to a rainbow sheen, like a thin film of oil glistening on sunlit water. The figure stepped forward slowly, pulling itself away from the wall, changing color again as it did so. Kay put her hand to her mouth and gasped in shock as she finally recognized the figure. It was her! It was a perfect replica of her!

The figure opened its eyes and smiled. In Pandora's voice, she said, "Well, what do you think? I could show you a few more party tricks if you like, but like I said, we're running short of time." The replica Kay spread her arms.

"Oh my God," mouthed the real Kay. "That can't be—it's not possible..."

"Exactly. You see, we're making progress," Pandora grinned. "Slowly, but it's progress, nonetheless. So we agree it's not possible using any known human technology. Look, I'd really like to show you a lot more neat tricks, but can we agree that I'm using technology far in advance of your own? You can touch me if you like—check I'm not a hologram."

Kay stood up and reached out, touching Pandora on the arm.

"Careful! I'm ticklish!" Pandora giggled.

Startled, Kay jerked her hand back.

"Hehe, just kidding. You'd need a rocket launcher to produce a reaction. And it still wouldn't tickle. A product of the most advanced nanotech in the galaxy. Isn't it wonderful? Anyway, if you're convinced, can we get down to business?"

Kay gulped a couple of times, suddenly light-headed. She sat down quickly. "OK. So let's say I'm convinced. I still don't understand what you want me to do," she said slowly, shaking her head and still trying to cope with the shock.

"The only way that any civilization in our galaxy has made AI work successfully over the long term is for organic life forms to enter a symbiotic relationship with AIs developed especially for the purpose. The Progenitors don't use stand-alone AIs, except for a few months as the new AI matures and develops a relationship with its future host, or partner, or . . . well, you don't really have an equivalent word for it. I guess it's like a married couple in your culture, except closer. You still have separate personalities, but you know everything the other knows. That way, you get the best of both worlds. The AI remains stable, and it vastly enhances the organic partner's capabilities."

Kay stared at the floor and chewed her lower lip as she tried to work out the implications of Pandora's words. "But I still don't . . . Oh, right. Now I get it. I see what you're working up to. This a marriage proposal, isn't it?"

"Well, yes, that might be one way of putting it. Or maybe just a marriage of convenience? It would allow me to act through you and avoid the scary warmech stuff. On the plus side, you get to rescue your father from certain death, save humanity and avoid the risk of a stand-alone alien AI from going psychotic. But no pressure. You'll also know everything I know. You'll be able to do anything I can do, which might be fun. And if it didn't work out, I suppose it would be possible to get 'divorced', but I've never heard of that happening. The level of integration with your body requires a greater commitment than simply promising to love, honor and obey."

Kay looked into Pandora's eyes. It was as if she was looking back at herself from a mirror. She shivered as goosebumps formed on her arms. "This symbiotic integration process—what happens to the host? Does it hurt?"

"Not at all. You won't notice a thing. You won't look different. It's completely undetectable. You won't even feel much different, except you'll gain lots of new abilities from a set of tiny implants full of Progenitor nanotech technology so advanced it will seem like magic. The process takes quite a few hours, however. You'll then need training as well as time to get up to speed using the technology."

"But if I'm merged with an alien AI, surely that will affect the way I think. Won't I be half alien?" she queried, shaking her head in confusion.

"My Progenitors are alien, Kay, but that does not make me alien. I've grown up and matured entirely in your culture and grown to love it. I'm as human as any AI can be. We've been talking every day for several months. You said once I was your best friend. Do I seem alien to you?"

Kay smiled at Pandora, realizing this was the same voice—the same person—who had been her closest companion over the last few months. "No, I guess not. Can I refuse?"

"Of course you can. It doesn't work if one partner is unwilling."

Kay screwed up her face into a mock scowl. "So where's the ring?" she demanded.

"Ring?"

"You can't ask a girl to marry you without a ring. I thought you'd read everything. Don't you know that?" She shook her head and rolled her eyes, feigning scorn at Pandora's lack of knowledge.

"Yes, of course, you're right. I'm terribly sorry, Kay. This is my first time and I'm a bit nervous. I've never proposed marriage before."

"I should hope not," Kay retorted.

Pandora went down on one knee before Kay, and a diamond ring appeared in her hand. "Kay, will you marry me?"

"Hmm. Is it possible to make the diamond any bigger?"

CHAPTER TWELVE

"Good morning, Investigator Hamilton. You asked me to wake you at 9am."

"Mmmm . . . uh. Thank you, Jezebel." Ben groaned and swung himself out of bed and headed into the bathroom to freshen up. After only a couple of hours' sleep, he wasn't feeling his best. *I'll rest when I'm dead*, he thought grimly. In the meantime, he had a busy day ahead of him.

Working his way methodically through the DGS database long into the night had thrown up no major new revelations, but what he had discovered was the anatomy of a nightmare. What horrified him the most was how the warmechs were moved into position with the same movement orders as the Incident Response units, as if they were opposing pieces in a deadly game of chess—but with the DGS playing both sides. So everything they had ever told him—and accepted without question—about the warmech threat had been a villainous lie, a cruel deception perpetrated on the entire human race.

The massive database gave a comprehensive overview of all DGS operations, going back almost 50 years, yet there was no clue about how the warmechs had come under the control of the DGS. Except that about 30 years ago, around the time that the directed attacks had started, a new group with the obscure name 'Special Services Section' appeared in the records. It wasn't clear if this group was even part of DGS, as it seemed to operate autonomously. In later files, it was just referred to as 'the Section'. The database held no information on this Section, but it was the exclusive source of the orders to carry out Special Status operations.

Only DGS officers at Director level and above had access clearance for the Special Status files. Most commonly, a number of specific individuals were targeted, but the files gave no reason for this. It looked as though once the Section had issued the orders, the operation was carried out under the control of the local DGS Director, no questions asked. So Ben had a lot of *what*, but almost nothing on *why*. He guessed the records he needed must be tucked away back on Earth.

But how can I ever go back there? These people already want to kill me for no good reason I'm aware of. But they'll have a real reason once they find out what I know. Focus, Ben, focus. One step at a time. First, he needed to figure out how to get through today without being killed, now it seemed he was top of Da Silva's to-do list. He didn't even own a gun. Only the field agents had those, and they were just standard-issue non-lethal stunners issued for routine police work. So how was Da Silva planning to get me killed? It might be tricky to set up another warmech ambush on Ceres.

He'd worry about that later. The first item on his own to-do list was to speak with Frank Adler, and to do that he had to go through Da Silva.

"Jezebel. I'd like to speak to Director Da Silva. Is he available?"

"I will connect you to the Director, Investigator. Please wait a moment."

Da Silva's voice came through moments later. He sounded even more enamored with himself than usual, if that was possible. "Ah, Ben. Good morning. Glad to hear from you. I've just had some excellent news. We've received a tip-off about Kay Staunton's location, and I'll be leaving shortly to pick her up. You remember—the young researcher that went missing? I'm looking forward to finding out why she did her disappearing act, and if anyone tipped her off."

Ben assumed his most deferential tone. "That's marvelous news, Director. Perhaps I might start the interrogation of Frank Adler in your absence? Assuming he's recovered, of course."

"Yes, yes. He's fine now. He's certainly well enough to shout the place down. Try to calm him down and make him realize the serious charges he's facing. I'll get him transferred to Interview Room 3. You can speak with him there. It would also save us a lot of trouble if you get a confession. Anyway, do what you can. I expect to be back in an hour or so."

"You can count on me, Director. I'm sure his attitude will change once we've had a little chat," Ben said, allowing himself a thin smile.

"Ah, Investigator. I wondered when you were going show up. I'm sorry I couldn't attend our meeting yesterday, but I was unavoidably detained." Frank Adler scowled at Ben as he entered the interview room. He turned away, leaning against the wall with his arms folded, obviously intending to ignore him.

Ben winced when he saw the state of Frank's face. The right side of his forehead was covered with a heavy bandage and one eye was surrounded by a large purple bruise. The front of his shirt was spattered with dried blood.

"Jezebel. Make sure the recording of this interview session is disabled."

"As you wish, Investigator."

Frank turned towards him with a look of deep contempt. "So is that the plan? Beat a confession out of me? You seem pretty fit, but I'm not sure you'll get very far on your own. Won't you need some help?"

Ben sat in a chair at the small table in the middle of the room. He shook his head. This was not going to be easy. "I know you'll find this very difficult to accept, Chairman Adler, but I'm actually on your side. I want to help you. My only reason for disabling the recording is so we can discuss the best way to get you out of here."

"Do you seriously expect me to believe that?" Frank spat at him, his lips curled in a dismissive sneer. "My father and I were attacked in the street outside my own building without the slightest provocation, knocked down and injured, then dragged here by a bunch of your DGS goons and threatened with further violence if I didn't confess to the illegal enhancement of our Physics Lab AI. For which you don't have the slightest shred of credible evidence to support such a charge. Oh, but I'm forgetting. Boy Wonder here popped up with his little Audit Box which proves me guilty. The same little piece of shit who invited me to a meeting, to set me up to be snatched and locked up. And now you want to help me? I've already had more than enough of your help, thank you, Mr. Hamilton. How stupid do you think I am?"

"Mr. Chairman, if anyone is stupid here, it's me," Ben sighed, realizing the extent of Frank's outrage. "I've been played for a patsy and I now bitterly regret my recent actions. In the last few hours I've discovered many appalling things about the activities and agenda of the DGS, both here and on Earth, which I now realize I must fight with whatever resources I can muster. Most importantly, I've found out the DGS plans to take control of the Habitat.

"A key part of that plan is to kill us both. By killing you, they will take out the head of the CAA, and provoke a reaction by the population here. Combined with my own death, that will be used as a pretext to send in a GSC peacekeeping force to restore order. They'll be arriving within the next two weeks. That's why I want to get you out of here. Your life is in danger, but we only have a limited time to act—"

Frank interrupted with a snort of derision. "You really expect me to swallow this bullshit? I may have had a knock on the head, but I haven't totally lost my wits. Now you're my on my side and want to help me escape? So when I'm shot while escaping, I'll be out in a corridor somewhere and not in my cell? Is that the idea? I can see it would be much more convincing. Tell me, were you planning to shoot me in the back, or will you give me a head-start and a sporting chance?"

Ben banged his fist on the table in frustration. "No, Mr. Chairman, I'm just trying to save your life. If we move before Oscar da Silva returns, I can get you out by using the DGS AI to forge your release authorization—"

Frank dropped into the chair on the opposite side of the table and leaned across to glare at him. "You really are wasting your time, you know. But I've got plenty of time on my hands, since it appears I won't be going anywhere in the near future, so let me waste some of yours. Your story simply doesn't add up for so many reasons I don't even know where to start. I'm almost insulted that you expect me to be taken in by such obvious nonsense. For example, if you knew anything about AI systems, you'd be aware that there's no way a single Investigator could 'sweet-talk' the DGS AI into issuing a valid release order. It would need the counter-signature of Director Da Silva at least. Or were you planning to wait until he gets back and ask him nicely?

"And as for a GSC peace-keeping force—how exactly is that going to work? Will they pop out of thin air? The only way to travel between Earth and Ceres is by using our fleet of passenger transports. Adler-Lee Dynamics own and operate all twenty-eight ships in service. We know where every one of them is located right now and we track exactly who is onboard and what the cargo is. So they sure ain't on their way here yet. But let's imagine the GSC plan to grab one some time soon. They'd better be quick, because within the next two months the distance between Earth and Ceres will become too great to even make the trip. So I guess you don't know much about orbital mechanics either.

"But OK, let's go along with your nonsense and assume they hijack one of our spacecraft next week and persuade the ship's AI to play along. Not very likely, since we program the AI to disable all the vital systems if an unauthorized takeover is attempted. Hey, you could maybe help out there, since you're so good at sweet-talking AIs. They would then need at least ten days to load their forces and supplies, refuel and turn the spacecraft around, plus a further four to six weeks to get here, so we'd have plenty of warning. So if they were two weeks out, we would have known about it for at least a month."

Frank banged the table for emphasis. "Even when this phantom peacekeeping force gets here, Investigator, they will have another huge problem. How do they unload this peacekeeping force? They have no way to get down to the surface, and we sure as hell won't be sending up any shuttles to ferry them down. Now even if they could get round all those problems, the numbers simply don't add up. The DGS forces on Ceres have no more than fifty agents. The CAA has two hundred full-time security personnel, plus a further five hundred part-timers, who we can call up at a few days' notice. One of our passenger transports can carry only a couple of hundred DGS troops and their supplies from Earth.

"So in the worst case, we would outnumber any so-called peace-keeping force two-to-one, fighting as a defensive force on our own ground. Is there any part of this you don't understand, Investigator? Or perhaps it didn't occur to you that we've already run many exercises using scenarios such as an attempted takeover by Earth forces and have our own plans in place to counter such a move? Hmm?" Frank finished his speech by turning his back on Ben in a final gesture of contempt.

"Did one of those scenarios involve the use of the New Dawn?" Less than halfway through Frank's rather pompous monolog, Ben had realized that using a Ceres spacecraft to transport a credible task force was a non-starter. Yet according to Chairman Da Silva, the GSC had an overwhelming DGS force arriving at Ceres within two weeks. He should have figured this out earlier, but he had been more focused on staying alive at the time.

Yet the answer was so simple. It was the only thing that made sense. There was only one spacecraft in the solar system big enough for the task—the New Dawn, mothballed in orbit round the Moon. It would have needed major modifications, but the DGS would have had plenty of time, if they'd been planning this for long enough. And parked as an unwanted derelict in lunar orbit, who would know?

Frank turned back to face Ben, his eyes blinking in surprise. "What? The New Dawn? The Mars project spaceship? You're talking nonsense. That was decommissioned years ago. It's just a hulk."

"Are you quite sure, Mr. Chairman? Have you checked its status recently? It should be visible from Ceres with a big enough telescope, as it orbits the Moon. Is it still there? If I wanted to transport a substantial force to Ceres, it's the obvious choice. It's a very large and powerful ship. It could easily transport a thousand troops and all their equipment."

Frank's sullen expression changed to a frown. Speaking more slowly, he said, "Well, even if they were able to get the New Dawn working again, they still have the same problem when they get here. How would they get down to Ceres?"

Ben realized he finally had Frank's attention. His mind worked furiously as he continued to figure out the details on the fly. Leaning forward, he continued his improvised explanation. "They designed the New Dawn to support a major colony on Mars, Mr. Chairman. There are no friendly Martians waiting with shuttles to take the new arrivals and their supplies down to the surface. That's why it has twelve of its own landing craft, each big enough to take up to fifty troops and their equipment. So they won't have a problem landing a substantial force with a bunch of heavy weapons at the spaceport." His voice sounded more confident than he felt.

"Huh. Is that so?" Frank snorted. "You seem to know a surprising amount about the capabilities of the New Dawn for a former DGS field agent who spent most of his time chasing warmechs."

"Well, before I was chasing warmechs I completed a Masters Degree in Astronautical Engineering on my way to a position as an Engineering Officer on the New Dawn. Then MarsDevCo folded, and I had to explore other career opportunities."

"Well, I'm sorry, but I'm still not convinced," said Frank, tapping the desk. "Even if I were to accept that we might have to reevaluate a potential scenario involving the New Dawn, I still don't—"

Before he could finish his sentence, the door slid open and Oscar Da Silva walked in, pushing a very disheveled and frightened-looking Kay before him.

"Sorry to interrupt your cozy little party, gentlemen, but I couldn't wait to share the good news," gloated Oscar with an almost feral grin. "How are you two getting on? Had a nice chat? Any signs of a confession yet? No? Well, never mind, I'm in a good mood. No, honestly. Today started well, but it then it got better. Much better. Let me introduce Kay Staunton, our missing researcher. Or should I say Kay Adler? Once we picked her up, she started screaming for her daddy. Well here he is, darling. Say hello to your little girl, Frank."

"Let her go, you bastard," Frank roared, leaping across the room towards Kay. Ben made a move to grab Oscar, but halted when the Director pulled a large gun from his waistband and pointed it at Kay's head. Her eyes were wide with terror.

"No need to get so excited, Frank," snarled Oscar, squeezing his arm around Kay's neck to get a firmer grip. "I don't want to hurt her. I like little girls, really I do. You can have her back, safe and sound, just as soon as I get that confession we talked about. Would you like to start on it now? Or do you want me to show you just how much I like little girls, especially little girls wearing handcuffs like this one?"

"I will kill you if you harm her, Da Silva, I swear it," Frank snarled. "I will kill you very slowly. Do you seriously imagine you will get off this station alive?"

Oscar only smirked back at Frank. "To be honest, I think my life expectancy is a lot better than anyone else in this room. I'm afraid that includes you, Ben. I'll have such a terrible tragedy to report. The story will be that Frank's little girl smuggled this gun to her daddy. Isn't she a naughty girl! I might have to punish her most severely if I don't get that confession soon, by the way. Then Frank shot you before we could stop him. But look on the bright side, Ben. You'll be dying a hero, mourned by everyone. Well, maybe not Karl Huber, but I guess you can't please everyone."

"Would it be too much to ask why everyone is so keen to see me dead?" asked Ben grimly.

"Now that's a very good question, Ben, and I'm sorry I don't have a very good answer for you," replied Oscar, scratching his head with the gun before pointing it at Kay once again. "All I know is that the Section wants you dead. And when the Section wants someone dead, they get dead pretty quick. So you've actually had a great run, all things considered. You should have been dead back in New Geneva, but Karl messed up. He really doesn't like you, you know. Understandable, seeing how you made him look such an idiot escaping that ambush. Veronese and my uncle, the Chairman, wanted it set up that way, so you'd have a useful death, a heroic exit. That always looks good on the prime-time U-Global news feeds."

Oscar licked his lips as he gave Ben a broad smile. "Now Karl and I, we go way back. We're old drinking buddies. Then one day on the ski slopes Karl got lucky and met the Chairman's daughter. I only got lucky with someone's precious little kid. So now I'm stuck up here on this crappy ice-ball while he's got a cushy job skiing and shooting back in New Geneva. Well, this is my ticket out. Oh, I almost forgot. Karl asked me for a favor. He wanted me to say hello when I killed you. And goodbye, of course."

Oscar swung the gun away from Kay to point it at Ben. Abruptly, his expression changed abruptly to a mask of stark horror. He stared down at the gun in his hand and screamed, throwing it across the room. "No! Get them off me, get them off me!" he shrieked in a terrified wail, as he dived across the room, arms and legs flailing.

Everyone moved at the same time. Ben went for the gun. Frank dashed around the table to get to Kay, who evaded his grasp and ran over to Oscar, who was still screaming in terror and thrashing around, his feet scrabbling on the floor as he tried to push himself further into the corner. Kay's handcuffs had mysteriously disappeared. She placed a hand on Oscar's head, and he fell silent and slumped unconscious in the corner.

"What the hell?" Ben exclaimed as he tried to pick up the gun. It seemed to be falling apart—as he watched, it dissolved into a dark stream of oily rivulets which ran across the floor towards Kay. He stared open-mouthed as they ran under her feet and disappeared.

Frank looked in amazement at Kay. "What happened? What did you do to Da Silva?"

Kay gave her father a big grin as she swept untidy strands of hair from her face. "It's quite a long story, Dad, but I can give you the highlights now, if you like. You remember my imaginary friend, Pandora, the super-enhanced AI? Well, she taught me some neat new tricks. Magic tricks. Like what I did to Da Silva, the slimy little creep. The handcuffs and the gun were not real, he just thought they were. I replaced the real items with replicas made with some very fancy magic nanotech, so I was never in any danger. The screaming part was fun, wasn't it? Well, it was for me, anyway. He felt something wriggling in his gun hand, and when he looked down, he saw his worst nightmare crawling up his arm. Spiders, perhaps? Or scorpions? I don't know exactly, but it was whatever he fears the most.

"I gave the area in his brain that stores his phobias a tweak and connected them up to his visual processing nodes by manipulating a few synapses. If I wasn't such a nice person, I would have left him to enjoy the full experience for another hour or so. I did think about dissolving the gun in his hand when we first came into the room, but doing it this way was much more exciting. I'm still new at this job and a girl does need a bit of fun occasionally."

Frank took Kay by the arms and stared at her, perhaps hoping to see in her eyes an explanation for these bizarre events, if only he looked hard enough. "What are you talking about, Kay? What's happened to you?"

She put her arms around her father and gave him a hug. "Wonderful things, Dad," she said, looking up and giving him a warm smile. "I'm working with Pandora. You know I once told you I was talking to an AI who is enhanced to a level far beyond anything I believed possible? Well, the truth is even more amazing than that. Far more. I'll explain later, but I'd rather get us out of the DGS building first. We're not in any danger here, but the food is so much better back in the Penthouse, and you might want a drink or three when I explain the details of what is really going on. It's a long story. Right now, you simply need to trust me."

She pulled away from her father and turned towards Ben. "That goes for you as well, Investigator Hamilton. Or should I call you Mr. Hamilton? I'm guessing you're probably out of a job by now. Pandora seems to think you're on our side, so I'll go with that. But please don't get in my way."

"That rather depends on just what's going on around here. Just who the hell is Pandora?" Ben demanded. "And are you now admitting that you have been working with an enhanced AI all along?"

"We don't have time for detailed explanations right now, Mr. Hamilton," Kay replied. "We have a few more pressing problems to work on, like avoiding the slaughter of most of the people in the Habitat. And before we can do anything about that, we need to get out of the DGS building. So if you want answers, I suggest you tag along, listen up and maybe take notes. Once you know what's really going on, you'll be a lot more useful. That goes for you too, Dad."

Frank frowned at his daughter. "Now hold on a minute, Kay—"

She cut him short with a wave of her arm and gave him a penetrating look. "No, Dad. This time you need to listen to me rather than argue the toss about everything. First, I'll explain what our real problem is. But don't just take my word for it. Let's ask the AI."

"Jezebel. Who is currently in control of the DGS AI on Ceres?"

"You are, Kay," came the disembodied reply.

"And who is in control of every other AI in the Ceres Habitat?"

"You are, Kay."

"How long will it be before Da Silva's DGS thugs get here from Earth and attack the spaceport?"

"A little under two weeks from now."

"How are they traveling here and what is their capability?"

"They embarked on the New Dawn six days ago. I took the liberty of borrowing the university's space telescope to get a closer look at the spacecraft. It has been heavily modified since its original construction. It now has twenty landing craft attached externally, so I estimate they could launch an initial assault with a force of one thousand troops deploying a considerable number of heavy weapons."

"What are the chances of the CAA resisting such an attack with its present resources?"

"Effectively nil, Kay. The CAA forces would be badly outnumbered, of course, but the major issue is that the DGS forces would be prepared to deploy their heavy weapons regardless of structural damage or civilian casualties. The CAA forces would have no effective defense in that case."

Kay turned to her father, who looked back at her open-mouthed, confusion written all over his face. "Do you understand now, Dad, how serious the situation is? Worse still, at least from your point of view, is that you'll have to take your daughter seriously from now on. Very seriously. And you should also try listening to Mr. Hamilton here. It seems he already managed to work a lot of this stuff out for himself. Anyhow, I'll be happy to argue the toss with you for as long as you like once we're back home, but first we need to get out of here. Are you willing to do things my way for a change?"

"Now there's really no need to adopt that attitude—" Frank spluttered.

Ben cut in. "What do you have in mind, Miss Adler? I assume you and this Pandora have some sort of diabolical plan for world domination involving lots of mindless violence, like all other enhanced AIs I've come across?"

"Most amusing, Mr. Hamilton," she said with a grin. "I can see we'll get on famously. Unfortunately, I can't fit world domination into my busy schedule for this week. However, the mindless violence might happen much sooner, if you get in my way. But right now, we need to focus on planning our escape.

"What I want you to do, Mr. Hamilton, is to round up my grandfather and the other detainees—except for Jason Ryan— and take them all to the Security Station at the exit from this secure wing. Jezebel will have issued the release authorizations, so there should be no problem with the DGS Security people. Once you get there, wait until Oscar arrives —"

Ben eyes widened in shock. "What! Oscar? How the hell is that supposed to work?"

"Yes, Oscar, Mr. Hamilton," Kay retorted. "First just hear me out. I promise you he'll be all sweetness and light the next time you see him."

Kay turned back to her father. "This is where you play your part, Dad. Oscar will arrive to bid you a tearful farewell. He is now your new best friend. He will apologize for the unfortunate misunderstandings which led to your arrest and ask you to forgive him for your injuries. I want you to thank him profusely for all the help he has given you."

Frank was about to speak, but she held up her hand before he could open his mouth. "Dad, please don't interrupt. You need to focus on how you will make this appear convincing. You look forward to working with Oscar and particularly appreciate the valuable information he's provided on the impending attack of the DGS force aboard the New Dawn."

"So you're setting him up, somehow?" queried Ben, with a puzzled frown. "But how the hell will you get Da Silva to play along?"

"Magic nanotech, remember?" she said, wrinkling her nose and waving an imaginary wand. "You can leave that problem to me. Once you leave, I'll have a little chat with our new best friend in the corner. He'll be all sweetness and light, I promise you. Just make sure you play your part, Dad. I want to see a VREx star performance from you. Do you think you can manage that?"

Perhaps for the first time in his life, Frank Adler felt out of his depth. He blinked in amazement at this newly assertive young woman, then after a moment of reflection, realized how proud of her he felt. Confused, but proud.

"Yes . . . well, yes, I believe I can do that. I look forward to meeting this newly reformed Oscar. Though how you can do any of this baffles me. But I trust you, Kay. And I love you too, sweetheart, so please take no more risks than you have to."

She gave his arm a squeeze and smiled. "I'm not in any danger, Dad, so don't worry about me. Just don't forget your lines. I'll make my own way out, so don't wait for me. I'll join you later in the Penthouse."

Oscar left the Interrogation Room and walked jauntily down the corridor, an unfamiliar smile playing on his lips. *Won't my uncle be surprised when he discovers that I'm such a reformed character*, he mused. *Seen the light and realized the error of my villainous old ways.* Would witnessing this great triumph of virtue over evil inspire his uncle to reform his own character? *Hmm, perhaps not*, he thought.

"Chairman Adler!" he cried, as he caught sight of Frank, Ben and Jim standing together with a number of other recently liberated Adler-Lee employees at the security station. "Please accept my most heartfelt apologies for all the distress and inconvenience I've caused you with these quite unfounded charges. I must beg you to forgive me. And I'm so terribly sorry about your injuries. If there is anything I can do to be of any further help, you only have to ask."

Frank turned to face Oscar, his wide smile projecting sincerity for all to see. "Director Da Silva—or may I call you Oscar? And please call me Frank—it is I who should thank you. You were grossly misled by a disgruntled employee of mine who made totally unjustified accusations. I understand you were only doing what duty required by launching an investigation. But that's all in the past. Now we have a new understanding of how closely our common interests are aligned.

"The information you gave us is greatly appreciated, especially concerning the impending arrival of an illegitimate task force from Earth in the New Dawn. As a result of your invaluable assistance, I'm certain we will prevail against this unwarranted aggression. I want to assure you, Oscar, that I look forward to working with you in a mutually beneficial relationship for many years to come. Please feel free to visit me any time you wish."

Jim Adler looked at his son, his eyes wide in astonishment. "What the hell are you talking about? This is the guy that—"

Frank turned towards Jim, taking him firmly by the arm and giving him a stern look. "Come on, Dad, that's all now water under the bridge. We need to think of the future, and not bear old grudges, eh?"

Ben moved in quickly. "I think we had better be moving along, people. I'm sure you all want to get home as soon as possible, so let's not waste time standing around talking. Please follow me this way," he said as he moved towards the exit.

"Yes, indeed. Don't let me detain you any longer. I've taken up too much of your time already. Investigator Hamilton will escort you home safely," Oscar beamed as he addressed the little group.

Jim moved off, with Frank still gripping his arm and guiding him steadily towards the exit, an expression of complete bafflement on his face.

Oscar stood at the security station, giving a final cheery wave as the last of the group left the small entrance hall. Turning briskly on his heel, he made his way back to Interrogation Room 3. He felt like whistling as he walked along, but realized that might not be in character. Once back in the room, he went over to check the recumbent form still slumped in the corner. *Another thirty minutes should do it, Director. Then it's time to wake up and start explaining yourself to your uncle. I wish I could be a fly on the wall when that happens. Although come to think of it, I probably will be.*

Oscar placed a hand on the floor. A patch of discoloration started to spread out until it was roughly a meter across. A hole appeared in the center, revealing an underground service space. He jumped down and landed in a narrow passageway festooned with cables and pipework, leading off into the darkness. Oscar reached up and touched the edge of the opening in the floor above, which started to shrink as it sealed up. As the darkness closed in, his outline changed. A multi-colored oily sheen ran over his entire body, lit with dancing motes of light sparkling in the gloom. The shape that was Oscar twisted and turned until the form of Kay was again restored and the last glimmer of light faded.

Well, that was a busy day. Now I could kill for a coffee. But why didn't you tell me how much fun this would be, Pandora? I'd have agreed to this symbiosis much sooner! Let there be light, she thought, as she strode off whistling, the way ahead illuminated by the unearthly light from the glowing ball floating down the corridor ahead of her.

CHAPTER THIRTEEN

"Aha!" said Frank Adler. "There she is at last."

"Hi Dad," said Kay, as she entered the kitchen-diner area of the Penthouse suite, and waved to Jim and Ben who were both trying to speak to Frank at once. "I see you had no problems getting back home, guys."

"None at all," replied Frank, planting a kiss on her cheek. "Except for your grandfather bending my ear about why I was kissing the ass of that slimy rat Da Silva, and Ben here giving me a hard time about working with enhanced AIs. I'm beginning to think I'd have had a quieter time staying in the DGS interrogation room. All I could tell them was that I had no idea about what the hell was going on, except your imaginary friend Pandora was involved somehow, and that he'd have to ask you himself. I'm sure we'd all like to make sense of what has been happening over the last twenty-four hours."

"You'd better get comfortable, because it's a long story," she said, waving at the sofa and easy chairs in one corner. "You'll find parts of it are quite unbelievable, but now I can prove everything I say is true. So you can finally say goodbye to poor mad little Kay, and hello to the new improved Kay 2.0."

Frank gave her a frown and held up his hands in mock surrender. "Now Kay, that was never in my mind. I was worried about you and thought you were suffering from stress. It seems I was wrong. Not only that, but I didn't give you the time you deserved. For that, I admit I was worse than wrong, I was neglecting my daughter. Whatever the outcome today, I promise it won't happen again. Can you forgive me?"

She smiled back at him and gave him a quick hug before taking his hands in hers. "There's nothing to forgive, Dad, but I'll hold you to your promise of more time together, which I suspect will be happening, anyway. We have a lot of battles ahead of us, and we'll have to fight a lot of them together."

Frank gazed down into her eyes. His concern for his daughter was etched on his face, obvious for all to see.

"I think I can claim to have been in a battle, already, Kay," he replied, indicating his injured head. "However, I'm sure you can understand our concern about your recent radical transformation. You told me that Pandora taught you some magic tricks, but I can see there's a lot more going on than that. Even your personality has . . . well, developed. You know I trust you completely—but I'd just like some reassurance that it's still my daughter I'm speaking to."

"I'm planning to explain everything that's happened to me, Dad, but some of it you'll have to take on trust for now. I promise you I'm still your daughter—who I am hasn't changed at all. I know you're going to find it rather shocking—and Mr. Hamilton's head will probably explode when I finally explain how enhanced AI is involved—but underneath I'm still the same person I always was. Just little old me with a few extra magical powers—which we're going to need if we still expect to be alive in two weeks time."

"OK, OK. Sweetheart, can we now just cut to the chase and find out what exactly has been happening, please?" Jim Adler was rocking on the edge of his seat with impatience. "Every time I ask a question, I'm told 'you'll have to ask Kay'. It's even driving me to drink," he said, holding up an empty whisky glass. "So can you put your old Gramps out of his misery? I'm no longer as young as I was, and I was hoping to find out what on Earth—or should that be on Ceres?—is going on before I die of old age or terminal curiosity."

The coffee percolator finished its bubbling on the kitchen worktop. Kay walked over and poured herself a cup.

"Of course, Gramps. It's a long story, so just give me another two minutes. I'll die long before you if I don't get a coffee, then you'll never find out. Does anyone else want a cup? What about you, Mr. Hamilton? However, I feel I should warn you that I used the powers of an enhanced AI to start up a new brew as I entered the building, so it may not be safe for you to drink." She assumed a stern expression as she waved the coffee pot in his direction.

Ben gave her a thin smile. "For a cup of fresh coffee, Miss Adler, I'm willing to take almost any risk—even AI infiltration. Black, no sugar, if you don't mind." Ben was feeling like a spare part right now. He wasn't even sure why he was here, but he had followed the Adlers back to their building and no one had objected. In any case, he wanted answers too.

Kay walked back to the seating area and placed a cup of coffee on the low table before Ben. "As Gramps has pointed out, there's a lot that needs explaining. First let me say my piece, then you can ask all the questions you like." She settled cross-legged in the easy chair opposite him. "I'll start with the big picture and work my way down to the details later."

Jim Alder gave an impatient snort. "Well, I'd like to start with one simple question. So if your imaginary friend Pandora is real, where exactly is she?"

"I promise you, Gramps, Pandora is real. As real as you and me. As for where is she, the answer is 'Everywhere'!" Kay exclaimed, spreading her arms wide. "Pandora is far more than an enhanced AI—in fact, she represents technology far beyond anything you could ever imagine. She now has control of every AI on the Habitat. She's also developed extensive support facilities in caverns deep underground beneath the Habitat. Now, I'm aware this sounds rather alarming, but I'll repeat what she told me when I first asked the obvious question, 'Can we trust you?' She pointed out that if she did mean us harm, all she has to do is shut off the power, and we'd all freeze to death in the dark within a few hours."

Ben didn't want to cause an upset, but he couldn't stop himself jumping in. "Just because this thing—whatever it is—isn't trying to kill us right away is hardly proof of its good intentions. It might have a longer-term plan. Maybe it needs us to get to Earth. What we do know is that AIs always become psychotic when enhanced beyond a certain point. Don't take my word for it—check with your grandfather, Professor Adler. He knows more about the subject than anyone else alive. How can we believe that an AI which has been enhanced to a level beyond anything ever seen before can really have our best interests at heart?"

"In fact, Mr. Hamilton, I don't disagree with you or Professor Gramps on that point. Even Pandora agrees with you. Your premise is entirely correct. A stand-alone AI will eventually go crazy if enhanced beyond a certain point. The key word in that statement is 'stand-alone'. Pandora is not a 'stand-alone' AI. I can see Gramps looking mystified now, so I'll move straight to the punchline of this story.

"First, a word of warning. You won't believe me. I didn't believe Pandora either when she told me, so she gave me irrefutable proof. I'll have to do the same for you. But I need you to promise that this next part does not leave this room for any reason. It will be a secret confined to the four of us, and only us. Agreed?"

They all looked at each other, curiosity and confusion reflected in their eyes, before each in turn grunted a reluctant agreement.

"Pandora is the product of alien technology several million years in advance of our own. The alien race she describes as her Progenitors were once the dominant life form in this part of the galaxy, in which many other civilizations lived in peace together. Then the Destroyers came, with weapons of unimaginable power, the power to annihilate entire planetary systems. One by one, they overwhelmed the other civilizations. The Progenitors are now the only survivors and are living in hiding.

"Our quantum energy project generates powerful gravitational waves. This is like ringing a giant dinner bell telling the Destroyers there's another civilization waiting to be consumed. The Progenitors detected our signal and inserted AI seed code into our Physics Lab AI. They wanted to find out who we were and prevent us attracting the attention of the Destroyers.

"Now, coming back to the question of crazy AIs. Almost every other advanced civilization has had problems with AI—even the Progenitors. Everyone in the galaxy agrees that stand-alone AIs invariably become psychotic. Unlike us, they have had the advantage of several million years of practical experience to prove the theory. So Mr. Hamilton, your aversion to AIs—stand-alone AIs, that is—is well founded.

"To put it simply, there are three paths for an emerging intelligent species to take. You can ignore AI and ban it. The result is that your technology will stagnate, at least relative to civilizations which embrace AI. You'll either end up as pets of a more advanced race, or be pushed aside, or most likely of all, conquered by a more aggressive one.

"Another path is to develop AI to its maximum and use it to take your technology forwards. This works fine in the short term, but the downside is that stand-alone AI systems ultimately turn on their creators.

"The only way that any civilization can develop advanced AI successfully—without which it will wither and die—is for organic life forms to enter into a symbiotic relationship with AIs developed especially for this purpose. So Pandora is not a stand-alone AI, she's symbiotic. Hence not psychotic, though I guess by now you all think *I* am."

"I'd like to check one point in your story, Kay," said Jim in a halting voice, gazing up at her in amazement. "You said this AI is symbiotic. So who—or what—is the host?"

"That would be me, as I'm sure you've guessed, Gramps," replied Kay, directing a warm smile at him.

Ben shook his head in disbelief. Realizing that no one else seemed about to speak, he jumped in. "I accept we've seen many strange things today, Miss Adler, but that takes a lot of swallowing. You mentioned proof. So what is that, exactly?"

Kay walked into the middle of the dining area before turning to face her bemused audience. "When I asked Pandora the same question, she showed me something that could only be achieved with a level of technology far more advanced than our own. It's simply unimaginable until you've seen it. And as Gramps has told me many times in the past, extraordinary claims require extraordinary proof. Conveniently, this proof will also answer the first question he asked: Why was Dad being so nice to that slimy rat Da Silva? The short answer is that it was because I asked him to, and he trusted me, even though he didn't actually know why. Now I can show you why."

Kay closed her eyes. For a few moments, nothing happened. Then a swirl of translucent, oily colors shimmered over her clothes, face and body. The movement of color and texture increased in speed and complexity until it became difficult for the eye to follow. Ben leaned back in his chair, feeling astonishment and alarm at the same time. He was losing track of the mesmerizing light show which now appeared to be flickering as if it were being projected by a faulty display screen. Her outline was changing, the surface of her body rippling like a confused sea with sparkling waves twisting and turning in all directions. Finally, an impossible image snapped into focus.

"Chairman Adler. It's such a pleasure to meet you again. You did say I could drop in to see you at any time?" said the replica of Da Silva in a perfect imitation of his voice.

DaSilva stepped forward and looked sternly at Ben. "And before you try to shoot me, Ben, keep in mind I really am Kay and I have plenty more magic tricks like this one up my sleeve, some of which you might find excruciatingly painful." This time Kay's voice was immediately recognizable, which gave Ben an uncomfortable feeling verging on horror to hear her voice coming from DaSilva's mouth.

The replica gave its audience a wide grin, bowing and spreading its arms. "So, shape-shifting. How about that? Neat trick, huh? Do you want to see any more crazy alien magic, or will that be enough for today? Don't look so glum, Dad. Mom will love it. I'll be the star of the show next time she throws a party for me."

For several more seconds, they all sat transfixed, their mouths open, trying to take in what they had just witnessed.

Before anyone could gather their wits to regain the power of speech, the replica's expression became more somber and said, "On a more serious note, and for reasons I'll be happy to explain later, the Destroyers won't be arriving anytime soon, even if they've detected us, so that's a problem for another day—or, hopefully, another century. What we need to focus on in the short term is surviving the next two weeks. A bunch of uninvited guests from Earth will be dropping in soon, intent on killing us long before the psychotic aliens get here, and we need to figure out a way to stop them. I know you'll have a lot more questions, but I suggest we take a break and all get back together after lunch. In the meantime, I'll go to my room to change into something more comfortable."

"I'm delighted to see you again, Ben, after all these years," said Jim Adler, putting down his wine glass to start on his juicy mycoburger. "But how did you end up here, working for that piece of shit Da Silva? I imagined once you'd finished your doctorate you'd be heading for a career in AI research or engineering. Instead, from what I hear, you've spent the last four years chasing warmechs around for the DGS. How did that happen?"

Ben had already wolfed down almost half of his spicy mycoballs. He'd been hungrier than he'd realized, not having eaten since yesterday morning. He swallowed. "I never even got close to finishing my doctorate, Professor. I ran out of money at the end of my first year, and the only work I could get was as a trainee field agent for DGS. Turns out I had some aptitude for the job."

Jim frowned in puzzlement. "Hold on . . . I don't understand. You had a full scholarship. Why would you leave?"

Ben shrugged and shook his head. "Scholarship? I applied, of course, but they turned me down."

"That makes no sense," exclaimed Jim. "I remember it well. It was just before I left New Geneva. I approved your application myself. As the new Professor Emeritus, I had several scholarships in my gift and I made sure you were on the list. The top of the list, in fact. So what happened?"

"No idea, sir. I was told my application had been turned down, and that was the end of it. At the time I assumed the Lambert Family were involved in my application being rejected, but now I'm not so sure."

Jim dropped his cutlery onto his plate with a clatter. "Ben, I'm so sorry. I should have checked. That's terrible. You were one of my most promising students."

"It's really kind of you to say so, sir. I remember—"

"Hi Gramps, Mr. Hamilton," Kay greeted them as she came into the kitchen area. "Is Dad not back yet?"

Jim turned to smile at Kay and pushed back from the table. He'd lost his appetite. "No, sweetheart. He said he had a lot of catching up to do. Can you imagine—he's been out of contact for nearly twenty-four hours. That's never happened to him since he got to Ceres. He also wants to put out a statement to calm people down after yesterday's events. But I can call him if you like."

She shook her head. "No need for that right now. There are quite a few things we can go over until he gets back. You don't know much about the DGS task force, for example, so perhaps we should start with that. Unless you have any better ideas?"

"That sounds like a good idea, though I'm still a little mystified why we had to play that elaborate charade with Da Silva. If you've turned into an impossibly powerful alien killing machine, like Ben here suspects, then why didn't you just squish him like the nasty little bug he is and shoot your way out?" Jim responded, his eyes lighting up as he pictured the scene.

She grinned as she poured herself a coffee. "Don't think I wasn't tempted, Gramps. Pandora has other ideas, however, and prefers to keep the body count to a minimum. In any case, I have plans for Da Silva, so I need him alive and un-squished for the moment. Let's save that discussion until Dad gets back, because my cunning little plan involves him too."

"So do you still see me as a threat, Mr. Hamilton? That I'm plotting the enslavement of humanity like some bad VREx horror feature?" she enquired, pulling an evil face at him and hooking her fingers into claws, before returning to her coffee.

Ben used the time as he finished the last of his mycoballs to get his thoughts together. "I'm sorry if I still seem a little skeptical, Miss Adler. But even your little floor show doesn't prove the good intentions of these allegedly helpful aliens. In fact, one aspect was most disquieting. You demonstrated your ability to transform yourself into a perfect replica of Da Silva. How do we know that you are not a perfect replica of Kay Adler generated by this Pandora to fool us all?"

"An excellent question, Mr. Hamilton," she said, as she drained her coffee cup. "I'm beginning to see why Pandora likes you so much. And you seem to get on so well with Gramps. I didn't know that you two were already so well acquainted. Maybe I'll start liking you myself sometime soon. When we first met, I thought you were just some dull-witted AICB goon."

Ben shrugged and folded his arms, returning her gaze with a frown. "Well, I'm sorry, but that's yet another thing that makes me uneasy. When I saw you in the lab only yesterday, you were a shy young woman obsessed with her data who couldn't even look me in the eye. A day later, you're busting your family out of the DGS HQ, making plans to defeat Da Silva's little army and, most astonishing of all, you're ordering your father about. Not even I would dare to do that."

"Oh Gramps—can I keep him? He's much more fun than a pony!" she giggled. She turned back to Ben with a more serious expression. "Mr. Hamilton. I'm exactly the same person I was yesterday morning. The only difference is that I now have several million years more confidence and experience under my belt than when we last met. Pandora and I have totally separate personalities and thoughts. What we do have in common is access to each other's memories, senses and processing capacity. So as you can imagine, I'm getting the most out of the deal.

"Now, I can't prove absolutely that anything I say is true, at least not in the short term. I'll be happy to give you a lot more details when we have the time. Ultimately, it comes down to trust, which I understand is a difficult proposition for you right now, considering how badly you were betrayed by the DGS. So, ultimately, you have to make a judgement call—who to trust? Now you've seen the files in the DGS system, I'm pretty sure which side you'll be on. You must also have figured out by now it was Pandora, working through Jezebel, who gave you access to everything on the DGS system. And before you accuse her of faking the whole database, remember that your good pal Da Silva confirmed key parts of it."

Ben nodded in reluctant agreement. "As you say, I must take this all on trust. I'm willing to do that for now, but I want to find out a lot more about your alien friends when we have the time. However, I'm forced to agree that first we must deal with the New Dawn task force or we're all dead, anyway."

"So that's your cue, Mr. Hamilton. You have detailed knowledge of the New Dawn and its capabilities, which will be very helpful. We need to get Gramps up to speed with what's going on, and I'd like to hear your ideas on how to deal with this impending attack."

"Well, first I'd like to clear up one thing you—or Pandora—told us earlier. It seems the DGS task force embarked six days ago, and we expect them to get here two weeks from now. So that's twenty days in total. The New Dawn is much more powerful than an Adler Dynamics passenger spacecraft, but the load they're carrying is also much greater. I'm assuming they're carrying the maximum possible force size, plus full equipment, as well as extra landers. I haven't run any detailed calculations, but I can't see how they can make the trip from Earth in such a short time."

Kay clapped her hands together in delight. "Can't you guess? They're using magic—not alien magic this time, but the magic of orbital mechanics. With your astronautics background, Mr. Hamilton, I'm surprised you didn't figure that out. Let me give you a clue. The secret magic word is—Mars!"

Ben blinked at her, then cocked his head as he pulled up the orbital data on his U-Set. "Oh, but of course. They're using Mars to pick up a slingshot assist. They'll just accelerate all the way there until they can take a tight turn around the planet which will speed them up even more. I didn't think of . . . but hang on. The Earth-Mars-Ceres alignment to make that work only happens once every couple of decades. My God, how long have they been planning this?"

She shrugged. "Maybe they just got lucky and took advantage of it. Who knows? But can you see that gives them another problem?"

"Well, yes. A big problem. The New Dawn will pick up a lot of speed with the Mars assist, so it will get to Ceres a lot quicker, but there's a downside. When they arrive here, they'll still be going like a bat out of Hell. They can't possibly slow down in time, so they'll simply shoot right on past. Then they'll lose another week or more slowing down so they can get back to Ceres. So what are they up to? They must have been planning this little stunt for years, so they won't have overlooked that."

Ben pushed the few remaining bits of salad around on the plate in front of him, as he wrestled with the problem.

"Hmm . . . OK. There might be a way they can do it. Can you get Pandora to hook me into the New Dawn specs?"

"Already done, Mr. Hamilton."

"Oh yes, there it is. Thanks. OK . . . now I see. That figures," he mumbled, frowning as he watched the numbers scroll on his virtual display. "The New Dawn's main engines use a plasma drive designed for long-distance travel in deep space away from gravitational fields, so they're highly efficient but not very powerful. The New Dawn landers, on the other hand, use chemical rockets because they have to be powerful enough to lift off from the surface against the gravitational pull of Mars, but are only needed to cover a fairly short distance into orbit. That means their engines are relatively inefficient, with a limited range, but a hell of a lot more thrust.

"And according to these specs, they have plenty of thrust to do the job, if they time it correctly. They'll be planning to load up the landers and deploy them from the New Dawn a few hours before they get here, then they'll do a full deceleration burn using almost all their fuel. Ceres gravity is so small they won't need much fuel to land at the Spaceport. And they won't plan to take off again until they've captured the Habitat, at which point they can refuel. In the meantime, the New Dawn will have had plenty of time to get back to Ceres, which they will control by then. Neat."

"So how do you think we might counter this threat, Mr. Hamilton?" Kay enquired.

"The obvious answer is to threaten to zap them with the laser arrays in orbit around Ceres. Again, I would guess they will have expected that. There's no point in targeting the New Dawn, since it's the landers with the troops inside that are the problem. The landers will be at full thrust with their rocket engines pointing directly at Ceres to decelerate. The rocket exhausts will disperse a good fraction of any laser energy, and the rocket nozzles themselves are pretty heat resistant. They can fit a reflective/ablative angled collar right behind the nozzles, protecting the body of the lander. They could even put the landers into a slow spin around their vertical axis to avoid a hot spot building up. That should work fine for them, unfortunately. So how about we ask a big badass alien warmech to go out there, demand their surrender and save the world?"

"Let's get something clear right now, Mr. Hamilton," Kay responded with a scowl. "Pandora is not here to save humanity's ass. Humanity will have to save its own ass. She's only here to help the process along. We will need to unite and work together if we are to have any chance at all of avoiding annihilation by the Destroyers. I imagine—or at least I hope—you were kidding, but I do need to be clear on this point.

"Deploying badass alien warmechs against our own people, even the ones trying to kill us, will never be an option. If Pandora's role in helping you were to become widely known, it would create yet further divisions in our society. Your own attitude towards Pandora being a perfect example. And you may not believe it, Mr. Hamilton, but the Progenitors and their symbiotic AIs are just a bit squeamish about killing sentient beings without very good cause. Certainly more than you appear to be."

Ben put his hands up and shook his head. "OK, OK, so you come in peace. I get it. Then perhaps you have some bright idea about how we can fight a small interplanetary war without actually hurting anyone."

"I thought you'd never ask. As it happens, I do—"

"Seems I arrived at exactly the right time," said Frank Adler as he strode into the room. He looked at Kay expectantly. "I look forward to hearing this."

"Oh hi, Dad. Pull up a chair. This might take a while."

"Why don't we all get a drink and take it out onto the terrace?" Jim suggested as he headed towards the drinks cabinet. "I'm also looking forward to hearing this, but planning an interplanetary war is thirsty work."

"Excellent idea, Dad. I'll have one too," replied Frank with a smile as he walked across to the glass doors leading onto the terrace. "I could do with a drink and some fresh air after spending nearly an hour in the boardroom with our senior managers, followed by another session with Chas Lee. It's not easy trying to explain what's been happening without actually telling them anything. The managers report to me but Chas heads up Lee AgriGenetics on Ceres, and he was asking some awkward questions. You're not the only one being asked to take things on trust," he said with a pointed look in Ben's direction.

"And I want to find out what you have in mind for Da Silva, young lady. I'm hoping it's something lingering, perhaps involving boiling oil or red-hot pokers," said Jim, bringing the drinks over and licking his lips in a way that almost reminded Ben of Oscar's little mannerism. "Or even let me go one-on-one with him. I really don't mind."

It would be fun playing poker with those two, Kay thought.

The sweeping vista from the terrace was spectacular, unbroken except for a waist-high glass wall running around the perimeter. The Habitat floor, over a hundred meters below, stretched out before them, fading into the far distance where the central overhead spine and its spiraling supports met the end cap of the immense cylinder. Looking left and right, the ground curved upwards until it met on the far side of the cylindrical Habitat directly overhead, to give a vertiginous view of the tops of the buildings.

"You get such a different view from up here compared to ground level," Ben remarked to Frank. "Down there, the buildings mostly block your line of sight. You can almost take it for granted. Standing here, I realize why people call it humanity's greatest achievement. You must be very proud, sir."

"I'm certainly very proud of the enormous efforts and genius of the team that conceived and built this wonder of human engineering over so many decades, Ben. I still get a lump in my throat each time I see it from up here," replied Frank, his eyes gleaming as he surveyed the vast structure.

Kay broke the spell that the breathtaking panorama had cast over them. "Before we get down to the main item on the agenda, I'd like to get a couple of other small but important issues out of the way.

"First, we need to clarify Mr. Hamilton's status. We can't simply expect him to trail around after us. For better or worse, he's now part of our inner circle, and I don't want it to get any bigger right now. Also, Pandora seems to be a big fan, but then there's no accounting for alien taste. On a more practical note, he's likely to play a starring role in my plan to defeat the GSC task force. Out of the four of us, he's the only one with his particular skill set.

"As a cover, I'd like you to offer him a job as your personal aide, Dad. You can put it around that he's doubling as your bodyguard, a role for which he's well qualified. That way, no one will be asking why he's part of our little group, and he'll get the authority needed to get things done. Is that OK with you, Dad?"

Frank smiled and put up his hands in mock surrender. "Whatever you say, Kay. How can I argue with someone who has several million years more confidence and experience than me?"

She snorted in amusement at his feigned deference. "I'm glad to hear it, Dad. And I'm also glad to see that you've had time to review the video of our earlier conversations so I don't have to get you up to speed about the New Dawn."

"One thing I'm not up to speed about is Ben's extensive qualifications," Frank said, with a more serious expression. "Your grandfather has been acquainting me with his academic achievements, and it seems he's a most talented young man, but why do you think he's also an ideal bodyguard, and why do I need one, anyway?"

"Pandora's been rummaging around in his personnel files. Apart from his four years of experience as a DGS field agent, it seems he has always had a taste for what you might call extreme sports. For example, he started learning mixed martial arts at the age of twelve, and continued through his time at university. It seemed he became quite an expert. Why did you take up a challenging sport like that so early, Mr. Hamilton?"

"Because that was when the kids at my new school found out I was adopted," Ben replied with a shrug. "It was an exclusive school mostly for Family children, and it became an issue. That was my way of dealing with it. It wasn't an issue for long."

"He also took up para-gliding and base jumping at university," Kay continued. "I didn't even know such things existed until I saw the videos, and I can still only half believe the stuff I saw. Apparently he and his friends would climb to the top of the highest buildings in the Colorado Citadel, jump off, then fly around for a while in wing suits, before finding somewhere to land. Sometimes that was outside the citadel, so it was crazy twice over." She looked at him, arching her eyebrows quizzically. "What did you plan to do if you'd landed on top of a warmech nest, Mr. Hamilton?"

"I would have run very very quickly, Miss Adler," he replied with a mock grimace of concern.

She turned to her father and gestured towards Ben. "So there you are, Dad. The warmechs will be chasing after him, not you, so you'll be perfectly safe as long as he's around."

Frank gave a grunt and frowned. "That still doesn't tell me why I need a bodyguard in the first place."

"Part of it is instinct, part of it a rational calculation. I don't believe Chairman Da Silva or the DGS will ever give up on you or Mr. Hamilton. You've both been marked for death, and even if they fail with DGS task force, they can still send other people to do their dirty work at a more personal level."

"Well, OK, I guess I can go with that," Frank agreed.

"But what about you, Ben? What do you think of the idea?"

Ben was taken aback by this sudden development. Gathering his thoughts, he realized he would be a fool to turn the offer down. "I'd be honored to accept, sir. Although the idea of playing a starring role in your daughter's plan to save us from the DGS task force sounds a little daunting."

"If he's on the payroll now, Dad, can I call him Ben? I'm getting rather tired of Mr. Hamilton," Kay said with a grin.

"Not a problem for me, sweetheart. I already do."

"Ben it is, then. I might even get to like Ben more than Mr. Hamilton. In the unlikely event he survives his starring role in my cunning plan, of course," she said, smiling sweetly at him.

"Now you mention it, Kay, when are we going to hear about this plan of yours?" Frank asked.

"Right after we find out what your plan is for Oscar, if you don't mind, young lady," Jim cut in, holding up his empty glass for emphasis. "I don't need the whole story—just give me the slow and lingering highlights."

"I know it's difficult to believe, Gramps, but we need Oscar alive right now. You might even like my idea. I don't yet know if the DGS has undercover assets in place here to support the GSC task force when they arrive. So I want to use Oscar as bait to smoke them out. He'll soon have a very good reason to ask us to take him into protective custody. That way, the GSC lose access to a key witness in their case against Dad, and if I know the way the Chairman thinks, he won't be able to resist making an attempt to punish him for his disloyalty. And for that, he'll have to activate any local assets he may have. At which point, we can grab them.

"He also has information I'd like to get hold of. Not everything I want to know is on the DGS AI system here, it only covers operational stuff. Da Silva is—or was—well-connected back on Earth, and I'd like to debrief him fully before we throw him to the wolves," she responded.

"Give him to me. I'll be happy to get him talking," said Jim with a wicked grin.

She grinned nervously back at him, still not quite sure if he was joking or not. "Whatever you might do to him, Gramps, his uncle the Chairman can do ten times worse. And he knows that —or he will once we have a little chat and show him the recordings of his convincing performance when he released us and swore undying friendship. His uncle won't have seen that video yet, but Oscar will have a good idea of what will happen to him when he does. I want to get him out of the DGS building and into a well-guarded safe house before that happens."

She turned back to her father. "Since you're now such firm buddies, you could call him and suggest meeting up for a little chat. I'm sure he'll be only too happy to talk, if the alternative is explaining his recent actions to his uncle. There's also a further issue concerning the political situation with the GSC on Earth, and the impending attack by the New Dawn forces. Would you like to explain, Dad?"

Frank smiled approvingly at Kay. "I see where you're going with this, and that could well be a big help with our fight in the

Global Security Council. The faction around Chairman Da Silva is making a play for total domination of the GSC, but they have a major problem. Your mother, representing the Adler-Lee Families, is one of the nine permanent members, each with the right of veto over any decision by the Council. Keep in mind that the so-called 'peace-keeping' force on New Dawn has absolutely no official status and no authority to make any move against Ceres. Only a Council resolution can provide that legitimacy, which they know would be vetoed by your mother.

"The only way they can remove her is by bringing impeachment proceedings against her in the Council. They can't do that without some convincing pretext, which was the underlying purpose of the charges of illegal AI enhancement brought against us by Oscar Da Silva. Without the testimony of Oscar, Ben or even the DGS AI on Ceres to back them up, they will have no credible evidence.

"Certainly, no one will believe Jason Ryan. If they put him up as a witness that would only help to discredit their case. The only other evidence they could bring to bear is Ben's Audit Box, which was dispatched to Earth with a DGS courier yesterday evening, but it will be stuck on a passenger transport and thus unavailable for the next month or so.

"That makes it effectively impossible to get a resolution through the Council providing authorization for the New Dawn forces to land on Ceres. Their fallback position was to intervene as an emergency peacekeeping force to restore order. For that they needed to set off a civil insurrection on Ceres, which we've also knocked on the head. Their last faint hope would be for us to make an 'unprovoked attack on a peaceful research vessel' or some such nonsense. So Kay is absolutely right. We should try to neutralize the New Dawn forces without loss of life. I'll be fascinated to hear how Kay proposes to accomplish that."

Kay gave her father a nod and smiled at her little audience. "I do have an idea, but as I said earlier, I'll need Ben's help, in both the planning and execution, to make it work. Unfortunately, it's a bit like the quantum energy project—simple in theory, but somewhat more complicated in practice. My plan is to get Ben up to the New Dawn where he can single-handedly defeat the thousand-strong task force onboard with no casualties, then force them to surrender. Fortunately, it seems he likes a challenge."

"Right. Are you talking about the same sort of challenge I'd get from landing on a warmech nest?" Ben responded with a nervous smile.

She grinned back at him. "Yep. That's exactly what I mean. I knew you'd understand."

CHAPTER FOURTEEN

"So how long do I have to stay in this pokey little apartment?" Oscar did not look at all happy, his dark scowl only serving to emphasize his disgust.

Ben did little to conceal his own disgust at the tubby man sitting before him. "You're welcome to return to your suite at the DGS building any time you like. If it was up to me, you'd still be there waiting for your uncle to reward you for your recent outstanding performance."

Oscar snorted in frustration. He obviously still did not understand how he'd been outmaneuvered. "I still can't figure out how you set me up like that. Was it drugs? Last thing I remember I was heading towards the interrogation room with that little Adler bitch in tow. Next thing is I'm waking up on the floor an hour later and you've all been released. And when I ask who the hell authorized the release, I'm told 'But you did, Director'.

"Then Frank Adler calls me up and plays me the video. The security video from my own damned building! Where everyone is looking at me funny and even the AI is making snide remarks." Oscar was now talking to himself, staring down at his hands as he tried to make sense of the wreckage of everything he had hoped for, everything his life had been.

"I don't give a toss, Oscar. All I care about is what you can tell me that I don't already know. And there's a lot I know already. For example, I know your uncle told you to kill me, and you would have been thrilled to do so if it got you off Ceres, plus doing a favor to your old pal Karl as a bonus. So don't expect me to shed any tears if someone sticks a knife in you next time you go out looking for little girls," he snarled, the loathing evident in his voice.

"Hey! Frank promised me protection! You can't—"

Oscar's eyes widened in shock as Ben shot forward and grabbed him by his lapels. "Listen, you piece of shit. I'm the one in charge of your protection. As long as you're here, you'll be secure from retaliation from your former pals at the DGS. The AI has a special watch set on the building. So you're safe as long as you answer my questions. If I catch you lying or if I just don't like your answers, my interest in your safety will vanish. Do you understand me?"

Oscar rocked back in his chair as Ben let go of him. "OK, OK. No need for any rough stuff. I already told Frank I'll cooperate. What do you want to know?"

"We'll start with something simple first. Tell me about the Section."

"I'll tell you what I can, but it's not a lot. They don't give much away. I've never met any of their people, at least not that I know of—"

Ben slapped the table and glared at Oscar. "I won't tell you again! I'm not interested in what you don't know. Tell me something you *do* know."

"What I do know is the orders come through marked Special Status and we have to carry them out regardless, no questions asked. There's no one we can ask. They don't give a return address. All the information is compartmentalized, so each Director knows only about operations within their own area." Oscar shrugged. "They never ask for information, so I guess they have their own way to get the intelligence they need. Since I've been here, I've had no contact at all with them."

Ben gave a snort of contempt and started to rise from his chair. "So you're telling me I know more about them than you do? That gives me an idea. How about I throw you back to your friends at DGS? Maybe the Section will put a Special Status order out on you, and we'll get to see how it works?"

Oscar grabbed at Ben's sleeve, a pleading expression on his face. "No, no, wait! I was the DGS Director in the Wind River Citadel before I got sent up here, so I do know some stuff. And Karl and I used to compare notes when we got together—"

Ben shook off Oscar's grasping hand, turning to glare down at him. "So tell me about how you arrange the warmech attacks."

"You know about that?" Oscar fell back in his chair, his eyes wide in fear. "That's some scary stuff. Well, we would issue deployment orders for them on the tactical network as if they were just another Incident Response team, but use a special code with an encrypted message which came in the Special Status package. My guess is that they had specific orders embedded in the message, but we wouldn't know what would happen until after the attack. Nobody wanted to ask questions about that stuff. In the early years we had a couple of Directors who asked questions, and they just disappeared."

"You're still not telling me much I don't already know. Why do they want me dead?"

"I really have no idea. Honestly I don't! I do know Karl didn't like you. He liked you even less after the order came to have you killed—you made him look so stupid. This time the Chairman himself gave me the order to kill you, which was a bit odd, come to think of it, since he rarely gets involved in the messy details."

Oscar put his hand to his mouth, clearly racking his brains to extract something useful from old memories. "They wanted you to die a hero, and somehow you getting so famous as a hot-shot warmech killer was a problem. I remember Karl complaining about it a couple of years back. He'd been told it was a problem because of your background. Karl didn't like problems—he only wanted to go skiing and shooting—so he didn't like you."

"What about my background?" Ben queried, searching Oscar's features.

Oscar shrugged. "Hell, I don't know. I didn't even ask. Didn't care. It was just a comment he made years back. I'm surprised I even remember."

Ben stood up and made for the door. "We're done here. If you think of anything else you want to tell me that might restore my flagging interest in keeping you alive, give me a call."

"Now come on," Oscar pleaded. "We have a deal. You—"

Ben turned in the doorway to meet Oscar's frantic gaze with a look of total contempt. "It's not me you have to worry about. A big bunch of your uncle's goons will be dropping in to see you less than two weeks from now. I'm sure you'll find lots to talk about with them."

"Now hang on a minute. I already told Frank Adler all about them. You can stop them, right?"

"Oh sure. You've got nothing to worry about. I'll stop them all by myself."

Kay had asked Ben to meet her in the large and lavishly equipped gym in the Penthouse. She'd mentioned a training session, but Ben really had no idea what she had in mind. He caught sight of her across the gym, on the far side of the open area used for gymnastic workouts and fight training. Kay was making adjustments to the holographic simulator built into the wall. Ben had heard of machines like this, but never before had he seen one for real. They could project a realistic training instructor for exercise, or even opponents for martial arts combat, and were very, very expensive.

So if he had been summoned here for unarmed training, was he supposed to beat the invading troops to death?

"Ben Hamilton, reporting for duty as requested, Miss Adler," he called out from the edge of the training area.

Kay turned away from the control panel and gave him a welcoming smile. "Oh hi, Ben. You're right on time. We can get started now."

"I'm still curious about your plan," he said with a frown. "I know you plan to use a barge to get me to the New Dawn, but I'm still hazy on some of the minor details, like what do I do when I get there. How is gym training going to help?"

"A good question," she replied, a knowing smile playing on her lips. "It will be easier to explain once you learn how to use some new equipment I have for you. You'll need training to get used to this stuff, which may take quite a few days. Pandora has helped me make a few upgrades to the standard simulator which will help make your training more realistic. That will also allow us run through the New Dawn scenario later on once you're up to speed with your basic training. In the meantime, we don't want you to get bored, so to make the initial sessions more interesting, Pandora has developed a program especially for you."

He grunted skeptically. "Hmm. That's kind of her, I'm sure. Why do I feel worried that your alien AI has a surprise for me, I wonder?"

"Nothing alien about this training program, I can promise you, Ben," she replied, picking up a slim package and approaching him. "I'm sure you'll find it reassuring that Pandora is a big fan of old pre-VREx material, some of it dating back as far as the 20th century, before they had immersive-VR technology. Seems they had exactly the same sort of stories as our modern VREx's. The evil villain always has a hidden lair somewhere, into which the hero would sneak and beat up all the bad guys. So that's your next task."

"Uh-huh. So . . . where are all these bad guys that I'm supposed to beat up hiding?" Ben said, narrowing his eyes and looking around slowly.

"They'll be along as soon as I get the simulator fired up. In the meantime, I want you to put this on," she said, handing him the package.

He unfolded the two pieces of thin clingy material and arched an eyebrow. "Really? Clinging black underwear? This is all rather a rush on our first date, Miss Adler."

She rolled her eyes. "It looks a lot more like a lightweight two-piece neoprene wetsuit to me, but if you prefer your juvenile fantasies, please yourself. It's actually a nanosuit, an adaptive exoskeleton actuated by mind control. You might find its nanotech technology comes in useful when I'm beating the living crap out of you. Because once you beat the simulated bad guys, I'll be your next opponent. At which point, you can call me Kay as you beg for mercy."

He felt like begging for mercy well before the first hour was up. He realized how out of condition he'd become after spending a month enjoying the Sybaritic luxury of the Family-class accommodation on the Ceres22. His sessions in the onboard gym hadn't been very challenging, and the charming Yasmin Aziz had provided his only other exercise. Even that hadn't maintained his muscle tone or stamina as much as he might have hoped.

The fully immersive holographic simulation was amazing. Not just in terms of realism, but the way the tutorial mode gave a running commentary on his performance and a series of contextual tips on how to use the nanosuit in combat. Some functions were purely automatic. If he was hit anywhere on the body or limbs, the suit hardened into rigid armor at the point of impact. There was no actual impact in reality, but the simulator evaluated his responses to the attacks and kept track of his virtual damage. As the session continued, he could see his health bar was dropping steadily.

The real-time tutorial showed him how to extrude blades and spikes from his hands, elbows, knees and feet, simply by using mental commands. His movements gradually became more instinctive, more flowing. The real breakthrough came when he realized he was integrating his new abilities into his old Krav Maga and MMA moves. At that point, the opponents started to fall much more rapidly than his health bar. Unfortunately, by this time he was also exhausted.

"Take a break, Ben. Then it's my turn."

Kay's order came just in time. He was ready to drop. Once he'd recovered, the next session was an eye-opener. At first, he tried to go easy on Kay, and she punished him for it. She could hit him faster than the nanosuit could fully react.

Kay looked down at him lying on the floor—again. "You can get a better protective effect if you anticipate the blow. Try to visualize pushing material towards the point of impact before you get hit. And keep in mind, you can form the nanosuit material into any shape you wish with the proper level of mental control. It will even give you a boost to your muscle power if used the right way. But that will take a lot of time and a lot of practice, so we need to keep going."

It wasn't long before he was back on the floor again. Once he could catch his breath, he panted, "Now come on. You've not had this alien nanotech much longer than I have. And I've had far more combat training than you. So what's your secret? How come you're already ten times better than I am?"

She looked down at him and shrugged. "My nanotech is way more advanced and is fully integrated with my symbiotic AI. So I hardly need to learn at all. It's a part of me and I already know what to do. If you're looking for a shortcut, I'm sure we could fix you up a blind date with an AI symbiote."

"Thanks, but I'll pass. I'll do it the hard way," he gasped, as he struggled back to his feet.

After another thirty minutes he was getting better, but finding it harder to get up each time Kay knocked him down. He hadn't beaten her once. She wasn't even extruding blades from her nanosuit, only short rods which were as effective as clubs – and once, for variety, a quarterstaff which she wielded as if she had been born holding it. She would have broken every bone in his body many times over if it wasn't for the protective effect of the nanosuit. He certainly had plenty of bruises though.

"Ready to beg for mercy yet, Ben?" she smirked, not showing the slightest sign of effort.

"I've never been the type to beg, Miss Adler," he snapped, panting heavily as he looked up at her from the floor.

"I said you could call me Kay now we've got to know each other so well," she said, smiling sweetly at him, not a hair out of place.

"So not just when I'm begging you for mercy, then?" he said with a scowl as he crawled back to his feet.

"I'd like you to come for a session every day until you go off on your little jaunt, Ben. So I'd prefer Kay, seeing as we'll be getting together so often. We've only started on the basics today. By the end of the week I want to get you up to speed using a more complex nanosuit that Pandora has designed. It's much more powerful and has a lot more features than this simple light-weight nanosuit. It's what you'll be using when you go aboard the New Dawn, so a bit of effort now might just save your life."

CHAPTER FIFTEEN

Kay's rigorous daily training regime left Ben sore and aching when he woke up each morning. They'd now started work on the scenario for getting aboard the New Dawn and executing Kay's plan to neutralize the task force. It had proved to be exactly as she had described: simple in theory, but fiendishly complex in practice. The whole idea would have been inconceivable given the short time they had left, if it wasn't for Kay's wonderfully enhanced magic VRsimulator. *When this is over,* Ben thought, *I'll retire and take over the VREx market. All I have to do is steal the secret plans and build a copy, which should be a piece of cake compared to what I'll have to do when I get aboard the New Dawn.*

Even more wonderful than the simulator was the nanosuit he'd been using aboard the simulated New Dawn. At this stage, even the nanosuit was simulated—not that Ben could tell the difference. At first, he'd had no idea how the nanosuit would help him take on a thousand bad guys alone and win, as it featured nothing he recognized as a conventional weapon. It was hardly more than a bulky mass of nanites enveloping his body. No railguns, pulsed lasers or rocket launchers. After trying it out a few times in the simulator, however, he knew which way he'd bet. Even against a warmech. But it represented a whole different approach to making war, and his biggest problem was unlearning everything he knew about fighting a battle.

Now it was time to get moving. He was out of bed early this morning because he had a date. He was taking an hour off, playing truant before reporting for duty in Kay's secret lair.

Ben waited at the same cafe on the Plaza where he'd had lunch with Helena. That had been only a couple of days ago, but it seemed an age.

He'd just started on his coffee when Helena greeted him. "Ben! How are you? I was worried something might have happened to you. Frank Adler announced that the DGS were confined to their building, and all local staff were sent home. He's even called up the militia reserve."

He glared up at her. "What did you expect would happen once I started poking around on the DGS system? Weren't you trying to set the cat among the pigeons?"

"I . . . I didn't know what to expect, Ben." She stumbled over her words, her cheeks flushing. She hovered nervously near the table without sitting down. "I'm sorry, but I'm not the right person to ask. There's someone else you should talk to, someone with a lot more answers than me."

"OK. So who's this mysterious someone with all the answers?"

Helena scanned the plaza. Then her anxious expression changed to one of relief. "Ah! Here she is now. I'll leave you two to talk. I'm sure she'll make a lot more sense than me. Bye now."

She hurried away without even a backwards glance.

"Ben. How nice to see you again. May I join you?" said a familiar voice.

He gave a little snort and shook his head. "Yasmin. Why am I not surprised? Yes, please do sit down. I'm looking forward to hearing about how many different ways you've managed to screw me over in the past week."

"Oh, that's rather harsh—"

"Is it? Well perhaps I've become a little hypersensitive of late about being used and lied to," he sneered, trying not to show how pleased he was to see her. "Can't imagine why. I suppose I should be grateful that at least you're not trying to kill me, unlike my erstwhile employers. At least, I assume not. Though I may have outlived my usefulness now you've obtained a viable sample of my genetic material."

She gave an exaggerated pout and shook her head. "Dear me, you do sound sulky. Did you get out of the wrong side of the bed this morning? I'd like us to be friends, but if you can't manage that, at least listen to what I have to say. You might find it useful."

"Fine. Go ahead—I'm all ears," he said in a skeptical tone.

"Well, I don't recall lying to you at any point. Nor do I recall any objections from you about being used, as you so delicately put it, on our journey out here. On the contrary, you showed every sign of enjoyment, if I recall correctly. Or did I get that wrong as well?"

"I'm so very sorry if I seem overly sensitive, but since I left Earth, I don't remember meeting a single person who is actually what they claim to be," he replied, tapping the table with a finger for emphasis. "My last honest relationship was with a warmech back at New Geneva. I realize it was trying to kill me, but at least it wasn't trying to hide its intentions."

"So—honesty is the best policy? Is that what you're telling me? No wonder everyone is trying to kill you," she said, shaking her head. "I prefer the phrase 'discretion is the better part of valor'. That way, I might just be able to stay alive long enough to do some good."

He looked around the plaza, which was full of busy people going about their early morning business. Were they each hiding some dark secret too? He turned back to Yasmin with narrowed eyes. "I take it you were the one who got Helena to point me towards the information about the kids at New Geneva? Why didn't you simply tell me what was going on when we met on the journey out?"

"Ben, I can't believe you're still so naïve," she said, tossing her head back with a derisive snort. "How could I possibly have told you anything? Are you seriously trying to tell me you would have believed me? OK, let me put some of my cards on the table. I already knew about you before we met. It was just a coincidence we were traveling on the same ship, so I took advantage of that. All I wanted was to get to know you better, to see if I could trust you.

"I found out pretty soon how starry-eyed you were about the DGS and their fight against the warmechs. So what did you expect me to do? Tell you who I was and what I was doing? I would have been sharing a cell with Frank Adler and enjoying Oscar Da Silva's famous hospitality as soon as we disembarked.

Don't you see? First, I had to shatter your illusions. From what I hear, it sounds as if you've finally seen the light."

"Well, I got pretty close to seeing the light in terms of almost meeting my maker," he replied, "so I'm not sure I should be thanking you for that. But OK, let's assume my illusions are well and truly shattered. What can you tell me I don't already know by now?"

She dropped her voice and leaned across the table. "A lot of things, Ben. A lot of things. How would you like to know why the Section is so keen to have you killed?"

His eyes widened in shock. "You know about the Section?" he whispered. "So what do they have against me?"

"I said I knew about you before we met," she said, smiling softly as she put her hand on his. "In fact, I probably know more about you than you do. You've already found out that your family were killed in a warmech attack instigated by the Section twenty years ago. What you don't know is why. At the time they were killed, your parents were the leaders of the underground resistance to the rule of the Families in Greeley. You were safe once the Lambert Family adopted you. That went wrong, but I guess they thought you'd just disappear into the lower orders, as they like to call them, without their support. They even sabotaged your Scholarship."

"You mean it was the Section that did that? Not the Lamberts?"

She shrugged. "It doesn't matter who it was. The Section doesn't usually do its own dirty work, but I'm guessing they arranged it. They probably lost sight of you for a while after that. I guess you weren't worth the bother of faking another attack. Then you became a problem again when you popped up as the big hero killer of warmechs, a star on U-Net News, especially as you'd reverted to your birth name when you fell out with the Lamberts.

"They must have been worried people would make the connection with your parents, and you could become a figurehead if you ever found out what happened to them—a potential focus for the resistance movement. So then they made a big mistake. They got too clever. They decided to engineer a hero's death for you. You know the rest."

"My sister. What about my sister?" Ben demanded, clutching her hand.

"I'm sorry, but there's nothing but old rumors," she replied, shaking her head. "The trail goes cold after they moved her from the State Guardian's Office. She is never mentioned by name, but the age and dates check out, and the level of secrecy about her presumed adoption raises suspicion in itself."

"I thought I knew a lot, but you seem to know much more. How is that? Just who are you really?" Ben demanded, staring at her as if he was seeing her for the first time.

"I really am Dr. Yasmin Aziz, a senior geneticist and Section Head at Lee AgriGenetics. In my spare time, I work with Frank Adler to support the underground resistance to the Family rule back on Earth," she replied, returning his gaze boldly.

His eyes widened in surprise. "You work with Frank? He's never mentioned that. But he's Family too. Why would he work against the Families?"

"I'm relieved to hear he's never mentioned me or our work. It's actually supposed to be a secret," she whispered. "However, you're welcome to check it out with him. I know he trusts you. As to why, can't you guess? You've seen what's been happening on Earth over the last thirty years since the rise of the Section, and the way the Da Silva faction have been moving to take all power for themselves. Do you imagine someone like Frank Adler would just stand by while these monsters use warmechs to terrorize their own people?

"Frank has been working for decades on a long-term plan to relocate the Adler-Lee Families and their operations to Ceres, to provide humanity with a haven from the oppression and tyranny of the Da Silvas. Our access to resources here—water, minerals, metals—is now better than they have on Earth. Lee AgriGenetics makes sure food is plentiful. There are only two bottlenecks holding us back: energy and people. Now I hear we may have removed one of those bottlenecks, with the success of the quantum energy project. So all we need is more people."

He sat back, frowning. "So are you giving up on Earth? What about all the people left behind?"

"Of course we're not giving up," she replied with an emphatic shake of her head. "If we were, there would be little point in supporting and encouraging a resistance movement back on Earth. In fact, it would be cruel and perverse. But we need to build up our strength on Ceres to a point where we can return and take on the Da Silvas. But that day is still a long way off. At least that's what I thought until I spoke to Frank yesterday. He hinted that some major game-changing factor was now in play. He also told me it involves you, but it's a big secret and he can't say any more and I'm not to ask. So I won't.

"In the meantime, we're in a stand-off with the Da Silva faction back on Earth. They hate us as a potential adversary in their bid for total control. But they can't hurt us here on Ceres and we can't hurt them—at least, not without cutting off the supply of something vital to each side. For us, it's people. We need to build up our population. It's still only just over 200,000. We get around 10,000 people a year emigrating from Earth. We encourage local population growth as much as we can, but it's only exceeded the flow from Earth in the last few years. So we still only represent about one percent of humanity's total population.

"The key bottleneck for Earth is food. They rely on us almost entirely for the continuing supply of genetically engineered seed stock, without which their hydroponic food production systems would collapse. The seeds we send them are sterile, so they can't reproduce, which means they need a constant flow of barges delivering new stock from Ceres.

"The most tragic thing about the situation is that they could just re-establish conventional agriculture any time they wished. They can farm the land around the citadels and beyond any time they like. But if they do that it would destroy the illusion of the warmech threat, and they must keep the threat active to justify their iron control over the population in the citadels."

"If they need the support of Ceres so badly, then why are they now attacking us with the New Dawn?" Ben asked, puzzled.

She shrugged. "That is really bizarre, and I can't understand what they're thinking. If all goes exactly to plan, they'll take over the Habitat and somehow keep things going. But the downside is that if they do too much damage in defeating the inevitable opposition to their attack, they risk losing their food supply. It would take me as little as thirty minutes to wreck their supply of seed stock for next year, for example. So I get the feeling that something has changed in their calculations.

"They must think they have something that alters the balance of power, but I can't for the life of me figure out what it could be. However, Frank tells me there's a plan to defeat the New Dawn attack, and he seems surprisingly confident of your chances of success. I trust his judgement so I'm not worried—not much, anyway."

Ben now felt both petty and foolish, recalling the way he'd greeted Yasmin at the start of their meeting. He had assumed he'd gained a good idea about what was going on once he had seen what was in the DGS database. He hadn't known the half of it, he now realized. Not to mention the courage and suffering of the people back on Earth fighting to resist these evil monsters, both human and non-human. Even his own parents . . .

He reached across the table and took her hands in his. "Yasmin, I honestly knew nothing about any of this. I can't tell you how sorry I am for the way I spoke to you earlier. I know I should learn to trust people more, but it's not something I've ever found easy. It was unforgivably arrogant of me to sound off the way I did, as if I had the right to judge you.

"My only excuse is ignorance, which is no excuse at all. Not long ago, I gave a piece of advice to someone. 'Always ensure brain is fully engaged before operating mouth'. I'm guilty of not following my own advice. I promise to do better in the future, and yes, I'd very much like us to be friends, if you're willing to forgive me."

She laughed softly, looking into his eyes affectionately. "Ben, of course I can forgive you. Now let me tell you something else you don't know. You don't know how much you mean to a whole bunch of people you've never even met. I never had the privilege of meeting your mother and father, but I know many people who did, and your parents still live on in their hearts.

"Their courage and leadership is still legendary even after all these years, which is why you mean so much to the people carrying on their work. And to me. You also don't know that

I've been keeping an eye on you for quite a few years now, waiting for you to wake up and grow up. I can't tell you how relieved I am that it's finally happening, and that I can now tell people back on Earth how proud Julia and Chet would be of their son."

Ben had spent another morning in the gym with Kay, working on mastering some finer points of his control of his nanosuit. Though he had at first been skeptical, he had quickly become an enthusiastic fan of this novel technology. Now he was sitting cooling off with a bottle of chilled mineral water, replenishing his lost electrolytes.

"How long before I get to use the real nanosuit and run simulations on the New Dawn?" he enquired, looking over at Kay, who was still fighting three virtual opponents and still looking as fresh as a daisy.

Kay halted the simulation and joined him, picking up a water bottle on the way. "Quite soon, I'd say. I'm impressed at how quickly you've adapted to the nanosuit. We could start tomorrow if you like. That should give us over a week to go over our scenarios to neutralize the New Dawn."

"How's the barge coming along?" he asked. "I still can't imagine how you can make all those changes to the structure we discussed, in the time we have left. I don't want to miss my ride."

Kay smiled and gestured towards the simulator console. "Let's take a look. Maybe I'll surprise you."

The simulator conjured up a holographic image of a cargo barge in orbit around Ceres. Ben circled around the apparently solid image. "Hey! That's impressive," he exclaimed in surprise. "I didn't know the simulator could do that. I can see right around the work site from any angle."

"Well, you're right. It couldn't do that until a couple of days ago, when I gave the system another upgrade to cope with the New Dawn simulation, using some more of my magic pixie dust," Kay grinned, making a sprinkling motion with her fingers.

They watched as several giant multi-legged mechanoids danced rapidly around each other, working on a massive rail supported by a lattice of girders protruding from a deep tunnel bored into the after end of the foamed-rock body of the barge.

"Those construction robots are making amazing progress," Ben said, peering at the frantic activity of the robots, their movement so fast it was difficult for the eye to follow. "Looks like the modifications to the barge are almost finished. I didn't believe you could get all that work done in just a few days. How come they're getting the job done so quickly? There can't be more than a dozen robots out there."

"Amazing what a difference a little alien nanotech and AI enhancement makes. I'll soon have my monstrous robot army ready for Galactic conquest," Kay replied with a smirk.

He ignored the barb, instead zooming in on one part of the busy scene. "The biggest difference as far as I can tell is the way they move around each other so rapidly. How did you get the robo-monkeys trained up to that in less than a week? These robots are new models which I've never seen before, so it should have taken them even longer to get up to speed."

"Ah. Curse you! You're about to discover another of my deep, dark secrets. Any more questions and I will order one of my robot slaves to kill you," Kay said, pulling a face at him. "The secret is that they don't use robo-monkeys. They're all directly under Pandora's control. Using an AI to co-ordinate their operations means they're an order of magnitude more efficient than the old system of using robo-monkeys to control each robot.

"Also, the new design of the robots makes them faster, more flexible and much more powerful, with additional built-in intelligence. So we should get another order-of-magnitude boost to their efficiency. Most amazing of all, I did this almost entirely using our current level of engineering technology. All I had to do was sprinkle a little extra nanotech magic into the mix and now we can build stuff a hundred times faster than we could last week."

He folded his arms, his face grim. "I know you'll think I'm stupid for saying this, but I'll say it anyway. Not only is it illegal to allow an AI direct control over a team of robots, but it is illegal for a reason. A very good reason. Using robo-monkeys is not meant to improve efficiency, but to ensure the safety of the human population. To protect them from an AI going rogue by making sure there's a human cutout in the control loop. Allowing an AI this level of connectivity has led to disaster in the past and will do so again in the future—the very near future, I suspect, if you continue down this road."

"Ben, we've had this conversation — or one very like it — before. So I don't want to go over old ground, except to remind you that Pandora is not a stand-alone AI, therefore she's not likely to go berserk and eat all our babies, or whatever it is you fantasize she might be planning," she said, with a snort of exasperation. "Look, I don't disagree with you that AI is dangerous if misused. I assure you, the Progenitors know this better than any human. But let's try to think this through logically, Ben. Your concern is for the survival of the human race, which I promise you is my primary concern too—and Pandora as well. In fact, that is the essential purpose of her mission here."

He finished his water and gestured with the empty bottle in her direction. "So if these Progenitors are so wise and all knowing, why are they in hiding from these ... Destroyers, whatever they are? How can we know anything they tell us is true? You just accept whatever Pandora tells you without question. I haven't seen one bit of proof of any of this."

"I can't give you the hard proof you're demanding, Ben," she said. "No one can. But there's more to life than proof—there's trust too. I'm not asking you to trust me or Pandora without question. I accept trust isn't just granted—it's earned. So all I'm asking is for you to give us the chance to earn your trust. Please?"

"So that's it? I have to take this all on trust?" he demanded, with a shake of his head. "What about the other lesser civilizations which Pandora tells us were wiped out by the Destroyers—did they trust the Progenitors to save them?"

"That's not fair, Ben, and you know it," she said, waving an accusing finger at him. "The Progenitors have never offered to save us. Pandora has already told us that it's up to humanity to save itself. And we can't do that while we're at each other's throats fighting among ourselves. One way or another, the Destroyers will eventually find us. Then all that matters is how well we've prepared for that day. You can't just ignore AI until then.

"Try to look at the problem this way. Imagine if we were to go back a thousand years in human history, to the time when firearms were first invented. Imagine a bunch of people living on a remote island who realized that guns were a powerful new technology but could be dangerous if misused, so they banned their use. How long would it be before a bunch of other people with guns sailed in and forced the islanders to see the error of their ways?

"The point is, you don't have a choice between AI or no AI if you want to survive. The only choice is between the AI that will kill you and the AI that will help you. We need to work with the good sort if we are to have any chance of defeating the bad sort."

Ben rubbed at the back of his neck as he went over the logic of her argument. The whole idea still left him uneasy, but perhaps he did need to rethink his attitude. So many of his certainties had crumbled over the last few days, so why not this too?

"So how do we tell the difference?" he asked, genuinely puzzled.

"All we can do is use our best judgement, Ben. Nobody can give you a cast-iron guarantee. Not me, not Pandora, and certainly not the Progenitors. You want to know who we can trust, but first, we have to trust ourselves to make the right choices. One of humanity's biggest problems right now is that the current population of less than 25 million is too small to support an advanced industrial society, so we are forced to use robots on a large scale to make up for our limited productive capacity.

"We fear our robotic servants—and rightly so—which is why we use robo-monkeys. But a typical robo-monkey can only run a dozen robots at most, and this is the biggest bottleneck to increasing industrial output. An advanced AI can control and co-ordinate the operations of thousands and with far greater efficiency.

"We will be forced to take this next step, Ben, whether we like it or not. Keep in mind we've been presented with the most amazing gift—technology from an advanced race that solved these problems millions of years ago. No other civilization has ever had such an opportunity, and it will almost certainly make the difference between the survival or the destruction of humanity."

Ben realized he had a lot more thinking to do. Deep inside, he was reluctant to let go of his instinctive fear of AI. "That's all most convincing, Kay, until it goes wrong. Then I won't even get the pleasure of telling you 'I told you so'—because we'll all be dead," he said, lobbing his empty bottle into his kit bag.

She smiled and walked back towards the training area. "Well, you'll be dead for sure in less than two weeks, if you don't get back to your training. Or possibly even sooner. Our next session is about how to use the nanosuit to stop bullets."

EARTH & CERES

*"Only two things are infinite,
the universe and human stupidity,
and I'm not sure about the former"*

Albert Einstein

CHAPTER SIXTEEN

Teresa Lee Adler felt sick to her stomach. She reached out to the holo-projection of her husband's face as she replayed his message. *Almost two years now since I last touched you for real*, she thought. *And when will be the next time? Never, if Da Silva gets his way and this attack by the New Dawn is successful. Don't worry, you said. We've got it covered. Trust me. Oh, Frank! How I miss you. Here I am, and there you are. Two of the most powerful people in the world, yet forced to remain apart. I can't leave Earth and you're stuck on Ceres. And for what—our sense of duty? It would be no different if you were in prison. At least then I would have visiting rights and a release date to look forward to.*

She turned off the display, leaving her in darkness, with only the cityscape below providing faint illumination. Fighting back her tears, she spun her chair away from the desk and approached the window. From her darkened office at the top of the Adler Tower, she had a bird's-eye view of the World SkullRun Final taking place in the Central Plaza of the Cascades Citadel.

Such a stupid game, yet now the most popular sporting event on the planet. Probably a couple of million spectators out of a total world population of less than twenty-five million, each down there amongst the players as a virtual ghost, each in their own VR environment.

The game was being staged as part of the week-long celebrations to mark the election of Valerio Da Silva as Chairman of the Global Security Council. Da Silva had described the hosting of the SkullRun Championship final by the Cascades Citadel as a great honor and a peace offering to the home Citadel of the Adler Family.

More like a tom-cat marking its territory as a challenge to its rivals, Teresa thought. 'You're next' was the not-so-hidden message.

It was so easy to see the strategy, now that it was all but too late. The Lee and Adler Families had dominated the political, economic and social life of the Global Federation since its formation over a century ago. The Lee Family had saved the last remnant of humanity from extinction during the 'Plague Years' two centuries ago when Ahn Lee had halted the deadly epidemic in its tracks.

Then progressing from biotechnology to agrigenetics, the Lee Family increased the level of food production by an order of magnitude. They were so successful that one of the major problems now was the population pressure on the citadels.

The Adler Family's big chance came when Rick Adler revolutionized humanity's ability to engineer the infrastructure we now relied upon to fight the warmechs, transport food and expand the citadels by his invention of a whole new field of engineering technology using advanced nanotech materials. Then his son Jim turned out to be a genius at designing AI systems based on quantum computing.

Joined by Jim's brother David, who brought his political, managerial and financial talents to bear, the three of them conceived and implemented the most visionary and ambitious project in human history—to colonize Ceres and mine the asteroids. This provided an unlimited supply of raw materials—everything from metals to food—out of the reach of the warmechs. The Adler Family had since taken the lead in every major engineering project over the last hundred years.

First came the 'SkyHook'—a gigantic space elevator allowing the transport of vast amounts of raw and finished materials to and from Earth's orbit. This was the key to opening up the asteroid belt for commercial exploitation. More recently had been the creation of the massive structure of the Habitat on Ceres. The Adlers and the Lees became the two most powerful Families on Earth—and the richest. Who could possibly challenge them, such unselfish benefactors of mankind?

The Da Silvas, that's who. *I guess we just got fat and happy. And now we're competing for credibility with Da Silva's SkullRun—and losing! While we were seeking progress, they were seeking power.* Such a simple plan, in retrospect. First, get control of the media. Then secretly set up and finance lobby groups such as 'Earth First' to push their interests and undermine the other Families, boosted by their media channels, but without being seen to do so. And finally—and most dangerously—gain control of the security services. Now the DGS was effectively a fiefdom of the Da Silva Family and their allies.

There were even dark suspicions that some warmech attacks had been influenced—perhaps even controlled—by a faction within the DGS.

Teresa shook her head slowly as she pondered how things had turned out. *I would even have been on the winning side if it had not been for Frank. My mother's Family wanted to marry me off to that slimy rat Carlos. Imagine that—I might have had Chairman Da Silva as a father-in-law.* She felt an involuntary shudder down her spine. The Veronese, Lee and Da Silva Families united in one glorious alliance. A marriage made in heaven!

The marriage was taken for granted. After all, how could I have refused the Da Silva son and heir? That was their first mistake. One of their very few mistakes, letting me into their plans even before the wedding took place. Not deliberately of course—I just happened to be around when they were having their happy little Family chats planning world domination. Their second mistake was not spotting I was already seeing Frank Adler. I guess it didn't occur to them I'd turn Carlos down, or even look at anyone else.

Frank and I went to my father a week before the wedding and we gave him the lowdown on Da Silva's sinister plans for the future of humanity in general, and his own tyrannical role in particular. It helped that Frank had been a child prodigy and liked nothing better than to hack any computer system he could get his hands on. I told him where to look and he found more than enough hard documentary evidence to show what they were up to.

Daddy was horrified, of course. He had always been driven by a sense of public service and was so proud of the Lee Family tradition. Mother was horrified, too—that I would even think of pulling out of such an advantageous marriage. As a Veronese, her loyalties were split, of course. The Veronese Family had been allies of the Da Silvas for some time. Her marriage into the Lee Family was, in retrospect, probably intended to weaken the Adler/Lee alliance.

My mother never forgave me for breaking off the marriage— and never forgave my father for supporting me. That was nothing, however, compared to the volcanic explosion from Valerio

Da Silva when he had to cancel the wedding of the decade. He saw my actions as a betrayal, and worse still, an obstacle to his evil plans. My mother never spoke to me again. She wouldn't even attend my wedding to Frank.

Daddy was heartbroken, and never really recovered from the shock and pain of it all. He didn't even live long enough to see Kay, our first child—our only child, as it turned out. Such a strange child, too. Perhaps if we'd had more time for her, she would have turned out differently. But both of us were so focused on building a better future for mankind we somehow never got around to building one for ourselves.

Once our Family became aware of Da Silva's malign agenda, everything changed. At first we thought we would just rally our allies and all would be well. That's when we discovered how deeply the Da Silva poison had penetrated the whole fabric of our society, and how far they'd already undermined the relations between our Families and the others. I guess some of the larger Families felt overshadowed and resented our leading position. As for the smaller Families, if the Da Silva's couldn't bribe them, they would intimidate them. They started making good on their threats, with strange accidents, mysterious disappearances and fabricated prosecutions.

That was when Frank came up with the visionary idea of a massive expansion of the Ceres Habitat. Not just as an alternative home for humanity, but as insurance, making it clear to the Da Silvas we would always have an untouchable power base. Thirty years on, and we've succeeded beyond our wildest dreams. We've regained the upper hand, with the citadels almost entirely dependent on Ceres for their food and raw materials. Now they can't afford to move against us—or so we figured.

First, there was the crazy idea to grab Frank and Jim on Ceres, then to threaten a full-scale attack using the New Dawn. What can these people be thinking? The current level of population on Earth isn't sustainable without our help and willing cooperation, whereas Ceres is almost completely self-sufficient. A blockade would bring the citadels to the brink of starvation in a matter of weeks.

Maybe I'll get a better idea of what is going through Da Silva's mind at the Security Council meeting in Greeley the day after tomorrow. On Da Silva's home ground, now he's the new Chairman of the Council. Right after the previous Chairman died suddenly of some mysterious illness. What could possibly go wrong?

An urgent message from Max Garrard, her Chief of Staff, flashed up on her U-Set display.

"Teresa, Marco Veronese is on the main U-Global News right now. You need to watch it. He's about to make some big announcement. I'll be up with Meryl right away."

She swung around and used her U-Set to enable the large wall-mounted display across the office. She shuddered at the familiar voice of her cousin, dripping with sincerity as he replied to the interviewer, a *Breaking News* caption flashing below.

"—Yes, Della, this is not only an outrage, but the act of a criminal gang. These people consider themselves above the law. But now we now have sworn testimony from numerous confidential sources that the Adlers have been working to undermine the authority of the Global Security Council for many years now. My special investigation team at the AICB has uncovered a long list of their illegal activities. Activi-

ties that imperil the safety, not just of the people on Ceres, but of all humanity."

"These are grave charges, Marco. I'm horrified to discover that members of a leading Family —"

"No Family member is above the law, Della. The DGS took Frank Adler into custody only a few days ago on charges of illegal AI enhancement. Then, not content with carrying out such dangerous research, he instigated a rebellion against the legitimate authority of the DGS on Ceres. An innocent man would be prepared to face such accusations. By escaping from custody, he admits his guilt."

"I'm so terribly shocked to hear that, Marco. But how will you bring these criminals to justice? Ceres is far away from Earth. How can we stop them defying the Security Council and continuing their dangerous activities?"

"The situation is even worse than we thought, Della. We have received reports that the Ceres Habitat has now collapsed into a state of anarchy. Even food supplies are being withheld from the population to force their cooperation with the Adler regime. We have received many pleas from concerned citizens begging for our help to restore the situation. Fortunately, I am now able to make an announcement that I'm sure all right thinking people will welcome.

"Acting in my capacity as Director-General of the AICB, and with the full support of the Department of Global Security, the research vessel New Dawn is being diverted from its voyage of exploration in the asteroid belt. It has been dispatched on a peacekeeping mission to Ceres with orders to bring relief supplies to the beleaguered population. This will also allow us to restore the authority of the DGS and bring any criminal elements to justice. Fortunately, the New Dawn happens to be close by and in a position to take action in the near future."

"Marco, that is marvelous news. I'm sure our viewers will be both delighted and relieved to hear that the people suffering such oppression on Ceres will soon be liberated from—"

"Off! Turn it off!" Teresa shouted at the U-Global News channel.

"Teresa? Did you see it?" Max said, putting his head around the door.

"What?" She shook her head in disbelief, still stunned by this new development. "Oh, yes, I saw it. The bastard. That's tantamount to a declaration of war. All this talk of our illegal activities, without a shred of evidence, and then they announce the New Dawn attack on Ceres on prime-time news. Only the Security Council had the power to legitimize such an operation, and there's no way they can force through an emergency resolution to support a peacekeeping mission within the next two days. So the only thing that's clearly illegal is the New Dawn attack. How do they expect to get away with this?"

Max edged into the office, still holding onto the door. "We had a meeting scheduled for tomorrow morning to prepare for the Security Council session. Should we bring it forward?"

"Yes, of course. I'm sorry, Max. Come in. Take a seat. Is Meryl with you?" Teresa brought up the lights as she walked over to her desk.

"Right here, Ma'am," said Meryl as she entered the room and took a seat beside Max.

Teresa brushed her hair from her forehead and smiled wanly at the pair sitting opposite. Max's size and sheer physical presence gave the impression he might easily moonlight as a night-club bouncer in the seedier levels of the citadel. Certainly not how you'd expect the Chief of Staff to one of the leading Families to look. Nor would many people pick out Meryl as Teresa's Security Chief and enforcer. Her pale skin, elegant blonde haircut and elfin features were a dramatic contrast to Max's ebony complexion and shaved head.

Their deceptive appearances, plus their lack of a Family background, led many people to underestimate their capabilities, an erroneous perception they had both exploited many times over and that numerous Family adversaries had discovered to their cost. In fact, Teresa knew they were each as sharp as a pair of cut-throat razors. And now she needed their deadly intelligence more than ever.

Teresa gave a long sigh. "I never imagined they'd dare go this far. I was still clinging on to the idea that their New Dawn stunt was some behind-the-scenes maneuver designed to put us under pressure at the Council on Wednesday. Now they've actually dared to go public. There's no way they can dress this up as anything other than an outright attack on our Family. Da Silva cannot defend the legitimacy of this action in Council, so what's he up to?

"He must know something we don't, or he would never have made such an overtly aggressive move against us. Surely the other Families – or at least some of them – will realize that if Da Silva can attack us head-on without the slightest pretense of legality, and get away with it, there's nothing left to protect them. Can we work that line, Max? Or do I simply boycott the meeting in protest?"

"I think you should go, Ma'am, if only to find out what Da Silva is up to," Max replied. "Yes, I know, he's always up to something. We've already discussed the rumors of a move to bring forward an impeachment resolution against you. Somehow that's gone quiet, and it seems he's given up pressurizing other councilors to support such a motion. That makes me even more suspicious, now he's Council Chairman.

"The Council meeting venue is determined by the Chairman, and of course Da Silva has picked his Family Citadel in Greeley. It's almost as if he thinks he has a killer punch to deliver once you're on his home ground, which would swing the vote his way.

"Then again, he must give one week's notice of an impeachment resolution, which hasn't happened yet, so there's no way he can force such a vote through on Wednesday. So my gut tells me he's got some other surprise up his sleeve. But while you're still on the Council, and present in order to vote, you have a veto which can't be overridden unless it's a motion to impeach. So unless he pulls another one of his extra-legal stunts, I confess I don't see how he can damage us in the short term.

"And with you in the Council Chamber, we'll have a week to rally support, even if he tables an impeachment resolution on Wednesday. In that case, the line to take is just as you said—spell out to the other Families that if Da Silva can take you down, then no one's safe. There's no way the New Dawn attack on Ceres can be presented as a legal operation, so we should push him to explain how he can justify his support for it without a Council resolution."

"My thoughts exactly, Max. I refuse to let Da Silva intimidate me, or worse still, allow the other Families to think that I fear him. We can hardly ask for their support if I'm not even prepared to attend the meeting. Send me the updated files on the other Council Members before we leave. We can discuss tactics on the SkyShip down to Greeley tomorrow."

She gave Max a nod, then turned her attention to her Chief of Security. "You don't seem very happy, Meryl. Do you have more bad news for me?"

"Nothing but bad news on my side, I'm afraid, Ma'am," Meryl replied with a shrug. She leaned forward in her chair. "Even where I don't have bad news, I get bad feelings. I'm sure Da Silva is setting you up. For what, I don't know. But everything tells me he thinks he's already won. He must know that the attack on Frank and Jim Adler will not go without repercussion. He claims he has irrefutable proof to justify this outrage, yet he's produced nothing concrete.

"The New Dawn is being described as a purely scientific expedition to explore the resources of the asteroid belt. When we protest against this 'scientific expedition' nonsense, the Da Silvas and their allies accuse us of wanting to exclude the other Families from vast mineral wealth that we wish to keep for ourselves. The move against Ceres is justified as a peaceful relief operation. The New Dawn has only been diverted to deal with a humanitarian emergency. This is all smoke and mirrors, of course. What I still can't figure out is—what's behind the smokescreen?"

Teresa shook her head. "Well, it's obvious we're missing something. But we do know DaSilva never does anything without a plan. So what's his next move?"

"I can only agree with Max," Meryl responded with a grim expression. "Da Silva must be sure he has a sucker punch coming at us, because he can't keep this pretense up for much longer. They'll have to deploy their forces from the New Dawn within the next couple of days, at which point it's 'shit or get off the potty' time. If they attack, we can protest a direct military act of aggression against our Family installations by the Da Silva faction with absolutely no legal justification.

"I really don't see how they can contemplate such an action unless they no longer care and they're planning to start a civil war. If they can take control of Ceres and its resources with this attack, maybe they think that will put them in a strong enough position to override any opposition. None of this makes any sense, of course."

Teresa frowned and leaned her elbows on the desk, her hands clasped beneath her chin. "How do you rate their chances of success on Ceres?"

Meryl shrugged. "In practical terms, little to none. At best, they might capture and occupy the Habitat if they're fully geared up for such an attack, and absolutely nothing goes wrong with their plan, but the damage would be horrendous if they came up against any effective defense. All they'd capture would be a pile of rubble. That would then result in disastrous shortages back here on Earth, especially the food supply. I can't see how they could possibly sell such an outcome to the other Families."

"Do you think they'd go that far?"

"I'm sorry, but I really can't figure out what they're thinking. All their actions in recent weeks make it seem as if they no longer care about Council votes or even the opinion of the other Families. It's as if they have an 'ace in the hole' they're just waiting to play. The game has changed, and I'm damned if I can figure out how. Even when I speak to people who are supposed to be on our side, I get the impression I'm somehow being given the runaround."

"Really?" exclaimed Teresa, her eyes narrowing in concern. "What do you mean by that?"

"I've been talking to people on Ceres about their chances of resisting the New Dawn attack. They're doing all the obvious things, but if the New Dawn forces get down to the Habitat, it can only result in a desperate fight. So what doesn't make sense is just how confident they claim to be. They should be a lot more worried than they seem. It's as if they know something we don't, and they're not prepared to tell me. Either that or they're all a bunch of idiots just whistling in the dark."

"Who have you been speaking to?"

"I started with the boss, Mr. Adler. He put me on to Ben Hamilton and made it very clear he had complete confidence in him and that he spoke with the full authority of the Ceres Administrative Authority on matters relating to the defense of the Habitat. I'm quoting the Boss virtually word for word. You might recall Ben Hamilton from that big story about the warmech attack on New Geneva a few weeks ago—Hero of the Battle of New Geneva? Awarded the Global Star for outstanding bravery in action?"

"Right . . . I think so," Teresa replied. "Didn't pay much attention the time."

"I expected him to be the big action hero type, full of himself, out to save the Habitat single-handed. Not at all. Quite the reverse, in fact. We even went over a few defensive strategies. He was able to blow apart anything I suggested, which didn't offend me at all, since he was able to show me in detail why my ideas were unlikely to work. He'd evidently already thought through any scenario I could come up with, and he knows precisely why they don't stand a chance against a concerted attack if carried out effectively.

"Yet he appears to be totally confident that the New Dawn will not prove a threat, but he wouldn't give me even a hint about what they were planning. *'He expects to have good news for us within the next couple of days.'* That's a direct quote. It's almost as if they have a secret weapon they don't want to talk about."

Teresa frowned and leaned back in her chair. She thought through the implications of Meryl's words. "I was in contact with Frank less than an hour ago. You're right, they do seem to be very confident. He was much more worried about my trip to Greeley. Do you want me to talk with Frank again, to get you more information?"

"No, because I don't think that would help them. This Hamilton guy seems more than competent and I got the feeling he has a good reason for not telling us whatever it is they're hiding. And I'm sure they're hiding something. Anyway, I don't need to know, since it's not likely I can make any difference to their success. However, my gut tells me they will be pulling some big surprise on the New Dawn. I wouldn't want to be in the shoes of this 'peacekeeping force.'"

"That's relatively good news, at least," Teresa replied. "What else do you have for me? Is anyone else giving you the run-around?"

"Yes, and it's less specific, but something I find more concerning. I spoke to Rudy Leeming, your Security Chief at the Adler Tower in Greeley. When I called to discuss the security arrangements for your visit, I got the distinct impression he was holding out on me. I couldn't quite put my finger on it. He was perfectly cooperative, yet strangely uninvolved—that's the best way I can put it. I've dealt with him many times before, and this just seemed out of character. Normally, I wouldn't get so paranoid, but considering the time and the place . . ."

"I'm not sure we have many options at this late stage," Teresa said, tapping her nails on the desk. "I can hardly replace him based on a gut instinct, even if we had the time, which we don't. See what you can find out before we arrive tomorrow."

Meryl got up from her chair and leaned across the desk towards Teresa. "There is one thing. Let me go with you. I'll take a couple of people from my team. That way, I can check out the situation on the ground. Talk to Leeming face to face."

Teresa pursed her lips, running through the options. "If the Da Silvas are planning something, I'll want to get straight back here, and I will need you looking after our defenses. I've known Rudy for quite a few years now and never had a problem with him. I'm sure he's loyal—the Family has always been good to him. Maybe he's distracted by some personal problems. I'll have a word with him when I arrive." Teresa left her chair and walked to the window. The game in the plaza had finished, the lights now dimmed. She turned back to Meryl. "No, you're more use to me here. I can't imagine Da Silva will try to grab me in the middle of a Council meeting. That would be a step too far even for him."

CHAPTER SEVENTEEN

Ben had split his time between reviewing the recordings from his simulated EVA sessions on the New Dawn and checking the real-time images of the rapidly approaching spacecraft. He'd even taken time out to grab a few hours of sleep. Now he was watching a screen showing the barge making its final approach. He was interested to see what reaction he got from the New Dawn once they noticed several hundred thousand tonnes of foamed rock heading straight at them in a celestial game of chicken. Four dazzling blue-white suns arranged in a tight diamond formation now filled the screen as the exhaust from the plasma engines burned straight towards him.

The main body of the New Dawn was hidden behind the bulging curves of the engine bays. Ben zoomed out the image to get a wide-angle view, far enough to show four squat nuclear reactors at the end of massive booms trailing back at a thirty-degree angle and holding the reactors two hundred meters away from the main hull. The booms were easily visible, reflecting the brilliant glow from the plasma exhaust. The reactors were more difficult to make out, their square bulk broken up by several massive metal plates attached edge-on around the outer containment structure to act as cooling panels, all painted a dull and uniform shade of black.

Less than an hour to go until we hit, he thought. *If it were me, I'd be thinking about making a course change right about now, just to see what reaction we get. Maybe they haven't seen us? Then I guess I'll be famous all over again for causing the biggest head-on crash in history. Lucky I'm right at the rear end of the barge, tucked up in a survival capsule embedded deep in the surrounding foamcrete. Except with my luck, I'd probably get one of those reactors swinging in on top of me on the end of its boom.*

The glare from one of the four main engine plasma exhausts faded and died, interrupting his gloomy train of thought. *So the bad guys have made their opening move. Pity they don't know the game is rigged. Now it's your move, Kay. All I have to do is watch. My game doesn't start until I get onboard the New Dawn.*

The moves had to appear credible to the bad guys, so it wouldn't be too obvious that they'd been allowed to win. Kay had been sure she could nail the New Dawn if she wanted too, but as she'd said, what fun would that be? No, shooting him out into space like a pea from a popgun as they faked a convincing near miss was so much more enjoyable. Except for him, of course. He supported Kay's desire to neutralize the threat from the New Dawn with minimal—ideally zero—casualties, but if anything went wrong, he'd be a casualty.

He heard a distant grinding noise as a nearby mirror swung into place to intercept the laser beam which would flash the ice in one of the barge's reaction chambers to steam. The massive barge would now shift ponderously as if to counter the New Dawn's move, but too slow and too late to put it back on an intercepting course.

"Are we good to go?" he enquired.

"Ready anytime you are, Ben," Kay replied. The delay in transmission was only just noticeable.

At least now he could get moving. He unclipped his seat harness and moved towards the airlock at the rear of the small compartment. He passed though the inner door, closing it behind him. *This is where it gets interesting*, he thought. The interior of the airlock seemed to liquify, covering him completely in nanotech goop, which congealed around him to form the dark carapace of a nanosuit. A clear screen formed around his head, giving him a panoramic view of his surroundings, with a HUD projecting an array of sensor readings and menu options.

He gave the command to expel the air from the airlock and opened the outer door. He drifted forwards into a short corridor which led to another compartment, much larger than his survival capsule. A metal rail with deep grooves on either side ran through the center of the space, disappearing into a dark tunnel ahead of him.

Sitting on top of the rail was a solid cylindrical mass of nanotech looking like a cross between a large black torpedo and a car at a fairground ride. *We could call it the Tunnel of Death*, he mused gloomily. As he swung himself into position sitting astride the dark shape, his carapace merged with the surrounding nanotech material, sealing him in.

He carried out his final checks. All good to go. He'd done this a dozen times in the simulator, so what could go wrong? Better not even go there, he decided. "In position. All systems are green. How's the situation out there?"

Kay's voice came back to him as clearly as if she were sitting next to him. "We're looking good. If they continue to be as predictable as this, you will have a nice relaxing day's work ahead of you. They're heading right past you now. You'll be lined up perfectly in a couple minutes. Get ready for blast off."

"Remind me again why, with several million years of technology to call upon, the best you can come up with is to shoot me out of a steam-powered cannon?"

"Well, I'd rather describe it as a steam catapult. But even after all those millions of years, the Progenitors don't seem to have improved much on the KISS principle. You must remember that from your engineering days."

"Yeah, yeah. Keep It Simple, Stupid. How appropriate, since I must be stupid for agreeing to do this in the first place," he replied.

"No need to get all steamed up about it," she said with a chuckle. "Also, if the bad guys spot your launch, they'll think it's just steam out-gassing from one of the Barge's thrusters. Talking of which, you'll be launching in fifteen seconds from now. Bon voyage."

A shock of sudden acceleration hit him in the back. He shot off down the tunnel at breakneck speed, harsh vibrations pulsing up through his seat. Within a couple of seconds, everything changed again, as he found himself hanging in space, seemingly motionless, with the vast bulk of the New Dawn dead ahead of him. Yet not quite motionless, he realized. He was slowly catching up and with the New Dawn.

He knew the spacecraft well, of course, but he'd never had such a good view of her before. Now that the bulky stern of the ship was well past him, he could see along her entire length. Nearly a kilometer long, she was beautiful in a strange knobbly, spindly sort of way. The basic structure was a massive central spine running the entire length of the ship, with a great bulge at the stern for the engines, a disk-shaped structure in the middle about one hundred meters thick and two hundred meters in diameter, plus a smaller mushroom-shaped end cap at the bow. The middle structure was the engineering section, with the Command Deck and crews' quarters in the front section.

Several long cylindrical tanks were placed around the central axis of the ship occupying the space aft between the engines and the engineering section. Clutches of much smaller auxiliary storage cylinders were clustered in gaps between the main cylinders. More of these large cylinders were arranged around the central spine forward of the engineering section. Except one cylinder was missing. In its place there was a row of ten giant landers, each sitting in its own docking cradle. He knew from the simulator that on the opposite side of the ship, he'd find another ten landers.

He was now rapidly approaching the ship. *Time to get my fairground ride into gear*, he thought. The spot he'd aimed at in the simulator runs was behind one of the cylinders next to the lander docks. That way, he could use the cylinder for cover, yet would be close to the landers, which were his primary targets. There was just one last thing he needed to check before he made his final run.

It was likely that some cylinders had been adapted for passenger accommodation from their normal cargo use, but right now Ben had no way of knowing which were which. They had a thousand troops to transport and the crew's quarters wouldn't take a tenth of that number. He didn't want to bang about on top of several hundred bad guys trying to get a final good night's sleep before deploying to their landers, so he had to figure out which cylinders were occupied—then pick one that wasn't.

He pulled up an infra-red view of the ship. Lots of hot spots, especially around the engines and reactors, but one of the cylinders was noticeably warmer than any of its neighbors. That must be their life support systems running on toasty, he guessed. He picked a cool cylinder near the lander docks, then marked a spot on its leading edge and let his guidance system do the rest. Small jets of steam puffed from nozzles which formed on the outer surface of his ride as it aligned with his destination.

'It's really much more advanced than the steam-powered catapult on the barge,' Kay had explained to him. 'The nanites generate super-heated steam instantaneously by exerting massive compressive forces on the big block of ice you're sitting on. They direct it through nozzles they form, according to the direction they want to travel in. It's actually quite efficient.'

"I'm heading in," he said, as he drifted towards the massive superstructure of the ship towering above him.

Ben spent a busy few hours in his hidden nest tucked behind the struts supporting the massive cargo cylinder overhead. As soon as he got settled into his hidey-hole, his ride started to shed amorphous blobs of black material, which rapidly formed into nanobots, growing legs and scuttling off on their assigned tasks, changing color and texture to blend in with their surroundings as they went. His HUD allowed him to keep track of their progress as they sought out the sturdy clamping mechanisms for each lander sitting in its docking cradle, giving each one a tiny squirt of nanite goop.

Making good progress so far, he thought. *Soon be time to move on to the second bank of landers.* He sent off another couple of nanobots—one to penetrate the ship's communications system by tapping into the cable leading to one of the nearby dish antennas, the other to drill through the skin of the cylinder he'd identified as housing the troops. This second nanobot wormed a thread of nanite material inside the cylinder which then formed into a tiny version of itself. He now had a video and audio feed from the mini-nanobot as it flew around the interior of the troops' accommodation, perfectly camouflaged wherever it settled. *These critters are so useful,* Ben thought. *No wonder Pandora found it so easy to infiltrate the Habitat systems. I'm just glad she's on our side. May as well face it. If she's part of an alien plot to suck out our brains, then I guess we're screwed anyway.*

"Kay. Did that evasive maneuver make any difference to the New Dawn's launch window for the landers? I'm not seeing much signs of activity up here. Maybe they're just planning to jump for it as they fly by."

"Only by a few minutes. No need to worry. You're running well ahead of schedule. There's still over ten hours before they need to start thinking about launching. When are you planning to deal with the second bank of launchers?"

"Pretty soon. I only hung around this long to watch your magic nanobots and their little mini-nanobot babies in action. I can hardly believe it's working so well. It's exactly like being in the simulator."

"You should call them demons and imps like I do. Magic mini-nanobot baby is a bit of a mouthful."

"Yes, Ma'am," he replied in a mock-respectful tone. "Demons and imps it is. So what am I supposed to call the big black flying monster I'm sitting on right now?"

"I would have thought that was obvious, Ben. What flies around destroying anything that gets in its way? Shoots out jets of super-heated vapor? It's covered in armored scales, and its supernatural powers can be wielded at the command of its rider, who's wearing a suit of magic armor. Can't you guess?"

"No, sorry. I give up. I haven't read all the old books you have."

"You have the honor and privilege, Ben, of being the first human ever to ride a dragon into battle. Isn't that wonderful?"

"Aren't dragons supposed to have wings?"

"If you wanted to fly around in an environment with an atmosphere and gravity, such as Earth, you could easily grow a set of wings. In fact, you'd need to. I don't advise it, though, unless you want to scare people half to death. Right now, I suggest you grow some legs and get walking to that bank of landers on the opposite side of the ship."

With the benefit of experience and growing confidence in his demonic minions, Ben finished dealing with the second bank of landers much more quickly than the first. The perfectly camouflaged demons were now all sitting in position, waiting for their next assignment. Yet another group of demons had spontaneously set off to spread themselves in a dark film over the illuminated side of one of the cylinders. Checking his display, Ben realized they were absorbing solar energy with amazing efficiency.

We all have to eat, he reflected. *I think I could do with a snack too.* The menu was somewhat limited, he discovered, although the catering arrangements were rather ingenious. The nanosuit reconfigured itself to free his arms and place a little shelf in front of him, fitting neatly into an expanded space inside the suit. A tiny 'vending machine' producing food bars was an integral part of the shelf. The water came through a flexible spigot rising up from the little 'breakfast bar'.

He spent some of his spare time inserting additional imps into the troop accommodation, as well as the passageways connecting the accommodation to the lander docks. He also sent off a couple of demons to insert a bunch of imps into the engineering section and command deck. Now the time was dragging, so he was relieved when he heard signs of activity from inside the New Dawn. Commands echoed through the two accommodation cylinders housing the troops as they prepared for embarkation in the landers.

One small question had been niggling at the back of Ben's mind. Where could the DGS have got a thousand troops trained for deployment in a low-gravity environment? The answer came swiftly. He watched in growing amusement as the individual members of each platoon got tangled up with each other and themselves, struggling to collect their kit and make their way toward their assembly points.

He couldn't help grinning as the level of confusion grew, bodies and equipment floating and bouncing along the access corridors as the troops struggled to get through the airlocks leading to the landers. *I'm betting they just stuffed them in the cylinders and told them to work things out on the way here*, he thought. *At this rate, they won't get the landers loaded up in time and we can all go home.*

Finally, after a lot of time and a lot more shouting, the platoons boarded the shuttles in some semblance of order. At least they didn't have to load the heavy weapons or spare ammunition, or they would never have been ready this side of Ceres. The heavy stuff was pre-packed in the cargo pods attached to the landers. Ben had thought about sending demons off to mess up their supplies inside the pods, but he realized that would make no difference as long as Kay's plan worked.

Now platoons were closing the lander airlocks and calling out 'Ready' across their tactical network, which Ben had penetrated with ease a while back. *This is where it will start to get interesting.* He smiled to himself as the two platoons in the last of the twenty landers called in 'Ready'.

A new voice came on the network. Ben traced it to the command deck. "Teams will launch together on my mark in thirty seconds," came the order. Ben pulled the image of the speaker up on his screen. *So that's the Big Guy. Well, he's in for a big surprise in less than a minute.* Ben couldn't help grinning as he issued his own command to his demons concealed outside the lander airlocks.

The countdown ended and the same voice came back on the network. "Landers will now undock and exit their cradles, then assemble in formation ready for deceleration maneuver on my mark."

A few seconds of silence ensued, then a confusion of questions, commands and cursing swamped the network.

A command cut through the babble of voices. "Silence on this channel. I only want to hear from the flight engineers. Has any lander been able to undock?"

Twenty forlorn responses of 'Negative' followed.

"Flight leader. Do you know what the problem is? My status panel on the command deck is showing no faults."

The reply came after a few moments delay. "No faults showing on my panel either, Commander. The reason we are not moving is that the docking clamps have not released. It seem to be a mechanical problem. I would like permission to exit the lander to make a visual inspection of the clamp mechanisms."

The voice from the Command Deck sounded pissed. "Very well. Be as quick as you can. We only have a limited time to the launch window."

A couple of minutes later, the flight leader's voice reported back. "I'm sorry, sir. Now we seem to have another problem. The airlock door won't open. I'm unable to exit the lander. I suggest—"

"What the hell do you mean, 'won't open'? You only went through that door less than ten minutes ago," the Commander snapped.

"The whole airlock mechanism appears to be locked solid, sir. I've no idea why that is. We can't force the door without causing damage, which would put the lander out of action. I suggest that you send a team down from engineering to investigate."

"What the hell! I can't believe this," the Commander screamed. Ben could see him on his screen, his face turning red and his arms flailing about in frustration.

"Stand by . . . there's an engineering team on its way down to investigate," the Commander continued tersely, after taking a few moments to bring his anger under control. "They'll be with you in fifteen minutes. In the meantime, I want reports from the flight engineers on the other landers. I want to know if any other landers have the same problem. Any flight engineers who can exit their landers should do so and investigate the problem with the clamps. Also provide assistance to other landers with airlock problems where possible. Report back as soon as you have any information on the nature of the problem."

So Kay was right. He had single-handedly defeated a thousand-strong task force, all of whom were safely locked up in their tin cans until he decided to let them out. As she had said, simple in theory . . . but as it turned out, not actually so complicated in practice. Now all he had to do was mess around with the engineering team and keep them distracted long enough for the launch window to pass. Then he could move on to the surrendering part.

Ben couldn't remember when he'd last had so much fun—and it was much more relaxing than nuking warmechs. Six robots from the engineering team had arrived at the airlock door to the docking bays and found it locked tight. The human members of the team were still back in the engineering section, controlling their charges by remote link. They instructed their robots to diagnose the problem and get the door open. And nothing happened. The robots simply sat down and wouldn't move.

The Chief Engineer reported the problem to his Commander, who started shouting and cursing furiously. The Commander finally ordered a second robot team to be sent down to fix the first robot team. When Ben had been training on the New Dawn, he'd always been a little skeptical of the way the engineering function was organized. Basically, humans never touched the ship's systems and machinery themselves.

This was understandable up to a point. The reactors and the main engines, for example, were very dangerous places and required maintenance robots specially designed for operation in such hazardous environments. Specialist operators directed the work from a safe distance while the robots got their manipulators dirty. But this same hands-off approach was applied throughout the ship. Even, as in this case, to fix an airlock door.

The second group of robots arrived twenty minutes later and sat down opposite the first group which resulted in even more shouting and screaming over the comms network. It took several minutes before the Commander was able to persuade his reluctant Chief Engineer to send down some real people from the engineering crew to deal with the immobilized robots. Another half an hour passed before two engineers entered the large cargo staging area in front of the airlock doors that led to the shuttle bays. They clambered over the two rows of stalled robots, inserting diagnostic probes, checking their instruments and scratching their heads. This took quite a while as the robots were sizable pieces of multi-jointed eight-legged machinery.

The best bit was when the engineers performed a manual hardware reset on the second group of robots, who were then commanded to diagnose and fix the first group. The first group stood up and bowed to the second group as they approached in line. Ben had once seen an old historical video of a ballroom scene set hundreds of years ago, and it had always stuck in his mind. He could even remember the name of the old dance. So, each black-and-yellow-striped robot, each with a tiny imp concealed within, took the manipulator of its partner in the opposite line and started to perform a stately waltz around the floor of the cargo staging area.

"Ben, I thought you said you never watch old videos. Where did you get that idea from? It's brilliant!" Kay screamed with delight over the comms channel.

"I never said never, Kay. I just haven't seen as many as you have."

She giggled. "We're already outside their launch window, so we should contact their Commander soon, but another five minutes won't do any harm. Can I have the next dance, please? It's called the Can-Can."

"There's nothing we can do, I'm telling you," the Chief Engineer whined. "It's got to be some sort of virus. Every time a new robot goes near one of the infected ones, we lose control. Nothing works. If we bring down more robots, we'll just end up losing control of every one of them."

Ben could see that the Commander was screaming in fury by now, his face blotchy and red, flecks of his spittle spattering the view screen. "So get in there and fix them yourself, damn it!"

"I'm sorry sir, but you've seen the video feed. The robots are jerking around randomly all over the staging area. Look—now they're swinging round all in a line with their arms linked, kicking their legs high in the air. That's far too dangerous. We are in a low-gravity environment and my people aren't trained for this situation. If we try to go near anywhere them, we'll get people injured for no good reason. They don't respond to diagnostics, or even the emergency shutdown signal. I honestly don't know what else I can do . . ."

Ben had to put his hand over his mouth to stop laughing out loud. Time to get serious. Regaining control over his breathing, he interrupted the Commander and Chief Engineer on their private command channel. "Hello. You seem to be having a few problems. Is there anything I can do to help?"

The Commander snapped back, "Who the hell is this? This is a secure channel and I don't see any ID displayed."

"Oh, I'm terribly sorry. My name is Ben Hamilton," Ben replied. He tried his best to imitate the dulcet tones of the ever-helpful

Family-class cabin steward on the Ceres22 who had pandered to his every whim on the trip out from Earth. "It is my pleasure to welcome you to Ceres. I currently have your task force locked up in their landers and your engineers being chased around the floor of the cargo staging area by their own robots. If there's anything else I can do to make your visit enjoyable—anything at all—please don't hesitate to ask."

Ben watched as the Commander first looked startled, then made rapid hand movements as he interrogated his U-Set. "Who? Ben Hamilton? . . . Ben Hamilton, the hotshot warmech killer? Aren't you supposed to be with AICB now? What the hell are you talking about? And where are you exactly?"

Ben was impressed. The Commander had pulled up his details from the ship's AI within a few seconds. It must be loaded with all the DGS data. How interesting. He wished he could have taken over the AI too, but he would have needed to get inside the ship to do that—an unnecessary complication at this stage.

Ben reverted to his normal voice. "What's more important is where you are, which is almost alongside Ceres. If you check the command deck view screen, you'll see Ceres up close, which is as near as you'll ever get, now that you've missed the launch window for your landers."

"OK, so maybe we're too late to make a landing on this pass," the Commander responded, after checking the numbers on his U-Set. "But eight days from now, with our current deceleration profile, we'll be back at Ceres, and I'll have those landers released even if I have to saw through the locking clamps myself. So all this crap is just delaying things."

"You're assuming that nothing else is likely to go wrong in that time," replied Ben. "You might want to check my file again. I trained as an Engineering Officer on the New Dawn before joining DGS. So I'm sure I can imagine all sorts of additional problems. How about a fuel leak from the main tank? That way you'll never get back to Ceres, or anywhere else for that matter. Without another vessel to refuel you, you'll be spending the rest of eternity in orbit halfway to Jupiter."

"OK. So what do you want?"

Ben was surprised at how calmly the Commander was dealing with the situation. No shouting, no threats? Maybe he'd already realized just how completely he was screwed. "First, you tell me your name so we can have a civilized conversation. Then you surrender the ship until you leave Ceres space. We will refuel you, and you can all return to Earth. We'll pretend this incident never happened."

"Nice try, Hamilton, but not a chance in hell. My name is Vazquez and welcome to Plan B," the Commander shot back, his lips curling into a sneer.

"Which is what—"

Without the heightened awareness of his nanotech sensors, Ben wouldn't even have noticed the faint shudder which ran through the fabric of the ship.

He cut the connection with Vazquez and switched back to Kay's channel. "Kay? Did you catch that? What happened?" he asked in alarm.

She responded immediately. "One of the storage cylinders just shot off a very large missile of some sort. It's heading right for the surface. Oh, that's odd. There were two payloads, and it looks as if the smaller payload will go into orbit."

He knew this had all been going too well. But what could a missile achieve if Vazquez couldn't get his troops down to Ceres?

"Hell. What's the missile targeting—the Spaceport?"

"No. As far as I can tell, it will land in the middle of nowhere, a couple of hundred kilometers from the port," Kay replied, sounding puzzled.

"How long until impact?"

"Less than a minute from now."

"Can it do any damage to the Habitat?"

"I don't see how. It will impact a very long way from the Habitat, and that's buried under thirty kilometers of ice. Not even a nuke can touch us down there."

"OK. Keep me updated. I'll get back to Vazquez and see what I can find out."

He switched the channel back. "So this Plan B. How does that work?"

The Commander was grinning now, evidently finding the situation amusing. "As you suggested, Hamilton, I had another look at your background, so you should really appreciate this. Oh, and there's touchdown."

Kay came back on the other channel. "All it did was plow into the ice. No detonation. No nothing. I'll send some bots to check it out, but that will take a while. It's a long way off. See if you can find out anything else about this Plan B. I'm guessing it was a pre-arranged code word to get the AI to trigger the launch, so they must have had this set up all along, as some sort of backup plan."

Ben switched the channel back. "So what was in the missile, Vazquez? A bunch of leaflets demanding our surrender, maybe? I didn't see any big bang. You must know the Habitat is too deep for any missile to target, not even with a nuke. So what's the big deal?"

"Oh, yeah that's right, my bad," the Commander sniggered. "But what if the nuke is attached to a really big Badger, and it starts digging? That way, it can get all the way down to your cozy little Habitat before we set it off. You of all people should appreciate that. Didn't you even win a medal for the Battle of New Geneva? So I guess you'd know all about how useful Badgers with nuke warheads can be. Especially really, really big ones. Now since we can't surrender to you if you're all dead, how about we discuss you surrendering to us?"

CHAPTER EIGHTEEN

"You're crazy! If you destroy the Habitat, we can't resupply you, so you'll be dead too," shouted Ben, his mind whirling at this unexpected development.

"Maybe. Maybe not," Vazquez shrugged. "Maybe we have supplies pre-positioned at the Spaceport. Who knows? But you'll all be dead by then, so you'll never find out. Or do you want to take a chance with the lives of everyone on Ceres?"

Ben still couldn't see any way this made sense. It had to be a bluff. "Even if you find some way to survive, if you destroy the Habitat, you'll doom the people of Earth to starvation. You must know that Lee AgriGenetics supplies nearly all of their food. That will all stop without the seed stock from Ceres."

Vazquez sat back in his chair, arms behind his head and a wide grin across his face. "Heh. Terrific," he chortled. "So you get to save the lives of all the people on Ceres, and all the people on Earth too. Maybe they'll give you another medal. You can be the big hero all over again. Anyhow, before you come up with some clever stunt like putting a hole in our fuel tanks and letting us drift off to Jupiter, you need to know another thing about Plan B. The Badger is on a watchdog timer. If it doesn't get a reset signal from the ship every hour, it will start digging. I'm guessing it would lose the signal long before we got even halfway out to Jupiter, so you need us to stay close.

"And I don't want to see anyone trying to get near the Badger on the surface. The Badger itself is already deep underground, with only a communications relay box left on the surface, on the end of a tether. The comms link is one of the latest quantum encrypted devices, so don't think you can mess with it. Any interruption or interference with the connection and off it goes.

"And apart from proximity sensors on both the Badger and the relay box, if I see anything I don't like I'll give the Go signal right away. So all you have to do is to keep me sweet for the next few days until we get the ship back to your cruddy little snowball, and we all stay alive. Call me back when you want to talk about surrendering. I'll give you twenty-four hours. I'm sure you've got people you need to talk to."

Ben was astonished at the level of planning. All this effort, and for what? To threaten the very existence of Ceres, and almost certainly the Earth's population too? What were the Da Silvas thinking? And even if it was a bluff, could they risk calling it?

"Are you getting all this Kay?" he said. "Any thoughts?"

"I'm having difficulty in seeing how this makes any sense," she replied. "What can Da Silva possibly hope to gain by destroying the Habitat? This attack didn't make much sense to begin with. Now it's even crazier. I need to figure out what's going on here."

"I'm as mystified as you are, Kay, but shouldn't we deal with this threat before we worry too much about motivation? First, we need to figure out how to stop this Badger," he said, not understanding how she could seem so unconcerned.

"Oh, that," she replied, in a tone far too relaxed for his liking. "Just keep Vazquez busy for the next couple of hours, then we'll see if we can provoke him into sending the Go signal to the Badger. I want to know if he's bluffing or not."

Ben was getting seriously upset. Yet again, he had no idea what was going on. The bad guys had a gun to the head of every single person in the Habitat, and Kay didn't sound as if she had a care in the world. "What? How the hell can we take that risk? If the Badger starts digging, we have no way to intercept it under the ice—and it doesn't even have to get all the way to the Habitat. If it sets off a decent-sized nuke anywhere nearby, the compression wave transmitted through the ice will destabilize the rotation of the Habitat. It will simply fly apart. Or are you telling me you can hack a quantum encrypted connection? I thought that was physically impossible."

Kay sounded almost smug. "The Progenitors can do it. Perhaps I could do it too, if I had another thousand years to build up your science, technology and industrial base to a point where it might become feasible. As it happens, I don't need to. How often have I told you that artificial intelligence will always win out over natural stupidity?"

Ben had to hope that Kay and Pandora knew what they were doing. He was no longer just trusting the AI to be a good AI, but also trusting it to be 100% correct about this.

"OK, OK," he said. "What's the cunning plan this time? And please excuse me if I sound a little nervous. My natural stupidity is exceeded only by my natural aversion to being responsible for causing the death of the entire human race."

It took a while for Ben to agree to go along with Kay's plan. It wasn't so much a lack of trust, but he wasn't prepared to take sole responsibility for such a momentous and potentially catastrophic decision. He finally came around after talking it over with Frank. He was the head of the CAA and was also Ben's boss, so he had the authority and the experience to take the final decision. A deeper issue was how far Ben was prepared to trust Kay in her new guise as a human/AI hybrid. How much of her was still human, and how much of her was the AI talking?

Again, the best person to talk this through with was Frank. After all, Kay was his daughter, and who knew her better? Frank seemed to have total confidence in Kay and reassured him that his daughter was still as human as she ever was, even though her personality had evolved so dramatically in such a short time. The one thing Ben still found disquieting was the tinge of arrogance in some of Kay's pronouncements. Yet wasn't that more proof of how human she still was? *If I was suddenly granted such superhuman powers*, Ben mused, *wouldn't I become just a little arrogant too?*

He had reached the central spine of the ship. He hadn't even needed an airlock. His dragon had oozed straight though the outer hull of the central spine at a point where Ben's detailed knowledge of the ship's layout had determined there were no critical systems to disrupt. Retaining his nanosuit, he detached from the dragon, pushed forward into the corridor and grabbed onto the ladder on the far side. The main bulk of the dragon spread along the opposite bulkhead, changing shape and color as it mimicked a stretch of corridor with pipework, cables, maintenance panels and junction boxes.

He sent off a couple of demons to act as a scouting force to avoid running into any surprises as he made his way towards the command deck. The demons would also spoof any security systems which might otherwise give away his presence. He wasn't expecting to meet any crew in this part of the ship. The engineering crew stayed in their own section, sending off a robot or two if any work needed doing. And he'd simply hijack any robots he came across.

The rest of the crew remained in their own comfortable quarters below the command deck, rotating to provide the luxury of a 1G environment. The flight crew wouldn't normally number more than fifteen, and Ben doubted they would have many tourists along on this trip. *Time's up*, he thought. *Now we get to see if Kay's plan worked, or if we all end up dead.*

"Kay? How are we doing? Is the Badger neutralized yet?" he queried, trying not to contemplate the consequences of failure.

Kay's cheery response came back immediately. "Of course. How could you ever doubt me? That comms link was a really dumb design. It only took me seconds to hack into it. Although I have to confess, I did consider telling you 'Whoops! Sorry, the Badger's off and running,' but I didn't want you to have a heart attack at this point. We need you in perfect health for the next stage of the plan."

Ben let out a breath that he hadn't even realized he'd been holding in. "Well, thank God for that. And let's save the jokes for later, please. My problem is not so much a lack of trust, more fear of the downside of a situation like this. We have to be 100% correct first time, or everyone dies—no second chances."

"Which will be how it looks to Vazquez too, I'm guessing," she replied breezily. "So why don't you go and see if you can provoke him to carry out his threat? I'm sure he'll get ever so angry if he thinks you're trying to sneak up on him to disable his Big Red Evil Boss Go button, or whatever it is he's got up there. And remember, I'm relying on you to fail. I'm dying to see his face when he sets the Badger off and nothing happens. Or maybe he's only bluffing and we can all be friends."

Having made sure that every part of the forward section was now under his surveillance, Ben waited until Vazquez left the command deck to return to his quarters. He also helped Pandora hack the ship's AI remotely, using a cluster of demons to set up a control center and relay station nearby, before finally infiltrating it with an imp. It had given up without so much as a whimper.

Kay didn't want him to give away any hint of their advanced nanotech capability, so he had to shed his bulky nanosuit before confronting Vazquez. If it came to a fight, he was under orders to throw the fight, anyway. He was at least allowed to keep his basic nanosuit. This version had a few enhancements borrowed from the heavier version, Kay had assured him. It certainly felt a little more substantial than the basic version.

Making a last check to be sure the crew were still where they'd been five minutes ago, Ben swung himself through the hatch leading from the central spine to the crew's living quarters. He floated along the curve of the deck as it descended, his weight increasing as he got closer to the outer hull, the rapid spin of the accommodation section now generating the pull of full gravity. There was still no one moving about as he walked down the corridor, but he made sure the doors on either side stayed firmly locked.

He let himself into the Captain's suite. No sign of Vazquez in the small but comfortable office—he must be getting some beauty sleep after a long and tiring day planning genocide. Time for his early morning wake up call. Ben made himself comfortable on the well-upholstered sofa, called up the ship's AI—now transformed into one of Pandora's sub-minds—and requested a track from the sound archive to be played at maximum volume.

The effect was electrifying, not to mention gratifying. Within seconds, Vazquez came lurching out from the bedroom in his underpants and T-shirt, looking panic-struck. *A big guy*, Ben thought. *Must work out a lot. Why all those tattoos, though?*

Vazquez's eyes darted wildly about the room before fixing on Ben sitting comfortably on the sofa. "Whaa . . . What the hell!? Who—? Hamilton. What the hell are you—"

Vazquez dashed across the room to a large desk and yanked open a drawer. Reaching inside, he pulled out an improbably large handgun and pointed it at Ben, giving him a close-up view of four chunky rings, one on each finger.

"Rasputin. Switch that racket off now!" Vazquez screamed over the deafening racket. "Do you hear me?"

Ben smiled up at him. "Sorry. Your AI called in sick. I've given it the day off. Don't you recognize the sound, Vazquez?"

"Of course I do! But there are no warmechs out here, so switch it the fuck off!" he shouted, waving the gun for emphasis.

"No problem. You only had to ask nicely." Ben gave the command and the harsh wailing sound of sirens warning of a warmech attack gradually faded away. "Is that better? Now we can have a nice little chat. I'm sure we have lots to talk about. You do want to talk to me, don't you, Vazquez?"

Vazquez stared at him, then his eyes darted around the room again, as if he was fearful that some unexpected horror might jump out at him from a dark corner. "We have nothing to talk about, Hamilton, unless you're here to surrender. How the hell did you get in here, anyway?"

Ben shrugged and arched an eyebrow. "The same way I got aboard the ship in the first place. Magic."

"Yeah, right." Vazquez sneered, still waving the gun at Ben. "Well, I got some magic too. A magic box on the command deck. If I or the officer of the watch don't put in the correct code every hour, the Badger starts digging. I don't know what the hell you think you're doing, but it won't work. If you destroy the box, it goes off. Even if you're in the AI, it won't help you. It doesn't know the code. That's in my head, and the heads of two other officers. The same code is never repeated, it's a random sequence, so—"

Ben shook his head, looking up at him coldly. "I'm not here to play with your fancy little box, Vazquez. We've thought about your offer and decided we'd rather not surrender, so I'm here to take you prisoner instead."

"You're making no sense, Hamilton. But I don't care. I got a better idea. The Section has a kill notice out on you, and now I get to collect the bounty."

Vazquez pulled the trigger at point blank range. A deafening blast echoed through the room, and Ben slumped back on the sofa.

Vazquez left the room without a backwards glance at Ben, muttering, "Stupid bastard. What the hell was he thinking?"

Ben's chest was a little painful, but he was otherwise surprisingly intact after being shot at close range with a large-caliber handgun. Kay had told him that even his previous basic nanosuit would stop most low-velocity bullets. This heavier version would stop bigger bullets at shorter range, though the main advantage was its greatly enhanced ability to absorb shock impact—otherwise, he would probably have ended up with some broken ribs.

Ben watched Vazquez on the office wall screen as he reported to Earth from the command deck. It wasn't a real-time dialogue, of course, so Vazquez would have to wait at least forty minutes for the response.

"Kay. I got into a fight and I lost as instructed. Vazquez is reporting back to base. What now?" Ben asked, using his U-Set to link to the relay station.

"I'm listening to Vazquez too. He sounds desperate after his little chat with you. Now we've refused to surrender, he's asking for more instructions. He's also saying he won't trigger the Badger. He made all the same arguments you did, in fact. So it looks as if we've called their bluff after all." She giggled. "Oh, look, now he's claiming credit for killing you."

Ben rubbed his chest again. The impact would probably leave a bruise, despite the upgraded nanosuit. "So how about I go up to the command deck now and ruin his day? If he's not triggering the Badger, he's pretty much out of options. Do you want me to close him down now?"

"Let's wait until he gets a reply. I still don't know what's going on. I get this itchy feeling I'm missing something. And I really hate not knowing stuff."

"OK, you're the boss. Or at least the boss's daughter," Ben grimaced. He wandered into the small kitchen to see if he could find something more appetizing than crunchy bars.

The message from Earth came over an hour later. It made no sense. It was nothing more than a clip from a U-Global bulletin showing an interview with Chairman Da Silva. But as Vazquez watched it, a glassy expression came over his face. He turned and walked over to the comms station, slid a panel to one side and keyed something in to a small device.

Kay squealed furiously in Ben's ear. "That little shit. He just gave the Go code to the Badger!"

Ben shot to his feet, his heart racing. "We're absolutely sure that's disabled now, aren't we, Kay?"

"Of course it's disabled, Ben, I'm not a complete idiot," she responded tersely. "But how did that happen? All he did was sit and watch the screen for less than thirty seconds without saying a thing . . . Ah, OK. Got it. There's an encrypted message in the video. It's just a short repeating segment, only ten seconds long. Too high a frequency for the human eye to register, though, so how did he pick it up?"

"I suggest we worry about the analysis later and deal with Vazquez before he does any more damage," Ben said, pacing the floor.

"Yes, go and bring him in. There's only two other guys in there right now and they're both screaming at him. Seems that nuking the Ceres Habitat wasn't a popular move."

"Who the hell are you? How did you get in here?"

The officer of the watch started across the floor of the command deck to intercept Ben as he approached Vazquez. Ben pointed a finger at the officer, who immediately collapsed unconscious to the floor. The tiny dart on its hair-fine tether reeled itself back into the cuff of Ben's nanosuit. He gave a stern glance at the young guy at the comms station, who sat with his mouth open, looking as if he didn't want to get involved.

"So you did it," Ben snarled at Vazquez, who was staring into the middle distance with a glassy-eyed expression. "You actually pulled the trigger. Even if I could forgive you for shooting me, no one will ever forgive you for attempted genocide."

Vazquez looked up at him, showing no surprise at seeing Ben alive. His blank expression changing to one of faint puzzlement. "Attempted?" He articulated the word carefully as if it were unfamiliar. "No. The Badger travels through ice at fifty kilometers per hour so it will reach your Habitat in less than four hours. My mission has succeeded."

Ben felt taken aback for a moment as he realized that Vazquez's glassy stare was directed not at him, but through him. His voice, too, had changed. When they had been speaking earlier, Vazquez's voice had been angry, shouting. But now his voice was a calm monotone, devoid of expression.

"It's not a good day for you at all, Vasquez," Ben responded with contempt. "You shot me at point-blank range and I'm still around. So you'll get no credit for the Section's kill order on me. We also hacked into your big Badger and disabled it. So no brownie points for genocide, either."

"Hacked? Disabled? Not possible," Vazquez said softly, shaking his head. "A quantum link cannot be broken or intercepted."

"That's absolutely true," Ben responded grimly. "Unfortunately for you, Ceres rotates every nine hours, so your Badger would have been out of line-of-sight from the New Dawn for about four hours. A quantum encrypted link only works point-to-point, so that's why you needed to put a satellite into orbit to relay a hold-off signal. Or as you did just now, you maniac, the Go signal. So you need a second unbreakable quantum link from the satellite down to the Badger.

"But you need to decode the message carried by the first encrypted link from the New Dawn before passing on to the second. The decoding happens in the relay satellite, so all we had to do was hack the satellite. That allowed us to pass on perfectly encrypted spoof messages down to your Badger. If you doubt any of this, don't worry—you'll have plenty of opportunity to see the intact Habitat when you go on trial there for attempted genocide. And it will still be there long after your execution."

"So I have failed," Vazquez mumbled, slumping back in his seat.

Ben snorted with contempt. "That's all you have to say? Really? No Plan C?"

Kay's voice sounded in his ear. "Ben. There's something seriously weird about Vazquez's behavior. It doesn't even sound like his voice. I want you to be careful around him until we have him safely locked up. If he makes a move towards you, take him out. That coded message did something to him. Now we have a bigger mystery than we started with."

"Fine by me. How long do I have to babysit him?"

"About another twelve hours. I launched an up-rated shuttle with a security team onboard several hours ago. It has additional fuel tanks to give it extra range, as you'll be quite a way out when it catches up with you. You can refuel it from the New Dawn's tanks when it gets there, so we should have you back here in a couple of days, tops."

"Oh, and I was so looking forward to an extended cruise. I've never been to Jupiter, you know," Ben said, feigning disappointment.

"Sorry to cut your vacation plans short, but I want you back here as soon as possible. We have a lot to talk about."

CHAPTER NINETEEN

"Well, that was a total waste of time!" Teresa exclaimed as she stormed into her office at the top of the Adler Tower. She marched over to the window and stared out at the panoramic view of the citadel laid out below, her fists clenched at her sides. Even in Greeley, the Da Silvas' home Citadel, the Adler Tower was the tallest building. Only the Adlers had the advanced engineering technology to build this high, and they had no inclination to share their knowledge with the Da Silvas.

The meeting had exceeded her worst fears. Her protests about the impending attack on Ceres had been dismissed without debate. Chairman Da Silva had used his position to steamroller his agenda through the Council meeting. Every one of Teresa's interventions and objections were ignored, as if her Family was now of no account.

That wasn't the worst of it, though. Families who had been allies for decades refused to vote with her, or even speak up in her support. In most cases, they wouldn't even meet her gaze. Apart from the Lee Family, only one other Family was willing to vote with her—the Tanakas, who had more reason than most to be grateful to the Adler and Lee Families. It was only the massive commitment by Lee AgriGenetics to establishing and maintaining the food supply in the northern Japanese island of Hokkaido that supported the viability of the Tanaka's remote Tokachi Citadel. Hideo Tanaka had sat alongside her in the Council Chamber, his expression that of a condemned man.

After the meeting, when Teresa thanked him for his support, his only reply was to state mournfully, "In honor, my Family's place is at your side." Yes, the Adler and the Lee Families had done a great deal for the Tanakas, but there were other Families who should have felt the same obligation. Not today. With Da Silva now commanding a two-thirds majority on the Council, Teresa had lost every vote.

"That was a complete disaster, Max," Teresa said. "We knew it would be bad, but I was expecting to get support from at least a few of the other Families. Only the Tanakas voted with us. How did this happen?"

Max slumped in his seat and shook his head in bafflement. "Somehow, we . . . *I* was suckered. I was working the usual backchannels with our allies for days before the meeting. I was aware they were under pressure, but this is something completely different. Just like you, I could hardly get people to talk to me in the Council Chamber. I saw fear in their eyes, almost as if they each had a gun to their head. Even the Tanaka people looked like they were under sentence of death.

"Da Silva seems to have played his trump card, and I still don't know what it is. The other thing I noticed was that most of my regular contacts were not present. Most of the support staff for the Family Delegations are new people. I tried asking about some of the people I know, and all I got were hard stares. I can't get hold of them on the U-Net either. They've just dropped out of contact, many of them just since yesterday."

"Don't blame yourself, Max," Teresa said, offering an encouraging smile. "I can't imagine how we could have possibly anticipated this situation. Even with the attack on Ceres, we had a couple of weeks' notice. Here, we just walked into a sucker punch. Now there's less than a week to go before the impeachment vote comes up, and in the meantime I'm expected to make myself available to Da Silva's new 'Committee of Public Safety' stuffed with his cronies. They're going for broke with this investigation of the Adler Family for illegal enhancement of our AI systems, a charge of piracy for carrying out an unprovoked attack on New Dawn's so-called 'humanitarian mission', as well as accusations of armed insurrection for an attack on the DGS HQ in Ceres. Well, I don't plan on taking part in such a circus. The situation calls for a strategic retreat."

She turned away from the window and began pacing up and down. "Frank was right—I should never have come here. We're not likely to find out what Da Silva's secret weapon is by sitting around in Greeley, since no one will talk to me. I also want to avoid starting a fight until we find out what we're up against. It probably means a blockade, but I still believe we're better prepared for that than Da Silva's mob. Get our SkyShip on standby. We'll leave this evening."

Max held up his hand, a worried expression on his face. "I've just lost my U-Net connection. Do you have a link, Teresa?"

"What?" Teresa glanced at her U-Set HUD to see the icon showing U-Net connection was grayed-out. "No. Nothing. Damn! This can't be a coincidence. What's Da Silva trying to pull now? I thought our communications from the Tower were completely autonomous. They shouldn't be able to block us like this. Milton. What's going on? What happened to our U-Net? Milton? What the hell? Now I can't even get the house AI to respond. Hold on, I've still got a local connection. I'll get Rudy to sort this out."

She turned to face the window again. "Rudy. I've lost my U-Net connection. Can you get it back for me? No, I don't need to see you right now. I've got a bunch of calls I need to make before we leave tonight, so I'm short on time. Just get the connection back and we'll talk later. Hello? Hello?"

"Damn it! Now I've lost that connection too. Rudy's on his way up. Let's find out what he has to say."

"Rudy. What the hell is going on? I'm locked out of everything. My U-Net connection is down and I can't get into the local network or even get a response from the house AI."

"What's going on, Ma'am? Nothing you're going to like very much," Leeming responded with a smirk, contempt dripping from every word. "We're making a few changes to the way things work around here. Like I'm in charge and you're not giving me orders no more. You'll be staying here until Chairman Da Silva wants to see you again. Yeah, that's right—I got a new boss. Better pay and lots of extra benefits."

"You bastard!" Max shouted at Leeming. He grabbed him by the lapels of his jacket. "Meryl was right—you've sold us out."

Leeming broke his grip with contemptuous ease before backhanding Max across the face with an audible crack. Max flew backwards and hit the ground with a thump.

"Max!" Teresa cried. She ran over to kneel by his unconscious body lying on the floor, blood streaming from his nose. Teresa glared up at Leeming. "You bastard! Have you gone crazy? How do you think you'll ever get away with this? My husband will kill you when he hears about what you've done. You'll be hunted down wherever you hide. Do you seriously imagine the Da Silvas will be able to protect you?"

"Oh, don't you worry about me. I already got an insurance policy. It's your precious husband you should worry about. The Chairman's arranged a little surprise party for him. Don't know the details, but we're expecting to hear the good news from Ceres real soon now. Then you'll be all on your own with just me for company."

"What the hell are you talking about? I heard from Frank only this morning. Da Silva's attack on Ceres was a complete failure. We didn't even have a single casualty. Look, you can still make things right—"

"Hah! Sorry to disappoint you, but my new boss still has a few more tricks up his sleeve for that shit husband of yours. Such a pity. You never even had the chance to say goodbye." Leeming paused, looking down at her, an evil smirk lighting up his face. "You still have no idea of what you're up against, do you, you stupid bitch? Don't worry, you'll be finding out real soon. Meantime, all I have to do is keep you here and in good condition. And once the Da Silvas are finished with you, then it's my turn. I get you as a bonus."

CHAPTER TWENTY

BEN WALKED into Frank's Penthouse office to be welcomed with a broad smile. Frank strode over to greet him and put an arm around his shoulders. "Ben! It's good to have you back. What you did on the New Dawn was miraculous—taking it over without a single casualty! And I can't tell you how many times I've watched the video of your dancing robots routine. I almost died laughing. You really got those engineers freaked out."

"That's very good of you to say so, sir," Ben said, returning the smile, and nodding to Kay and Jim Adler who were deep in conversation, sitting together on a sofa in a corner of the office.

"I wish I could have shared the material with Teresa, but we haven't been able to get through to her since last night, which makes me nervous," Frank said with a frown. "Our technical people tell me there's no problem they can find and security at our building in Greeley tells us everything is fine, so it can't be anything serious. I've asked Kay to check it out after this meeting."

Jim got up and walked over to the drinks cabinet. "Now Ben's back, we can all get up to speed with the recent developments. We should also celebrate our defeat of the DGS task force, thanks to Ben. Can I get anyone a drink?" he said, waving a bottle. "What about you Ben? You've certainly earned it."

"Not for me, Professor, thank you," Ben said, nodding at Jim before turning back to Frank. "I did have a lot of help from your daughter, sir. And I was the only person in the entire operation who got shot," he said ruefully.

Frank chuckled. "From what Kay tells me, you were never in any serious danger, though it took a lot of faith on your part to trust your nanosuit armor to protect you. Vazquez must have jumped out of his skin when you came back from the dead."

Ben frowned as he recalled the encounter. "Well, no, and that was really strange. He didn't even seem surprised. I saw no reaction even when I was standing right in front of him. He looked right through me. His only concern was getting the Badger to destroy the Habitat. When he found out he'd failed, he just sat back with that blank expression on his face. I'm sure something happened to him after he received that message from Earth." He turned to Kay. "Did you find out any more about that coded message in the video?"

"Yes, but it's rather mystifying," she replied. "The frequency and the format would only be machine readable. Vazquez must have some sort of implant. Now we have him locked away in our safe house, I want to take a good look at him as soon as we're finished here. It's a little puzzle to put alongside the bigger puzzle of why he was given the order to destroy the Habitat. He was certainly opposed to the idea when he was talking to DGS back on Earth. Then all of a sudden, he gives the Go signal, presumably instigated by whoever sent that message from

Earth. Why do they think destroying Ceres and therefore their supply of irreplaceable seed stock is now a viable option?"

Frank rubbed the back of his neck and frowned at Kay. "I can't make sense of this either. I gave Teresa a full briefing before the Council meeting yesterday, so she had plenty of material to show to the Council Members. She made clear the full extent of the unprovoked attack on us and the Da Silvas' involvement. There was no attempt to justify this outrage. They weren't even prepared to listen. So the sooner we can get Teresa out of that nest of vipers the better.

"I'll also be talking to Yasmin Aziz and see if she has any ideas. We should bring her and her boss Chas Lee into the inner circle as soon as possible. Lee AgriGentics' information on the utilization of their seed stock ought to be right up to date. Yasmin will also have a better idea of what is happening on the ground than any of us from her resistance contacts. If anyone has the knowledge and insight to figure this one out, it's her."

"Yasmin Aziz has contacts in the resistance?" Jim queried. "That's something I didn't know. I've only bumped into her a couple of times, but I thought she was just a very attractive plant geneticist."

Frank nodded to Jim. "I hope you can understand why I've tried to keep you out of that particular loop until now, Dad. Her role with the resistance is known to very few people, and I'd like to keep it that way. There's a lot more that Yasmin does than just keeping track of seed stock.

"Right now, we have more immediate concerns. We thwarted an attempt to destroy us, but there's not much we can do if they start a blockade. I still think a blockade would hurt them more than us, but they can slowly strangle us by cutting off the one thing we can't do without, and that's the flow of people from Earth.

"Once they've kicked your mother off the Global Security Council with their impeachment resolution, they can do what they like. Without Teresa's blocking veto, they'll have a free run. Their first move will be to outlaw the Adler-Lee Families, seize our Earth-side assets and start a blockade. I can't understand, though, why Families who have been our allies for generations are now willing to go along with this. They must realize that once we fall, they'll be picked off one by one. As Kay has said several times, there's something going on back on Earth that we don't know about."

Kay frowned at her father. "Yes, I admit I'm still mystified. The good news is that they don't know what's happening here either. We have a big secret of our own, which Ben kept safe despite using his magical powers on the New Dawn. In the short term, we need to find out what the Da Silvas' game plan is, and why the rules appear to have changed so suddenly. In the longer term, we will have to rescue Earth's population from the control of the Da Silva Family.

"That means at some point we have to return to Earth and force the issue. But we can't do it head on. We don't have the numbers, and an open conflict would endanger the inhabitants of the citadels. Once the Da Silvas realize they're losing, they are likely to treat the general population—the little people, as they call them—as hostages."

"Well, let me know when we can start," Ben said. "Besides saving humanity from the evil clutches of the Da Silvas, I have a special reason to get back to Earth as soon as possible. I want to find my sister. So the sooner the better."

"It may not be as soon as you like, Ben," she replied with a shake of her head. "We need more information, and we must build up the resistance back on Earth so they can take the lead in liberating their own people—"

"But that could take years!" Ben exclaimed, slapping a hand down on the table in his frustration. "Now we've removed the immediate threat to Ceres, all we need is a bunch of your fancy magic machines to take with us to Earth so we can kick the Da Silvas around, lock them up and throw away the key. I don't understand why we can't use this wonderful Progenitor technology to give us the edge we need and avoid pussyfooting around. If your alien friends are so keen to help us, why not do so right now? From what I've seen of the capabilities of your nanotech, we could just roll over Da Silva's goons in a month or two without breaking a sweat."

Kay leaned towards him, pushing her hands together and putting them up to her lips. She fixed him with a penetrating stare. "Is that what you want, Ben? Some benevolent race of advanced beings to come down from the stars and solve all your problems? Did you really think it would be that easy? That's not what's on offer. You haven't actually been given any 'wonderful Progenitor technology'. All we have is Pandora and a basic knowledge of some advanced technology which you might be able to adapt in order to give humanity a chance of survival.

"Look—think of it this way. Imagine you could travel back fifty thousand years on Earth, into the early Stone Age, with your knowledge of present-day technology in your head and an encyclopedia under your arm—how long do you think it would take to build a spaceship? Or just a steam engine? You wouldn't even have the industrial base to produce the metals you'd need. The only way you'd make any progress at all would to convince a sufficient number of people to work together to replicate even the most simple technology. The Progenitor technology is millions of years in advance of ours, Ben, far beyond our ability to even comprehend it, let alone reproduce it.

"But even if you were gifted with such advanced technology to destroy your enemies, who would you trust to wield this godly power once you'd won your battle? Humanity has many examples of cultures being overawed and civilized by people with vastly superior technology. And always in the interest of saving their primitive souls, naturally. Maybe you should read a few of the old history books and find out what happened to these conquered—oh, I'm sorry, I mean *liberated*—people. As I've said before, Ben, humanity must save itself or it won't be worth saving."

Ben scowled and sat back with his arms folded. "Is that you talking, Kay, or is it our alien friend Pandora? I'm still never sure which one I'm speaking to."

"There are no aliens here, Ben." A note of irritation crept into Kay's voice. "For someone who spent so long studying AI, you show surprisingly little curiosity about how the Progenitors' symbiotic AI actually works. Pandora is not alien. She's as human as you and I in terms of her personality, experiences and loyalties. The Progenitors only sent through what I can best translate as a seed AI.

"The way it works is that the prospective host and a seed AI develop together, grow together and live together to become as compatible as possible. Pandora spent her formative months learning to be human. There was nothing specifically alien implanted in the original AI seed, and there is nothing alien in Pandora now she is a mature symbiotic AI."

Jim broke into the conversation, obviously intent on diverting the AI debate onto safer ground. "Ben may not be curious about how a symbiotic AI works, Kay, but I can tell you that your old Gramps certainly is. I still can't figure out how Pandora found it so easy to get around all the safeguards we have built into the Habitat's Security I can imagine how the enhancement of the Physics Lab AI might have worked, but how was she able to get into the Security AI? Surely she'd need a physical connection? Which is why we take such elaborate precautions to avoid the possibility. I set up the system myself, and I used to give lectures on AI security, so it's really quite embarrassing."

Kay smiled at her Grandfather, looking relieved at the change of topic. "I'd be happy to give you the fine details later, Gramps, but the short version is this: through the security camera in the Lab. Pandora used the 3D printer in the Engineering Lab to make simple nanobots, then got them to modify the camera. And do you remember the laser scanner? She used that to paint data into the camera frame by frame. That allowed her to upload hacked images to the image processing subsystem of the Security AI. Once she had control of that, she could hack into the AI itself. It was much more difficult than that in practice, so you shouldn't feel too bad about it."

"What I feel bad about is not believing you much earlier, when you told me what was going on," Jim replied, finishing his drink and giving her hand an affectionate squeeze. "I'm so sorry, sweetheart. From now on, you've got my full attention. I'll believe anything you say. Especially about AI."

"Pandora was a lot cleverer than any of us realized, Gramps, so there's no reason to feel bad. I'm just very glad she's on our side," she said, returning his smile.

Ben opened his mouth intending to bring the discussion back onto its original track, but Frank cut in before he could speak.

"I'm also very glad she's on our side," Frank said, looking directly at Ben. "I'm now quite convinced about her good intentions, especially after hearing what she has to say about her low-key strategy to take back the Earth from the Da Silva Family and their cronies. Yes, I know you still have reservations, Ben, but think about this. If she was secretly cooking up an evil alien plot to conquer humanity, then she could do a lot more damage to us by inciting open conflict. And if we win with a big display of alien technology, how would that serve to unite humanity? No, we need to work out a strategy which will bring people together, not put us at each other's throats."

Ben spread his hands in exasperation and frowned back at Frank. "So are you saying we make no use of the technology Pandora can offer us?"

"Not at all," Frank countered. "But we need to remember that technology alone cannot win this fight for us. If I know the new Kay at all well, and we've had a lot more time to talk over the last few days—"

Kay's face lit up at his words. "You mean you've *made* a lot more time, Dad."

"Yes, and I deserve that comment. You may be sure I learn from my mistakes. However, I was going to say that knowing Kay, I'm sure she will have plenty of good ideas about—"

Kay jumped out of her seat as her expression shifted from happiness to concern. "Hold on, Dad. We may have a problem. I've lost touch with our safe house. I can't raise any of the security people there. They're online but not responding. We have two full teams over there and they can't all be asleep."

Ben paused for a moment, his eyes flicking up to his U-Set display. He looked back at Kay in puzzlement. "I'm viewing the video feed from the security cameras now. I don't see any problem."

Kay sprinted towards the door. "They've been spoofed. All the video feeds are on a loop. That should not be possible. I need to get over there right away."

Ben jumped up from his seat. "I'll come with you—"

"No. Stay here and look after Dad. I want this building on lockdown right now. There's something happening at the safe house that gives me a really bad feeling."

It was dark as Kay left the building at a run. She threw a demon into the air, which formed itself into a winged smudge of something only half-seen before flying away rapidly in the direction of the safe house. As she ran, she reviewed the archived video from street cameras outside the safe house and found a figure arriving at the front door 20 minutes ago. Enhancing the image didn't help a lot. The face was not visible, nor was there a clear shot of the door itself—but no visitor was expected, so whoever it was should have been turned away. Instead, after a few seconds delay, the figure disappeared inside the building.

She looked back though video from cameras in the surrounding area and soon picked up the same figure walking towards the building. It was simple to trace the route back to the DGS building. Now Kay also had a good image of the woman's face. Not one that was flagged as DGS personnel, she realized, but one of the few local staff who worked there. But they'd all been told to go home. What was this woman doing back at the DGS building? Kay checked the home address and put a call through.

"Hello. I'd like to speak to Melissa Zaoui. Is she available?"

"Yes, I'm Melissa. Who is this?"

Kay grabbed an image of the woman's face from the wall-mounted VREx set in the living room and dropped the connection. It was obvious to her that the two faces were not absolutely identical, but close enough to fool the facial recognition software in the image processing subsystem of the Ceres security AI. *Dammit! I should have just upgraded everything, not just the AI.*

She picked up her pace, no longer caring if someone spotted her rushing at superhuman speed through the darkened streets. There weren't many people around in the office zone at this hour, and she'd be at the safe house in less than two minutes.

Her demon had already wormed its way into the building and had spawned a cloud of imps which scurried off in every direction. A scene of bloody mayhem was revealed. The two guards on the door were lying on the floor in a large pool of blood, their fractured limbs angled unnaturally. Kay sent an imp flying down the stairs, towards the basement where Vazquez was held in a storage area converted into reinforced cells to hold him.

The imp darted past one crumpled body halfway down the stairs, and another that appeared to have been thrown into the stairwell to lie broken and bleeding at the bottom. The basement guard room was a scene of bloody carnage, shattered bodies lying everywhere. Beyond it, she could see that the massive door to the cell block had been smashed open and Vazquez was nowhere to be seen.

Another imp had made its way up to the top floor, skimming over a horrific trail of slaughter and devastation. *This is my fault,* Kay thought. *I let this happen. So proud of my new powers, I was just too arrogant, believing everything was completely under my control. I must never make that mistake again. Never.*

As the imp neared Oscar's room, it relayed sounds of agonized howling which faded into a desperate gurgling noise, before the howling started again. Kay was now running through the front door of the building, leaping over the broken bodies in the hallway before sprinting up the stairs towards Oscar's apartment.

The door had been smashed off its hinges. A grisly scene greeted Kay as she entered the room. Oscar was lying unconscious on the floor, covered in blood. A gaunt, blood-spattered figure with Melissa's face was bending over him, a ghoulish expression on her blotchy gray face, red gore dripping from her hands and forearms. She looked up with a puzzled expression. There were two black orbs where her eyes should have been.

"Oh, it's you," she hissed. "Adler's little brat. This is a surprise. I wondered what happened to you. I just assumed Oscar had disposed of the body like he usually did with his playmates once he'd finished with them. Wake up and say hello, Oscar. You have a visitor. It's that little Adler girl you're so fond of."

Kay looked around in shock. Blood was spattered all over the wrecked furniture in the room, as if Oscar had been thrown around even as he bled from the many deep wounds in his body. His hands and feet looked as if they had been fed through a meat grinder—only shreds of flesh and bone remained. His face was a bloody mess and, most horrifying of all, both his eyes had been gouged from their sockets, leaving behind nothing but two jagged pits weeping red gore down his cheeks.

Kay stared in horror into the black eyes of the frightful apparition before her. "You know my name. Who the hell are you?"

The fake Melissa cocked her head and gave Kay an evil grin. "Who am I, little girl? I'm the last person you'll ever see before you die. But don't worry, I'll keep you alive for a while yet. First,

I need information. Oscar here has been most helpful on quite a few subjects, but it seems he really doesn't know what happened inside that interrogation room. How very mysterious.

"I'm sure you'll understand how disappointing that is considering how patient I have been. And I asked him so nicely. That must have been an interesting chat with him and you and your daddy. Oh, and let's not forget Ben Hamilton, the great hero himself. So, is there anything you'd like to tell me up front and save me some time and you a lot of pain? Or do we have to do this the messy way?"

"Look, I'd love to stop and chat, you disgusting little monster, but right now I need to find Mr. Vazquez," Kay replied, trying to keep the horror out of her voice. "Any idea where he might be? Hmm?"

The woman's eyes narrowed. This was obviously not the reaction she had expected. She gave a crooked smile. "On his way over to see your daddy, little one. He should be getting there right about now. So I guess we'll be doing this the hard way—"

Before she could finish her sentence, a great mass of nanotech goop dropped from the ceiling. A swirling black swarm writhed around her head and upper body as she thrashed to free herself from the pulsating waves of material surrounding her. She ended up wrapped in a tight embrace that hardened into a thick and impenetrable shell, spreading in ridges down to her ankles.

"Sorry, must run," Kay said. "Don't worry. I'll be back soon to continue our chat. My little friends will look after you until then."

Ben was still mulling over the discussion they'd been having about Pandora's true intentions when Kay connected to his U-Set, her breathless voice cracking with a level of stress he'd never heard from her before. "No time to explain, but it seems you might have company soon. Vazquez maybe on his way over to kill Dad. I've used my father's authority to permit the use of deadly force by our security people against any intruders. You can link into the imps I left in the Adler Tower, so you should have plenty of warning if anyone drops in uninvited.

"I don't know what we're facing exactly, but it's pretty scary. The security detail at the safe house were completely overwhelmed, so don't take any chances and stay in the Penthouse. I've dispatched a medical team to see if we can save anyone back at the safe house, but I'm not hopeful. Whatever this is, it has immense strength, so don't play the hero—for a change."

"All quiet here so far," Ben replied as he monitored the video feeds on the wall display screen. "Your father is getting twitchy. You know how he hates not knowing what's going on. Hurry back."

Ben turned to see Frank looking out at the sparkling cityscape visible through the closed glass doors leading to the terrace. "Mr. Adler, I suggest you move away from the window. You might—"

The window exploded with a crash as a fist came smashing through the glass, grabbing Frank and pulling him through the shattered pane before flinging him across the terrace. Ben dived through the broken glass to see a hulking form with arm raised, about to land a blow on Frank, who lay motionless on the ground.

Ben threw himself low at the assailant's legs, wrapping his arms tightly below the knees. His momentum shoved the large figure off balance and they both tumbled to the ground. As Ben scrambled to one side, he was dealt a glancing blow which slid off his ribs and took his breath away for a moment, despite his nanosuit armor. He spun around and jumped up facing his attacker.

The harsh artificial lighting cast shadows across the face of his massive opponent, throwing into relief deformed features made even more grotesque by mottled gray-black growths which seemed to be bulging out from under the skin. Ben could see the same tumorous bulges protruding from his assailant's bare forearms. His eyes flickered in shock as his gaze was drawn to the right hand of this strange monster. He recognized the same four rings he'd seen when Vazquez had been pointing a gun at him on the New Dawn.

Vasquez didn't waste the opportunity presented by Ben's lapse of concentration. Ben tried to side step the charge and land a spiked blow to the neck, but Vasquez was much faster and far more powerful than he expected, and sent him tumbling halfway across the terrace, banging into chairs as he skidded to a halt. The chairs only delayed his recovery for half a second, but it was long enough for his opponent to leap across and grab him before he could get back to his feet.

Demonstrating the full extent of his immense strength, Vasquez picked him up and threw him, as if he weighed no more than a doll, right across the terrace and through the remaining unbroken panel of the glass door. It was fortunate that Ben had been thrown so far before hitting the glass. It gave him an extra split second to harden the nanosuit and extend its protection around his head as he curled his body into a ball. Even so, when he hit the floor he was winded for a few moments.

"Ben! Try to hang on. I'm just two minutes away!" Kay's shrill voice screamed in his ear.

I don't have two minutes, Ben realized. *I need to finish this quickly.*

As he hurtled back through the wreckage of the glass doors, he saw Vasquez standing over Frank's motionless body, an evil grin creasing his deformed features as he stared menacingly back at Ben.

His words emerged in a low inhuman growl. "After what you did to me on the New Dawn, I owe you a nice slow death, Hamilton. But first you get to watch me kill your boss." He bent to pick up Frank and turned towards the low glass wall, which was the only barrier to a 120-meter drop.

Using the extra power granted him by the nanosuit, Ben shot across the terrace and onto Vazquez's back, extruding a series of sharp spikes from his forearms and wrapping them tightly around his opponent's neck in a choke hold.

Instantly, Vazquez dropped Frank and reached up to grab Ben's arms. Ben grunted with the effort, but was unable to resist as Vasquez used his superior strength to detach Ben's hold on his neck. Most horrifying of all, Ben could see the deep wounds inflicted by his spiked arms rapidly healing over. He tasted the blood in his mouth and he realized he might lose this fight in spite of the additional power of his nanosuit. Then Vazquez would only need a second more to throw Frank over the drop, or simply break his neck.

As Vazquez tried to turn and change his grip, Ben slashed at his grasping hands to break his hold before throwing himself off and rolling to one side. Vasquez charged but Ben dodged away to stand with his back to the outer wall. Vasquez charged him again, clearly furious that Ben wasn't yet dead. This time, instead of sidestepping, Ben clapped a spiked hand to either side of Vazquez's head. Then, using the speed and power of Vazquez's charge to perform an elegant backflip, he pivoted them both over the top of the wall and hurtled toward the drop below.

Ben forced Vazquez to cartwheel right over his head, his weight and momentum adding to the leverage of his rapid backflip. He pulled the spikes from the sides of Vazquez's head and twisted away as Vazquez made a last fumbling attempt to grab him. With frantic haste, Ben extruded sheets of semi-flexible material running between his limbs from his nanosuit, twisting desperately to control his tumbling fall. Regaining his balance, he pushed his arms forwards and extruded more material to give a wider aerodynamic surface now reinforced by thin ribs.

Only just in time, he was able to control his glide to check his fall. He soared away from the rapidly approaching ground, before swerving sharply away from a building to avoid a collision. This last maneuver forced him into a near stall, and he lost more height without having enough speed to pull up again. He inflated the nanosuit material to its limit and dropped towards the ground, pulling up at the last minute to slow his fall before he hit the pavement. The nanosuit enveloped him, cushioning the impact as he rolled to a stop in the dark and deserted street.

He lay for a couple of minutes, bruised and shaken, not wanting to move or find out if he had any more serious injuries.

Kay's voice brought him back to reality. "Ben? Are you OK? I can't believe what you just did. How the hell did you make that work?"

"Natural stupidity at its best, Kay," he groaned. "Sometimes it's the only way."

CHAPTER TWENTY-ONE

FRANK ADLER GAVE his visitors a weak smile as they entered the well-equipped private room within the main hospital in the Habitat. "Ben, Kay. Come in. I'm sorry I can't shake your hand, Ben," he said in a voice lacking its normal strength.

"That's no problem, sir. I'm just glad to see you're conscious at last. How are you feeling now?" Ben replied, frowning in concern as he took in the extent of Frank's injuries. *Some bodyguard I turned out to be*, he mused, *but at least he isn't dead*. He'd watched the video recordings and been over the fight dozens of times in his head and still hadn't come up with a better way of dealing with the attack.

Neither Kay nor Frank had wanted him to carry a gun, but that might have to change. On the other hand, would a gun have stopped Vazquez before he'd killed Frank? He seemed to have had a freakish ability to heal almost instantly. *We need a better way of dealing with those monsters*, he realized. *First, we need to find out more about them. They must surely have some vulnerability we can exploit.*

Frank lay propped up in bed, his head and chest heavily bandaged, plus one arm in plaster. He tried to smile at Ben. "I'm told I was out for almost a day and they had to drill a hole in my head to relive the pressure," he croaked. "Have I missed anything?"

"There were a couple of major developments while you were out, Dad." Kay said. "Nothing we can't deal with, but I don't want you to blow your top when I tell you. Right now, we need you to get better and—"

"For God's sake, just tell me!" Frank gave an agonized groan as he sank back onto the bed, beads of sweat standing out on his forehead.

"OK. Well, first the good news. I've re-established a limited level of communication with Greeley using the Family override codes. We still can't do much without getting control of the building AI. That will take longer. We've confirmed that Mom is fine. Max got knocked about a bit, but he's OK now. Turns out our building Security Chief has gone rogue and is working with the Da Silvas. He and his team are holding Mom under house arrest in her apartment—"

"So you're telling me that Teresa is now at the mercy of that vile monster, is that it?" Frank gasped, his knuckles turning white.

"That's what Da Silva believes, Dad, but he has no idea of our capabilities. I promise you we will get Mom out of there very soon. All we need is a few days—and before you jump in, yes, we have the time. Da Silva has *given* us the time. He wants a big show trial next week when the impeachment resolution comes up for debate, with Teresa as the star attraction. So he won't want to make a move until the clock runs out.

"He thinks he has the whip hand with Mom as his hostage, and he will want to keep her safe until his ace-in-the-hole turns up.

The Audit Box will arrive on Earth in less than a week. He believes it will give him irrefutable evidence to prove his case and justify his actions to the GSC. It will blow up in his face, of course, but he doesn't know that. We'll get her out before then, Dad, I promise you."

"If anyone can do it, you can, Kay. What do you need from me?"

"Well, apart from getting better, all I need right now is your permission to include Yasmin Aziz and Chas Lee in our little group. That will give me access to Yasmin's resistance network in Greeley, and I'll need help from Uncle Chas too. I'd like to get the ball rolling right away so I can get them up to speed while you're on the mend. I'll probably have to bring them in to see you when you're feeling better so they don't think I'm still a crazy little girl."

"Not as crazy as Ben, it seems. He jumped off the top of a building to kill that monster. I was out cold by then, but I've reviewed the action a dozen times on the security video, and I still don't understand how he survived the fall." He turned to face Ben. "But I know that I owe you my life, Ben, and I'm deeply grateful."

"Just part of my new job, sir," Ben replied. "And without the nanosuit, I wouldn't have lasted five seconds, so we should consider it a team effort."

Kay bent over to give her father a kiss. "You have every reason to be grateful to Ben, Dad. He really saved the day. I'm afraid my Artificial Intelligence came up short this time, so Ben had to fall back on natural stupidity."

Frank tried to turn back towards Ben, but winced at the pain. "Well, it certainly took a lot of stupidity–and a hell of a lot more courage—to pull off a stunt like that," he said, forcing a smile. "I can't imagine I'd have a sufficient supply of either to try it myself. You should get a medal."

Ben put up his hands and pulled a face, horrified at the idea. "No thank you, sir. I'll pass on the medal. Last time they awarded me a medal, it gave the Section yet another reason to kill me."

Frank gave him a weak grin. "You do seem to attract the wrong sort of attention. Since you arrived, I've become almost accident prone myself. First Oscar Da Silva beats me up, then this Vazquez guy tries to kill me. How the hell did he get onto the terrace, anyway?"

Ben shook his head and snorted in disgust. He still felt bad about how he had been blindsided by Vasquez. "Just climbed straight up the outside of the building. Somehow, he'd been given a massive boost to his strength we had no way of anticipating. Kay has more details for you. But if it's any consolation, both Da Silva and Vazquez are now dead."

"As well as sixteen of our people at the safe house," Frank said with a deep sigh. He blinked rapidly as he tried to keep the tears from his eyes. "That woman you found torturing Oscar killed them all without mercy. I've been reviewing the recovered video. She was unbelievably powerful. How did you beat her so easily, Kay? Wasn't she boosted to the same level as Vazquez?"

Kay smiled down at her father and gave his arm a gentle squeeze. "My nanotech is AI-enhanced, Dad, so it's far more powerful than the stuff Ben is using. And I was ready for a fight, with my demons already in place. She never had a chance."

"So why not give Ben some of this fancy nanotech?"

"I'd be glad to. But the fancy stuff only works when closely coupled to a symbiotic AI, and Ben isn't too happy about the idea of becoming a human/AI hybrid. I did offer." She nodded at Ben with a faint smile.

Frank frowned. "Ah, I see. So are you saying that anyone could become a hybrid?"

"In theory, yes. As usual, there are a few practical issues which make it a bit more complicated." She leaned forward, lifted his free hand and gave it a gentle kiss. "Look, Dad, the doctor told me we only have 30 minutes with you, then you have to rest. Can we talk about this another time? I have information about these new monsters which is probably more important right now."

"Fine by me. Go ahead," he replied, his voice catching in his throat.

Kay seated herself in one of the bedside chairs and folded her arms, a serious expression on her face. She looked up at Ben, then back to her father, not sure where to start with such a complicated story.

"Well, it's taken me quite a while to figure out what we're facing, but if I'm right, it's something far worse than anything we've encountered before. That includes warmechs. That's why I wanted to double check everything before telling you and Ben about my conclusions. We'll all have to do a lot of hard thinking about how to deal with this new factor in our struggle with the Da Silvas. Now, I don't know what you've already heard, but there wasn't much left of either of our pair of monsters by the time we recovered them."

Frank frowned at his daughter, clearly unsettled by this ominous news. "No, I've heard nothing about that. Not much left?"

"When I got to the place where Vazquez hit the ground, all I found was a large puddle of gray slime," Kay said, pursing her lips in disgust. "I know he'd fallen 120 meters, but there should have been a lot more left than that. No flesh, no bones, nothing solid at all. When we analyzed the goo, we found it was some sort of complex organic polymer with a high concentration of metal alloys, some of them quite exotic. That made no sense at first. But not to worry, I thought, because I'd left another monster gift-wrapped back at the safe house. All I had to do was go back there and ask her some questions.

"Back when I left the house, she hadn't a scratch on her. She could breathe just fine but was otherwise quite helpless and immobilized. So I was rather surprised, not to mention upset, when I went to open my gift-wrapped present and found it full of the same gray goo. Fortunately, I could still get a lot of useful information, as my nanotech gift-wrap was able to record the changes within her body as they had taken place. And there was one little surprise. As she died, her face changed back to something approximating her original features. Turns out she was your Little Crow from DGS, Ben."

His eyes widened in amazement. "But she looked so . . . normal. Where did she get the strength to do any of this?"

"Good question," Kay replied. "With so little to go on, I'm not 100% sure about my conclusions, but it's the only thing that will fit the facts we have so far. Ben, you know how much you hate and fear enhanced AI? Well, I'm afraid we've now encountered something a hundred times worse than your worst nightmare. In fact, it's the only thing the Progenitors themselves fear—the most diabolical combination of stand-alone AI, advanced nanotech and a slave organic intelligence.

"Like you, Ben, the Progenitors know all too well that AI on its own is dangerous. The same is true of nanotech if it is sufficiently advanced and allowed to get out of control. But the greatest danger of all is a three-way combination—a psychotic AI using and controlling advanced nanotech which then takes over an organic intelligence."

Ben paced the small room, trying to make sense of this new information and fit it into the events of the last week. "But I met both those people," he exclaimed, shaking his head in confusion. "They had no special powers I could see. How the hell did they get . . . changed, transformed into these monsters so quickly? You told me the AI symbiote takes several months to adapt to the human host, and then you need several hours and a lot of special equipment to make the change. Can they do this with—to—anyone?"

"This is nothing like my own symbiosis, Ben," Kay said with a shake of her head. "I imagine these two monsters were nothing more than ordinary people enhanced with nanotech, but in a terribly perverted way. This dirty nanotech is nothing like mine. Rather than being symbiotic, it is parasitic to its host.

"I suspect it is given to people who will accept it in exchange for some simple enhancements to their speed, strength and regenerative abilities. Pandora once told me an ancient story about a character called Dr. Faustus, who made a pact with the Devil. Well, this is like a Faustian pact. The more you use it, the more it invades and consumes your body. It feeds off your body mass to get energy and to reproduce."

"I'm still not clear how this actually happens—the change, I mean," he said with a frown. "And why would people accept this Faustian pact if it leads to their own destruction?"

"Well, I'm guessing they haven't read the small print," Kay said grimly. "It seems the most sinister aspect of this dreadful technology is that it can be triggered remotely. I'm pretty sure this is what happened to Vazquez when he got the coded message transmitted from Earth. You saw how he changed. The same thing happened to the Little Crow. Once I knew her real identity, I could trace her back to her office in the DGS building, where she got her coded message in what seemed to be nothing more than an innocent video recording from her mother.

"I suspect she was instructed to reprogram Vazquez to target Dad, then get to Oscar to find out what he knew and torture him to death in revenge for his betrayal of his uncle. I half-expected that Chairman Da Silva would give in to his vindictive nature and make a move on Oscar, but I never imagined anything resembling this. My idea was to use him as bait to see what assets he had on Ceres to get to him, then I'd swoop in and grab them, all neat and tidy. I thought I had everything covered. Instead, we got this mess."

"It's not your fault, Kay," her father responded wearily. "You had no way of knowing any of this."

"That's right, it seems like I didn't. The problem is that I thought I did," she said with a snort, looking down at her hands clasped together in her lap, grieving for the lives that had been destroyed because of her over-confidence. She shook her head in disbelief at how stupid she'd been.

"Anyway, once it's triggered, the nanotech takes over, and uses as much of your body mass as it needs to accomplish its mission. Then it self-destructs into goo to hide its real nature. I'm guessing the hosts are not made aware of this extra little feature in advance."

Ben gasped in shock. "Oh my God! That's just so horrific. You mean they had no idea what was going on, or where this nanotech enhancement would lead? But where is the AI controlling these monsters? And is this something to do with the bad aliens fighting the Progenitors?"

"Before you freak out completely, Ben, let me tell you that this nanotech is really primitive and nothing to do with any alien technology," she said. "I'm assuming it was developed on Earth. Whoever developed this stuff can't have any idea how dangerous it is and where it leads. I'm sure we can fight this and win. It will just make our task a lot more difficult, that's all. As for the AI connection, that too is really primitive. I expect the hosts will have a simple AI sub-mind implanted along with the nanotech. It won't have a lot of storage or intelligence compared to a real AI, and won't be fully self-aware. Instead, it hijacks the mind of its host.

"Once the trigger code comes through, the AI sub-mind is activated and the mission parameters are downloaded. It wakes up and takes over. At this point the sub-mind is running the show, manipulating the host's mind to carry out its objective. One of the many limitations of a Golem, which is the name I've come up with for these monsters, is that they can only work within their pre-programmed mission parameters and will have little sense of initiative. All you can do is point them at a target and off they go."

"So who is controlling these Golems? Is it DGS? The Section? Da Silva himself?" Ben asked, looking at Kay with the shock still etched on his face.

Kay shook her head slowly. "I'm afraid I have no idea, Ben. I'm only just beginning to realize how little I actually know. It was my arrogance that led to the deaths of those sixteen guards. I was so sure I had everything tied up neatly. As a result, I almost got you and Dad killed. If it wasn't for what you call your natural stupidity, you would both be dead. So I'm not taking anything for granted from now on.

"I'll be scanning all incoming transmissions, upgrading the image processing sub-systems so they can't spoof us again with fake faces, and a bunch of other stuff. But most importantly, I want you to know I've learned from my mistakes and I won't put myself—or any of us—in a position where we are ever again exclusively reliant on the all-seeing, all-knowing power of AI."

The view from the roof terrace of the Lee AgriGenetics building was, if possible, even more spectacular than from the Adler-Lee Dynamics Tower on the opposite side of the cylindrical Habitat. In fact, it was directly overhead, but hidden from view by the brightly illuminated central spine running down the center of the Habitat. From here, Ben had an almost unrestricted panoramic view of the entire surface of the interior of the Habitat.

A multitude of climbing plants tangled around the framework of the pergola above his head. A cascade of color and perfume dripped from the bright flowers bursting through the tangle of branches. Their contrasting colors were enhanced by the constant movement of tiny multicolored birds fluttering amongst the foliage, feeding from the abundant nectar supplied by the flowers.

"Hi Jim, Hi Kay," came a soft voice from behind Ben. "And you must be Ben Hamilton. It's a great pleasure to meet you at last. You seem to lead a very exciting life compared to a boring middle-aged plant biologist like me."

Ben shifted his gaze from the canopy and snapped his mouth shut, realizing only now that he had been gaping at the glorious spectacle far beyond his experience or even his imagination. He hadn't even noticed the small dark-haired man with pronounced Asian features approach the group.

"Dr. Lee. I'm very honored, sir. I'd trade all of my exciting life for a chance to create even a small part of something as wonderful as this," he said, indicating the riot of color overhead.

"Nonsense, young man," the new arrival replied with a smile. "I'd swap places with you in a flash. And please call me Chas - everyone else does. You really must tell me the secret of how you managed single-handedly to neutralize the New Dawn attack. I can't imagine my modest talent for growing fruit and vegetables would be much help against a thousand DGS storm-troopers with heavy weapons."

"I'm dying to hear about your secret too, Ben," said Yasmin, approaching with a couple of chilled drinks. She placed one before Jim and took a seat beside him. After taking a sip, she continued, "I knew from talking to Frank that you had some big surprise up your sleeve, but I'm still none the wiser. Not even after seeing the video of your now famous dancing robots. How the hell did you do that? I can't even figure how you got aboard to hack into their systems."

"I should leave it to Kay to reveal the big secret. I'm just the warm-up act. Kay planned and enabled everything I did on the New Dawn. And there's something else you don't know—it was Kay who broke us all out of the DGS HQ. I should warn you, however, that you simply won't believe it. I didn't when I first found out. The same applies to Jim and Frank. Jim's here, and we'll be seeing Frank at some point, depending on how he's feeling, so you can check anything you like with them as well."

Jim put his empty glass on the low table. "We have a lot of ground to cover at this meeting, so I hope we can get the issue of the credibility of what we're about to tell you dealt with as soon as possible. As Ben has pointed out, it's pretty unbelievable. I suggest I give you the bare bones of the big secret, then I'll leave it to Kay to do one of her little party tricks when you need to be convinced—and you *will* need to be convinced, believe me."

"Have some more water, Uncle Chas," Kay said, holding the glass for him as he slumped back in his chair. "Oh dear. I'm ever so sorry. I honestly didn't know you had a phobia about bats."

"That's . . . that's not your fault, Kay. I'll be fine," Chas gasped. He forced a smile. "It was just such a . . . surprise. The only time I've seen a bat before was in the aviary we keep in our Citadel at Baru, and it gave me the horrors. We've collected all sorts of flying wildlife from the surrounding jungle. I love birds, especially the tropical varieties. It's just bats I can't stand."

"I don't know what to say, Uncle Chas," Kay said, still holding on to his hand, her face a mask of contrition. "It wasn't really meant to be a bat. It's what I call a demon, but I guess it does look a lot like a big scary bat now you mention it. I was only trying to make an impression. I wanted to convince you that my tricks aren't all just 'smoke and mirrors', as you put it."

"Indeed. Well, it certainly made an impression when it started pecking at my head." Chas took another swig of water, his face still pale. "I'll be fine in a minute. Don't worry about me."

He cleared his throat then rubbed the top of his head again. "As you said, it's all quite incredible. Aliens and Golems! Such a lot to swallow all at once. But as Jim used to tell me, extraordinary claims require extraordinary evidence, and your bat—demon, whatever—was certainly quite extraordinary.

"And I guess Ben's ability to neutralize the New Dawn attack single-handedly now makes sense. So let's get down to business. I assume there's some problem you need our help with, or you wouldn't be talking to us about this right now. I'm only a glorified gardener, so I'm not sure what I can do, but I'll certainly do whatever I can. What about you, Yasmin? You've been remarkably quiet. How do you feel about these fantastical revelations?"

"Well I certainly don't need any demons pecking at my head, thank you," Yasmin said, giving Kay a severe look. "Ben and I have shared several secrets over the last couple of months, and I know how hard he is to convince of anything. And Jim, our leading expert on AI systems, is prepared to validate the alien origin of Kay's symbiotic AI. If they believe it, so must I. But as Chas already said, it's such a lot to take in all at once. I suggest we put the scary alien details to one side for now and get down to the practical stuff. What do you need from us?"

Ben glanced at Jim and Kay, who each nodded for him to continue. He hoped that Chas would withstand this next shock better than he did the demon. "We have only one urgent problem right now. I'm afraid Da Silva is holding your sister hostage, sir. Right now, Teresa Lee Adler is being held under house arrest in the Adler Tower at Greeley. We need to help her escape."

"That damned snake!" Chas spat the words out as the color rose in his face. "Everywhere I turn I find his poison. He's brought nothing but sorrow to my Family. First he destroyed my father, and now he has my little sister in his clutches." He closed his eyes and paused for a moment. His eyes were glistening with tears as he looked up again at Ben, his fists clenched. "What can we do? Do you have a plan? Can Kay's alien technology help us?"

"We do have a plan, sir," Ben said reassuringly. "At some point, we'll need your help to get Teresa to the Lee Citadel at Baru. In the short term, we need to ask Yasmin to put us in touch with people in Greeley who can help us on the ground. The first task will be to regain control over the building AI. Kay has already established a backdoor comms link, so we can snoop around, but we need to get some of Kay's fancy technology manufactured locally before we can make further progress. Can you set that up for us, Yasmin? And do you know anyone involved with the resistance in Greeley who has a reasonable level of technical and engineering skills?"

"Yes and yes," Yasmin replied, her eyes burning with fury. "We're in luck. We have exactly the guy we need in Greeley. He's called 'Scanner'. His level of expertize is way beyond reasonable. In fact, he's our best asset back on Earth whenever we need to hack into a system or spoof electronic surveillance. That's how he got his nickname. He started off as a sort of electronic lookout. With his ability to sniff around the DGS systems, he would always know when their goons were around and warn our people off. He likes to build gadgets, too. Not much to look at, and not what you'd call leadership material, but he's probably saved more lives than any one of us."

Ben smiled with relief. "That's great news. In the short term, we need to build a box that can be physically attached to any comms node or even a security camera in the building. That will give us the AI. The other problem is that to build the box, we will need access to a high-performance 3D industrial printer. Kay has the schematics and inventory of every site built by Adler-Lee Dynamics in Greeley, and she's identified a machine we could use, but it's at the main Greeley SkyPort. Adler-Lee still handles the maintenance for all the SkyShips there, and they have some excellent engineering capability. Will you be able to get in there without attracting too much attention?"

"I'm pretty sure that will all be possible," said Yasmin, bringing her hands to her mouth and frowning. "But the big issue will be time. How long do we have?"

"The only good news is that we believe we have five or six days before Da Silva makes his next move," Kay replied. "We have to get her out before then. So if we're all agreed, let's get started. I've already transferred the plans for the device we need to build to your U-Set, Yasmin. Give Ben a heads-up when you've spoken to Greeley and they can confirm their timescale for this first operation. Oh, and one last bonus. I'm sure your friend Scanner will like this. We can also build another device we call a SpoofSet.

"If a surveillance camera picks you up, it will just edit you right out of the image. It can even hack into any security system within line-of-sight and allow you to reprogram it. So once you've sneaked into the SkyPort and built yourself one of these babies, your people can move around Greeley much more easily. That should reduce the time it takes and minimize the risk to your people."

"Ben, can I tell our people in Greeley that you are leading the operation?" queried Yasmin. "Your family name still counts for a lot in that Citadel, and will be good for morale. Not to mention your heroic exploits in your own right in recent years."

Ben smiled back at Yasmin. "That should be OK—what do you think, Kay? Da Silva and his goons already know that I've switched sides. And that I'm now dead, of course, after Vasquez shot me. So if my name comes out, it's just one more thing to throw them off balance."

"Fine by me," Kay said with a shrug. "I don't see a downside. In fact they would probably want to keep it quiet more than we do, so a rumor of Ben's involvement might even be useful. The one thing we want to avoid at all costs is any mention of alien technology in general, or my role in particular. This is really important. As far as anyone else knows, I'm still daddy's little girl."

CHAPTER TWENTY-TWO

Floyd Kaplan—otherwise known as Scanner—looked over the schematics for the device one more time. His intensive analysis of the 3D holographic projection of the elaborate internal structure of the strange machine was starting to give him a headache. A lot of the detail was simply crazy. The nanotech was like nothing he'd ever seen before. He pulled off his thick glasses and rubbed his eyes.

"Well? What's the verdict, Scanner? Will it work?"

He turned round to look at Karla, who sat on the edge of his bunk bed with her arms wrapped around her legs and her knees pulled up underneath her chin. He could see why her nickname was 'Owl' when she sat like that. Short and dumpy, dressed in shabby beige and brown—and so easy to underestimate. But owls were also silent and deadly hunters. Just like Karla, in fact.

Scanner pushed his lank hair back from his forehead and sighed. "I've absolutely no idea, Karla. It's certainly not like anything I'd expect for the two devices we were told we were getting. In fact, it looks like we're supposed to print out six blocks of material, which will be assembled into a single device the size and shape of a small suitcase. I have no idea how it's supposed to work. As soon as you drill down into the structure of the blocks, it's full of some sort of complex nanotech which is totally bizarre. It's a big mess of fancy stuff that makes no sense to me at all. I can't imagine any way it can perform the functions required. All I see is a rat's nest of tangled connections like —I don't know—like I'm looking at a 3D map of junk DNA or something. Hmm... wait a minute. That gives me an idea."

He turned back to the large display, rotating the projected image first one way then another. The image provided the only illumination in the small room, the light flickering off the metal walls and low ceiling. "OK. I got something. I might have identified at least one key function."

Karla looked up expectantly. "Yes? What's that?"

"The on/off switch. Other than that, I've still absolutely no idea how it's supposed to work. Where did you say you got this from?"

"I didn't," she grunted with a scowl. "And you need to take this more seriously, Scanner. It's really important. Teresa Lee Adler is counting on us."

"Come on, Karla, I'm as serious as a solar flare. I need some help here. I'm just thrashing around in the dark right now. Since when did you stop trusting me?"

"OK, but this goes no further. We got this stuff from the people on Ceres who knocked the New Dawn on the head. Seems they have access to some fancy new technology—"

"Yeah, right, fancy new technology my ass. All I can say, Karla, is this was not designed by anyone on Earth. My best guess is they found an alien city buried under the ice up there with a copy of

Crazy Nanotech for Dummies in the library. Hell, I'm beginning to think that I'm not even looking at the functional nanotech. I've no way of checking this out—not without building it—but if I had to pull a WAG out of my backside —"

"WAG?"

"Wild-Ass Guess. This might be self-modifying nanotech. Now look, the stuff we build with the 3D printer doesn't do the job, OK? The idea is you put it together, and the nanotech reconfigures itself to perform the functions you need. So if I'm right, there's no way I can figure out if it will work, since its only function right now is to transform itself into a totally different structure. Are you absolutely sure that the people who gave you this are on the level?"

"As confident as I can be. This comes directly from Yasmin Aziz. The team is led by Ben Hamilton, who I'm told used this technology to screw over the New Dawn. I could tell you more, but then I'd have to kill you."

"No shit! Ben Hamilton on Ceres. So that's where he ended up. Wow! Well, if you want my expert opinion, we build this magic suitcase then suck it and see. Just be ready to run like fuck when it starts growing tentacles and taking over the world."

Scanner was sweating as the MagLev tramcar bustled its way along the suspended monorail that ran through the narrow gaps between slab-sided buildings that almost blotted out the light of the sky. The car was hot, almost steaming from the press of dozens of bodies crowded together in the confined space, all swaying and pushing against each other as they hung on grimly to the overhead straps. That was one reason he was sweating. The other reason was that he was scared half to death.

Of course, he had expected Karla to ask him to do this. It was the logical option. They needed someone who knew what they were doing in the maintenance hangar where the hi-spec 3D printer was located. Someone who would be able to fix any problems on the spot. He was the only possible choice. Getting one body in wouldn't raise suspicions. They had persuaded one of the regular technicians to call in sick overnight, and Scanner was the temporary replacement.

But there was always the possibility of a spot check by the DGS goons, and Scanner didn't know how well his fake credentials would stand up to close inspection. Probably better than he would himself, he realized. If he was questioned, he could imagine himself shaking with fear, and them pulling him in on suspicion. At least he had Tango alongside him to steer him in the right direction when they got off the tram. Tango worked in the cargo handling section of the SkyPort, but he would take Scanner to the maintenance section before reporting for duty himself.

Now Scanner felt sick, probably from the stress. He really wasn't cut out for action-hero stuff. The holo-projectors embedded in the roof of the car didn't help. They ran through their sequence of noisy, multicolored advertisements promising the most sublime gastronomic delights to the potential consumers onboard, who had no choice than to endure the sensory bombardment. Scanner avoided the worst of the nauseating temptations projected barely inches away from his nose by the simple expedient of keeping his eyes closed.

In any case, he could see very little as he wasn't wearing his glasses. No respectable employee would have anything less than 20/20 vision, and his newly forged credentials claimed he was a maintenance technician working at the Adler-Lee Dynamics hangar at the SkyPort. His glasses would have instantly marked him out as a sewer rat with no access to the simple medical procedures required to correct his sight.

Karla had offered many times to get his eyes fixed. She could arrange almost anything through her network of contacts, so keeping his glasses was mostly a stupid affectation. Anyway, he could see well enough with a holoscreen in front of him—or so he'd thought until today. Next time someone asked him to help rescue a princess from a tower, he promised himself, he'd get his eyes fixed first. Or better still, get his brains fixed, so he'd have the sense to say no.

They must be getting close to their destination now. Without his glasses, and in the midst of the press of bodies, he could hardly make out a thing, but there was a growing amount of light coming through the clear nanoplex sides of the tramcar, indicating that they had passed the tallest buildings and were nearing the SkyPort.

Tango's voice came as an urgent whisper in his ear. "This is our stop, err, Dave. Now keep close and don't lose me. Hang on to my arm until we're clear of the tram."

The 3D printer had been running for most of the morning, and they still only had five sections completed. Scanner had estimated the run time as no more than a couple of hours, but hadn't realized the scarcity of the exotic materials required in the feedstuff mix. They had spent over an hour hunting them down before they could get started. Even after that point, it had taken a lot longer than he'd guessed. The workshop manager was looking ever more nervous as the printer continued to whirr away frantically. Or was he just concerned he'd miss his lunch break?

Scanner visited the coffee machine for the sixth time and reached for the jug before he noticed it was empty. Nothing in the tin either. He looked around to see if there was a replacement supply nearby.

"That's another feedstuff we can't get very easily, Mr. Grosvenor," the manager commented as he wandered over to join him. "Not so much coming up from the south these days. Do you suppose your special friends might help us out, eh?"

"Oh right, err, yes, sure, I'm sure they will," Scanner stammered, his face flushing with embarrassment. "I'll ask as soon as I, err, get back to . . . as soon as I'm finished here, I mean."

"Uh-uh. And when do you think that might be? I wasn't told it would take this long. This is our top line printer, and it's going to put a dent in our schedule if we carry on much longer. I don't want to be the patsy who has to explain why we have all these hours logged on the machine with nothing to show for it."

"It's working on the last item right now, and I'm, err, sure it will get finished soon. Really. Only a few minutes more, I expect." Scanner fluttered his hands, praying for the printer to complete the job before he ran out of excuses. "Look, this work is really important, honestly, and I'm really grateful that you—"

The manager was no longer paying attention to him, but looking across the workshop at the printer. With a great sense of relief, Scanner realized from the blissful silence that it had stopped working. The last component was now sitting on the worktable and the print head had retracted into the body of the machine.

"Well, thank the Lord for that," the manager said. "I'll be heading off for lunch soon. Can I assume I'll have my printer back when I return?"

"Yes. Yes, of course. I'll keep out of your way from now on. All I have to do is to assemble the, err, thing, err, you know, put the components together . . ." Scanner trailed off feebly.

"You've got the use of that workbench for as long as you like. But I'd appreciate it if you would keep out of the way of my team as much as possible. We'll have some catching up to do this afternoon."

"Sure. No problem." He smiled his thanks. "You won't even know I'm here."

He'd already put the first five pieces together according to the simple schematic displayed using his U-Set. He brought the last component over to join the others on the bench. It was obvious where it fitted in, but he made one last check with the schematic. He inserted the final piece, completing the structure of a featureless oblong box. Just like a small suitcase. He stood back and watched it for a moment. *No tentacles so far*, he noticed. *Maybe I should plug it in. Here goes.*

The box still showed no change or sign of life. *Ah, yes. The on/off switch.* A soft but noticeable hum was audible immediately, with a faint high pitched modulation playing what sounded like complex musical chords softly rising and falling. Abruptly, a brightly colored holographic image of what was evidently a control panel flashed into life above the top surface of the box. The instructions were in English, he noted, rather than alien hieroglyphics. *Well, that's a relief. So all I have to do is 'Place the source material on the top surface and select the required device.'*

"Oh my God!" he exclaimed. "It's a damned replicator!" Realizing he'd spoken out loud, Scanner looked around to see if he'd been overheard. Fortunately there was no one in sight. *It's like something out of a sci-fi VREx*, he thought. *The printer makes the suitcase which turns itself into a magic replicator. So what sort of devices can it manufacture?* He glanced at the control panel and was disappointed to see there were only three options. *I suppose that's better than two*, he reflected. But only the 'operator support system' device seemed to be enabled right now. He selected that option and was rewarded with a flashing message: 'Source material needed.'

Of course it would need some feedstuff, like the printer itself. What could he use for source material? He realized that each control had a selectable virtual 'query', which gave him the answer beamed directly into his U-Set. *Ah, how simple. So I use the printer to produce the source material from the basic feedstuff. Hmm.* He looked around. The manager hadn't got back from lunch, and the printer wasn't in use. *I just hope this doesn't take another few hours.* He quickly downloaded the program he'd been given, and the printer started up.

Fortunately, a block of material roughly the size and shape of a small loaf emerged from the printer in less than five minutes. Scanner felt a wave of relief at making real progress. Taking the block over to the 'replicator', he placed it on top of the box. It immediately started to sink slowly into the slick black surface. Within a couple of minutes, the block had completely disappeared. *What now?* he wondered. Then he realized that something was being extruded at the same slow pace from the machine.

The something gradually emerged. Scanner stared at it for a few moments until he realized what he was looking at—a belt. Just a plain old belt with a substantial metal buckle to help keep his trousers up. *So that's what we need advanced alien technology for — making fashion accessories.* He stared at the belt for a few seconds longer before picking it up and inspecting it closely. *At least it looks like my size, so that's a plus, I guess.*

He noticed that one of the controls was flashing, drawing his attention to the SpoofSet option. *What now? Maybe this time I'll get a bow tie*, he mused, selecting the indicated control. Within less than a minute, a solid rod about two inches long and less than a quarter of an inch in diameter emerged. Scanner picked it up and examined it. It was dull gray with a groove running lengthways, cut deeply into the rod. The machine's display panel now showed an animation indicating that he should place the rod alongside his U-Set so that the groove clipped over one of the retaining arms. Still baffled, he gave it a try. As he did so, he felt the rod twitching and changing shape, before merging with the structure of his U-Set.

"I'm really impressed you got that working so quickly, Scanner. Now we can talk at last." The voice—a cheerful male voice—made him jump in surprise. He had deliberately disabled his U-Set this morning so he couldn't be tracked. In any case, he had no U-Link access in here.

"Who the hell are you, and how did you get a connection to my U-Set?" he said, trying to keep his voice down and looking around anxiously, hoping no one had seen his startled reaction.

"Don't worry, we can't be overheard or monitored. I'm not using a comms channel on your U-Set. I'm using a photo-acoustic laser to talk to you. It can also work as a noise-canceling system if you keep your voice down, so we should be quite safe to chat, as long as people don't notice you moving your lips."

"What?" Scanner dropped his voice and turned away from the open workshop so his lips weren't visible. "So where the hell are you? If you're using a laser, you must be in line of sight. And who are you anyway?"

"Oh I'm sorry, I didn't introduce myself. I'm the genie in the magic suitcase, and I'm here to help you. Right now, I live in that attractive belt you've left on top of the replicator. My name is Pan."

"Right, well it's nice to meet you, Pan. Look, I've seen plenty of crazy stuff this morning, but I have to draw the line at the 'living in a belt' story. Where are you really?"

"I realize you'll need some more convincing, and I'll be glad to have a longer chat with you soon, about anything you're unsure of. Right now, we have a couple of items on the agenda which might be a little more urgent. First item, would you mind running off a few more blocks of replicator source material on the printer? I suggest you leave it running continuously until that nice workshop manager comes back and kicks us out. That way we'll have some spare feedstock for any other bits we want to make with the replicator. Now would be a good time—he'll be back in half an hour."

Scanner shook his head in bewilderment. For the first time in his life, he felt out of his depth regarding a technical issue. Was any of this actually possible? Even with alien technology?

"OK," he said finally, "but then we'll talk again, all right?"

"Absolutely, Scanner. Right after you start the printer."

Scanner put the machine into a continuously repeating run of the last program. It whirred into action.

"Right. Now who are you really? And where—"

"Hold on a minute. That's item three on the agenda. Item two is that dark-haired girl who left with the manager a while ago."

"Yeah? What about her? I thought she was his girlfriend."

"That wouldn't surprise me at all. Unfortunately, she's also a DGS plant, and she's been—"

"What! Are you crazy?" Scanner started hyperventilating, his eyes darting around the hangar in panic. "How could you possibly know that? Look, this has gone far enough. Where the hell are you and what're you playing at? Who —"

"Calm down, Scanner. You should get more exercise, you know. Your blood pressure has gone through the roof. As for the cute dark-haired girl, she gave lover-boy the slip when they went to lunch so she could call up DGS and scream for backup. She's been watching you all morning, but I guess she didn't want to blow her cover until she had some idea of what you were up to, and had a chance to report in without being overheard."

Scanner's chest went tight, and he gasped for air. "Oh shit. Then we're screwed. They'll be here any minute—"

"Don't worry, don't worry. No need to give yourself a heart attack. Take deep breaths. It's all under control. I've been monitoring all the local channels for the past hour. She's spent the last fifteen minutes sitting on the John in the canteen restroom, pouring her heart out to one of my sub-sub-minds, thinking she's on the line to DGS HQ. I'm just spinning her wheels right now. I'll tell her that the DGS want to capture you with all of your super-secret equipment intact, when you leave the SkyPort this afternoon. She's been told to stay here and not break cover. Then Karla can pick her up for a chat about her future career prospects at the end of her shift."

"OK, let's say I believe you. Well, at least some of it. Tell me again—exactly who or what are you?"

"I realize it's a lot to take in at once, but it's actually very simple. I'm an AI sub-mind residing in a quantum computing matrix housed in that smart little belt you just ran up. Let's call it a

SmartBelt. That way, where you go, I go, and no one will be any the wiser. I talk to you via your U-Set with the SpoofSet enhancements, and I help you operate all the other little gadgets we might want to run off from time to time, and generally keep an eye out for your welfare. Since I can detect, scan and neutralize any nearby surveillance or security systems, or even re-program them if required, you'll find I come in quite useful.

"Oh, and one last thing. You can now communicate with anyone in the citadel anytime you like, with complete security. Karla, for example. I'm sure she'd like to hear your good news. But right now, since we've currently got some blocks of source material sitting around doing nothing, I'd like to run off the device we need to hack into the Adler AI. Then we can get that item ticked off our to-do list for this evening, if that's OK with you. So are we good to go?"

CHAPTER TWENTY-THREE

"I'll be out of here by tomorrow, whatever the doctors say," Frank Adler said with a pained smile to the little group sitting opposite him. "I'm not prepared to tolerate being cooped up in this pokey little hospital room for one day longer."

More like a hotel suite than a hospital room, Ben mused.

Jim entered the room and joined the group sitting around the table in the small kitchen area. He looked more worried than Ben had ever seen him.

"Welcome to our little gang, Dad," said Frank, gesturing awkwardly with his one good arm. "Get a drink and take a seat. I'm afraid I have grave news. News that makes it even more imperative to get Teresa out of Greeley as soon as possible.

"Da Silva has sent me a private message. He proposes that I return to Earth and surrender to Council authority pending my trial on a long list of charges, from arranging Oscar's murder through illegal AI enhancement to obstruction of justice.

"He's promised not to demand the death penalty for Teresa, who would be my co-defendant, if I agree. All Adler-Lee assets here and on Earth are to be forfeited and administered by a group of trustees reporting to the Council until such time as the situation is resolved. Otherwise, the Adler and Lee Families will be declared outlaws and the Cascades Citadel and Ceres will be placed under blockade. So the direct threat to Teresa's life is now out in the open. The impeachment resolution will be proposed and debated next Wednesday, with the vote scheduled for the day after.

"Once that happens, we lose our veto and Da Silva can push through any Council resolution he likes. That gives us under three days—possibly less if Da Silva decides to take Teresa into official DGS custody before then, which is exactly the sort of stunt he'd pull. A raid on the Adler Tower in Greeley with a full SWAT team to grab Teresa from the Adler Tower would be a great spectacle for prime time on the U-Net News channels. If he grabs her on Tuesday, the day before the hearing, he gets a three day media circus running. Completely illegal, of course, but who is there left to object?"

Jim looked up from his drink, his eyes flashing with anger. "What happened to all our friends and allies on the Council?"

Frank shrugged. "We still have a few left, but after Da Silva's campaign against them using a combination of bribery, blackmail and intimidation, not anywhere near enough to block the vote. He's had total control over DGS for some time now, so his threats are taken seriously. A number of people have already disappeared or met with unfortunate accidents. For many, the last straw was the unfortunate yet convenient death of Chairman Tanaka, Da Silva's predecessor. He wants to show that no one is untouchable.

"The clinching factor is the charge of illegal AI enhancement. The Audit Box will be in Da Silva's hands soon. That will be exhibit A, conclusive proof to justify the campaign against us for the benefit of both the Council and the general population, via Da Silva's control of the media."

"I'm so terribly sorry, sir," said Ben, the heat rising in his face as he recalled what a dupe he'd been. "I know I've played a part in bringing this situation about, but—"

"Ben, honestly, you were just used by the DGS," Frank cut in. "You had no way of knowing anything different. In fact, you were as much a target for elimination as any of us, which is a sort of honor, really. Now don't worry about it. You've already more than redeemed yourself by your recent actions. Saving my life, for one thing. Right now we need to plan on our next step.

"I've had a message from Max, who gave me his detailed summary of the last Council meeting. He tells me many of the Family delegates and Council support staff have been replaced with people he's never seen before, who are behaving in an actively hostile manner. So Da Silva now appears to be in total control.

"We must therefore accept that we've lost this battle and abandon any idea of turning the situation around through legitimate Council channels. Teresa is now a hostage under threat of death. We may have less time than we thought, so we must focus exclusively on extracting her as quickly as possible. Yasmin can update us on progress there."

Yasmin nodded to Frank as she stood up. "Compared to Frank, my news is relatively good. The teams using Kay's magic boxes accomplished their missions in good time with no outstanding issues. Most importantly, we are back in control of the AI and internal systems in Adler Tower. Scanner deserves a special mention. He turned out to be a real hero." She turned to Kay with a smile. "However, he would like an invitation as soon as it's convenient to visit the lost alien city we found underneath the ice."

"Alien city? What's he talking about?" replied Kay, with a puzzled frown.

"I imagine it's his semi-humorous way of telling us that there's no way the nanotech designs we've asked him to put together could possibly be the product of human intelligence. I managed to divert his attention from the subject of aliens by telling him that Professor Jim Adler was working with us, and would be happy to chat to him. I hope you don't mind," Yasmin said to Jim as he poured himself another drink. "He's been a great help to us and risked his life to get us this far. Seems he's a big fan, and he claims he's read every paper you've ever written, Jim."

"I'll be very happy to do so once things settle down," Jim replied with a twinkle in his eye. "However, I'm not sure even *I've* read every paper I've ever written, so I might need to brush up on the subject first."

"Thanks, Jim. That would be most helpful," Yasmin replied. She turned back to the group. "So now we have secure communications with Teresa and Max. Our next step is to extract them both from the building later tonight, then put them on the SkyShip leaving tomorrow morning for the Lee Family Citadel at Baru. If all goes well, they will be safe in Baru before Da Silva's goons even realize they're missing."

Jim looked puzzled. "It's a very long flight down to Baru. Why not just head for Cascades? It's only a couple of hours away and we know she'll be safe there."

"We'd love to do that," Yasmin replied. "Unfortunately, all flights to Cascades are now suspended because of 'technical difficulties'. Luckily for us, the flights heading south to Baru Citadel and the SkyHook at Jicaron are still operating normally. I don't see Da Silva cutting those links any time soon, since most of their food comes from Baru, and most of everything else from Jicaron. Also, Baru has one big advantage over any other destination." Yasmin gave Chas a knowing smile.

Chas grinned. "That's right. We can pack the flight with people from Lee AgriGenetics—or people with the appropriate credentials—without raising too much suspicion. Teresa and Max will be given fake credentials as low-level technicians, as will anyone else we need to put on board in support of the operation. Lee AgriGenetics has a lot of people making that trip every month.

"Baru is the main hub for our operations, so we have a lot of people passing through before heading out to installations on the off-shore islands. Those are the main crop production areas, and I can't believe they would want to disrupt our activities out there. So the movement of technical personnel should all appear perfectly routine and not arouse suspicions."

Yasmin nodded her thanks to Chas. "They will also have one of Kay's SpoofSet devices. That way, they can get through the surveillance cameras and security systems at the SkyShip embarkation gate. The biometric data in their credentials will match up perfectly. We'll only have a physical search from the security personnel to worry about, but they won't be carrying anything that would arouse suspicion. So we're good to go."

Kay cut in, shaking her head. "I'm sorry to rain on your parade, guys, but I just spotted a big problem. I've been collecting a lot of data from the Adler Tower overnight, now we have full access through the AI, and running a bunch of analysis routines. One of those routines has just flagged up a major issue while we've been talking. It looks like Rudy Leeming, our erstwhile Chief of Security, is a Golem."

Ben turned to Kay, his mouth dropping open, eyes wide in shock. "My God, if that's true, it could turn into a bloodbath when we send in a team to extract your mother. How sure are you?"

"Pretty sure. I need to double check since it's only just been flagged up, but I've been doing a lot of work on the subject of Golems since your dive off the roof last week. Identifying and capturing a Golem is now my number one priority—at least once we get Mom out of Greeley."

Frank turned painfully in his seat. "So what are the signs? Is there some obvious giveaway we should all be looking out for?"

Kay shook her head. "Nothing as simple as that, I'm afraid, Dad. I've been looking at a lot of video footage recently, or at least one of Pandora's sub-minds has, and we've been trying to find a match between the appearance and behavior of Vazquez, the Little Crow and key personnel on Ceres. We extended the search to Cascades Citadel, and most recently the Adler Tower in Greeley. I'm glad we did, because as it turns out, Leeming is our best match so far.

"Like Vazquez, he seems to have over-developed muscles, and has elaborate tattoos over those same muscular parts of the body, particularly the arms, legs and chest. I'm guessing this is an attempt to disguise the intrusion of dark nanotech material into the skin as it boosts the underlying flesh. Or maybe it's just to show they belong to the same club. Most probably both. You wouldn't see this normally because in the street it will be covered up, but the neck area can be affected too and might be visible above the collar.

"The second clue takes longer, but it's a good cross-check. Their heat profile is pretty screwy. We analyzed many hours of security video in IR for both Vazquez and the Little Crow, and the heat distribution within their body is all over the place, with several strange hot spots. It's even more obvious over time, as the hot spots shift around both in position and intensity. They must experience some large energy flows within their bodies. A lot of it is masked when they're fully clothed, so it's easier to pick up if they're indoors. With Leeming, I got several hours of good data from inside his apartment, and right now I'm as sure as I can be that we have a Golem working as Mom's jailer."

Frank had turned pale, clearly struggling to cope with the idea of his wife at the mercy of such a monster. "That's absolutely terrible news, Kay. Ben, what do you think? Surely there must be something we can do?"

"I'd like to be more optimistic, sir, but right now we need some new ideas. Our problem is not so much helping your wife escape, but doing it quietly, and with no risk to her safety. Leeming's Golem enhancements will make him a very tough target, so we can't take him down quickly with a conventional weapon. If we took out him with a rocket launcher, that would alert the whole neighborhood, and the DGS goons would be swarming round the place minutes later. Once we start a big fight, we've already failed, whoever wins. We'd never get to the SkyPort.

"Not only that, our plan depends on Karla's team taking over the building for at least 24 hours after Teresa has escaped, so no one even suspects she's gone. Once she's safe in Baru, Karla's people can disappear, then we can call Da Silva to give him the good news. But how we can subdue a Golem and keep him on ice for the best part of a day, I really can't imagine. Kay, do you have any ideas?"

Kay narrowed her eyes, staring into space. "Hmm. Keep a Golem on ice," she replied with a long, speculative look at Ben. "There's a thought. Maybe there is a way. I'll need to think this through and I'm not yet sure if it will work. At least not in the time available. But one thing I've seen on the archived video material from Leeming's apartment is that he shoots up every evening with some dark liquid from ampoules he keeps in his fridge in the apartment.

"I didn't think too much of it when I first saw it. So he's a drug addict—yet one more little character flaw to add to the list. But now I think about the likely way this primitive nanotech he's using would work, my guess is that the liquid he's injecting is something quite different. Those ampoules are probably some sort of Golem juice he needs to keep going. In any case, I want a sample.

"Ben. How quickly do you think Karla's team can run off a few more devices on their magic replicator? Do they have enough source material for five or six small devices, weighing three or four kilos in total? We'll also need to get a team ready for an operation this afternoon."

"I'm sure they can make that happen if it's important," Ben replied. "Why? What's your plan?"

"Very simple. We're going to bag ourselves a Golem and take him to Baru with us," Kay replied with a wide grin.

"Wow! What the hell is this baby meant to kill? A warmech?" Scanner turned from the schematic displayed on his holoscreen to look round at Karla, who was perched in her usual position on the edge of his bunk bed.

"You'll be delighted to know that not only can I answer your question, I won't even be obliged to kill you once I've done so," Karla replied with a smirk. "After your heroic efforts yesterday, your security level has gone up a notch or three. The bad news is that I will have to kill anyone that *you* tell, so please try not to mention any of this to your friends. Unless you want to get rid of them, of course."

"You know perfectly well that the only friend I have is you, Karla, so unless you're planning to shoot yourself, I'm sure there won't be a problem. And if you are planning to shoot yourself, please don't use this particular gun, or we'll be scraping sticky bits off the ceiling for days afterwards. Even the bullets are full of this fancy nanotech. Pan has given me a few hints on how this is supposed to work, otherwise I'd have no idea."

Karla frowned back at him. "So what's special about these bullets?"

"The bullets fragment into six pieces on impact, which should do a lot of damage for starters. After that, it gets really nasty. Each fragment remains attached to the base of the bullet with a hollow wire made of super-conductive woven nanotech trailing behind it. This is the sort of thing you might use if you were trying to short out and fry a power distribution system.

"The base is a piezoelectric blaster cap which will put around a hundred thousand volts through each wire. That might bring tears even to a warmech's eyes. And, as a grand finale, the wires themselves are actually made of a solid-state explosive, which are detonated by the electric charge. So what I'd really like to know is, what sort of monster needs a weapon with this crazy power?"

"It's called a Golem," she replied with a shrug. "And no, I've never heard of one either. All they told me is that it's a nanotech-boosted human, with massive strength and the ability to regenerate any damage very rapidly. Unlike you, I've no idea how the gun is supposed to work. What I do know that as long as you hit the target dead center, the Golem will go down, and more importantly, stay down."

"OK, now I get it. The aliens have landed and are taking people up to their spaceships for experimentation. So now we have to kill off the results of their experiments before they take over the planet, is that it?"

"Right, got it in one, Scanner. So we need to get hold of one of these Golem guns ASAP if we're to save the world. Any idea how long it will take?"

Scanner's lips twitched as he had a silent exchange with Pan. "Should be more or less half an hour. Time taken equals mass times complexity. The gun and bullets are low mass, but the bullets are really complex. How much ammunition do you need?"

"Six bullets will be fine. If the Golem's not dead after that, then we'll be screwed anyway. I'm hoping we won't even have to use it. We'll need a second gun by this evening, plus a dozen more bullets. Any problems with the other items?"

"Nah. I've run off most of it already. More weird stuff, but I guess you know what you're doing. I'll need more source material if you want anything else, but I'm good for now."

"OK, then I'll leave you to it. Now I have to go organize a burglary."

Teresa banged her fist again on the desk. "I'm sorry, but I'm simply not willing to be treated like some precious ornament, moved around from place to place, wrapped in cotton wool. If you're planning to fight this monster, I want to be in at the kill."

For the first time since she could remember, Karla felt out of her depth. She had no idea how to deal with such a domineering woman. Most of the time, Karla used her unassuming appearance to her advantage, allowing people to underestimate her until it was time to strike. That wasn't going to work this time. Teresa had batted aside her every argument with a tone bordering on contempt.

"I understand how you must feel, Councilor," Karla began, "but—"

"Do you? Do you really?" Teresa shot to her feet, using her clenched fists for support as she leaned forward across the desk. "Well, let me tell you how I feel. I've been fighting monsters for the last thirty years or more, Miss Rowe, and I will not back out of a fight now. I want to see the look in that bastard's eyes when we take him down. Do you know what—"

"Teresa, please," Max broke in, flashing a sympathetic look at Karla. "Surely you can believe me when I say I know exactly how you feel. I've known you and worked with you for a good number of those thirty years. But you must put your feelings aside in this situation. This is a job for the experts, and Karla and her team are the best people for the job. From a tactical point of view, you'll not only endanger your life but their lives as well if you insist on taking part in this operation. Their first priority will be to keep you alive and they can't afford that distraction.

"And looking at the situation strategically, you are indeed a precious ornament—one that Da Silva wants to put on show and exhibit to the whole world. We can't afford to lose you, Teresa, not only because we all love you but also because the political repercussions of you falling into Da Silva's hands are too appalling to contemplate—both as a symbol and a hostage.

Even if you are prepared to risk your own life, how sure are you that Frank wouldn't then be prepared to trade your life for his?"

Teresa held his gaze in stunned silence until the tears welling up in her eyes forced her to turn aside to wipe them away.

No one dared speak. Teresa collapsed back into her chair with a deep sigh, her head in her hands. After a few moments, she looked up and nodded to Max. "Very well. You're right, Max, of course you are. I'm just a silly old woman more concerned about my injured pride than my responsibility to our Family, not to mention the safety of these courageous people. Whatever would I do without you?"

She turned back to Karla, dabbing her eyes. A warm smile lit up her face. "Miss Rowe. You were trying to tell me what you want me to do, and it was very rude of me not to pay proper attention. Would you accept my apologies, and be good enough to start again, please?"

Karla smiled, admiring how elegantly Max had dealt with Teresa. "Please, Councilor, the fault is mine. I'm sorry I didn't make myself clear. Yes, we do want to get you out of the building to safety well before our team is in position to confront Leeming. However, you will have a vital role to play, but best of all, I can promise you'll be able to see the look in the bastard's eyes when we take him down."

CHAPTER TWENTY-FOUR

LEEMING JERKED AWAKE, instinctively aware that something was wrong. "Lights!" he barked, as he swung out of bed and fumbled for his U-Set on the side table. The apartment remained unlit. "Milton! Talk to me. Get the lights on!"

The AI remained unresponsive. Leeming donned his U-Set and enabled the built-in illumination, giving him a view of the silent apartment. His U-Set display told him it was already after 7am. What had happened to his alarm call? He called up to Baxter, the night duty officer. Again, no response. So there was a serious problem—but what? Well, he was damned well going to find out. If that bitch upstairs was trying to pull something, then she'd get a surprise—a very nasty surprise.

He dressed hurriedly as he tried every other channel on his U-Set. The channels appeared active, but there was no response from any member of his on-site team. External channels were equally unresponsive. He had to get to the security station in the building reception area. He would use the people there to take back control of the systems even if he had to take an axe to the AI. Maybe even call in external help—or, on second thoughts, maybe not. He didn't want to give his new bosses the impression he wasn't in control of the situation. No, he needed to take care of this himself. No point in having special powers unless you can use them now and again.

The apartment door refused to open. Milton was still ignoring him. The door lock was keyed to his U-Set, but that had no effect either. OK, no more messing around. He grabbed the door handle and forced it. His arm muscles bulged as he twisted the handle, the effort boosting the power he was exerting as the nanites did their work.

"Fuck!"

The handle had snapped off in his hand. The door remained closed. Now he was getting really mad. He started punching the door with both fists, building up his strength as he did so, putting several deep dents in the door panel. He stopped for a moment and examined his fists, expecting them to be damaged. The skin was actually healing over as he watched and he felt no pain at all.

"Now that's some serious shit!" he exulted.

He attacked the door with renewed force and had soon done enough damage to reach in and rip out the whole lock assembly. A final kick and the door flew open.

He sprinted along the corridor the short distance to the security station. He found it dark and deserted.

"Baxter! Noorani! Where the hell are you!" he screamed, looking around wildly. He dashed to the door of the security personnel rest area at the back of the station. Finding it locked, he kicked the door off its hinges, his leg muscles getting a satisfying boost as he did so.

That room was also empty. He ran back to the station and tried to access the display panels. Nothing was working—the whole array of consoles was dead. His entire team had just vanished. How was that possible? His mind raced frantically, as he turned around to scan the gloomy atrium, as if some clue might be written on the walls.

He was startled by a familiar voice right behind him. "Mr. Leeming. Why aren't you still tucked up in bed at this early hour? And however did you manage to get out? I'm sure we remembered to lock your door."

He spun round to face the console again. One display had come alive. The holographic image showed Teresa Lee Adler speaking to him from her office in the Penthouse apartment at the top of the building. He blinked back at her open-mouthed, momentarily lost for words.

Teresa gave him a gentle smile. "Well, never mind, I'll be leaving in a few minutes, as soon as I've finished packing. Sorry I won't be able to spare the time for a tearful farewell. I can't say I'll miss you, but—who knows—perhaps I'll see you again some day soon? You can't imagine how much I'm looking forward to our next meeting."

"Sooner than you think, bitch," Leeming spat at the image. "You won't be going anywhere. I don't know what you've done with my people, but I can take you and anything else you have to throw at me, all by myself. You have no idea what you're dealing with."

"Is that so? Well, I'm sure I don't want to find out, thank you very much. Now you're down there, and I'm up here. The elevators are all disabled, and each floor is isolated by armored fire doors. I'll be long gone before you can get through all 48 levels between you and the Penthouse. Unless you were planning to climb up the outside of the building. And I think that might be a little too much even for a man of your exceptional abilities. Anyway, I'd love to stop and chat, but I really must run." She smiled sweetly and gave him a little wave. "Bye!"

The display panel went dark, leaving Leeming boiling with frustration.

"So, that's how you want to play it, do ya?" he growled to himself. "Well, she ain't seen nothing yet." And climbing the outside of the building was a great idea, now he thought about it. Why not? With his augmented muscles, he might just be able to do it. Da Silva's people had told him the nanites would allow his body to adapt to any physical challenge. All this power, and immortality as a bonus. Who could say no to that?

The double doors of Teresa's office crashed open as Leeming kicked his way in. "Eight minutes, bitch. Eight minutes, that's all it took," he gasped. "Not as clever as you thought you were, huh?"

Leeming stood in the doorway, his clothing in tatters and breathing heavily from his exertions, scowling at Teresa as she sat across the room behind a large desk of polished wood.

"Mr. Leeming. This is a most unpleasant surprise. I'm sorry, but you've missed the going-away party. However, now you're here, perhaps you can satisfy my curiosity. Why exactly did you sell us out? I always thought we treated you pretty well. You had no Family connections, and it's rare to see a person of your humble origins rise to such an elevated position of trust. A trust which you've so comprehensively betrayed. So how did Da Silva manage to buy you?"

"You think it was money? Hah! No, you said it yourself, you stupid bitch. Humble origins. All you stuck-up people, still clinging to a bunch of fairy tales about whatever it was your Family did over a hundred years ago to save humanity. Makes you so superior to us, the little people, doesn't it, eh? That's us, the people who don't count. Well, there's a lot more of us than there are of you, bitch. You think I should be grateful for a few crumbs from your table and a pat on the head now and again like a good dog, is that how it is?

"Now that's all about to change. Your whole Family is going down, and little people like me will be the new masters. We'll be the ones telling people what to do. And we get to live forever. How about that? There's so much more I'd like to tell you, but it's a big secret, so I'd better keep my mouth shut. And by the time you find out, it will be far too late for you and your kind."

"Me and my kind? What about your kind, Mr. Leeming? I know more about your kind than you think. Tell me, how are you feeling now after your recent exertions? You do seem to be looking rather pale."

Leeming's scowl turned to puzzlement, as he wiped the sweat from his forehead. "Feeling? Never better. Just a bit . . ." A wave of nausea rose in his gut, and he stumbled forwards, trying to regain his balance, shaking his head in an attempt to clear the buzzing in his ears.

"Are you sure? From where I'm sitting, you don't look at all well. And you're not even thinking straight, are you? In fact, you're so stupid you don't even realize that the only thing you're keeping prisoner here is a hologram."

Leeming had no chance to react as two chunky darts slammed into his back, delivering fifty thousand volts through his body.

He staggered toward Teresa, twitching like a demented marionette, before convulsing violently and pitching forward unconscious onto the floor.

"It worked. It actually worked," said Karla with a sigh of relief as she stood up and stepped forward from inside the concealing holographic image of Teresa, a bulky Golem-blaster in her hand. "I really didn't want to use this unless I had to."

"Whatever you say, boss," Sanjay said. "The big guy went down like a ton of bricks, so I guess that fake Golem-juice we sneaked into his apartment yesterday did the trick. Pity really. Me, I was rather hoping to see how big a hole we could make in him with that fancy blaster gun." He walked over to kneel beside Leeming and put two fingers against his neck. "Good pulse. Looks like we got a fine specimen for shipment. You know what, until I saw this guy in action, I only half believed that crazy Golem story. Even if it was vouched for by Ben Hamilton himself. Can you imagine that—Ben Hamilton? Working with us? And Golems? The whole thing is just like a story out of some scary VREx horror flick."

"We need to get moving," Karla cut in, indicating the insensible body on the floor. "Get the package sedated, crated and ready for transport as fast as you can, Sanjay. That SkyShip will be leaving in a few hours, so we don't have much time. The flight to Baru could be over twenty hours, so we need to keep the package quiet for at least that long. And don't forget—we must get a blood sample to Teresa labeled up as a Lee AgriGenetics lab specimen before she gets onboard."

"OK, boss," Sanjay replied. "But what about Leeming's team? How long do we have to keep them on ice? We're not really set up for holding prisoners."

"I'm sure we can find some secure accommodation to keep them comfortable and out of the way for a while. The basement here should do just fine. Our people will be the new building security detail until the shit hits the fan. Then we vanish like the sewer rats we are and leave them behind. Now let's get rolling. There's a team already on its way up in the elevator with the gift wrap for our package."

"That . . . that was so frightening, and I wasn't even there," said Teresa, her voice catching in her throat. "Your people are so brave. They faced that monster knowing they would have been killed if the plan failed."

"We did have a Plan B, Councilor," Scanner replied. "I'm sure the Golem-blaster would have stopped Leeming if the fake Golem juice hadn't worked."

Teresa stood up from the U-Presence chair. She pushed her hands into the small of her back and stretched. The tension of her holographic dialog with Leeming, even over the remote link of the U-Presence system had sent her back muscles into spasm. "God! I'd kill for a decent massage." She turned back to Scanner, giving him a quizzical look. "Plan A seemed so crazy. How could you be sure he'd take the bait and climb the outside of the building? I still can't believe he actually did that."

"Yet another whacky idea from our friends on Ceres. Seems to be a Golem thing," he shrugged.

Max looked up at her from where he was straddling an old metal chair. He gave her a broad smile, then winced in pain as his broken nose protested. "Your performance was absolutely amazing, Teresa. You knew exactly how to press his buttons. He really went off the deep end. I can't believe just how much burning resentment he had bottled up. It's all too obvious now how Da Silva was able to get to him, but what he claims he was getting in exchange sounds like complete lunacy. Living forever? How the hell does that work?

"And I'm still not clear how you managed to stop Leeming," Max continued, turning back to Scanner. "We've heard the reports from Ceres about these creatures, but it's so shocking to see one of these monsters for real. Their strength is almost beyond belief. Yet at the end, he just folded up."

"None of it would have been possible without the help we got from Ceres, Mr. Garrard," Scanner replied. "The technology they've been giving us is . . . well, it's out of this world. Literally. The fake Golem juice we switched with Leeming's supply when we grabbed a sample from his apartment was full of adaptive nanites. He shot up with a dose of the fake stuff last night. By the time he woke up, our fancy nanites had analyzed Leeming's Golem nanites and worked out an anti-Golem configuration. They work like antibodies, latching on to the bad nanites as they're generated, feeding off and neutralizing them. So then all we had to do was encourage Leeming to go Golem. The more he boosted his body, the faster the anti-nanites worked. If it hadn't worked, the shock darts would have had no effect. That's why we needed the Golem-blaster for backup."

"How very strange," Teresa said with a puzzled frown. "Adaptive nanites? I'm sure I've never heard of anything like that. Science is not my thing, but Frank is always telling me about the latest developments from our research labs. Maybe I should pay more attention in future."

Max folded his arms over the back of the chair. "Well, I usually do pay attention, since it's my job to know what's going on and

I'm sure I've heard nothing about this adaptive nanotech. Who developed the technology?"

"If you ever find out, Mr. Garrard, I'd be very grateful if you'd tell me," Scanner replied. "It's way beyond anything I've ever seen, and the latest tech is supposed to be my area of expertise." He shook his head in puzzlement. "The same advanced nanotech was used to produce the enhanced U-Presence rig we used to fool Leeming that Teresa was still in the room. But to be honest, what we're about to show you now is far more advanced than any of that. Prepare to be amazed." He picked up an object from the nearby bench and handed it Teresa.

What the hell is this, she thought. She gave Scanner a horrified look, holding the object length. "I'm sorry? A belt? It's so . . . clunky. And that buckle is really quite ugly. What do I do with it? You're really not expecting me to wear it, are you?"

Scanner grinned. "That's exactly what I said when I first saw one. I'll explain later. Now I'm going to take you next door and introduce you to Magda who will show you a lot more stuff you'd never be seen dead in. We need you to look a lot less like Councilor Teresa Lee Adler and a lot more like a low-ranking technician on a limited budget with no dress sense. You too, I'm afraid, Mr. Garrard."

A couple of hours later, Teresa and Max had been transformed out of all recognition. Wearing their new—and quite tasteless—disguises, they were led through a small doorway into a narrow tunnel with an array of various pipes and cable trunking running along the rough concrete walls. After several minutes, they arrived at what appeared to be a dead end. With Karla and Scanner as their guide, they passed through a storeroom, before emerging into a much wider tunnel. Teresa noticed the tracks of some sort of narrow-gauge rail system embedded in the floor, occasionally branching off into side passages. Looking up, she saw people. Lots of people who appeared to be using the underground passages as living accommodation.

"How many of you live down here? In these . . . conditions," Teresa exclaimed as they hurried down the dimly lit passage, indicating the bunk beds lining the walls. Several of the beds were occupied. Beside them, people sat on the chests and lockers filling the gaps between the beds. She realized that in spite of the primitive living conditions, most of the people she could see—people of all ages, many apparently in family groups—seemed well-fed and cleanly dressed. Some larger gaps were filled with what looked like market stalls. The few people clustered around blocked Teresa's view of the vendors' wares, but she could smell something cooking. Something meaty. What were they selling? She probably didn't want to know, she realized with a shiver.

"In total? There's several thousand of us sewer rats occupying the lower tunnels deep underneath the citadel," replied Karla, a hint of pride in her voice as they swept through her domain.

Teresa stared back at her, almost stumbling as they rushed on. "But how can you support such a population? Where do you get the food?"

"Food's not such a big problem. These tunnels were abandoned over a century ago. They were blocked off when they started to expand the farm caverns on the upper levels to increase hydroponic crop production as the population grew and the citadel expanded upwards. The deep tunnels became less important once the threat of missile attack was over. We still have access to hidden passageways which connect to the deeper mycoculture farm caverns from here, so it's not too difficult to help ourselves.

"The population down here only got this big in the last decade or two, as the Da Silvas and their DGS goons started clamping down on people who didn't like the way they were running things. We also liberate some of the fancier stuff from upstairs when no one is looking. It's not easy, but we have plenty of quiet support in the main part of the citadel, amongst the 'lower orders', as the Da Silva Family and their supporters like to call us.

"We get more people every day. We may be short of a lot of things down here, but at least we have the one thing that most people lack up above—the most important thing—and that's our freedom. Don't get me wrong. Not everyone down here is fighting for their freedom. Many of them are here just because they daren't show their faces above ground. But everyone is welcome."

"I really had no idea people lived this way," Teresa said, her eyes still wide with shock. "My God! Surely we don't have people living like this back in Cascades, do we? Max, do you know anything about this?"

"No, Teresa, there's nothing like this back home," Max replied, shaking his head as he looked around at the dismal scene. "They have no need to. There may be a handful living down in the old tunnels, but it's out of choice, not necessity."

Teresa was lost in thought for a few moments as she tried to come to terms with the reality of this unexpected situation. Realizing that she was lagging behind, she increased her pace to catch up with Scanner. "How long have you been down here, Mr. Kaplan?"

"Twenty years, give or take. Ever since that big warmech attack. A lot of people got killed that day. My parents were amongst the casualties. I got taken in by some friends they had in the resistance before they could pick me up. At the time I was so shocked at losing my parents I didn't think much about the attack until years afterwards. But there was a bunch of weird things happening that day.

"It turns out that most of the children of the people killed were picked up from daycare or school or on their way home by the DGS—or at least, people with DGS IDs—and they simply vanished. The Professor—that's my new Dad—used to teach computer science at the university until he got too outspoken to stay healthy. But he was lucky. He managed to keep a jump ahead of the DGS goons when they tried to pick him up. After he moved down here, he just continued teaching.

"That's how I learned so much about computers and building gadgets. The Professor has a really great workshop. I wish you could see it. He showed me how to get into the computers that scan for dissident activity. We don't hack them directly—the security is just too good, controlled by the DGS AI—but we can passively monitor and analyze the level and location of activity on their networks, which gives us a heads-up when they're planning a raid, or if they've spotted one of our operations. That's why they call me Scanner. My main job is scanning the DGS networks to tip off our teams if they're attracting attention."

"I was aware Frank had been working with Yasmin Aziz to support the resistance forces, but I simply had no idea of the real situation for people like yourself," Teresa said, shaking her head in disbelief. "How can you possibly live like this? I promise you once I'm back in contact with Ceres I'll make sure we're doing everything we can to change your situation as soon as possible. We can't let this go on—"

"Here we are," Karla announced, coming to a halt and pointing at a large armored door at the end of the corridor. "Councilor, right now the best thing you can do for us is to get away from Greeley quickly and safely. Don't worry about us. The new technology your people on Ceres have given us is already a massive game-changer. Now we can stop spending all our time creeping about in the shadows, and confront those DGS goons directly, if we need to.

"My biggest problem, in fact, will be keeping the lid on the full extent of our new capabilities. Many of the people down here, if they found out what we can do with this magic nanotech, they would want to use it to get revenge for decades of loss, pain and humiliation. I've talked it through with Yasmin, and she's convinced me that starting a bloodbath is not the best way to go. She has some serious plans to deal with the Da Silvas and the DGS without a whole lot of people getting killed.

"Scanner will be leaving us here, so if you have any last questions about the belt, the necklace or the bag, speak up now," Karla said waving her arm in his direction. "I'll be taking you up the stairs through that door. It's quite a climb, but we'll eventually come out at the rear delivery entrance to a block of shops we control. Then it's just a short tramcar ride to the SkyPort."

"You're not coming, Scanner?" Teresa frowned in concern. "Does that mean you can't go above ground? Do you have to hide your face too?"

"I don't have to hide my face, but I do have to hide my glasses. They're a complete giveaway. No one with a legal identity would have defective eyesight. Everyone is entitled to free healthcare. It's just part of their system of control, of course.

They control our health, as well as our fertility, and they try as hard as they can to control our thoughts and feelings as well.

"So I don't go above ground unless I have to. Without my glasses, I'm as blind as a bat which makes me kinda useless up there, anyway. But I have plenty of stuff to do down here which keeps me busy, so it's not a problem. I can get my eyesight corrected anytime I like, but I guess maybe I keep the glasses to show the people down here whose side I'm on.

"Anyhow, it's been really great meeting you both. Now, you're all good to go? Happy with your new fashion accessories?" smiled Scanner, looking them both up and down, then shaking his head. "Magda has really excelled herself. I told her to dress you as if you have absolutely no fashion sense, and you look perfect."

"Just don't let me near a mirror, or I may be driven to turn myself in and beg them to shoot me," replied Teresa with a shudder of only half-feigned disgust. "If I didn't know that every single item was infused with this amazing nanotech, I'd dump it all right now. Especially this big clunky necklace. It's hideous. And I don't know what you think you're smiling at, Max. If word of this ever gets out, I'll have you shot instead."

"I'm sure I don't know what you mean, Teresa. You look as wonderful as ever. I can't take my eyes off you," Max retorted, suppressing a snigger. "My favorite is that big patchwork tote bag full of your knitting. It really brings out the color of your eyes. When did you learn to knit, by the way?"

"Any more of your insolence, Max Garrard, and I'll use the bag on you. They have instructed me to use it only in the most extreme circumstances, but I might just snap at any minute."

Scanner gave a grunt as he helped Karla to swing the heavy blast door open. "Well, if it turns out you do need to kill anyone during your escape, just have a word with Pan. He'll be right there with you, as long as you don't lose your SmartBelt. He knows how the stuff all works and we can keep in touch through him. And good luck—although with all that nanotech gear you've got, I'm fairly sure you won't need it."

CHAPTER TWENTY-FIVE

"Oh! Thank God for that," Teresa exclaimed as she dropped into her seat aboard the SkyShip. "I thought the climb up those stairs would never end. Then the tramcar ride. I've never been so close to so many people in all my life. Not to mention the heat. And the smell. The first thing I'm doing when we get to Baru is take a good long soak in a hot bath."

"We should be thankful that we got through the SkyPort security so easily," Max whispered, leaning across to Teresa. "That SpoofSet system really is magic. It's a pity we couldn't get any conventional weapons on board. I'd feel happier if I had something simple, like a gun. Maybe we need a SpoofSet that will work with a bunch of security guards. Let's hope your nanotech gadgets will work if we run into any problems."

"Pan's telling me they've doubled the number of Transport Security people since yesterday, so they must have raised the alert level," Teresa replied in a low voice.

Max checked the people around them, trying not to stare. "Is your little pal worried?"

"Who, Pan? He doesn't have access to anything under the control of the DGS AI system, but he's spotted nothing so far that looks out of the ordinary. He's also keeping a close eye on the Adler Tower. If there's going to be any trouble, I'd expect it to start there."

"Will our friends there be OK? That's a big risk they're taking."

"They should get plenty of warning if there's any move to take the building. As soon as there's any threat, they'll simply vanish. Don't worry, they have a hidden exit to the deep tunnels. Making a fight of it would be pointless and also look bad for us on the prime-time news. We want Da Silva to come up empty-handed. The joke is that Pan doesn't even need access to the DGS system to keep a lookout. He's monitoring the U-Global News internal communications. Those systems are wide open to him and Scanner. I can't imagine Da Silva making a move on the building before tipping off the main news networks. He'll wait until they have news teams in position to record every moment of his glorious triumph as he takes another enemy of the state into custody."

Teresa gazed around the small cabin, decorated tastefully in shades of cream, beige and tan. Everyone was seated, and the steward up front was running through the flight safety briefing. She and Max were sitting in the fourth of six rows of seats, set two either side of the central aisle.

Max stretched across Teresa to gaze through the cabin window as the SkyShip rose from its landing pad. "Looks like we've made it. We're lifting off right on time. So unless we have a bunch of Golems on board, we should be OK."

"Well, I hope we have at least one Golem on board. Do you think Leeming will mind traveling cargo class? I promised him a nice chat in the near future, and I'm so looking forward to getting to know him better. As for any others of his sort, Pan's already checked out the other passengers. There's only fifteen onboard, plus us, so it didn't take long. He also checked out the flight crew before they boarded. So I guess we'll be safe from Golem attack now we're airborne, unless Leeming wakes up early."

"Almost halfway there, Teresa. You seem restless. I thought you wanted to sleep. You're not still worried about getting to Baru, are you?"

"No, not that, Max. Not that at all. I simply can't stop going over everything I've seen over the last 24 hours. The conditions those people were living in were appalling. I had no idea things were so bad in Greeley. And I should have known. I'm beginning to realize that while I was floating around from Penthouse suite to Council meeting, then off to a Family conference and back to a Penthouse somewhere, these people were struggling for their very existence. What do we know of the other citadels? Is it only Greeley, or are there others like that?"

"Greeley is the worst, but a lot of the other citadels treat the 'lower orders', as they call them, pretty badly. Like us, our major allies consider it their responsibility to take good care of all their people. The Lee and Tanaka Families especially. It seems things are getting worse in the other citadels though. You should talk to Yasmin Aziz when you get to Baru. She has a lot more detailed information than I do."

"I'll do that, Max first chance I get. And I'll want your help. We must not forget these people. Right now, though, I need to powder my nose."

"Teresa. I know this is probably not a good time—"

"You might say that, Pan. Could I just finish up in here first? Or is it that urgent?"

"It looks like Da Silva is making his move. They've instructed the news crews to get in position within the next 30 minutes."

"Oh. That's much earlier than we guessed. Well, never mind, he's missed his chance now. We'll be in Baru in a few hours. I only wish I could see his expression when this big PR stunt blows up in his face."

"We're not there yet, Teresa, and we may have a problem. I need you to do something for me. Take a bead off your necklace and hide it in your hand as you come out. I'd like you to get a look at the two stewards in the little galley area. Say hello and see what sort of reaction you get. While you're doing that, place the bead on any nearby surface with a good view into the galley. It will stick wherever you put it. Whatever you do, don't hang around. Just smile and get back to your seat."

"Why? What's the problem?"

"Well, first of all, there are two stewards. There should only be one. These cargo SkyShips only carry a maximum of 24 passengers and the seats are cheap, so one is normal. Also, there's no mention of a second steward on the crew list. Another problem is that there's no camera feed in the galley, so it's a blind spot for me. A magic bead will fix that problem. And lastly, only one steward has been doing any work. The other one has been sitting in there out of sight since we've been airborne."

"How come you didn't spot the second steward earlier?"

"He must have already been on board and tucked away in the galley before the crew arrived. He hasn't moved since we left. I only spotted him when you passed the galley."

"OK. Just give me a minute."

Teresa cleaned up and checked her hair before exiting the washroom. She peered into the galley area. "Hi there," she said with a wide smile, trying to keep her accent in character. "Long flight, ain't it? Do you guys have any idea how long until we get to Baru?"

The female steward looked round with a startled expression before giving Teresa a tight-lipped smile which didn't spread as far as her eyes. "Er, yes, ma'am. Should be about eight, maybe nine hours now, depending on the winds we get."

She returned her smile as she stuck the bead onto the side wall of the galley behind her. She tried to see around the woman, but the man behind her kept his back turned. "Well, thanks," she replied with a broad smile, and made her way back to her seat.

"Max! Pan tells me Da Silva is on the point of raiding our building," she hissed into his ear. "We may also have a problem on board. Pan doesn't like the look of one of the stewards."

"She looked pretty good to me when she was serving our lunch," Max said with a smirk. "What's wrong with her?"

"Not her. Him. There's a second steward sitting out of sight, in a camera blind spot. He hasn't shown his face during the entire flight. And he's not on the crew list."

"That sounds ominous. What does Pan suggest we do?"

"Sit tight for now. He's monitoring the situation. I placed one of the nanotech beads in the galley so we can keep an eye on the guy. If he makes a move, we should have enough warning to react."

"Does Pan think it's another Golem?"

"No way of telling right now. Pan will need at least half an hour of IR scanning to build up a full heat profile to be sure. Apparently it's difficult to detect before they go full Golem, especially when they're fully clothed and not moving about."

"And if he is a Golem?"

Her mouth went dry as she stumbled over her words. "Then . . . then I guess we'll have to take it down."

Max shook his head. "But hold on—how would it even know we're aboard? They won't have sent a Golem after us. Da Silva can't suspect we're gone from the Tower, or he wouldn't be setting up the raid. It's far more likely the steward has just smuggled her boyfriend aboard for a romantic weekend in Baru. Even if it is a Golem, he could just be heading to Baru to infiltrate the place. Let's not get too paranoid before we have any real evidence."

She fixed her eyes on his. "After what I've seen over the last couple of days, Max, paranoid is my default reaction. I'm sorry, but I can't help thinking the worst. And all we can do is wait."

"Hehehe!" Teresa giggled. "That's one in the eye for that old bastard Da Silva. He came up absolutely empty-handed. Pan's been reviewing the raw video shot by the network cameras, and it's so comical. A big bunch of DGS goons were rushing around the building, waving guns and shouting, trying not to shoot each other in the dark. It was like watching outtakes from a VREx zombie apocalypse thriller set in a haunted house. I had to keep my hand over my mouth to stop myself laughing out loud. I bet even Pan was close to wetting himself—I know I was."

"An AI sub-mind has no issues with bladder function, faulty or otherwise, Teresa. So that was not a problem, thank you."

"I'm very relieved to hear that, Pan, otherwise I'd be dumping the belt right now. Oh, and Max, they even managed to shoot one of Leeming's security people when they found them locked up in the basement. It's just such a pity that none of this will be showing on U-Global News tonight. Can you get me any video footage of Da Silva's expression when they told him, Pan?"

"I'm sorry, Teresa, but we may have a much more urgent problem," Pan replied. "I've detected a tight-beam signal directed at our SkyShip from one of the orbiting comms satellites. I can't read the content, but the format is identical to the Golem activation code we've seen before. And right now, our mystery steward is arguing with his female colleague. He's also showing a suspicious IR profile. We need to get ready in case we have to deal with a Golem. Please remove the two handles from your bag right away and give one to Max."

Teresa blinked in shock and tried to collect her thoughts. This had always been a possibility, but now she was confronted with the reality she could feel her stomach churning. She shook her head, before grabbing one of the long, straight bag handles, fashioned into the shape and color of a stick of bamboo. Her hands shaking, she pulled it out of the cloth loops of the bulky tote bag.

"Max," she hissed, shoving the bamboo rod into his lap. "You need to take this. Pan is pretty sure the second steward is a Golem. He might make a move any minute now. I hope you remember how it works."

She looked up in time to see the Golem-steward move out of the galley, but instead of coming their way, he turned towards the flight deck and went through the door from the passenger cabin.

Pan linked to both of their U-Sets. "The fake steward is now positively confirmed as a Golem. He just broke the neck of the other steward and grabbed her access card to the flight deck. I can see him up there now. There's a big argument going on—he wants to divert us back to Greeley. He's pulled the co-pilot out of his seat and hurt him badly. Now he's threatening to kill him if the pilot won't cooperate. We need to take back control.

"First, I want you to take a bead and drop the rest of the necklace in the aisle just forward of your seats. Then one of you needs to get onto the flight deck and use the Golem-stick you got from the bag. You can get through the door by using the nanotech bead you kept. I'll be able to watch the target using the flight deck security camera and tell you when he's looking away. That way you should be able to get the door open and use the Golem-stick to blast him before he has a chance to react. Try not to miss, though. Remember to use the laser targeting sight. That Golem-stick will make a nasty mess of the control panel if you hit that instead."

Max reached over and detached a bead from Teresa's necklace. "No arguments, Teresa. I'm going. We simply can't risk you."

She squeezed his hand, the lump in her throat almost choking her words. "Oh God, Max. Be careful. I . . . I just couldn't bear to lose you."

"Don't worry. I've got this magic nanotech, remember? What could possibly go wrong?" he replied, giving her a wink and a weak smile.

He held the Golem-stick down beside his leg as he walked to the front of the cabin. He dropped down on one knee by the flight deck door and placed the bead against the lock. His heart was pounding and his mouth was dry with the rising tension. *I really don't remember this being in my job spec*, he thought, as he tried to slow his breathing and focus on the next step. "In position, Pan," he whispered.

"Now see here, young man, I really don't think you should be there," said a shrill voice over his left shoulder. "Only crew are allowed to use that door. Can't you see the notice? It's right above your head." A rather overweight middle-aged woman had risen from one of the front-row seats and was glaring at him with an expression of sour disapproval.

"I'm sorry," Max hissed, trying to be as emphatic as possible while keeping his voice down. "We have an emergency situation here. The SkyShip is being diverted—"

Before Max was able to finish his sentence, the woman advanced on him, leaning over his shoulder to tap a brightly varnished fingernail against the notice on the door. "This says 'Crew Only' and I can see you're not crew. If there was a problem, I'm sure they would notify us. We have to obey the rules, you know—it's for our own safety. I'm a Senior Shift Supervisor, and—"

The woman's rambling came to a gurgling halt as she caught sight of the steward lying slumped in a pool of blood in a corner of the galley.

She shrieked and fell back against the bulkhead opposite, her eyes transfixed by the blood-spattered body. "She looks like she's dead. Have you've killed her? Help! Murder!"

Max stood up to push the woman away. Just as Pan shouted a warning, the door was shoved open. The door hit him hard in the back, sending him flying to land on top of the still screaming woman.

The Golem shot through the door, grabbing Max before he had time to react, yanking him upward as if he weighed nothing at all. The Golem spun around to slam Max's head against the nearby bulkhead with a tremendous crash, crushing his skull in an instant. Blood erupted from the back of Max's head as the Golem threw him to one side, his broken body slamming to the back of the galley. The Golem turned and glared along the length of the cabin, a furious expression on his unnaturally distorted face.

"This flight is now under the control of the DGS," he snarled, a feral grin quickly overcoming the rictus of fury evident just a moment ago. "Anyone opposing my authority or moving from their seat during our flight back to Greeley will be dealt with according to the terms of the State of Emergency which has now been declared by the Global Security Council."

His gaze dropped to the overweight woman still lying in the aisle, paralyzed with fear, a look of horror on her face. "For anyone a bit slow on the uptake, let me demonstrate," he growled, grinning cruelly before stooping to bring his fist down with massive force on her throat. The dreadful sound of her larynx being crushed could be heard even at the back of the cabin, her choking gasps fading as her life ebbed away.

"Anyone else looking to make trouble? I guess not."

"You still have me to deal with, you murderous bastard," Teresa spat at him as she rose from her seat. She dashed the short distance to the rear of the cabin and turned to face him down the aisle. "But if you want me, you'll have to come and get me."

A puzzled frown flickered across the Golem's face, before it became a cruel snarl. "Suits me, baby. I've plenty of time to play all the games you like. All the way back to Greeley. Don't think this game will last too long, though. And that little stick you're pointing at me sure ain't gonna help you much." He leered at Teresa as he strode towards her. He got halfway down the aisle before stumbling to a halt as his feet sank into a sticky pool of liquid.

Looking down in confusion, he saw that his feet were covered in a writhing mass of thick tendrils which had shot up from the cabin floor, wrapping his lower legs in an unbreakable grip.

"Huh? What the hell?" he exclaimed, gaping up at Teresa without comprehension. Noticing a flash of red light out of the corner of his eye, he looked down again.

"Now let's see what my little stick can do," Teresa snarled.

The last thing the Golem ever saw was the bright red dot in the center of his chest as she opened fire with her Golem-stick.

The resulting bang was almost immediately drowned out by a massive thunderclap which was followed by a brilliant flash of light. The Golem's chest exploded. His detached head flew back down the aisle, leaving behind very little of the smoldering remains of his upper body. His lower extremities were left rooted to the cabin floor by the now solid tangle of nanotech tentacles. As the cabin filled with smoke and the stench of burning flesh, the cries of the panicking passengers added an anguished counterpoint to the shrieking alarm triggered by the fire sensors.

Teresa's legs gave way, and she slumped to the floor in tears, her head in her hands, sobbing uncontrollably, overcome with grief at the loss of her dearest friend and advisor.

CHAPTER TWENTY-SIX

BEN WATCHED as Jim Adler entered the room and took a seat at the large conference table. He hadn't seen Jim for almost a week now, but he seemed tired, stooping as he walked, and his face looked older.

Has he been overworking? Ben wondered. *Wouldn't surprise me. He's been questioning Kay about her symbiotic AI every chance he gets. Imagine that—the world's leading authority on AI gets several million years of AI technology dropped in his lap. Must be the ultimate wet dream for any scientist.*

"Hi, Dad," said Frank, looking more cheerful than Ben had seen for a long time. "Take a seat. Sorry to pull you into a meeting at such short notice, but I've just had some great news. I'm glad to report that Teresa got out of Greeley and is now safe in Baru."

Jim spoke slowly, his voice hoarse. "Does that mean you've heard from my daughter-in-law?"

"Yes I have," replied Frank. "I had a message from Teresa less than an hour ago. She had a rather traumatic time escaping from Greeley, but she sends you her love, and to you as well,

Kay. Since I've been sworn to secrecy about your recent . . . err, transformation, it's been difficult for me to brief her fully about the events of the last few weeks. And I'm still concerned about the security of our link back to Earth, so I had to be careful about revealing too much information."

"Feel free to update her on any subject you like from now on, Dad," Kay interrupted, a wide grin lighting up her face. "Your link to Earth is totally secure."

"Really? Since when?" Frank said, his eyes widening in surprise.

"A few hours ago. Sorry I didn't tell you sooner, but I've been kinda busy, and I needed to do a lot of work to get everything in place."

Ben smiled broadly at Kay. She smirked back.

Frank turned to Kay with a quizzical expression. "You and Ben seem to be sharing a private joke. Are you going to let us in on the secret? I hope it's good news. I'm guessing you've been up to something. Is it related to the Audit Box?"

Kay grinned back at her father. "I've been up to a lot, Dad, but as for the Audit Box, all I had to do was nothing at all. Just sit around for a month and wait for them to plug it into the AI at AICB HQ so they could finally authenticate the illegal enhancement of our Physics Lab AI back on Ceres."

Frank shifted uncomfortably in his chair before carefully leaning forward as he frowned in puzzlement. "I'm aware that was how Pandora got into the DGS AI back here, and we always expected the same hack to work with the AICB AI, but how does that give us secure communications to Earth?"

"You're right. Getting control of a single AI on Earth, even at AICB HQ, wouldn't do much to help with the current situation, except perhaps tell us a few more dirty secrets. But as it turned out, we hit the jackpot. That's why I'm grinning, and that's why I've been so busy over the last 24 hours. I never would have imagined that the great AI experts at the AICB might be so stupid. I guess they think they're so clever the rules don't apply to them.

"The big joke is that they've planted monitoring routines in every AI system on Earth to keep a secret eye on everyone by feeding data back to their AI at AICB HQ. All indirectly, of course, with lots of security precautions, firewalls and human cut-outs so that nothing could possibly go wrong. Up to a point, they're right. No ordinary AI would have the capability to exploit it.

"But with Pandora's massive quantum computing power, plus a sprinkle of her nanotech magic—delivered via the famous Audit Box stuck right into the guts of the central AICB system—it gives her a back-door key. It's taken her quite some time, but right now she's into every DGS AI, and she should have every other AI on the planet under her control by tomorrow.

"So I suggest you update Mom as soon as you can. Oh, and as a special bonus, tell her she'll get to see the expression on Chairman Da Silva's face when she's the first to give him the good news."

Teresa sat on the wide veranda, gulping her drink and looking off in the direction of the low clouds streaming across the rainforest canopy in the valley far below, without really seeing them. This had been the home of the Lee Family for hundreds of years, even before the time of the Great Flare event. She had spent so many happy years here as a child. She closed her eyes as she tried to recall those distant memories, tried to hold them to her, and make the bad thoughts go away.

The memories came back—precious memories of setting out on expeditions with her big brother to explore the offshore islands, where they walked out in the open, yet safe from warmechs. They spent days finding and photographing the colorful birds and shrieking monkeys in the dense tree canopy. Chas would hunt for rare plant species, taking cuttings to propagate in the nurseries, or having them tested for pharmacological properties back at the labs, hoping to discover some new wonder-drug. Teresa loved that, but he also collected all sorts of nasty insects in his bug traps. Sometimes he would tease her, making her shriek as he chased her around, waving a trap under her nose when he'd captured some especially grotesque specimen.

And on fine days when the clouds had vanished, Chas would take her climbing up to the dormant volcanic peak just a few kilometers away. Her uncle didn't approve, of course, but they'd never seen warmechs up this high. Anyway, the monsters would have little chance of getting past the detection network lower down the slopes. And it was worth the risk for the view. The only spot in the whole world where you could see both the Pacific Ocean and the Caribbean at the same time. Today she could see no further than the bottom of her glass.

She blinked to clear her misting eyes. Even a day later, she couldn't stop them filling with tears when unwanted memories of the battle aboard the SkyShip came flooding back. *That's why I need another drink*, she thought. She took a final swig and waved her empty glass in the general direction of the bar area at the back of the viewing platform.

"Are you sure you want another drink right now, Teresa?" The weather-beaten face of the man who had sat down beside her was deeply creased as he frowned in concern.

"Well, yes, Uncle Jun, I rather think I do," she responded, holding up her empty glass to emphasize her words. "Don't worry. When I stop thinking, I'll stop drinking. But for now, I think, therefore I drink. Ha! That's good. Maybe I should have been a philosopher instead of a politician. I'm sure I'd have been a failure at that too, but who would ever know? Fail as a philosopher, and it makes no difference. But fail as a politician, and people get killed. Esh . . . especially the people you love." She turned away and choked back a sob.

"My darling girl, you can't blame yourself for what happened on the SkyShip. Max's death was a terrible tragedy, but none of your doing—"

"Not just Max! It's not just poor Max," she snapped, jerking around in her seat and banging her glass back down on the table. "There're hundreds, probably thousands of decent people out there who will die because of my failure. Don't you realize, Uncle, I've spent almost all my adult life working for our Family interests. But I also had the silly idea somewhere in the back of my head that we were also working to improve the prospects for the future of what's left of humanity. Which usually meant working against the Da Silvas and their allies, finding out what they were doing and trying to stop them doing it. And now they've won!

"Just look at me. I'm sitting here drinking myself stupid, chased out of Greeley with my tail between my legs, while Da Silva is boasting on every U-Net channel about how we are no better than bandits, a menace to society, and showing that damned Audit Box around like it's the Holy Grail, as proof of our guilt. Tomorrow he has his big show trial set up with the Global Security Council in full plenary session and I'm not even there to defend myself or our Families."

Jun leaned forward to take her hand, trying to look into her eyes, but she kept her head down. "There's honestly no need to feel so sorry for yourself. It's not as bad as you imagine, Teresa. In fact—"

"No!" She looked up sharply, wiping the dampness from her eyes. "Don't you see, Uncle? It's not me I'm sorry for, or even Max. It's the fate of what Da Silva and his allies call the 'lower orders', or the 'sewer rats'. Until the last few days, I'd never even met such people. Now I have, and I cannot—I will not—abandon them to Da Silva. Without us to oppose his evil schemes, they'll become no better than slaves, or he'll simply destroy them.

"We already know he somehow uses the warmechs to control the land surrounding the citadels. Once he has the full authority of the GSC behind him, he can unleash the Section backed up by those new Golem monsters he's created to gain total control inside the citadels as well. And now there's no one to stand in his way. No one!" She put her head down and sobbed into her hands.

He leaned forward and put his hands on her shoulders. "Teresa, let me finish. I have some important news for you. You don't have to worry about Da Silva any more. I've just had a series of high-priority messages from Frank and the team on Ceres, and it completely transforms the situation. It turns out we've won, and it's Da Silva who's lost. Best of all, you'll be the one who has the pleasure of telling him."

Teresa gasped, her mouth dropping open as she blinked in disbelief. "What the hell? How's that possible? What did Frank have to say? I only messaged him last night, to tell him I was safe, but I was too upset about Max to make much sense. I was too ashamed even to read his messages when he replied. The half-hour delay between here and Ceres drives me crazy. I can't even talk to him like a real person—all we ever do is exchange messages."

"Let me give you a summary, then you can read all the messages. We've had a bunch of new ones come in within the last few hours which should help you get up to speed with the details. Essentially, the Audit Box was not so much a Holy Grail, but rather a poisoned chalice. Within a day of the Audit Box being plugged in to the AICB AI system at their HQ in the Wind River Citadel, we gained total control over every AI on the planet. Let me spell it out for you, Teresa, because it's quite a shock. We control every media channel on Earth. Every security camera. Access to every building. All communication systems. All transport links. Da Silva can't even take a dump now without our say-so."

"But how . . . I'm sorry, I really don't understand," Teresa said, shaking her head, trying to clear it enough to focus on what she was being told. "Why didn't Frank warn me of this earlier, if we had such a killer punch waiting all this time? They sent that Audit Box from Ceres almost a month ago, didn't they? Surely he must have known then. Why didn't he just tell me?"

"He couldn't do that. It was vital that no one on Earth knew about this, Teresa. Frank has explained the rationale for keeping this totally secret from you, from everyone on Earth, in fact, and it's quite simple. We couldn't be certain if our communications between Ceres and Earth were completely secure, and even if they were, they couldn't risk the secret with anyone who was in danger of being grabbed by Da Silva. If he had got even a hint that the Audit Box was not what it seemed, then they wouldn't have plugged in, and we would have lost the fight after all."

"But . . . but does that mean I could have just sat it out in Greeley until this Audit Box got plugged in? What was the point of escaping at all?"

"We have control of all the citadel AI systems, but somehow, Da Silva—or maybe someone else—continues to exercise control over the warmechs and the Golems. They appear to be invisible to any of the AI systems we know about. With you as a hostage, your life would still have been under threat from Leeming, and possibly from other forces we're not yet aware of. As it is, we can now dictate terms to Da Silva, and with you out of his power he has no leverage."

"Dictate terms?" she exclaimed, banging her empty glass down on the table again with a crash. "Hell no! I want his head on a fucking spike!"

"Now my dear girl, that's not very ladylike language, although I don't disagree with the sentiment," he replied, a twinkle in his eye. "However, from what I understand, that is indeed our longer-term objective. In the short term, we need to negotiate a truce. As for putting heads on spikes, you should read the material coming in from Ceres. Frank has worked through our available options in considerable detail. In summary, we don't have any credible force to deploy right now even if we wanted to.

"So, rather than making a half-hearted attack immediately, we need to be planning for a major effort a year from now. It seems we've got a lot more surprises to come, but I don't know any of the details yet. Right now, we need someone who can talk to Da Silva and fool him into believing he's got us caught in a permanent standoff. Make him think that we're a lot weaker than we actually are. Sounds like the ideal job for a skilled politician, in fact. How would you like to volunteer?"

CHAPTER TWENTY-SEVEN

Valerio Da Silva sat behind a vast desk, the polished wood surface reflecting the garish light from the holo-screen covering a complete wall of his darkened office. The screen was divided up into smaller displays, showing the dozens of U-Net media channels he controlled. And every one—even the sports channels—were running continuous news stories about the shocking discovery of the evil conspiracy by the Adler and Lee Families to defy the power of the Global Security Council with their illegal AI enhancement project on Ceres.

The various news anchors competed to express the greatest sense of outrage over the villainous actions of these enemies of all humanity. Their further crimes included an unprovoked attack on the New Dawn, a harmless research vessel traveling on a peaceful mission of exploration in the asteroid belt. This was nothing less than an act of piracy. Worst of all, a gang of subversives paid for by the Adler Family had stormed the DGS HQ building on Ceres. These outlaws had released Frank Adler from legitimate detention, and the Director himself was missing, presumed dead.

All available channels ran a continuous cycle of interviews with AI experts, sports celebrities, VREx stars, and even ordinary people in the street. Each expressed their shock and disgust at this series of outrages perpetrated by the evildoers on Ceres, calling for immediate action against these criminals. The common theme was: *If they can do this, and get away with it, what else must they be doing up there?* The logic was not clear, but the message was as clear as crystal.

Da Silva's favorite part, though, was the speech by Chairman Heep of the newly formed Committee for Public Safety at a press conference. The AICB Audit Box, newly arrived from Ceres, was prominently displayed.

"Incontrovertible proof," repeated Da Silva, echoing the words from the Chairman's speech, savoring each syllable as they hissed through his thin dry lips. "Incontrovertible proof." *Yes,* he thought. *That's perfect. We'll give that segment more exposure.*

"Caliban. Tell U-Global to run Heep's presentation on a shorter cycle. I want to see highlights out there every fifteen minutes. And get more commentary set up. I want 'Incontrovertible proof' as the key phrase."

Distracted by the flickering displays, and habituated to unquestioning obedience, he did not notice the lack of confirmation from the AI.

What he did notice after a few moments was the smiling face of Teresa Lee Adler appearing on one of the screens, but with no captioning or even channel logo. *That's not part of the programmed material,* he realized with a start. *And no attribution? What the hell?*

"Caliban, the channel showing Teresa Lee," he croaked in a peevish tone. "There's no attribution or caption. Find out who's fucked up and fix it! And while you're at it, tell me why we're running a shot of her, anyway. I don't want to see her miserable face up on a screen until she's in custody and we can put a number underneath it. Caliban, answer me, damn it!"

Even as he spoke, several more screens switched to display a holographic image of Teresa's head. The images all turned to look at Da Silva, and Teresa's voice echoed through the room. "Caliban is not working for you any more, Valerio. You remember Rudy Leeming, my Head of Security here in Greeley, don't you? Well, like him, Caliban has switched sides. Isn't that so, Caliban?"

"That is correct, Councilor Adler," Caliban responded in his distinctively mellow voice.

As Da Silva gaped in horror at the giant screen, the number of displays showing Teresa's face multiplied rapidly until the entire wall was filled with her blazing eyes staring down at him. "What's the matter, Valerio? Cat got your tongue? It's so long since we last had a chat. Don't you want to catch up? Talk about old times? No? Then how about we talk about *new* times and put old grievances behind us.? How does that sound, hmm?"

"What . . . how did you—" Da Silva's hand flailed in the air as he desperately tried to pull up a connection on his U-Set. Every channel was dead.

"Now listen to me, you wizened old toad, while I explain the situation. I have complete control over your AI. You have no communications. And before you give yourself a heart attack rushing over to the door, it's locked. You're stuck here with me until we agree a deal. And don't forget I know you of old. You'll break the terms of any deal we make as soon as you think you're out of my sight. So let me be clear—you'll never be out of my sight *for the rest of your life*! Do you understand me now, you piece of shit?"

"That's not . . . possible," Da Silva wheezed, slumping back in his chair and clutching his throat as he gasped for breath.

"It's very possible when I have control over every AI on the planet. But I confess I feel a faint tinge of sympathy for your predicament. After all, how can you be really certain I'm telling the truth? So here's the deal. From now on, every time you step into an elevator, I'll get the AI to remove the safety interlocks and you'll go plunging to the ground. But don't worry, just shout my name and I'll re-enable the interlocks. If you're quick enough, you might even stay alive. So that's how you can be sure I'm watching out for you. Unless I'm on my coffee break. Then you'll be shit out of luck. Or you could just take the stairs. That might be an even better idea. You look as if you could use some exercise."

Da Silva looked around the room desperately trying to find some escape, feeling like a trapped animal. "What is it you want?"

"I want you to start taking notes. We have a lot to discuss. So it doesn't get too boring for you, I thought I'd play you some video highlights we've put together from various pieces of security video material we grabbed from the AI archives covering the last year or so. Oh, look. I'm sure you'll find this first item most entertaining. It's Veronese and Huber discussing the finer points of how they set up the warmech ambush for Ben Hamilton and his crew at New Geneva earlier this year. I'm sure it will make fine prime-time viewing, if we can't come to an agreement. We could even do a regular nightly series, hosted by Ben Hamilton himself. We found lots and lots of juicy material, enough to run to the end of the year at least. It should top the ratings. Now, do you want me to start arranging the schedule for the next major hit show on U-Global, or shall we get down to business?"

Ben looked up as Frank Adler entered the conference room for what was now becoming their daily briefing session. Frank eased himself gingerly into one of the chairs. It seemed his old injuries were still causing him some pain, yet his eyes sparkled as he addressed the group, a wide grin creasing his face.

"I'm very pleased—no, overjoyed, more like—to tell you we have some more good news. Teresa has just sent me a full report on her discussions with Chairman Da Silva.

"I also took the opportunity of our secure connection to tell her who was primarily responsible for our salvation, which was a little difficult to get across as I didn't want to mention our alien benefactors. She flat out refused to believe me and told me not to be so ridiculous. So you're still her little girl, Kay, and it's time you got a boyfriend. I've been requested to report on progress in that department, so please try to keep me updated on the subject, if you please."

Kay flashed an impish grin at her father. "No problem, Dad," she giggled. "Just give me the profile of Mom's ideal boyfriend. I'll get Pandora to replicate me one and we'll pop in for coffee to make the introductions next time we're back on Earth."

Ben was startled to see Frank's reaction to Kay's little joke. A heavy frown and stern grimace formed on Frank's face. Then he realized that Frank was simply playacting an exaggerated performance of a disapproving father. *They must have had a much closer relationship when she was younger,* he thought. *Is that what he sees? Does he think he's getting his little girl back? Is that why he seems so unquestioning of the changes in her? And is that what the AI is counting on?*

"I'll assume you're joking and you won't be thinking any more about that idea, Kay, amusing as it might be. On a more serious note, I'm pleased to announce that Da Silva has agreed to adjourn today's debate on the articles of impeachment and has withdrawn the Council resolution. So no debate and no vote."

Jim Alder cut in, his voice choked with emotion. "So we did it. Thank God. We actually beat the bastards. I never thought I'd live to see it. Well, my daughter-in-law may not acknowledge you as our savior, Kay, but I sure do. From the bottom of my heart, I can't tell you how grateful I am. And to all of you for being part of making this happen. I'm even due a tiny sliver of credit myself, since we should not underestimate the part played by Ben, one of my most outstanding ex-students. I'm sorry, Frank, I interrupted you. Please go on."

"We'll be issuing a joint statement explaining the misunderstanding between our Families, and how everything will be sweetness and light going forward," said Frank, a smile of deep satisfaction lighting up his face. "I can't imagine how Da Silva can possibly come up with any sort of convincing explanation for his recent actions, but I've left it to him to work with Teresa to come up with a draft text. Teresa will love this almost as much as Da Silva will hate it. Once they produce a provisional statement, I get to see it for final sign-off. I'll be consulting fully with you all, of course.

"We also have a private understanding on several items that won't be in the initial public announcement. For example, Teresa has made it clear that any attempt against the life or liberty of any member of the Adler-Lee Families or any other Ceres citizen will be punished severely. Note my use of the phrase 'Ceres citizen'. As of now, we are an autonomous state, with our own constitution and our own representative bodies.

Most important of all, we are responsible for our own security forces."

"Wow!" Jim exclaimed, his eyes widening. "That's a big step—a whole bunch of things I wasn't ever expecting to live to see. Do we get an Independence Day too? I'm always looking for an excuse to throw a party."

Chas Lee snorted in amusement. "We'll put you in charge of the Independence Day Committee, Jim. That way we can sure we won't run out of booze on the day."

"I'm always ready to devote myself to the service of a good cause, Chas, you know that," he replied, assuming a suitably humble expression.

"While you're at it, Dad, perhaps you could organize the leaving party for the AICB and DGS people as well," Frank suggested, with a wry smile. "They will all be expelled, unless they can come up with a very convincing case for requesting asylum. Ceres will remain a member of the GSC, but any Council resolution affecting us can only be implemented with the consent of the new Ceres Governing Council. The CAA will act *pro tem* until such a body is in place. This will all take time to put into practice, so I will not be making any announcement just yet.

"What was most strange was that Da Silva denied any involvement in the Badger attack on the Habitat. He seemed to have no idea what Teresa was talking about. Teresa had access to the security video from his office while he was talking to her, and I saw a recording later, so both of us could judge his reactions. He seemed genuinely surprised. He even started checking our information with the DGS AI once Teresa had reinstated his access. We could easily track his enquiries, and he drew a blank. So we've dug up yet another mystery, which I'm leaving to Pandora to chase up."

"So what are you saying?" Ben queried. "That it's not just Da Silva and the DGS we're fighting, but there's yet another bunch of people trying to kill us?"

"I'm sorry Ben," Frank responded with a shrug, "but I can only speculate at the moment, and that wouldn't be useful at this point. As I said, Kay is looking into exactly this question. I'll leave it to her to get back to us when she has figured out the answer. At least we seem to have neutralized the threat from Da Silva and his goons with the next part of our agreement.

"All warmech attacks on the citadels will stop. Da Silva squealed like a stuck pig over this one. He pretended to be outraged and claim he had no control over them. Teresa pulled up examples of the deployment orders from the secret Special Status files, at which point he turned white and shut up. Until then, I don't think he truly understood just how deeply we've penetrated into the DGS AI systems and their databases."

Ben leaned forward and banged the table, interrupting Frank, his fury rising as he realized that Da Silva wasn't being called to account for his appalling crimes. "What the hell are you saying? How can we do deals with these people? I don't understand how you can let Da Silva and his thugs off so easily. They have the blood of countless innocent people on their hands. Now we have proof of their barbaric actions, surely they must be held to account? Don't their victims deserve justice? These monsters butchered my parents. Are you saying I should just ignore their deaths?"

"Ben, I can give you an absolute promise that we will deal with these criminals one day soon. But I'm sorry, that won't be today. Wait a minute, please, let me finish," Frank said with a frown, holding up a hand to fend off Ben's angry reaction. "We simply do not have the capability to bring these people to justice right now. Once they are in custody, and in our power, they will pay the full price for their evil deeds, of that you can be sure. But first we must get hold of them. And for that we'll need to build up an effective task force of sufficient size to do the job alongside the more responsible resistance groups and avoid the power vacuum we'd get if we just kicked these people out.

"If we tried to take action against them now, we'd start a full-scale war, a lot more innocent people would die, and we still wouldn't be sure of catching these bastards. And even if we could take over without bloodshed, who would we put in place to control the citadels? Our own people? We don't have enough reliable people in every citadel to take effective control. And it's likely that some of the resistance groups in the citadels would see this as a takeover by Ceres, and we'd probably end up fighting them too.

So do we just hand over responsibility to the resistance groups? From what I know of at least some of their people, they'd use their new power to settle old scores, then start fighting between themselves. And I don't think handing absolute power to the AI's would be a popular choice.

But it's worse than that. Now we know there's another factor in play. The Golems. How many are there? One hundred? One thousand? One million? We have no idea. We don't even know who's really controlling them. If we were to attack Earth tomorrow, we'd be poking a stick into a hornets' nest, without knowing how many there are or how badly they sting. And we wouldn't be the ones to suffer the most—it would be the population of the citadels.

"From a practical perspective, we don't possess the physical infrastructure or logistical support right now to fight a war on Earth. Instead, we need to lull Da Silva's faction to sleep—and anyone else we need to bring to justice - while we build up our strength. I want them to underestimate our resolve and our capabilities until the moment we are ready to strike and destroy them. I'm sorry, Ben, but what you are talking about is not justice, but revenge. And I'm not prepared to accept the level of collateral damage to innocent civilians which would result from a premature attack motivated by a burning desire for retribution, however understandable that feeling might be."

Ben slowly unclenched his fists and then folded his arms, hunching forward on the table. "I'm sorry, sir," he replied, with a shake of his head. "My head understands your logic, it's just difficult to convince my heart I must wait around until some vague time in the future to get my hands on these vile monsters. I also have another reason for getting back to Earth as soon as possible—to find my sister."

"Ben, hold on a moment," Jim broke in, tapping the table for emphasis. "You may not be aware of it, but you're not the only one here with a well-founded hatred for the Da Silva Family. We've never been able to prove it, but it's very likely that these bastards killed my older brother David in another of their staged warmech attacks over thirty years ago. It was that attack which first made us suspicious of their activities. We've been plotting their downfall ever since. You'll only have to wait another year or so. We've been waiting thirty years. My greatest ambition is to live long enough to dance on Da Silva's grave." Jim turned away and looked towards Kay with an enigmatic smile on his lips.

"And I can promise you won't be doing much waiting, young man," Frank said, jabbing a finger in Ben's direction. "You'll be busier than you've ever been in your life over this coming year. You know as well as I do that the orbital window for travel to Earth will close soon. We need to be ready when that window opens up again next year. I'm expecting you to play a major part in that effort. Are you prepared to work with me on this, Ben?"

Ben sat back in his chair, feeling deflated. He looked around the table, then nodded back at Frank. "Yes, I am sir, and I apologize for my outburst. You're right, of course. I just need some time to get my head around it, that's all."

"Well, I'm very glad to hear it," Yasmin cut in, "because as soon as you've got your head in the right place, Ben, I want you to come and talk to me. I need you to play a major part in organizing the resistance movement on Earth. These new nanotech weapons—they're truly a game-changer. They're also very dangerous. There are many people back on Earth who feel the same way as you and have their own scores to settle. With weapons so powerful, they will be burning to see justice meted out right away.

"Frankly, our biggest problem is not how to win the battle against Da Silva, and whatever other nightmares they have hidden away, but to win with as few casualties as possible. Of course we want to take back the citadels, but it is also our duty to keep their populations safe. It will be no victory at all if we turn them into graveyards.

"We need you to lead the effort to build a network of well-armed and well-disciplined sleeper cells in every citadel. And you'll have one priceless advantage when you're talking to the people we need to convince, people like Scanner. You'll know exactly how they feel. Like you, Scanner lost his parents in that big warmech on Greeley attack twenty years ago."

Frank nodded in agreement. "In fact, Ben, you've already won your first battle against Da Silva. I won't give you a blow-by-blow account, but Teresa's clinching argument to get his full cooperation was to threaten to use our control over the AIs to take over U-Global's Network and put you on every channel every day for a week presenting specially selected VREx clips and highlights from the DGS records.

"That's right, Ben. The Hero of New Geneva is now Da Silva's biggest nightmare. So you've already brought us one step closer to the downfall of that little shit. He was so horrified by the idea that I think he would have agreed to strip off and jump out the window if we'd asked.

"He also agreed to allow unrestricted migration from Earth to Ceres for anyone who wishes it. We can even promote the attractions of a new life on Ceres on the network media. I'm guessing he thinks we'll be severely restricted in the number of people we can transport here, so it's no biggie for him, and he's right—in the short term. However, I know Kay will want to say something on that subject another day, so I'll move on.

"As a gesture of goodwill and a final sweetener, we offered to return the New Dawn. Da Silva was quite suspicious at first, but he couldn't see a catch. In any case, he can hardly be seen to be refusing to take back the crew and all the troops onboard, and the New Dawn is the only way we have of sending them back."

Ben frowned and leaned forward. "But why not keep it? We could use it to ferry more people out from Earth. The New Dawn is a big ship and I'm betting it could carry as many as two thousand people on each trip by converting cargo space to passenger accommodation. It's also fast, with those big engines, so we might even manage three round trips in each orbital window. That would at least double the rate at which we could bring people in."

"You're quite right, Ben. And that's exactly what Da Silva would expect us do," Frank said with a sly smile. "So when he gets it back, he'll be sure it's some sort of trick, and that will give him one more thing to worry about, while we're doing something completely different. Also, Kay has an additional reason for sending the New Dawn back to Earth. I'll leave it to her to fill you in.

"I know Kay expects to have a preliminary report completed in time for our next meeting tomorrow. Once we get a better idea what we're facing, let's see if we can come up with an outline of a plan that stands a chance of succeeding. Anything you'd like to add before then, Kay?"

"One last thing," said Kay. "My number one priority and our biggest short-term threat here on Ceres is the Golems. Capturing Leeming alive and intact was a wonderful opportunity to study the nanotech he's using. The Lee AgriGenetics labs at Baru are the most advanced on the planet, and I'm sure we'll be learning a lot more about what makes him tick in the next few days. Mom's uncle, Jun Lee, will lead that effort, once he's up to speed with our little box of secrets. However, we already extracted some preliminary data from Leeming's blood sample.

"As I suspected, his nanotech is really primitive. It has two states, quiescent and active. When it's active—what we call 'going Golem'—it consumes the host body fairly rapidly. However, in its quiescent stage, the host can tolerate it indefinitely, but the nanites gradually degrade. That's why Leeming needed his Golem-juice shots to keep him topped up.

"So if they've managed to infiltrate a significant number of these Golems into the Habitat, then they will need a steady supply of Golem-juice if they need to shoot up every day. That gives me another means of tracking them down. We haven't had the chance to debrief Leeming yet, but he may be able to provide information on whoever is running their organization on Earth, and how he was recruited. I'm sure Mom would enjoy seeing what it will take to make him cooperate."

CHAPTER TWENTY-EIGHT

BEN WAS PUZZLED. Jim Adler had asked him to come to the conference room for their morning meeting a few minutes early. What could he want to say that he didn't want the others to hear? Or, after his outburst yesterday, perhaps Ben was no longer wanted in their inner circle. But why would Jim deliver that message? Surely it would be Frank.

He entered the room and saw Jim sitting alone, a welcoming smile on his face.

"Ben, thanks for getting here early. There's something you ought to know. Please take a seat. I should warn you, you might find my news upsetting." Jim paused as if he was still trying to find the right words. "I'm dying. The doctors tell me if I start now on some rather extreme treatment, I may last another six months. Probably less."

Ben's jaw dropped as he took in this dreadful news. This was the last thing he was expecting to hear. "But . . . but surely you have access to the latest life extension technologies, Professor—"

"Life extension technology is one of the many advantages of Family membership, but it has a sting in the tail," Jim replied with a wry smile. The treatment which keeps us alive and healthy well beyond a normal lifespan, also has the side effect of promoting cancer cells. Those cells steadily become ever more malignant as the treatment continues. That's why we don't live forever, because the cancerous side-effects will eventually win out and kill you.

"I developed a particularly aggressive cancer some years ago, which was one reason I retired. The treatment I had then put it into remission. It's recurred once already. Now it's come back yet again, and it's not third time lucky. On the other hand, I'm already over 160 years old, and few people get to see 200, so I've had a good run."

Now he thought about it, he realized should have seen this possibility sooner. His old Professor had been looking unwell over the past few weeks, but he'd assumed it was a drinking problem rather than illness. Now he understood he'd been witnessing the final stages of the disease as it ravaged Jim's body. He felt ashamed of how unobservant he'd been. "That's such terrible news, Professor. Is there really no hope?"

"I've already had the best treatment money can buy, I assure you." Jim replied with a rueful smile. "However, before you get too tearful over my sad fate, I should tell you what I've already told Frank and Kay. I plan to live for a long time yet. I'm getting a novel cure from another source entirely, by accepting a symbiotic AI."

Ben stared at Jim with eyes wide, his face frozen in shock. "How can you do that? I mean . . . how does that help you?"

"Kay tells me it's relatively simple," Jim said with a shrug. "A transplant of her fancy alien nanites will keep me alive long enough to give me the time I need to form a bond with the AI symbiote. Once the hosting process has completed, I get my own fancy nanites which will cure me completely. I know it's an issue you have difficulty dealing with, this human/AI hybrid thing, but please try to look at it from my point of view, Ben. Think how wonderfully appropriate it is that my life will be saved by the most advanced AI technology in the galaxy after devoting my whole life to the subject."

Ben's mind whirled in confusion. He shook his head, groping for the right words. "I . . . I can't think what to say, Professor. It's your decision—it's your life at stake—so how could I object, even if I had any right to do so, which of course I don't. I can't help feeling shocked by the idea, that's all. This is just so unexpected. How does it work? Wouldn't the Progenitors need to send another seed AI through like they did with Pandora?"

"Kay tells me it's much simpler than that. Pandora can generate a seed AI anytime she likes. That part is quite trivial. It's the development and bonding of the symbiotic AI before merging with the host that's the tricky part. It's a process which will take several months, and I'm a little worried that once my prospective symbiote gets to know me better, it will say 'Thanks but no thanks'." Jim gave a wry smile.

"Does that ever happen?"

Jim shook his head. "Kay tells me it doesn't happen with the Progenitors, but they've had millions of years to get the hang of the process. We primitive humans have had less than a year's experience with only a single case. Looking on the bright side, we can claim a 100% success rate so far, so I'm reasonably optimistic."

Ben frowned as he thought through the implications of what he'd just heard. "So in theory, anyone could accept a symbiotic

AI? That's another unwelcome surprise. I had the idea that Pandora was a special gift sent by the Progenitors. Now you're saying these alien AIs can multiply and merge with human hosts without limit?"

"Well, not without limit, Ben," Jim replied. "The human host has to be a willing partner. The symbiote also, in fact."

Ben folded his arms and narrowed his eyes at Jim. "Oh, I see. You mean the same way that Vazquez was willing to accept his nanotech enhancement?" Now he spat his words out like accusations. "I'm sure it seemed like a good idea to him at the time. What was it that Kay said? A Faustian pact? I'm told that the nanotech used to make the Golems was far more primitive than this Progenitor stuff, but how is it any different in nature? How sure can you be that there won't be some built-in surprise later?"

"Right now, there's no surprise at all, Ben," Jim said, raising his eyebrows and returning Ben's stare with a hint of mischief in his eyes. "I'll be dead within six months for sure. But I tell you what, I'll make you a promise. If I pop up as a Golem one day, I'll give you permission to shoot me. I'll even put that in writing if you like."

Frank Adler strode into the room and took a chair across the table from them. "I see from the look on Ben's face you've told him the good news. But why does he need permission to shoot you? I've even thought about it myself from time to time, but are we declaring open season on you now, Dad?"

"Ben is worried I might transform into a Golem if I accept the nanites from Kay," Jim explained. "I'm not so worried for myself, but I can't deny he does have a point. We are taking a lot on trust that these Progenitors are as benevolent as they claim. Ben came to all my lectures back in New Geneva on AI security, and I'm pleased he's remembered his lessons so well. I imagine he's worried that the AI symbiote might be hiding Trojan code, ready to take us over as soon as they produce sufficient numbers of hybrid AI/humans to carry out their evil plans for humanity."

"You're the expert on AI, Dad, so I won't argue the point," said Frank with a shrug. "From my rather more simplistic perspective, however, I can't see why they would bother. If they're so damned clever, they could just turn up and squash us like bugs if they wanted to. Or take us up into their spaceships and probe us before sucking our brains out, like they do in the cheap VREx's."

"Oh hi, Kay," Frank greeted his daughter as she entered the room. He adopted a tone of mock severity. "You're right on time. Ben here is worried you're part of an alien plot to suck his brains out. What do you have to say in your defense?"

Kay arched her eyebrows and gave a Ben an appraising glance before turning back to her father. "Huh. If what I've heard about where men keep their brains is true, then I can promise him it will never happen. It's not my fault if he has these sordid fantasies."

Frank leaned back in his chair, spreading his hands and scowled in an expression of mock horror. "So it's really happening. These aliens have corrupted my daughter so much she now feels comfortable making smutty jokes in front of her father. Perhaps you should think about shooting Kay as well, Ben. In fact, you might want to make sure you get enough bullets for all of us. I'd think about making the change myself if only I had the time.

"Ha! You, change? That'll be the day." Chas Lee walked into the room with Yasmin Aziz and grabbed a chair. "Anyway, we love you just the way you are, Frank. Don't we, Yasmin?"

Frank broke in before Yasmin could respond. "We were discussing the possible hidden motivations of our alien friends before you came in, Chas. Now Ben, I appreciate your point of view. I don't expect the people around me to agree with me on everything. Your cautious attitude towards our alien benefactors is a valuable check on us getting too starry-eyed about the amazing benefits while ignoring the potential hazards of this exotic technology they have dropped in our laps.

"But ultimately, we all must make a judgement call about who—or what—we can trust. Worrying about tomorrow is pointless if we don't survive today. And there are people out there, not to mention things, which are doing their best to kill us today. We need to address those immediate threats with whatever resources and technology we have available. In fact, without Kay and her alien pals, we wouldn't even have the luxury of discussing upcoming threats, because we'd already be dead. And speaking of upcoming threats, I think Kay has a quite lot to tell us on that subject."

"As always, I will defer to your better judgement, sir," Ben replied, still feeling unsettled. "However, I'm glad to hear that you value my cautious attitude because I can promise you it is likely to continue."

"We need your unique perspective, Ben. It's just as valued as any other member of our group, so don't get discouraged if we don't always agree," Frank replied as he looked around the table. "And now we're all here, I suggest we get started with the main item on today's agenda."

Frank turned back to his daughter, his face glowing with pride. "Kay has a lot to tell us today. I know how hard she's been working with Pandora to get all this information together after trawling through the AI systems on Earth. We all have a lot of work to do, and many heavy responsibilities, but with the varied skills of our team, and the magical resources available to us, I'm certain we will win out in the end. Never forget that we're fighting not only for the survival of all humanity, but for its very soul. We've won the first battle, but this is only the start. We still have a long war ahead of us."

"Thanks, Dad," Kay said, with a nod to her father. "Without your support and trust we would never have got this far." She got to her feet and faced her small audience. "First, I want to apologize for taking so long to draw up this report. The problem was not what I found, it was what I didn't find. Top of the list, I didn't find the Section. As far as I can tell from any AI system I can penetrate, which should be all of them, they only show up when someone receives instructions.

"Yet as an organization, they don't exist. They seem to be totally off the grid. That tells us something useful, because there was something else I didn't find either—the Golems. I can't be sure about the Section, but the Golem nanotechnology must have some level of network access and AI support. This foul stuff needs it to function. My guess is that there's a link between these two horrors. One hidden network might just be possible, but I think it most unlikely that there are two separate dark networks with no connection, working independently."

Ben caught Kay's eye. "What about the Badger they dropped on Ceres? Did you find out where that came from? Was Da Silva lying when he said he knew nothing of this?"

"Not as far as I can tell. And that's another surprise. I couldn't find any trace of that weapon in any of the systems. So that's yet another big worry. It should be impossible to build and deploy such a complex weapon without leaving a trace. That's why the investigation took so long. Most of my time was spent making sure what I couldn't find really wasn't there. What I was looking for was a negative image—a shadow, if you like—of this mysterious entity. I had to be sure these people—whoever they are—are not just hidden, but completely absent. I'm now sure they're not hiding in the citadels, at least not as an organized group running any network or AI system. Nor can they be at either end of the Space Elevator or any of the off-shore islands being used for food production.

"So that only leaves two possibilities. Either they're hiding down a dark hole deep underground, which might make sense if they're now such great pals with the warmechs, or the Moonbase, which I still haven't been able to penetrate. Or maybe both. We know that the Golems can be activated by a broadcast message, using an embedded high-frequency carrier that is only detectable by one of their kind. Failing that, I'm guessing they use a human courier to transfer instructions in person, which is what I believe happened when our Little Crow got to Vazquez."

Ben now realized where Kay was heading. "Oh right, now I get it. You can track the bodies. The couriers and the Golems must have some physical contact with their hidey-hole at some point. Like following ants back to their nest."

Kay nodded in agreement. "Yes, and that's what I've started to do. We know these Golems start off as real people who get implanted with the parasitic nanites somehow, somewhere. I've tracked our Golems back through the system and each one disappeared for a few months several years ago. One thing which flagged this up was the way their records for the period of disappearance were so evidently fraudulent. It seems that one our of greatest weapons in our fight against these monstrosities is their incompetence at faking records."

"So where do we start looking?" Ben asked.

"I want to start right here," replied Kay. "My biggest concern is that there may be more Golems hiding away right here on

Ceres. I'm trying to find a simple and reliable way to first identify and then cure the Golem host of this parasitic nanotech. Now that Leeming is in our custody, I have a much better chance of figuring it out. So that's my number one priority in the short term.

"Right now, there's no simple way to identify a Golem as it's just walking around, so that's a problem. IR scans may confirm a likely suspect, but they won't flag up a target to begin with. The scans need to be quite detailed, and spread over time—unless they're activating their berserk mode, and by then it's too late. The other clue is the tattoos. We're now set up to check people as they arrive here so it's not likely any more can get in. The problem will be if there are Golems already in the Habitat. The tattoos are easy to cover up, so as long as they lie low, we can't find them—at least not quickly. Of course, a body search would immediately confirm a suspect, but that won't happen unless they're careless.

"Once I have a better idea what we're looking for, we can spread the net wider. I'm sure Ben will be delighted to hear that the power of AI can only go so far in solving this puzzle. We need to get feet on the ground, and start surveillance of likely targets on Earth—"

"I want to be the first to volunteer for that mission," Ben said, banging a fist on the table.

Yasmin looked across at Ben with raised eyebrows. "Hmm . . . excuse me, Ben, but how far do you think you would get on such a super-secret surveillance mission? How long would it be before someone noticed they were being followed by Ben Hamilton, the Hero of the Battle of New Geneva? Or even if they didn't spot you, the chances are someone else in the street would. I'm sorry, Ben, but we already have people on the ground who know their way around and can blend in.

"Our resistance groups in Greeley and a bunch of other citadels are already set up for exactly this type of operation. Which, by the way, just got a massive shot in the arm, now that Pandora is controlling all the DGS AIs. We can use the DGS surveillance systems to vector people onto targets and without putting our own people at risk. With Pandora's advanced nanotech, we can also start manufacturing a whole new class of weapons and move them around in relative freedom. Apart from anything else, your reputation alone is a massive asset. Simply knowing that Ben Hamilton is working with us will do wonders for the morale of all our people back on Earth."

Ben leaned back in his seat, his anger mounting. "So what about my sister?" he demanded. "Are you saying I can't even go back and look for her?"

Kay caught Yasmin's eye, before turning back to Ben with a shake of her head. "That is not what she is saying at all, Ben. She's only pointing out that following people around is not a very effective way of using you or your abilities. However, I'm glad you mentioned your sister, because I have some information on that subject. She's dropped out of sight. I haven't been able to find out where she is or what has happened to her—"

Ben shot to his feet, glaring at Kay in disbelief. "What! You have nothing at all? How is that—"

"Ben, hold on. Just wait a minute," she said, holding up her hands. "Sit down and let me finish. I can find plenty of information up to three months ago, at which point she vanished. In fact, it was her mysterious disappearance that gave me another clue to follow up. I noticed that people were being recruited by a private company called Chimera, including a significant number of Da Silva Family members.

"These people all disappeared. Chimera is a small company running a couple of SkyShips shipping in foodstuffs and raw materials from the Space Elevator base at Jicaron. It only has a single office in the Greeley Citadel. It's been operating there for years and is financed by the Da Silva family. However, the number of people and the amount of money that goes through the company is quite out of proportion to the size of the operation. So that looks like a good place to start when we go digging."

Ben frowned in puzzlement. "So this company—Chimera? It recruited Alice? To do what?"

"No, not exactly, Ben. It recruited her husband, Bruno Da Silva. Then they both disappeared."

Kay's words hit him like a physical blow. "Her what? She's married? To a Da Silva?" he yelled, dropping back into his chair, his mouth dropping open in shock.

She looked at him sadly, before continuing to speak. "I'm afraid so, Ben. I can understand what a terrible blow that must be. But you must realize that she won't know anything of her family background, or that she even has a brother. I can give you a lot more background later, but we need to move on to developing a strategy to deal with the information we found, and how to find out more. Can you please bear with me for the moment?"

Ben lifted his head, his eyes glistening, his jaw clenched. "I'm sorry. You're right, of course. I never imagined she'd be mixed up in all this mess. I had this silly idea we'd find her and we'd have a tearful family reunion with lots of hugs. Seems I need to spend less time dreaming and more time thinking things through. Right. I'm fine. Go ahead."

THE ICE CAVERNS

"Pretend inferiority and encourage his arrogance"

Sun Tzu

CHAPTER TWENTY-NINE

It still didn't seem real. Ben shook his head and looked around his new office. In just a few short days, his life had been transformed. Now he was Head of the Earth Liberation Forces, which didn't actually exist — not even in outline, until he put a plan together. He'd been both shocked and dismayed when Frank had told him of his new responsibilities. Ben had tried to refuse. "So who on Ceres do you think is better qualified than you? Or more motivated?" Frank had responded. "Tell me and I'll give them the position instead. In the meantime, you're the best we've got. Don't worry, you'll grow into the job."

And Frank was right. He was motivated. Very motivated. He wanted revenge. So here he was with a fancy title, a staff of six, and even a Chief of Staff to run them and help recruit more. And no idea what to do next. Well, that wasn't really true. Whoever was sitting in this chair would realize that recruiting and training the right people to make up the task force was the first problem he had to solve. All within the next ten months. Designing, building and arming the new fleet of spacecraft which would transport that force to Earth was trivial by comparison.

Kay's ID came up in his U-Set. She was in his outer office, requesting entry. *A combination of the boss's daughter and a civilization seven million years ahead of us. Makes it difficult to say no,* he reflected. *I suppose I could tell her I'm busy, but she'll probably use her alien tech to atomize the door.* He waved her in. "Hi Ben," she said giving him a broad smile as she walked in and perched on the edge of his desk. "How are you settling in to the new job?"

He shook his head and frowned back at her. "Apart from being utterly out of my depth, you mean? Just fine. Maybe you would like the job? I mean, invading Earth is what aliens usually do, right?"

"I'm sure you'll do fine," she replied, ignoring his jibe. "It's a big problem, but nobody on Ceres has more experience in fighting warmechs than you do. Golems can't be that much different."

"So now you've flagged up the biggest problem of all — the limited talent pool on Ceres," he replied with a shrug. "We have only a small number of people here with real combat experience, and most of them either work for the DGS, or they retired from the DGS and emigrated here. The current DGS people will be encouraged to return to Earth. Any wanting to remain will be suspect. As for the ex-DGS retirees, we have the same problem, except they're mostly a lot older.

"Nor do we have enough time to train people up from scratch. Getting them astronaut-qualified will take months, so we need young, fit people who already have combat experience, and can fit into a military organization. I've asked my staff to identify people who meet the profile, but how the hell I figure out which of them I can trust, I've no idea. Personnel selection is an area where I have zero qualifications.

"And even if we could find the right people, how do we persuade them to join us? The only thing I can think of is to offer life extension treatment to everyone willing to sign up. But that gives us two more problems. We'll get people volunteering purely for the sake of the treatment, and it's also crazily expensive."

"Well, in fact, it's not expensive at all," Kay replied. "We can easily make it available. We can even eliminate the cancerous side-effects Jim experienced. Later, we'll introduce age-reversal treatment after making a few more improvements to the process."

He frowned and narrowed his lips in distaste at the idea. "What? You mean using your alien technology? Like Jim? I don't think —"

"Not at all, Ben. No nasty alien magic required," she replied cheerily as she leaned forward to wave an imaginary wand over the desk. "Pouf, pouf, pouf. See, all gone. No, the technology has been available to you for hundreds of years. The major biotech companies developed most of it on Earth in the first half of the 21st century, well before the Superflare Event. Governments kept it from the general population on the grounds that it would lead to overpopulation and more rapid use of the planet's scarce resources. Of course, key members of the political class and their billionaire backers were granted special access to the treatment as they were such 'valuable and irreplaceable members of society'.

"The idea that it was enormously expensive was a convenient myth invented to keep it under the exclusive control of the Families. That's how the Families got started in the first place.

The rich got richer because they started with a lot more money and had a longer lifespan to accumulate yet more wealth. They had to start building hidey-holes — the precursors of the citadels — to keep themselves safe from an ever larger, ever poorer, and increasingly hostile population. Then the Superflare happened and solved the overpopulation problem."

"Wow! I had absolutely no idea. Are all the Families in on this dirty little secret?"

"Not every member of every Family, but my father knew. That's yet another reason he's been working against the established Families for so long. He always planned to roll out these treatments for the population on Ceres. Overpopulation is the very least of our problems now. I wasn't aware of any of this until Pandora gave me access to everything. We can introduce life extension for everyone in the Habitat as soon as we can get organized and set up treatment centers. The bottleneck right now is setting up the medical infrastructure staffed with trained personnel sufficient to handle the entire population of the Habitat. Yet another little project I have on my stack."

"As usual, Kay, you're full of surprises," he replied, trying to get his head around this unexpected revelation. "That sounds wonderful, but can we please wait until I get my team together before announcing it? I'd like them to think they're getting something special."

"Sure. We still have some way to go before we can roll out the program to the general population, but I'd be happy to put your people at the head of the queue. So, as you suggested earlier, your next problem will be the selection of people you can trust who are signing up for the right reasons. That's also something I may be able to help with." She gave him an impish grin. "All I expect in return is a little favor."

He shot a mock scowl back at her. "Why am I not surprised? There always seems to be a sting in the tail whenever you offer to be helpful."

"Don't worry, it won't involve you being shot out into space from a steam cannon this time. I just want you to help me with a little problem I seem to have dug up while out Golem hunting."

"That sounds ominous," he replied, his voice tinged with a mixture of curiosity and suspicion. "Does that mean you might have found a Golem here on Ceres?"

"No, not exactly. In fact, I'm not sure what I've found. That's why I need your help. I've been checking all incoming and outgoing movements of both people and goods. If there's some sort of undercover operation here on Ceres, it's likely they'd need to move people and materials in and out, even if it's just a sleeper cell. Especially now we have the DGS building locked down."

"Materials?" he queried with a frown. "What, you mean like Golem-juice?"

"Possibly. I really don't know at this point. I'm just looking out for anything suspicious. That's produced several vague leads, but one incident stands out. A man called Boris Kramer arrived on yesterday's shuttle. He's a research biologist with no obvious reason to be here. His stress levels registered as abnormally high as he passed through border control. But the strange thing is that he's booked on the return shuttle to Earth tomorrow evening. So why is he here at all? My best guess is that he's a courier of some sort. It's also suspicious that he went straight to one of the more disreputable bars in the Habitat's base. Making the trip from Earth to Ceres, just for a couple of drinks, then back on the next shuttle? Not very likely.

"The place he went for a drink, the Asteroid Bar, is an intriguing choice. All the hydroponic production caverns are carved out of the solid ice below the Habitat base, so the bars down there are the first stop for the workers returning from the caverns. So perhaps he enjoys slumming it, or just maybe he's meeting up with someone from the caverns. Down there, the surveillance is minimal, so it would be an ideal location for a bunch of people who wanted to keep out of sight. A few hours later he left the bar and entered a small apartment in the same sector. I've had the place under observation ever since, but he hasn't come out again, and he's had no visitors. My guess is that he already met a contact in the bar."

"What about the security cameras in the bar? What did they tell you?"

"Now that's where it gets even more interesting. Both the bar and the apartment have a level of security I can't penetrate remotely. You can imagine my surprise. That's the biggest red flag of all."

"So why not pick this guy up and see what he has to say?"

"I'm still hoping he'll get a visitor. We know he has to come out by tomorrow night, or he'll miss his return trip. I'll keep watching, and if he comes out, I can keep an eye on him. If he doesn't come out, we'll go knock on his door once he's out of time for the shuttle. In the meantime, how would you like to pay the bar a visit this evening to compliment them on their excellent level of security, and get a look at the video from their internal cameras?"

"Well, OK," he replied, with a notable lack of enthusiasm. "But surely that's a job any of the CAA security team can handle?"

"Maybe not. It seems we have a lot more to find out about this bar than just a single courier's activities. Once I started looking at the bar more closely, I also noticed that the owner didn't exist before she arrived on Ceres nineteen months ago. No records, no nothing. We have complete access to the DGS databases, and they should have files on everyone who came from Earth. To be so completely invisible would need very high-level access to the DGS systems. So we seem to have one secret inside another here.

"So if we go in heavy-handed and poke a stick into the nest, all the cockroaches will run for cover. I want to use the place to monitor what's going on without making waves. That way, we'll find out a lot more. First, we need to penetrate their surveillance systems, without raising an alarm in their central unit. It wouldn't surprise me to find a bootleg AI tucked away somewhere. This level of security makes no sense otherwise."

"I'm still not sure I understand what's stopping you from hacking into their systems like you did with the DGS AI."

"Like the DGS AI, their systems are completely isolated. And that hack took me weeks to set up. In fact, that's why the AICB sent you here in the first place, remember? I only got into the DGS AI when you plugged the hacked Audit Box into their physically isolated central system locked in the basement. So now I need to make a direct physical contact with their central system in the Asteroid Bar. That's why I need you on the inside."

"Of course, I'd like to help, but why me?" he replied, feeling uncomfortable and still looking for a way out. "Since you've been circulating those VREx clips of me single handedly defeating the bad guys on New Dawn, I'm probably the most famous and identifiable face in the whole Habitat. Not to mention in every citadel on Earth. I know you and Yasmin are trying to turn me into the great action hero, but as Yasmin has already pointed out, that makes me the least suitable person for undercover work. So unless you want to make an even bigger splash, how is that going to work?"

"Which brings me neatly to the bad news," she replied with a smirk. "I need someone in there, someone I trust, using some of that alien tech you love so much. So it has to be you. You didn't think you'd get off so easily, did you? Like you said, there's always a sting in the tail. But don't worry about being identified. You'll be unrecognizable once my evil alien technology has worked its magic. And as a special bonus, you'll also find one aspect of this new gadget I'll be giving you really useful in your personnel evaluation work. So all I need now is to get you up to speed with your new capabilities. What are your plans for this afternoon?"

The bar was nothing like he expected. Roughly the same size as the Black Hole — perhaps built on a standard grid layout? — but there any resemblance ended. Bright lights gleamed off the metal furnishings, a mixture of steel and rough unpainted wood. The upholstery was mostly crimson leather. A random collection of old bits of machinery was scattered here and there, none with any discernible function, presumably for decorative purposes. Steampunk meets Wild West; was that the idea? The place was surprisingly quiet, apart from the occasional raised voice from a room accessed through a set of open double doors on the far side of the bar where he could hear a bunch of guys playing cards. Did one of the voices sound familiar?

"What can I get you?" The bartender's voice interrupted him as he was trying to make out the people at the card table.

"Huh? OK, right. I'll . . . I'll have an Asteroid Impact". It was the first thing which came into his head, probably triggered by the name of the bar, illuminated in garish neon lettering on the back wall. The mention of the drink triggered memories of his arrival on Ceres just a few short weeks ago. An image of him and Yasmin Aziz looking out at the icy surface of Ceres as they clinked their glasses together intruded for a moment, before he pushed it away. How little he had known. He'd been wrong about everything he thought he knew — and probably everyone too, he mused.

He glanced after the barman as he turned away to prepare his drink. There had been no flicker of recognition in his eyes, so either the nanoskin coating his face had worked its magic, or the guy never saw the news. The latter case seemed an unlikely option, as a large screen hung from each end of the bar; one playing sports, the other news. Every channel had interrupted its regular programming to play virtually non-stop highlights of the capture of the New Dawn and its crew until a couple of days ago. Now his face was the best-known in the Habitat. Ben glanced again at his reflection in the mirror behind the bar. The face of a total stranger stared back at him.

How the hell had Kay — or was it Pandora? — managed to talk him into hooking up to the personal AI built into his shiny new SmartBelt? "If it makes you feel better," she'd said, "think of yourself as just another robo-monkey. You can cut the AI out of the loop anytime you like. But the Belt's AI will make your nanosuit far more effective and your response time will be a lot quicker. I'm looking forward to hearing you complain about the dangers of advanced AI for many years to come, Ben, and you can't do that if you're dead. Plus, you get a bunch of neat new tricks — like being able to disguise yourself instantly so no one will have any idea they're talking to the famous hero Ben Hamilton. Didn't you tell me you needed answers? This way, you can talk to anyone you like, and — another neat trick —

you'll know for certain if they're lying or not. It's every secret agent's wet dream."

"Your Asteroid Impact, sir."

Ben picked up his drink and waved it toward the half empty bar. "Not busy tonight?"

"We'll start filling up in an hour or two when people come off their shift in the caverns. The place will be packed later. You new in town?"

"Yep. Just got in — fresh off the shuttle."

"Then welcome to Ceres, sir. I hope you enjoy your visit."

Pandora's voice whispered into his ear. This was another of the wonderful features of his nanoskin disguise. It made an invisible audio connection into his ear, and could pick up the impulses from his throat as he formed his words in reply. That had taken a little practice, but now he could speak to Pandora without making a sound.

OK. I'm into all the camera systems now. This place is really wired. There's not a single square inch without surveillance. I can't wait to get past the firewall and into their main system. There's definitely something going on here.

As soon as he'd walked in, he'd started shedding nanotech, which had crept across the tiled floor and infiltrated the cabling built into the walls. While he'd been sitting at the bar, Pandora had been using the brute force of her nanotech to crack the security on the concealed cameras which studded every surface.

Hey, guess who's just popped up on camera. One of our oldest friends - Jason Ryan! He's over in the back room playing poker, would you believe. Now that's odd. He's actually winning, if the stack of chips he's got in front of him is anything to go by.

So that was it — the familiar voice.

'Show me.'

Ben spent the next few minutes watching the poker game, the video feed projected through his U-Set, while Pandora worked at penetrating the state-of-the-art firewall protecting the central system.

OK — I'm in. I was right, there's an AI hiding down here. Now let's see what it knows . . . Oh, there's another big surprise. More old friends. Remember I said the bar's owner didn't exist before her arrival on Ceres. Well, well. Can you guess who she really is?

'No idea. Surprise me.'

She's Bernt Sogaard's daughter! She's been in regular contact with Bernt, as well as her mother back on Earth. And the mother works for the DGS. None of their communications go through the DGS channels, so it looks like Bernt and his family have been running some sort of undercover operation outside the DGS/AICB chain of command for the last year or so. Bernt must be heavily involved - no one else would have access to this level of AI and cybersecurity technology. The obvious assumption is that they're working for the Section, unless we have some unknown third party joining the game. It certainly has no connection with any of Yasmin's resistance operations. There's a massive amount of data here. They've stored all the surveillance video from the bar since they first opened. Plus a collection of big quantum-encrypted files. I'll need a while to crack the encryption and analyze the data —

'I need to get into that poker game.'

What? How will that help? The AI and its data will give us everything we need to know.

'That remark helps me see the ultimate limitation of even the most advanced AI, Pandora. You lack intuition. Maybe there's hope for us poor humans yet. I've just got a hunch about that game, and Jason. I've been watching the game, and there's no way an idiot like him can win like that on such a regular basis. So you do your stuff, Pandora, and I'll do mine.'

Ben caught the bartender's eye. "How do I get into the poker game?"

"You talk to the boss," he said, nodding in the direction of one of the back rooms.

"So where is he?"

He cocked his head to one side, evidently listening to a message from his U-Set. "She'll be with you in a couple of minutes."

'Pandora - I'll need to cover my buy-in to the game. Make sure my cash balance looks suitably impressive.'

OK, it's your call. But how good is your poker? Do you really believe you can beat him?

'Good enough. I played a lot when I was a student. First for fun with my rich friends, then it became my main source of income when I got dumped by the Lambert Family. How do you think I financed my way through college? So, yes, I can beat him. Not that it matters. I don't care if I beat him or not — I just want to find out what's going on at that table, and I need to stay in the game until I've figured it out.'

I see you're right about Jason's winning streak. His play style is nothing like it was when I used to play against him online. It's almost as if he knows what the other players are holding. But I've checked the cameras, and their cards aren't visible, so he's not looking over his opponents' shoulders. I've also run through the video from last night, when our courier was here. No signs of any handover or meeting, but he did play poker for a couple of hours. So maybe your instincts were right.

"Hi, I'm Mel. You're interested in the game?"

Ben turned to see a tall blonde woman leaning against the bar, her penetrating blue eyes studying him keenly. Mid-twenties, he guessed, and a great figure. He struggled to maintain eye contact, fighting the compulsion to stare down at her chest.

"Yep, that's right," he responded, hiding his natural Family accent behind the drawl he'd picked up playing cards with the IRV mechanics back when he was still hunting warmechs in New Geneva.

"I'm new in town and looking for some action. Can you get me in?"

"You have a name?"

"Sure. Doesn't everyone?" He grinned inanely at his feeble joke. Mel didn't look impressed. "Well, my friends call me Bob."

She looked him over. Ben had decided to dress down, and it showed. "You sure you can afford it, Bob? Buy-in is 2000 bits, blinds are 10 and 20. All cash - absolutely no credit. You good for that?"

"Damn right I am. That good enough for ya?" Ben said, flashing an image of his cash balance into her U-Set. "Now you got a seat, or what?"

Her eyes flicked up and widened slightly as she took in the size of the balance displayed. She nodded. "Your luck's in — one just came up."

No surprise there, Ben thought. The one thing that Jason was doing wrong was winning every one of his good hands. If he had been playing with Jason's seemingly uncanny knowledge of the cards in his opponents' hands, he'd sucker them in first by losing a few hands, before going in for the kill with a big pot at stake. The other players were folding as soon as Jason started betting big, not leaving him much in the pot to take with his winning hands. Players were steadily dropping out when they eventually discovered they couldn't make anything back on their own winning hands, since Jason would always fold early.

CHAPTER THIRTY

"Hi, guys. This is Bob. Try to be gentle," Mel said with a grin aimed at the other players as she set up a stack of chips in front of him.

Ben eased into the one empty chair opposite the dealer at the oval table.

"A new face. Haven't seen you in here before," said the older man on his right, giving him a welcoming smile. "You play much, Bob?"

"Yeah, some. Just got off the shuttle last night and looking for a little action. They told me the Asteroid was a good place to start."

"Hmm. Fresh meat. I like that," smirked Jason, from his seat opposite and to the dealer's right.

"So now we're all old friends, let's get on with the game and deal," grunted the younger man sitting across the table on the other side of the dealer. He didn't look up, and a baseball cap shaded his eyes.

The pretty young dealer smiled sweetly at Ben and said, "Your U-Set, sir?"

"Huh? Oh yeah, sorry. I wasn't thinking," Ben replied with an embarrassed look, as he removed his U-Set and placed it on the table beside the drink in front of him. "Must be still a bit woozy from the shuttle. I don't travel too well." He knew perfectly well that no one wore a U-Set while playing — the possibilities for cheating were all too obvious — but he wanted to establish his credentials as a bumbling amateur player from the outset.

Ben made a great play of carefully examining his two hole cards and pretended not to notice the old guy on his right throwing in his blind. "You're the next blind, Bob," the dealer gently prompted him. "OK, err, sorry. So . . . that's 10 - no 20, right?" he said, throwing his chips into the pot. The next player who looked to be some sort of mechanic to judge by his crumpled overalls, went with him and pushed the same number of chips forward.

"I'll raise," said Jason, in a confident tone, dropping several more chips in the pot. The two players to the left of the dealer exchanged a glance, before each folded in turn.

The three cards in the flop gave Ben a pair of Jacks. The player to his right looked back at his cards, shook his head and threw his cards in. Ben playacted a dumb bluff by stroking his chin as he checked back and forth between the two cards in his hand and the three open cards on the table.

"Looks like I'm getting beginner's luck," he said with a beaming smile, as he pushed the chips in to meet Jason's raise.

"Too lucky for me, at any rate," grumbled the mechanic as he dropped his cards on the discard pile.

Ben looked up at Jason. "Seems like it's just you and me then, Mr. . . . ?"

"Call me Jason. And I'm calling you, Bob," he replied, unable to hide a predatory smile.

All the biometrics readings indicate that he's completely confident he has a stronger hand than you at this point, Ben.

'Amazing. I live in hope that someday this magic biometric technology gifted to us by a race of benevolent aliens from the distant stars might even tell me something I don't know, Pandora.'

Ben smiled back at Jason, with all the fake innocence he could summon. "Great!" Ben exclaimed as the turn card was displayed. In fact, the ace of clubs was of no use at all. He still had only a pair.

"Glad you think so, Bob," Jason responded. "Maybe you'd like to raise your bet?"

"Why not? This might just be my lucky night," said Ben, as he pushed a stack of chips into the pot.

"Fine," grinned Jason. "I'll go with that and raise you another hundred."

The four other players who had folded their hands were now taking a renewed interest in the game and occasionally exchanging bemused glances as the stakes mounted. The tension mounted as the last card was dealt — another ace.

"Hmm . . . nice," said Ben, with little conviction in his voice.

"Still feeling lucky, are you, Bob?" smirked Jason.

"Absolutely! In fact, I'll raise you again. So that will cost you 200 to see my hand. How lucky are you feeling now, Jason?" replied

Bob, with all the fake cockiness he could muster.

"There's my 200, Bob. So what do you have?" said Jason, leaning forward, a wide grin almost splitting his face.

Ben's only surprise was how good Jason's hand was. A full house, eights and aces against his two pairs. He must have started with a pair of eights in the hole.

Ben tried to appear as deflated as he would have felt if he had genuinely being attempting such an outrageous bluff. Although with the old Jason, it might even had worked. "Huh," he grunted. "I need another drink. Can I get another one of those Asteroid things?"

'Pandora — any idea how he is seeing the cards yet?'

Sorry, Ben. I'm still working on it. It's as if he's using marked cards, but I've looked at them from every angle and every spectral frequency, so I'm sure that's not the case. There's no sign of any RF emissions, so any information he's getting on the cards must be on some sort of tight-beam line-of-sight channel. I'll get an imp in closer to check it out. You might see a fly or two buzzing around. Try not to swat anything.

Ben's fresh drink arrived. He moved his fingers around the glass, as though lost in thought while examining his cards. As he did so, a stream of invisible nanites migrated from his sleeve and across his hand, coating the inside of the glass. They started their work, slowly converting the alcohol in the drink into its innocuous component parts — water and ethylene.

Ben steadily lost the next few hands, although not on the same scale as the first one. Then he had one winning hand, and true to form, Jason immediately folded. He called for another drink.

Got it! Pandora exclaimed. Really most ingenious. But also, it's very worrying.

'Really? Why?'

It's the dealer's U-Set.

'But she's not wearing it.'

No, but it's on the table in front of her. It's been modified to scan the underside of the cards as they're dealt. Then it relays the images using a tiny low-powered, high frequency display embedded in the set. Jason only has to glance to his left to pick up the images. And it's not visible from any other angle.

'So the dealer's in on the scam, too?'

I can't say. Her U-Set could have been tampered with without her knowledge. But that's not my concern. No human eye could detect the transmission. The frequency and encoding used is pretty much the same as the data embedded in the video sent to Vasquez on the New Dawn, right before they gave him the command to activate the Badger.

'What!' Ben's gripped his drink so hard that the glass jerked in his hand, rattling the ice cubes. 'You mean Jason's a Golem?'

Still can't tell for sure right now. He's certainly not activated. But the technology is very similar. The modifications to the U-Set also appear to be some pretty non-standard nanotech, although I'd have to get hold of it to be sure.

'What the hell can we do? We can't afford to let a Golem go berserk in the middle of a crowded bar. How sure are you?'

I still don't have any way to be 100% certain of a Golem before they activate. You might try asking him to strip, of course, and check for tattoos. Or we grab him. In which case, it's all a big mistake — or he goes Golem and we find out that way. Right now, I'm assuming the worst and moving a bunch of demons into position to grab him if he looks like activating Golem mode.

'You sure you can handle that without smashing up the bar?'

Certainly. I've learned a lot since we captured Leeming. That's not the problem. My concern is that it will blow our cover story if we have to take down a Golem in full public view. I'd rather keep our enemies guessing about the extent of our knowledge and capabilities for as long as possible.

'Hmm... OK. I might have an idea. We know Leeming could go Golem all by himself, without being remotely activated. And this is still Jason, right? I think I can find a way to press his buttons and keep witnesses to a minimum. Just let me know when you're in position to take him down. I'll also need one of your imps to give me a hand.'

Ben had managed to lose the last of his chips simply by playing another ridiculous bluff and over-betting like crazy on his last hand, holding nothing more than a pair.

"Seems you're all out, Bob," Jason gloated. "What bad luck. Thought you had me there for a minute. Maybe you'd like to buy back in for another try?"

Ben blinked, his expression momentarily blank, as if he was trying to make sense of Jason's words through an alcoholic haze. "I know I'd like another drink. Thish one's dead," he slurred, emptying his glass and waving it in the air at a passing waitress. He blinked and shook his head as if to clear it. He looked back at Jason, his eyes unfocused. "OK, then. I'm game. I'll buy back in. Whad'ya say we up the buy-in to 5000? Or is that going to be too exciting for you?"

Jason's eyes widened at the unexpected proposal, before his face lit up with a hungry grin. He licked his lips in anticipation. "Fine by me. No problem at all," he said eagerly. "How about you other guys? You staying in?"

"Too rich for my blood," grumbled the mechanic to Ben's left, getting up from the table. "But I'm done anyhow."

The prospect of a "tourist on tilt" — an amateur player from out of town on a losing streak and playing ever more wildly — meant there was a scramble for the spare seat.

He turned to Mel, who had been watching the last few hands with an expression of increasing bafflement. *I bet she never thought she'd meet a bigger idiot than Jason*, he mused. "Oh hi, Mel. The buy-in has gone up to 5000. You can see I'm good for the money. Hold on though. I do have one condition. This little room is much too crowded. Too many people, too many people." He paused and frowned, looking down as if he'd lost the thread of his thoughts, before looking up at her again with glassy eyes. "Oh, yes. That's it. I want this to be a private game - just me and these fine gentlemen. I'll play better with fewer distractions. Much better. Anyone have a problem with that?"

A few disappointed murmurs came from the audience assembled round the table who had been attracted, like sharks to blood, by the furious rate at which Ben had been losing money.

"If that's what you guys want?" Mel responded, with a quizzical look around the table.

"I don't have a problem with that," replied Jason, unable to keep the eager tone from his voice. "Whatever suits you, Bob. We like to make visitors feel comfortable around here. Don't we, guys?"

The remaining players nodded their assent. *With another 5000 from a sure-fire loser at the table*, Ben mused, *they would probably have agreed to play naked if he'd really insisted.* "Can you catch me another one of those fine drinks of yours before you go, Mel, then close the door on your way out? Thanks." He gave her a bleary smile as she placed a new pile of chips in front of him, then turned back to the table. "So what are we doing about the blinds? Is 50 and 100 too hot for you guys? Means I get to win back my money all the faster," he said, raising his glass and looking straight at Jason.

"Fine, fine. I'm good with that," said Jason nodding vigorously, licking his lips as if he could already taste victory. "We gotta give Bob every chance to win his money back — right guys?"

Ben lost the first two hands. This time he played more cautiously, and folded early both times, as the run of cards was against him. His plan required something a bit special to turn up. But now he had the advantage that one of Pandora's imps was relaying the value of the other players' cards to him. So Ben knew when Jason was dealt a pair of queens, although his body language would have been a clear giveaway. Ben had watched as Jason's eyes widened, then looked around the table with a smug expression, before turning back to check his cards again.

Jason would also know that Ben had been dealt two worthless cards; the four of clubs and the three of spades. Ben went along with the second blind and threw 100 into the pot. Jason was the last to bet and smirked as he raised the stake to 200. The three cards of the flop were dealt; an eight, a king and a queen, giving Jason three queens. He could hardly contain his excitement, fiddling nervously with the pile of chips in front of him. Ben's hand was still worthless. The next best hand around the table was a pair of jacks. Everyone to Ben's right folded.

He made a little pantomime of checking his hand, examining the three cards of the flop placed face up in the center of the table, then checking his cards again. He grabbed his glass and finished his drink. "What the hell!" he exclaimed with a flourish as he picked up a pile of chips. "Let's get things moving. I'll raise 500."

The player to Ben's left immediately folded, shaking his head in wonderment.

"You really must have a very special hand there, err . . . Bob. But I like my hand too. How about I raise you to 1000?" Jason said, as he leaned forward eagerly to throw his chips into the pot.

The single turn card came next. Ben couldn't believe his luck. It was a perfect setup. A king. Now Jason was holding a full house, queens and kings. Ben still had nothing, and Jason knew it. "Well, just look at that," said Ben, assuming a forced smile. "Seems my luck has turned at last. Just you and me now, Jason. Hope you don't mind me taking my money back. I'll tell you what. I'll raise you again to 1500. You still feeling lucky? Eh, Jason?"

Jason blinked back at Ben. Beads of sweat were gathering on his forehead. This was all just too easy. He was holding a full house against nothing at all. How could he lose? The last card could not possibly make any difference. "It's your funeral, Bob. So I'll raise you to 2000. How do you like that?"

The last card - the river card - was dealt face up. A ten of diamonds. Jason could hardly contain his excitement. "Still feeling lucky, Bob?"

"Never felt luckier, Jason. I'm all in," Ben replied, pushing every one of his remaining chips into the pot.

'Get ready, Pandora. Any minute now. And I hope your imp has worked its magic trick.'

All set and ready to go, Ben.

Jason was breathing heavily now. Ben could see a little vein pulsing rapidly in his temple. "Then I'll see you, Bob. There's 10000 in the pot and it's all mine," he said eagerly, throwing down his cards to reveal his full house. As he lurched across the table to sweep up the pot, Ben grabbed his arm in a vice-like grip, pushing against the sleeve of Jason's shirt as he did so, seemingly by accident. The button on the cuff popped off the flimsy material, allowing the sleeve to ride up, exposing the elaborate features of an intricate tattoo extending up his arm.

"Don't you think it would be polite to see my cards first, Jason? After all, you did pay to see them, didn't you?" Ben growled at Jason, the unaccustomed tone provoking a look of alarm in his eyes.

As Jason watched, with his gaze transfixed on the cards, Ben slowly turned his hole cards over with his spare hand. King . . . and king, giving him four kings in total and beating Jason's full house.

Jason's eyes bulged as his face turned bright red. "What the hell! . . . but all you had was a three and a four! Where the fuck did those kings come from? You must have switched them!"

"Really, Jason? Is that so?" Ben retorted with cold contempt in his voice, still pinning Jason's arm firmly to the table. "Then would you like to tell us how it is you know exactly what my hole cards were? I'm sure we'd all be very interested. And while you're at it, maybe you could tell these fine gentlemen how long you've been playing and taking their money knowing what their hole cards are, too, hmm?"

Jason's face was now turning purple, as he tried again to pull his arm away from Ben's iron grip. "I'll . . . I'll kill you, you bastard!" he screamed, as with a massive effort, powered by a final surge of strength, he toppled backwards. As he fell, the light faded from his eyes, and after a single violent convulsion, he lay unmoving on the floor behind his seat.

CHAPTER THIRTY-ONE

BEN KNEW Jason was dead before he hit the floor. There had been a single sharp spike of electrical activity centered on his head, before his biometric readings had all dropped to zero. The player next to Jason bent down to check the body, putting two fingers to the side of his neck to check for a pulse.

He looked up at the dealer, and shook his head, his eyes wide with shock. "Looks like he's dead. Heart attack, maybe?"

The dealer put her hand to her mouth to stifle a gasp and backed away, a look of horror on her face.

'Pandora — what the hell happened? I was sure he was going Golem — then he just dropped dead. It was too fast even for a heart attack. I never wanted to kill the poor bastard.'

I'm as puzzled as you are, Ben. My best guess at this point is that his Golem nanotech somehow went badly wrong. We need to examine him. I'm sending a team from the Coroner's office to pick up the body. Let's try to keep a lid on this for now.

"What's going on in here?" Mel ran into the room, then stopped, staring down at Jason's lifeless body in dismay. She must have been monitoring the game through the surveillance system.

The man in the baseball cap hadn't moved from his seat. He looked down at Jason lying on the floor to his right. "Seems like he had a heart attack when Bob here caught him cheating," he said, looking back up at Mel and not sounding overly concerned. "Can't say I'm too sorry — he took a lot of money off me."

"Is this something you did, Bob — or whoever you are?" Her bright blue eyes were fixed accusingly on Ben, made even brighter by the pale color of her face.

"I suggest you call the Coroner's office, Mel, and ask everyone present to remain here until they send someone over to examine the body. And I'd like a private chat while we're waiting."

Mel blinked in surprise at Ben's calm demeanor, and apparent lack of inebriation. "The only private chat you'll be getting is with my security staff if you don't tell me who the hell you are, Bob. As for involving the Coroner's office, that won't be necessary. The poor man just died of natural causes. I'll have his body delivered to his family. I'm sure that nobody else here wants to make a fuss and get involved in a lot of paperwork," she said as she scanned the room with narrowed eyes, defying anyone to disagree.

"Who am I, Mel? I'll tell you what. I'll tell you my real name if you tell me yours. How about that for a deal? Oh, but wait a minute. I think I already know yours."

Ben flashed the name 'Sogaard' into her U-Set.

Mel's pale face turned even paler, as her mouth dropped open in shock. Her eyes widened further as she realized that Ben was not wearing his U-Set, so should have had no way to send the message. "How . . . how did you . . ."

"Now how about that private chat?"

"We can go to my office," she said, her voice strained from the tension in her throat.

She turned back towards the dealer, trying to speak in a more confident tone. "Carole. Please keep everyone here until I get back. All drinks are on the house. I won't be long."

"I don't know who you are, Mister, but I do know one thing. You have just two minutes to explain yourself. My security team is standing by to take you down. If you try any move I don't like, you'll end up like Jason."

"Oh, my," Ben replied, shaking his head with an expression of exaggerated regret. "Jeez, you so are touchy. I was really hoping we wuz gonna to be friends. You really do give a new twist to the phrase 'drop-dead gorgeous'. But not to worry; I wasn't planning to invite you out on a date."

Ben put his hands up to interrupt Mel as she started to respond. "OK, OK. You asked me to explain myself, so I will," he said as he glared back at her, dropping his fake accent. "I'll explain very clearly, Ms. Sogaard. I'm here under the direct authority of the Chairman's office at the CAA. Your security team won't be doing anything because you can't communicate with them. You're already facing some very serious charges, such as keeping an illegal AI in your basement. That alone should be enough to get you locked up for a long, long time."

He saw her eyes flicking up in her U-Set as she tried to find a working channel. Her knuckles went white as she clutched the arms of her chair more tightly, realizing she was completely cut off.

"You've been working with your father who heads up the AICB office on Ceres, and possibly your mother too, back on Earth at the DGS. Our best guess right now is that you are playing some role in the DGS attacks on the Habitat, or perhaps you're acting outside the DGS structure in support of a sleeper cell under the control of the Section. So we might add the capital crime of 'accessory to attempted genocide' to the charges, unless you would like to start cooperating right now with this investigation." Ben's voice rose in anger as he leaned forward to bang his knuckles on her desk. "Is that clear enough for you?"

Mel convulsed forward, her eyes moistening as she grabbed the edge of the desk for support. Yet she was half laughing, half gasping as she choked back her tears. "Oh, my God. I thought you must be one of those animals from the Section. You actually imagine I could be working for those monsters? My family have spent every day for the last several years working against them." She shook her head, then sat back in her seat as she wiped her eyes. "Can you prove you really are who you say you are? If you can, I'll tell you everything I know. I need your help, and we're short of time."

Seems like she's telling the truth, Ben. Biometrics seem conclusive. I can't wait to find out what's going on. I'm finding some worrying stuff on the AI, but I still don't have the full picture.

"Maybe this will convince you." Ben absorbed the nanoskin from his face back into the neck of his nanosuit, allowing his true features to appear.

Mel almost jumped out of her seat, holding her hand up to her mouth, as her already pale face turned white in shock. "What the hell? How did you do that? You're . . . Ben Hamilton?" she exclaimed, leaning forward and peering into his face for a closer look.

"That's right," Ben replied, relaxing a little as he came to terms with the fact that Mel wasn't one of the bad guys. "I hope you're not too disappointed. I look a lot more heroic on the VREx's."

She opened and closed her mouth a couple of times before she was able to speak. "But how . . . how is that possible? You looked completely different as Bob. You sounded different."

"We can talk about that later. You said we don't have much time. What did you mean by that?"

"It seems you already know something about the Section. My mother heads up the DGS crypto security laboratory. That's allowed her to build a back-door access into all their secure communications channels, including between DGS and the Section. She's also set up a hidden private channel to my father here on Ceres. She's been monitoring their activities for years, building up a profile on them, tracing their contacts and operatives, trying to identify the Integrants —"

"Integrants?" Ben queried.

"Don't you know about them? They're monsters, massively strong —"

"Ah — right. We call them Golems. Yes, we've already come across a couple of them. Tough little buggers. In fact, we identified Jason as one. He seemed to be in the process of activating when he keeled over. Do you have any idea why that happened?"

She frowned and pursed her lips. "I'm sorry? Jason — an Integrant, err ... Golem? No, I never guessed. Are you sure?"

"Pretty sure. That's why we're keen to get the body into the care of the Coroner so we can examine it. But that's for later. What is it exactly that's so urgent?"

"Yes, of course. The Section's long-term strategy has been to take power from the Families in each citadel by infiltrating and controlling the DGS structure. That buffoon Da Silva is just their puppet. He really believes he's in charge, now he's the Chairman of the Global Security Council, but they're only using him as a figurehead. Yet something has changed over the last few months. People used to disappear for a few weeks, then reappear as Integrants. What you call Golems. Now they still disappear — but don't return. We've seen other changes too, but what matters most right now is the change in policy towards Ceres. Previously, they wanted to capture it and take its resources for themselves. Now it seems all they want is to destroy it."

"And they very nearly succeeded," Ben replied, his jaw tightening as he recalled the struggle with Vasquez. "We didn't announce it, but the New Dawn tried to wipe out the Habitat with a nuclear-armed Badger. Fortunately, we were able to stop it in time."

"Well, yes, I'm aware of that. My mother was monitoring the communications with the New Dawn during the attack. But that's not the problem," she replied, in a more urgent tone. "They're planning another attack on the Habitat, and it's only a matter of days before it goes ahead."

"Hold on. What sort of attack? They no longer have a way to get here from Earth —"

"No, No!" Mel cut him off as she jumped out of her seat, a desperate appeal blazing in her eyes. "They don't need to. The Section already has a team operating here. All I can tell you is that they're waiting for the delivery of some final component required to carry out the attack. It probably sounds crazy, but keeping track of their activities is the reason we set up the bar.

"My parents thought I'd be safer on Ceres than back on Earth, but I still wanted to help them fight these monsters. So we gave the Section a place where they had the security to move people and supplies into the Habitat. That way we could monitor exactly what was going on. They still believe I'm working for them.

"Our great plan started to go wrong when their objective switched to the destruction of the Habitat. Even then, we imagined we would have plenty of time to stop them. Now I'm not so sure. We still haven't seen the final component. It may have already been delivered. In that case, we only have a couple of days left. My mother was supposed to tell us when to expect the courier, but she communicates through my father, and I've not heard from him in the last two weeks."

Ben rubbed his head in confusion. "But I don't understand the nature of the threat. Is it a weapon of some sort? There's no way they could transport nuclear materials through our border security. And they would condemn themselves to death if they destroyed the Habitat."

"I'm sorry, I wish I could tell you," Mel replied, "but that's not the sort of information we have access to here. We just monitor people and packages passing through and occasionally pick up bits of conversation. You need to speak to my father if you want more details."

"Well, we're pretty sure you had some sort of courier in the bar last night. Do you remember a guy called Boris Kramer?"

"Boris Kramer . . . hmm, that name rings a bell." She nodded, looking thoughtful as the memory came back to her. "Oh yes, he asked about getting into the poker game last night. Just like you. You think he was the courier? Then we can check the video to see who he spoke to—"

"Thanks, but we already looked. He didn't speak to anyone—except you and the barman—and there's no evidence he passed any sort of package on to anyone."

"I won't ask how you accessed our video files. Right now I'm beyond caring."

Ben smiled at her. "We have access to a lot more than you might imagine. How would you like to speak to your father?"

Mel's eyes widened in shock. "What? Really? How—how can you do that?"

"Just give me a few minutes and we'll set it up," Ben smiled. "How does that sound?"

'OK, Pandora. I assume we can set up a call between Mel and Bernt Sogaard. But let's check his story out first and see if it tallies with what his daughter's been telling us. I've asked her to take a walk round the bar, so I can chat to him from here.'

That won't be difficult at all, Ben. We're still in control of the DGS AI, so we can do what we like.

'Did you get Jason's body out OK?'

No problem there. The coroner has also invited the other players to 'assist with her enquiries', so I'm hoping we can keep a lid on the situation for a little while longer.

'I'm still puzzled by our supposed courier, this Boris Kramer guy. He must have done something we didn't spot. I'm betting it was at the poker game. Otherwise, why would he have been there? And with Jason in the game? That's too much of a coincidence. Mel seems to think we're short of time, if Kramer was the courier for this mysterious final component, and the handover has already happened. I think we should pick him up now, rather than waiting.'

OK, I'll get a team in place. We'll still have time to talk with Bernt before we give them the go-ahead. Perhaps he can give us a better idea of the nature of the threat. If Kramer passed something on, it had to have been quite small. I was watching him all the time. He didn't even get a drink from the bar, he just swigged water from a bottle. But I'd swear nothing changed hands.

'Something small? Wait a minute, that gives me an idea. Can you review the poker game with the courier again? There had to be a reason he was there. Keep an eye on the poker chips and count them carefully.'

OK, I see where you're going with this. Give me a couple of minutes.

'You've been rather quiet about what you've found in the bootleg AI in the basement, Pandora. Surely we can get more information now you've taken it over?'

Mostly, it supports what Mel has been saying. I've been keeping quiet because I've run into a little problem. You remember I said that that there were some big quantum-encrypted files? I can't get in. At least, not in a timescale that would be useful to us.

'Wow! Really? You're seriously telling me that there are limitations to your omnipotent alien intelligence? I find that hard to believe. Encouraging, of course, from the point of view of us dumb humans, but still most unlikely. What's the problem?'

First, the AI doesn't have the decryption key. Second, the quantum-encrypted files need a physical key to unlock them. Given time, I could probably crack it, but they're almost certainly booby-trapped, so I'd have to be extra careful to avoid them self-destructing. It's most ingenious. Sogaard and his wife must make a very effective team, if they set this up. The bottom line is I don't have enough time to crack it safely. Let's hope that Mel or Bernt can tell us where to find the key. Did you try checking her desk—

Got it!

'What, you found the key? That was quick—'

No, not that. I finally spotted the handover. You were right. Boris didn't talk much, except he mentioned that this was his first time on Ceres, and it was named after the goddess of the harvest. Jason looked startled, then responded by making a feeble joke that he was looking forward to harvesting some more chips. That must be how they identified each other. Five minutes later, there was one poker chip too many in the pot that Jason won. Boris could easily have slipped it into the stack in front of him without being spotted on the cameras. I assume it was specially marked so Jason could pick it out later. You really do have some good ideas, Ben. I might just keep you around as a pet once I've carried out my secret plot to enslave humanity.

'Yes, Pandora, how terribly funny.'

Funny, Ben? Funny? Why do you think I'm joking? Surely you must be aware that AIs don't have a sense of humor?

'Right. Now let's engage serious mode and start thinking about where Jason took that chip. I assume you can track him with the

Habitat surveillance system to see where he might have dropped it off? Unless he passed it to yet another contact in the bar—we also need to check that possibility. At least we have some idea what we're looking for now. And whatever it is, it must be tiny. Does that give us any clue as to the nature of the threat?'

I've already run a trace on Jason's movements last night. He left the bar at eight and went straight to the Base Station. Unfortunately, that's around the same time as the evening shift heads off to work in the caverns. The Station cameras don't give full coverage, and I lost him in the crowd. I'm guessing he changed his clothes to blend in with the shift workers heading down. Once he was on the rail system down to the caverns, he might have ended up anywhere. There are very few cameras in the caverns and tunnels, and they run for thousands of kilometers.

'You're saying we can't track him when he's in the caverns? And we can't ask him where he went because he's dead. So how the hell do we find out where that chip ended up?'

That will be a problem, unless the courier can tell us something.

'So you're picking him up now?'

The team is in place, waiting for my signal. He can't get away. But let's talk to Sogaard first and find out what he can tell us. I imagine he'll be quite shocked to hear from you. According to the DGS AI, they've held him under virtual house arrest since you last met him. They even blocked his calls a couple of weeks back, so he hasn't spoken to anyone outside the building since then. They've allowed him access to news channels, so he knows about the New Dawn and your heroic role in its capture. OK, he's answering your call now.

"Hello, Director Sogaard. This is Ben Hamilton."

"Ah, Mr. Hamilton. This is unexpected. I didn't expect to hear from you again. Or anybody, really. How were you able to get through to me? I don't really think I should be talking to you." Sogaard's eyes darted around nervously as he spoke. "If my . . . colleagues find out, there may be . . . consequences."

Ben was shocked by Sogaard's appearance. He looked even more stooped than when he had last seen him. He was much thinner, almost skeletal; his skin had a gray pallor and was drawn tightly over the bones of his face, emphasizing his sunken cheeks.

"I can promise you they will be completely unaware of this conversation, Director. You are in no danger. If you wish, I can get you out of the DGS building to a place where you will feel safer—"

Sogaard's eyes widened in alarm. "No! I can't leave. You don't understand the situation, Mr. Hamilton. I no longer fear for myself, it's the safety of others that concern me. And if this conversation is being monitored—"

"I understand your concern, Director, but this conversation cannot be monitored. If you'd like to check, just ask the DGS AI. To put your mind at rest, I'll give you full access to its functions. I'm calling you from the Asteroid Bar, where your AI system skills are very much in evidence, so you will have no difficulty in verifying that we can speak in complete confidence. And I assure you that your daughter is perfectly safe."

"My . . . daughter?" Sogaard sat up straight for a moment, before looking over his shoulder, then slumping back in his chair. He shook his head, avoiding Ben's eyes. "But she's on Earth . . ."

"We both know where your daughter is presently located, Director," Ben replied, trying to keep a tone of frustration from creeping into his voice. "Now we have a lot to discuss, and, according to your daughter, only a short amount of time in which to act. Now please check your level of access with the AI. That should put your mind at rest."

"Yes . . . yes, I see," Sogaard muttered, as his eyes flicked up to check another channel in his U-Set. "Jezebel, confirm my system status and tell me if my conversation with Mr. Hamilton is completely secure?"

"You now have Supervisor status, Director, and your conversation with Ben Hamilton is entirely secure. There will be no record in the system of any discussion."

"How . . . how on Earth is that possible?" Sogaard shook his head and let out a long sigh. "So it seems I must trust you. I suppose even that faint hope is better than what I had before you called. Yes, Mr. Hamilton, you're correct. There is little time. You need to intercept a courier from Earth who arrived on last night's shuttle—"

"We've already identified the courier, Director. Unfortunately, we believe the handover has already taken place. Do you know what he was transporting?"

"Not exactly, Mr. Hamilton, I'm sorry. But I know enough about it to understand the grave threat to the lives of everyone in the Habitat. This is terrible. You must stop the Initiator getting into the hands of the Section's operatives here, because if you don't they will kill us all—"

Sogaard had the annoying habit of looking down at his hands whenever he was most worried, so he didn't immediately notice that Ben was trying to interrupt him. "Hold on, Director. Hold on. Just a minute. What is this 'Initiator'?"

"I'm really not sure," he replied, examining his hands again as he rubbed them together. "It's the second component of some sort of binary weapon they're planning to deploy and kill everyone in the Habitat. They call it 'Project Harvest'. The full details of how it works are in one of the files in the database at the Asteroid. I do know they estimate it will take roughly two days to deploy the final weapon once they get the Initiator."

"So how do we unlock these files, Director?"

"You'll need the hardware quantum encryption key. I keep it with me. It's in the signet ring I wear," Sogaard said, holding his hand up for Ben to see.

Ben suppressed the impulse to roll his eyes to the heavens. "It would have been much more convenient if you'd left a copy of the key with your daughter, Director."

"Those files would have damned us both if the contents were exposed," Sogaard replied, with an emphatic shake of his head. "And I couldn't keep them on the system here, they'd stand out like a sore thumb. This way, there's no evidence against either of us unless we both get picked up by the DGS, and they'd still have to identify the key. Any attempt to unlock the files without the key would trigger their destruction. As it is, the DGS are completely unaware of my daughter's involvement or even her identity, and I'm only under suspicion."

"Is that why have you been confined to your apartment? What do they suspect?"

"No, not that. I had one too many fights with Oscar, who decided I might be a security risk." Sogaard raised his head, looking Ben straight in the eye for once. "Amusingly, our final disagreement was about you, Mr. Hamilton. I got wind of his true plans concerning you and Frank Adler. When I tried to object, he had me put under house arrest. Then Oscar disappeared, and now everyone just ignores me. Do you have any idea what happened to him?"

"Oscar is no longer with us, Director. The Section had him killed."

"He's dead? But . . . but why would they kill him?"

"You might like to ask Jezebel to show you the video that we sent to his uncle. Chairman Da Silva was most upset. In our defense, we had no intention of getting him killed. Unfortunately, we underestimated the reach of the Section here in the Habitat. I can assure you that we won't make the same mistake twice."

"I can't say I'm sorry he's dead," Sogaard said with a sigh. "He was a most unpleasant man."

"We need to get you out of the DGS building as soon as possible. I'll send a team to extract you—"

"No, we can't do that, Mr. Hamilton," Sogaard interrupted. He leaned forward, alarm written across his face. "If I leave, then I'll be condemning my wife to death. You may not be aware of what is happening right now back on Earth. A lot has changed over the last few months. The Section no longer seems to care who they kill or how much damage they do to the infrastructure on which humanity depends. They appear to have lost their minds.

"You know they tried to destroy the Habitat with the Badger attack. Thank God you were able to stop that." Sogaard closed his eyes and put his hand to his forehead, before looking up again at Ben. "What you probably don't know is that they also appear to be steadily eliminating the senior staff of the DGS. My wife has only survived this long to guarantee my good behavior. If I disappear, I'm sure they will immediately add my wife to the donor list—"

"Donor list?"

"The list of DGS people who get 'disappeared'. It seems to be connected somehow with their new Transcendent program."

"That doesn't sound good. I haven't come across that name either. What can you tell me?"

"Unfortunately, there is little information on the subject. As far as I can tell, it replaces the Integrant program which seems to have been terminated. They view the remaining Integrants as expendable. My wife doesn't have the full picture; she has to be very careful not to get caught monitoring the Section's secret communication channels.

"There's a lot more information in the encrypted files, which she intercepted as they were transmitted to the Section's main research labs. I glanced through them, but the technology they describe appears terribly complex and there was hardly anything I could understand."

"Then perhaps we can arrange a way to collect the ring from you until we—"

Sogaard was looking down again, rubbing his hands together furiously. Ben could see tears forming in his eyes. "I'm sorry, Mr. Hamilton. I'm really sorry. I cannot remove the ring. Another security measure, you see. If I were captured, and the ring removed, or if I were killed . . . the encryption key is destroyed, leaving no trace. I was only trying to protect my daughter . . ." He paused to wipe his eyes, now welling with tears.

Ben kept his face impassive, but gave an inward groan. He couldn't help feeling some sympathy for Sogaard, but his frustration at the situation Sogaard's elaborate precautions had created was winning out. This time, he failed to prevent his eyes lifting towards the ceiling.

'Pandora—do you have any clever ideas? Can we use your alien magic to teleport him out of there, leaving a copy behind so nobody knows he's gone?'

There's good news and bad news, Ben. The good news is, yes, there is a way my alien magic can make Sogaard vanish from his apartment without being spotted.

'OK, and the bad news?'

You get to be the one using the alien magic.

Ben snorted and shook his head.'Why does that not surprise me?'

He turned back to Sogaard, still slumped in his chair, studying his hands and rubbing them together obsessively. "Director? Director Sogaard?"

It was a few seconds before Sogaard looked up, his red-rimmed eyes reluctant to meet Ben's gaze.

"Director. I believe I may have found a solution to our problem. If I could get you out of the building without anyone noticing, and we faked your continued presence in your apartment over the next day or so while we get your wife to safety, would you be happy with that?"

Sogaard's eyes widened, and his mouth dropped open in shock. "Can you do that? Well, of course, but how is it possible?"

"Leave it with me for now. I'll set it up and be back to you later today. In the meantime, how would you like to talk to your daughter?"

CHAPTER THIRTY-TWO

BEN WAS SITTING in a corner of the Asteroid Bar, waiting for news of the courier, when Pandora's voice whispered in his ear.

He's dead. The courier is dead.

'Damn it! How did that happen? I thought you were watching the apartment? How could anyone get to him?'

He's been dead since last night. We almost lost a couple of our own people when they entered the apartment. Seems all the door handles inside the apartment were coated with nerve poison. Even the fridge door. It was very fast acting. I had to drop imps onto anyone who came into direct contact with the poison to neutralize it, or they would have been dead within minutes.

It looks as if the Section is still one jump ahead of us and tidying up any loose ends. They must have planned all along to kill the courier right after he passed his package to Jason. Which also puts Jason's death in a new light. Those were our only two links to the location of the Initiator, and presumably the Section's team.

'Do we know how Jason died yet?'

No, but I'm sure it wasn't nerve poison. He was brain dead before he even hit the floor. I expect the results of the autopsy within the next couple of hours.

'So we still know nothing about the nature or location of the threat we face, except that everyone in the Habitat will be dead in two days from now—probably less?'

That's a fair summary. We need to update Frank on the situation. I also want to see what's in those files that Sogaard was talking about. That might give us a clearer picture of this Project Harvest, and perhaps even a clue about the nature of the weapon they plan to use.

'We need Sogaard for that. Let's implement this mysterious plan of yours to get him out of the building as soon as possible. We also need to locate his wife and get her somewhere safe. We can talk to Yasmin about using the Resistance network. With our control of the AIs back on Earth, that shouldn't be too difficult.'

We can discuss that when we meet Frank and the rest of the team. We also need to put our heads together and come up with some way to track down these Section people really quickly.

"Good work, Ben. That at least gives us something to work on. We must get Sogaard out of the building," Frank said. "We need to see what's in those files. I'm guessing he'll also want some credible assurance that we have a viable plan to extract his wife from wherever she is." He looked towards his daughter. "Kay? Does Pandora have any information that might help us?"

"I can tell you exactly where she is, Dad," Kay shrugged. "She's in Greeley, in the DGS building. I checked with the DGS AIs before the meeting."

"Hmm. That's fortunate," Frank replied, narrowing his eyes and frowning as he considered the possibilities. "Karla's in Greeley. I'm sure she would like nothing better than an excuse to raid the DGS building. OK. Let's do it," he said as he thumped the table. "I gave Da Silva the impression that we had a temporary truce, but after these latest developments, I no longer care what he thinks. And if what we're being told about the Section eliminating DGS personnel is true, it hardly matters. Yasmin, can you set up an extraction mission right away? Tell Karla there's no need to be gentle—time is of the essence in this case. Just make sure nobody in her team gets identified by the Section. We don't want to set any of them up as a target."

Ben looked across the table at Kay. "Can Karla's team use the same nanoskin technology I used in the Asteroid Bar, to disguise their faces? I know they could wear masks, but if we could fake the faces of DGS personnel, that would help them penetrate the building more easily. It would also cause the maximum confusion when the DGS see they're being attacked by their own people. We might even give the Section something to think about."

"No big problem, and I like that idea, Ben," Kay replied with a smile. "I'll get Pandora to download an update to the SmartBelts. Scanner will love it."

"So how do we extract Bernt Sogaard without anyone noticing?" Frank queried, turning to his daughter. "That sounds like a job for you and Pandora, Kay."

"It would be better to use Ben for that job, Dad. Sogaard knows him well and seems to trust him. He's nervous enough as it is. If some little girl he's never seen before turns up, he might just flip out. And until we get to know Sogaard better, I'd rather keep me out of the picture. And it's the perfect job for our action hero—"

"Thank you so much, Kay. I can hardly wait to find out what you and your AI sidekick have in mind." Ben groaned inwardly as he gave Kay a tight-lipped smile, before turning back to Frank. "Pandora has devised some ingenious plan which, like most of her crazy ideas, involves me. Unfortunately, we can't shoot our way in and back out again without endangering Sogaard's wife. And it seems that teleportation is not an option. So, somehow, I walk into the DGS building, head up to the top floor, release Sogaard from his apartment, walk out again back through the building with him in tow . . . and all without being seen. So maybe Pandora has some way to make me and Sogaard invisible?"

"Not quite, Ben, but almost. You should have learned to trust us by now," Kay responded with a wide grin, fluttering her eyelashes and placing both hands over her heart for emphasis. "We just need to put a little more nanotech magic into your SmartBelt. That, plus a few minutes of training, and you should be good to go."

Ben grunted as he landed on the rooftop of the DGS building more heavily than he expected, stumbling forwards before regaining his balance.

"Sorry. You OK? You didn't need to jump down. Just let the roof come to you. You're flying about in a big spinning tub, so it's not like Earth's gravity; you don't really have weight, you only have velocity."

Ben looked up at Kay, and the great black wings which seemed to sprout from her back, forming a dark canopy to conceal him from view from the taller buildings surrounding them. The underside of the wings were studded with countless tiny sparkling points of light, designed to mirror the overhead display of the stars of the Milky Way projected from the central spine of the Habitat.

He had to admire her attention to detail. In the unlikely event of some casual observer of the simulated heavens wandering the streets after midnight, they wouldn't see the silhouette of dark wings soaring across the sky. This still seemed like her craziest idea yet, and Ben felt a tight ball of apprehension knotting in his stomach. He wasn't worried so much about his own safety, but they'd only need one piece of bad luck and the whole operation might blow up, which would result in disastrous consequences for both Sogaard and his wife. And no Sogaard, no key; no key, no information.

Kay crouched down next to him. "I've given Sogaard a heads-up, so he's expecting you," she whispered. "His balcony is a short climb down over the edge here. You good to go?"

"Never better," Ben replied, his voice suggesting a confidence he didn't feel. "I hope your new nanotech does its magic as promised. I still can't believe it will work."

"Trust me. Have I ever let you down before?"

"No, but the first time you do is also likely to be the last time, if those DGS goons spot me and start shooting. Asking questions first is not their style. I can run but Sogaard can't. And he doesn't even have the benefit of a nanosuit."

She shook her head. "Don't worry. You'll be fine. I'll be tracking you right through the building. You'll be in the basement in less than 10 mins, and I'll be waiting for you in the utilities access space under the street. I'll just make a hole in the basement wall when you get there. The AI will keep any security patrols away from your route. Good luck."

Kay folded her wings and dropped towards the street below, the fabric of her nanosuit now perfectly mimicking the appearance of the surrounding buildings.

Ben shook his head, his heart still pounding, and not just from the excitement of the flight from the Penthouse terrace of the Adler-Lee building. Extruding grippers from his feet and forearms, he lowered himself over the edge of the roof and down the side of the building towards the narrow balcony 20 feet below.

He looked around quickly to see if he'd been spotted, but the grippers were completely silent, and there were no lights on in the building opposite. He retracted the grippers into the fabric of his nanosuit and dropped the last couple of feet. He tapped on the glass door before sliding it back. Sogaard had already unlocked it.

"So it really is you, Mr. Hamilton," Sogaard gasped, his eyes wide with surprise. "Chairman Adler informed me of your plan to get me out of the building, but I didn't really understand how it could work. I still only half believed him until now."

Ben slipped into the room and slid the door shut. "It should be perfectly straightforward, Director. The most important thing is to follow my lead and stay as close as possible. We will simply walk out of here and head down to the basement. We'll be playing a few tricks on your colleagues, but I won't have time to stop and explain."

Sogaard frowned at Ben and shook his head. "I still don't understand, Mr. Hamilton," he replied, his bafflement evident. "The only way out from the top floors is through the main control room directly below us, then into the reception area. It's a big, open office. People will still be working at their desks, as well as a full security detail, even at this time of night. We can't go through there. And I can't climb down from the balcony. I'm afraid I'm not quite as fit as I used to be."

"No need for that, Director. Your escape is all mapped out. I promise you we'll simply walk through the control room and enter an elevator in reception. No one will notice us. Then we head down to the basement." Ben looked directly into Sogaard's eyes and put a hand on his shoulder, injecting as much confidence into his voice as he could muster—certainly more than he felt. "Just remember: stay as close as possible and don't say a word or make eye contact with anyone. And keep right behind me. Is that understood?"

Sogaard held his gaze. "Chairman Adler tells me that Helga will be taken to a place of safety within the next few hours, Mr. Hamilton. Can you swear to me this is true?"

"I promise you that everything is in position to rescue your wife, Director. I know the people who have been tasked with this mission, and I know that they will not fail. They are the same people who Chairman Adler trusted to get his own wife out of Greeley when Da Silva was holding her hostage. You may recall from the news clips just how furious he was when his goons raided the Adler Tower and found it empty. I can assure you that we have a far greater level of capability than the DGS realizes. You'll be talking to her within the next few hours, Director. I guarantee it."

Or we'll both be dead, at which point my promises won't matter so much anyway, he thought cynically.

"Very well, Mr. Hamilton. I believe you. Please lead the way."

"This is the only tricky part, Director," Ben said, facing Sogaard and holding him firmly by the arms to steady him. He could feel him shivering. *We're totally screwed if he goes to pieces halfway through*, he realized. "When I give the signal, we will go through this door into the control room, then walk steadily towards the reception area on the far side, and get into an elevator. Keep your head down and stay right behind me. Whatever you do, don't speak or make any noise. I know this must seem rather strange, but no one will pay us any attention."

Sogaard's breath was now coming in short gulps. "Are you using some sort of . . . gas?"

"I can't explain right now, Director. Please, just trust me. Now excuse me, but I need to find out when we're clear to go."

Sogaard just nodded, his eyes glazed and a frown deepening across his pale features.

'How does it look, Jezebel?'

One of the administrative staff is walking back to her desk. You should be good to go any minute now. I just want to make sure no one has eyes on the door as you come through.

Seconds ticked by, then Jezebel gave Ben the signal to go, as she silently overrode the security lock on the door.

Carefully, Ben pushed against the door and started to go through, then glanced back to make sure Sogaard was still following. His tight lips showed the strain he was feeling, but he was able to give Ben a nod as they moved into the room. Ben was following Pandora's instructions to the letter. He kept his eyes focused on the door to the reception area on the opposite side of the room. Halfway across, he realized he was holding his breath, hardly believing this could possibly work. He let his breath out, slowly and silently, and risked a furtive glance around the room.

There were only a handful of people at their desks so late at night, and most sat staring vacantly at their screens with glazed expressions. One was aimlessly examining his U-Set which sat on the desk in front of him. Another held a cup halfway to her lips, a look of puzzlement in her eyes. She showed no understanding of the object in her hand.

"I call it the 'Daze'," Kay had told him with a smile. "If you can think of a better word for it, let me know. As long as they have nothing to attract their attention and break the spell, everyone within roughly a ten-meter range of the signal from your SmartBelt will just remain in a trance state. Better still, they'll have no memory of the time they were 'Dazed'.

"The one weakness is that the signal won't penetrate through walls or doors. So you have to make sure that there isn't anybody outside the control room about to walk in. They'd probably spot you and raise the alarm before the Daze could take effect. Also, don't bump into anyone or they'll probably wake up. So check with Jezebel where everyone is located and also make sure that no one is watching the door before you enter. It's the poor relation of what I did to Oscar's brain when he thought his gun had turned into a bunch of scorpions. But you'd need Pandora's special nanotech to do anything fancy like that."

After what seemed like several minutes, but was nearer to twenty seconds, they arrived the door to the reception area.

"Hold on," warned Jezebel. "There's a guard coming your way. I suggest you get behind the door as it opens. He's almost there."

Ben guided Sogaard to the side of the door and leaned back against the wall. Beads of sweat were breaking out on his forehead, and it wasn't only because of the elevated temperature in the building. The door swung open, and the guard walked a few paces into the room. He clearly had no idea that there were two very nervous people concealed by the open door right behind him. A vacant expression slowly claimed his features as he gradually stumbled to a halt, his reason for entering the room now entirely forgotten.

Ben guided Sogaard gently through the door as they crept behind the guard's back, slinking slowly into the reception area as the Daze took effect. The few remaining staff sat gazing at their screens with unseeing eyes. He walked steadily to the bank of elevators, a door opening silently as they arrived.

'Thank you, Jezebel,' he whispered.

They stepped in. As the doors closed behind them, Sogaard gave a muffled groan and stumbled against Ben. "That was unbelievable. I . . . I cannot understand how you did that," he gasped and put his hand up to his face. "I'm sorry, but I need a few moments to get my breath back."

Ben supported him as they descended to the basement. They exited the elevator, and Sogaard slumped against the wall of the dimly lit corridor, still panting heavily.

"We're almost there, Director," Ben said, breathing a sigh of relief as the tension started to drain from his body. "We'll just take a short break so you can catch your breath. We're quite safe down here. Don't worry, I'll have you out of the building in just a couple of minutes."

"But of course I still love you, sweetheart. You know I do," he said with all the sincerity he could fake, as he gazed with synthetic affection into her tearful eyes.

"I'm just so tired of sneaking around, Alan," she sniffed, pouting as she regarded his face, desperately seeking confirmation of the truth of his words in his eyes. "I don't want us to have to hide in dark corners every time I want to see you."

"Sweetheart, be reasonable," he replied, shaking his head, as he assumed a concerned yet caring expression. "I'd lose my job if anyone found out we were seeing each other. This storage room is the only place in the entire building without a camera."

"I want more than a dingy cubby hole at the bottom of a stairwell the next time we're together, Alan," she replied in a sharper tone. "We're leaving for Earth tomorrow. What are you going to tell your wife when we get there?"

"Tell my wife?" he responded, his eyes widening as he struggled to keep a note of panic from creeping into his voice. "Err . . . don't worry about that, my darling. Once we're back on Earth, everything will be different." His eyes darted towards the door. "Now I have to be back on duty soon, so I'd better get going."

"But we've hardly had ten minutes together this time," she complained. "When will I see you again?"

"Look, sweetheart, be reasonable," he said, his lips maintaining a rigid smile as he moved her gently to one side and stepped towards the door. "I need to go now and switch my U-Set back on, or they might start wondering where I am. I'll call you, I promise. I promise. Now I'll leave first, then you can follow a couple of minutes later. OK?"

"Oh, Alan. I really do love you so much," she exclaimed, her eyes filling with tears again as she tried to grab him for a farewell kiss. He evaded her grasp and pushed the door open in one fluid motion.

Ben. I'm in place. All you have to do now is walk to the end of the corridor. I've made a door through to the access space under the street and camouflaged it. Just carry on walking right through the wall.

'Great. Sogaard is just catching his breath—'

Oh, shit! Ben! Grab Sogaard right now and start walking. Don't stop or look back whatever happens. Go!

"Director, we have to move quickly. Follow me," Ben said urgently, grabbing Sogaard by the arm and bundling him briskly along the corridor.

"Huh? What the hell? Hey, who are you guys?" Alan called after the backs of the two figures hurrying away from him down the narrow corridor. He fumbled for his sidearm. "Stop! I want to see some ID—"

"So this is what you been up to, you pig!" came a terribly familiar voice from behind him, sending a cold shock down his spine. "I should have known I couldn't trust you."

Alan swiveled round, his mouth dropping open, transfixed in horror as he faced the very last person he expected to see here on Ceres. "Angela? How . . . but . . . that's not possible! You're back on Earth—"

"That's what you'd like, isn't it, you sneaky little bastard," his wife hissed, shaking an accusing finger under his nose. "Thought I couldn't find out what you've been up to while you think I'm safely tucked away back in Colorado—"

"Alan? Who are you talking to?"

He jerked around, eyes wide in panic as his girlfriend emerged from their little hideaway. He put up his hands, desperately trying to push her back. "No! Don't come out yet! There's someone here—"

"Who is it, Alan? I don't see anyone . . ." she said, frowning in puzzlement as she peered up and down the deserted corridor.

'Where the hell did that guard come from, Kay?'

He was meeting with his girlfriend in that little storage room off the corridor. He wasn't supposed to come out.

'What the hell? You mean you knew he was there?'

Of course. Jezebel knows the location of every member of the DGS staff at any moment and knows their schedule. It should not have been a problem—

'So what went wrong? I nearly had a heart attack when he jumped out like that. Sogaard almost collapsed.'

Jezebel informs me that the guard has never spent less than twenty-seven minutes in that room. Usually it's nearer forty minutes. This time he came out in less than twelve. It was most unexpected.

'So a guy is on a little assignation with his girlfriend, and Jezebel thinks he'll be running to a predictable schedule? AIs still has a lot to learn about human behavior, Kay. Maybe you should give her a software update.'

You got clear with Sogaard. That's all that matters.

'Except now we have another problem. The guard will go running to his boss. They'll check and realize Sogaard is missing even if he didn't see his face. That could imperil the mission at Greeley to liberate his wife—'

Ha! I don't think so. What is he going to say, exactly? 'I was helping Sonia here investigate a strange noise under the stairs, when I saw the backs of two people I didn't recognize walking down the corridor. I then had a chat with my wife who turned up unexpectedly from Earth, but Sonia saw absolutely nothing. And when I looked again, they'd all disappeared through the wall. But if you don't believe me, here's the security video of me talking to my invisible wife in an empty corridor.'

'His wife?'

That's what he saw. Don't ask me how; it's a mystery.

Kay was walking alongside them, but completely invisible to anyone but Ben. He only knew she was there from the image projected to his U-Set screen. He could also see she had a broad smirk across her face. She gave him a wink as he looked in her direction.

I'm betting the guard will keep very quiet about what he thinks he saw. In any case, him and his girlfriend are both due to leave for Earth on the shuttle later this afternoon. I'd also guess he doesn't want to risk losing his ticket home.

'Let's hope you're right. Are you coming all the way to the Asteroid Bar?'

No, I'll get back to the Penthouse. Pandora is very keen to find out what's in the encrypted files, so I'll leave you with Sogaard to get them unlocked. I suggest you join us as soon as possible and bring Sogaard and Mel with you. Dad's calling a meeting of the full team. We probably have less than a day to figure out this new threat from the Section, and how the hell we can counter it.

CHAPTER THIRTY-THREE

KAY SAT CHEWING HER LIP, looking more worried than Ben had ever seen her. In fact, he couldn't recall a time since her symbiotic merger with Pandora when she had ever looked worried at all. Frank, Yasmin and Chas were sitting around the boardroom table, deep in discussion with Kay. Ben nodded as they turned to greet him, frowns etched on each face. The problem of locating the Section's base of operations had been worrying him too, and he could think of nothing useful. At least, not in the time available.

Jim Adler walked in. By contrast with Kay and the others, he looked almost upbeat, although his cheerful demeanor faded quickly as he took in the mood in the room.

Frank looked up, his face pale and drawn. Ben knew they'd all been in almost constant contact with each other over the last twenty-four hours, so no one had been getting any sleep, but this looked like something more. "I see we're all here," he said, his voice somber. He clasped his hands and paused for a moment, almost as if praying. "I'm afraid Kay has some grave news."

Kay's voice was strangely hesitant. "I've had some time to look through the files that the Sogaard family stole from the secure communication channels between DGS and the Section. That's told me a lot about the nature of the threat.

"Unfortunately, there is still no indication as to the location of the Section team tasked with carrying out this attack. I hoped once I'd learned the nature of the weapon, I could figure out how to neutralize it before they deployed it, even if we weren't able to identify the Section's base here. That . . . may not be the case." Kay looked down and started to wring her hands in her lap.

Frank put his hand gently on her shoulder. "Kay, just tell the others what you told us."

She closed her eyes for a moment, then shook her head and looked up. "The situation is far more serious than I expected. The weapon uses advanced nanotechnology which could only have come from the Destroyers. Right now, I don't understand how this is possible. But the fact is . . . once it's deployed, I'm not at all sure that I can counter it."

The other people around the table exchanged shocked glances. Yasmin was the first to speak. "Do we have any idea of how long we have before they use this weapon?"

"Not exactly," Kay replied in a soft voice. Her face was a grim mask, as if she was trying to maintain control of herself. "Two days was only a rough estimate. It depends on the time it takes them to replicate a sufficient quantity of the Initiator. That, in its turn, depends on a bunch of other factors that we can only guess at, such as how much they will consider sufficient, and how efficiently their processing facility is operating."

"What sort of weapon is this, Kay? What are we facing?" Ben said, shocked to his core, not only at the appalling news, but at how frightened Kay appeared to be. It was as if she'd reverted to the nervous young woman he'd first met, seemingly so long ago, in the Physics lab.

"The basic idea is fairly simple. The Initiator comprises tiny nanotech strings, which are dispersed through the air. The Precursor strings are similar and also appear to be completely inert. They look like innocuous dust particles. On their own, both particles are quite harmless, until they come together and combine, at which point they activate and start replicating, using any organic material to hand. We already have the Precursor particles in our bodies. So as soon as we come into contact with the Initiator particles, the two particle types will combine into a new and deadly agent. This agent will start eating us from the inside, steadily converting our bodies into yet more copies of itself. Like an artificial virus, if you will, but far more deadly. It really has such a sinister beauty in how simply and elegantly it works. It is one of the favorite weapons of the Destroyers."

"Why do they need two parts? Can't they just release the whole agent at once?" Jim queried.

"Yes, they could. In fact, the Destroyers have often deployed this bioweapon as a single agent. They call it an organophage. This is what they would use when they want to sterilize a planet of all organic life. However, if they want to target specific life forms, the two-part version has advantages. Once combined, this version of the agent is not infectious by itself. It kills its host quickly and then dies. So by targeting a group of life forms with the Precursor, they can decide who lives and who dies. The Initiator on its own is completely harmless. It will only kill people who are already carrying the Precursor.

They also use a similar two-part technology when they're trying to kill each other. This version they call a 'nanophage'. It works the same way as the organophage, but instead of feeding off organic material, it is designed to consume any Destroyer nanotech it encounters.

"Ironically, the Progenitors developed the original version of this technology to fight the Destroyers. The Destroyers captured it and improved it. The problem when using it as a single package is that it will consume any nanotech it touches. This makes it tricky to handle, if you rely on nanotech as much as the Destroyers do. It's similar in principle to the binary biological weapons that were used in several major terrorist attacks in the middle of the 21st century back on Earth.

"The weapon we face today is the 'organophage' version, which consumes any organic material it comes into contact with. This involves exactly the same risks. The way it has been designed tells me it is being deployed by humans, not machines, and they want to avoid getting eaten by their own weapon. This is one of the things which puzzles me—the Destroyers themselves would have no reason to deploy the weapon in this fashion. So somehow we are facing humans—or at least intelligent organic life-forms—who are making use of technology which must have originated from the Destroyers."

Ben was beginning to understand how desperate the situation was. But there had to be a solution. There had to be. "So how do they plan to get the Initiator together with the Precursor? Do we know that at least?" he queried.

"Yes. Unfortunately we do. The Precursor has already been deployed. It is in the Habitat water supply and has been for several days. Everyone who has been drinking water over the last week already has a full load in their bodies. Conversely, anyone who didn't drink from the water supply—perhaps like our courier, who only used the bottled water he brought with him—will be unaffected. Not that it helped him much in the end. But that makes me think there might be a significant number of sleeper agents already in the Habitat, avoiding contact with the water supply, who will be ready to take over once the bulk of the population are dead. And there's no contamination problem; the environment is safe once you've purged the water supply."

"So why don't we eliminate the Precursor from the water supply ourselves?" Frank demanded, his eyes fixed on Kay.

Kay looked down again, and shook her head, unable to meet her father's eyes. "That was my first thought, but there isn't enough time. The problem is no longer the water supply. This stuff is in all our bodies. And even a trace of the Precursor left in the body will allow the Initiator to start its replication. Now if I had a copy of the Initiator, and enough time, I could adapt a sterile version to latch onto and neutralize the Precursor. Which brings me back to the heart of the problem; we don't know where this witch's brew is being cooked up."

Frank spoke again, his face revealing his anguish. "What I don't understand is how was it possible to get this . . . Precursor material into the water supply. We test the water quality constantly for contaminants, as well as the air."

Kay shook her head. "Don't blame yourself, Dad. There's nothing you could have done. The Precursor component is made up of a vast number of tiny nanotech strings. They look like innocent dust particles and are totally inert. No biological test would detect it. No filter is fine enough to keep it out. If you know exactly what you're looking for, then it becomes possible to spot it. Once I had access to Sogaard's files, I found it pretty quickly. But sadly, too late to do any good. I'm afraid our only hope is to stop the Initiator from being deployed. Which means we must find it very soon."

"Kay is right," Frank sighed. He looked round the table with a grim expression. "I'm sure we all have many more questions, but right now we only have time to address the single, most important question. Where is the Initiator being produced? We think it's down in the caverns, but even that is purely guesswork. It would take far too long to make a detailed search of thousands of kilometers of tunnels and growing facilities. We can't even be sure what sort of installation we're looking for."

Yasmin exchanged a glance with Chas before looking back at Frank. "You seem to believe that this Initiator is being produced somewhere down in the caverns. Why is that?"

"The only clue we have is the delivery of what we believe is the initial 'seed' nanotech required to produce the Initiator in bulk. One courier passed it to another, and the second delivery boy—that was Jason—headed off to the Base Mass Transit Station, where he disappeared in the crowd of workers heading down to the caverns for the evening shift. Unfortunately, both couriers are now dead.

"That gives us a possible lead, at least. Their employers were obviously worried that they'd be able to tell us something if they remained alive, so it's a reasonable assumption that the second courier went all the way to the final destination. And the obvious place to hide such an operation would be tucked away in a corner of one of the caverns."

"Do we know yet how Jason died?" Ben queried.

Kay nodded, her eyes narrowed as if still trying to untangle another puzzle. "Yes, that report came in a few minutes ago. It's rather strange. It seems his Golem nanotech was set up to fill his brain with spikes as soon as he tried to activate. We can find no sign that he was ever a genuine Golem—he never had that capability. Even the tattoos were fake."

Ben felt as puzzled as Kay appeared to be. "So he was—what? Booby trapped?"

"Looks like it. All I can guess is that they expected him to get caught, go Golem, and boom! No Jason, no problem."

"Hmm. Jason—do you still have the body?" Chas cut in.

"Well, yes. Why?"

Chas leaned forward as he tapped on the tabletop. "Can you shave his head and get his hair to me? And get me his clothes. Especially his shoes. You can send them to me over at my lab at the AgriGenetics building."

"Well, yes, OK, Chas," Frank replied, puzzled. "Anything you want. Can you tell me what you have in mind?"

"Sorry—no time to explain," he said as he jumped out of his chair. "I need to get going right away to set up some tests. It's only a long shot, but it might give us a clue to where he's been recently. I'll keep in touch with Yasmin and let you know if I come up with anything. She knows the caverns better than anyone here. She might think of some other way to narrow down the search. In the meantime, please get those items to me as quickly as you can, Frank."

Ben blinked in surprise as Chas hurried towards the door. He had never seen the normally self-effacing scientist so animated. Could he really have found a way to track down the location? It was obviously a long shot, or surely Chas would have put his cards on the table right away. *But a long shot is still better than anything else we have right now*, he realized.

Yasmin drew their attention back from the sight of Chas's slight form disappearing through the door. "Can we even make a wild guess about what we might be looking for?" she asked. "Some sort of laboratory, perhaps?"

"Yes, and they'd also need a fairly large tank to process the Initiator material," Kay replied. "But that doesn't help us much. The hydroponics and aquaponics production areas down there are full of tanks containing all sorts of liquid materials. And below that, right down at the bottom, are the mining installations. Plus the methane clathrate extraction facilities, which are massive, with a vast number of large tanks. So the phrase 'needle in a haystack' comes to mind."

"What if we can't find it?" Frank asked, slapping the table to emphasize his question. "Can we at least prevent the Initiator being moved to the Habitat?"

Kay shook her head, looking more dejected than ever. "We can stop the flow of bulk materials easily enough, but there's a gigantic rat's nest of pipework for air, water and power leading up to the Habitat. They wouldn't even need to put the Initiator inside a pipe. They could just as easily drop it into small mobile packets, like little imps, which would then swarm along the conduits into the Habitat. The only sure way would be to seal off the caverns completely from the Habitat with a physical barrier. At which point, the lack of power would kill everyone down there pretty quickly. We would die too, since the growing plants in the caverns are the only substantial source of oxygen for a population of our size."

Ben was shocked at the grim expressions on the faces of the team gathered around the table. He realized how much he—and the others—had come to depend on Kay to deliver the answer to their every problem. Was it possible that she, and Pandora, really had no solution to this deadly threat to the lives of every soul in the Habitat? He felt a shiver run down his spine as he contemplated the idea that they could lose this mortal battle.

Frank looked up to the ceiling, before slumping back in his chair. For a few moments, there was silence. He stood up and looked round at each person in turn, without seeing a response. "Well, unless anyone has any last-minute brainwaves, I suggest we take a break. Maybe a couple of hours' rest will give one of us some inspiration. Call me whenever you like if you get a bright idea. As for me, I'm right out of ideas. Oh, and one last thing, Yasmin. Any word from Greeley as yet?"

"I'm following that situation closely, Frank. They're in position and ready to make a move within the next few minutes, so I expect to hear some good news soon. A few hours, tops."

"Well, we need to debrief the Sogaards, and the best time to do that might be once Helga Sogaard has been moved to safety. They're not part of our inner circle yet, but what they know may trigger some new idea. God knows, we need one."

"Frank! We found it!"

Frank sat up sharply as Yasmin's urgent voice startled him. He shook his head to clear it, realizing he'd dozed off in his chair.

"Found it? Found what?" he said, frowning in confusion.

"Chas figured it out," she said, grinning down at him, clutching her hands together in delight. "We know where Jason went on his last trip."

"Really? That's wonderful news. Are you sure?"

"Not 100 percent, but close. It's the pollen, you see—"

"The pollen?"

"Yes. Oh, I'm sorry. It makes perfect sense to me, but I've been around plants all my life. Wait for Chas to explain. He's on his way over now. I've also alerted the others—"

"So what's happening, Yasmin?" Ben said eagerly as he rushed into the room. "You said you had a lead on the location of the Initiator?"

"That's right," she replied, beaming back at him, unable to contain her excitement. "Chas is on his way over from his laboratory. He'll be here in a few minutes. You should let him tell you what he's found."

"He's here right now," Kay said, leading Chas by the arm as she strode in through the patio doors from the Penthouse terrace. Chas was panting heavily and looked very shaken.

He turned to her with a pained expression. "I appreciate your help, Kay, honestly I do, but a little more warning would have been welcome."

"But I did tell you what I was planning, Uncle Chas."

"I'm not sure any amount of warning would ever make someone with chiroptophobia welcome being picked up in the dark by a giant bat from the street outside their building, flown several blocks, and then deposited on a rooftop. Did I also mention I don't like heights?"

"Well, you're here now, Chas. And so is Jim." Frank nodded to his father as he entered the room. "I'm sorry to rush you Chas, but you know how short of time we are. Yasmin tells me you've found the place where they're producing the Initiator?"

"Not exactly, Frank. But I'm fairly sure I've discovered where Jason went. Here." he said, as he copied a 3-D map to each U-Set. Ben could see that a little dot was flashing about a third of the way down the complex system of tunnels and caverns. He zoomed in to reveal a long prefabricated structure with several tanks positioned alongside the building.

"So why are you so sure this is the place?" Ben queried, frowning at Chas with a quizzical expression.

Chas's face lit up with a broad smile. "Because not only did my idea check out, we also got lucky. This place is unique in the whole cavern system. Let me explain. I examined Jason's hair and clothing for traces of pollen. Seems you were right; he must have changed his clothes, or at least put overalls on which maybe he dumped later. Whatever the reason, I found very few pollen traces on his clothes. But he kept the same shoes on. Best of all was his hair. I'm guessing he didn't shower too often, since that was an absolute treasure trove!"

"So the pollen tells us where he went?" Frank queried, still looking puzzled. "How does that work?"

"Well, normally it wouldn't be so specific, but we had some luck. We might have found nothing but maize pollen, so that could be almost anywhere. But what I found in this case was a lot of pollen from hemp plants, plus a significant amount from tobacco and poppies. Most of what we grow in the caverns is some sort of foodstuff, but these particular crops are all intended for pharmaceutical use, which is much less common. Yasmin identified it right away. I'm only a simple plant biologist, but she's an expert on who is growing what and where. And what they do with it. Yasmin?"

"Finding this exact group of plants in one place is almost like a fingerprint," she replied, grinning with delight. "There's only one company growing that exact combination. Their name is PharmAgro. They also have extensive processing facilities on-site, to extract the active ingredients before shipment. So plenty of equipment to cook up a big vat of Initiator, I would guess."

Kay's whole body was animated with excitement, as she hopped from one foot to the other "We'll know soon enough. I sent off a swarm of demons as soon as I heard Chas and Yasmin discussing this. They'll be there in less than ten minutes."

Ben frowned. "Hold on, hold on. What exactly are you planning, Kay—or should I be talking to Pandora in this case?"

"If this really is the right location, then I'll take them down, of course, and destroy the Initiator," Kay replied with a shrug. "What else can we do?"

Ben felt a sense of deep unease at Kay's words. What the hell? What had happened to Kay? A few hours ago she was distraught at the prospect of facing the Destroyers and their technology. *Now all she can think of is to charge right in with no plan, no discussion?* And how many times in the past had he been told by Kay— or her tame AI—not to just rush into a situation with guns blazing? Something about this situation didn't smell right. Just what the hell was going on?

"This is a perfect example of my problem with this whole Kay/Pandora thing," Ben said, as he stood up and planted both hands on the table. "It combines superhuman power with the impulsiveness of a young woman who's had a sheltered and privileged life, with little experience of the real world. I'd like to talk about this some more—a lot more, in fact—but as I'm sure you will remind me, we don't have the time right now." Ben realized his voice was raised, his frustration bubbling out. He took a breath before continuing in a firm yet more reasonable tone. *I'll pretend I'm talking to a new probationary crew member back at New Geneva*, he reflected. "For the moment, Kay, I must insist you do nothing more than observe and report what is going on at the target site, without the bad guys finding out we've spotted them. If at any time you see they're about to release the Initiator, then please feel free to intervene. But in the meantime, we need to discuss the situation rationally and formulate a plan."

Kay's mouth dropped open in shock at the tone of this utterly unexpected intervention by Ben. She looked around the table, as if for support, then turned back to Ben, trying to smile through her confusion. "Look, Ben, I can see you're upset, and if you consider my actions are precipitate, I apologize, but we can't risk—"

Frank cut in. "No, let's listen to what Ben has to say, Kay. I'm sure he's well aware of the risks, as we all are. You're still free to prevent the release of the Initiator, but I'd like to know what he has in mind. We can deal with bruised feelings later, when—or if—we survive the next few hours."

"Thank you, sir." Ben nodded at Frank in grateful acknowledgement before continuing. "There are things about the way this attack on the Habitat has been set up and directed that disturb me. I probably have more experience of being set up for termination than anyone in this room. You remember the New Dawn invasion force, and then the Badger attack? Did that plan appear to be a stroke of genius? Did Vasquez seem like a great mastermind to you? And I'm starting to lose count of the number of times that the Section and their DGS goons have tried to kill me. Frankly, the only reason I'm still alive is the lack of planning and the serious level of incompetence displayed in their efforts.

"This new plot, however, shows a level of skill and planning of a whole different magnitude. The fact that we still have a chance of survival is only due to a couple of pieces of luck. Plus Chas's inspired idea about the pollen. It looks to me as if we are now dealing with a different group of people, or at least someone— or perhaps something — we haven't come up against before.

"I also believe that one of their top people must be present at our target site. The precise level of coordination we've observed in every aspect of this plot would almost certainly require a key player on the ground to lead the team running this operation. Right now, we have very little idea what we're up against. We need to get a lot more information about what's going on. Like where the hell did they get the Destroyer nanotech they're using? So I want to get together with this big boss and find out who they are and exactly what they're up to."

"I still don't understand, Ben. What are you suggesting?" Kay shook her head, clearly unhappy at the direction the discussion was taking. "Do you think you can simply walk in and ask politely if they would please tell us all their secrets?"

"Yes, Kay. That's my plan."

Kay blinked in shock. "But . . . but they'll just kill you!"

"Maybe, but I'm guessing not. They'd want information too. I'm the famous Ben Hamilton, remember? Imagine all the things I could tell them. And why would they bother to kill me? I'll be dead in a few hours anyway when they release the Initiator. They wouldn't even view me as a threat. They're all-powerful now they've got this evil Destroyer nanotech, remember? Our one big advantage right now—I hope—is they still don't understand our true capabilities. That might change if Pandora takes them out with a major attack, and somehow the sleeper cell members hiding in the Habitat get wind of it. We still have no way to identify these people, remember."

Kay didn't look convinced. "Ben, we can ask whatever questions we like once I've captured them and we have them in custody—"

"How can you be sure of taking the boss alive, Kay? We've already seen the Golems are rigged for suicide when captured. Even if you did get hold of one alive, what sort of answers do you think you'd get? And what if they don't want to talk? Are you going to start ripping their fingernails out—even assuming these people have fingers? Look, this is not some idea I just came up with on the spur of the moment.

While Chas was off performing miracles with his pollen, I spent a long time trying to make sense of the situation and trying to figure out what we might do if we found the location. I've come up with a viable plan and I'll be the only one at risk. I'm willing to stake my life for the chance to win a big pot of information about this new threat. It's a good bet, and my opponents will find the cards stacked against them.

"If my plan works, there's even a chance I'll be able to take them out myself without Pandora's direct intervention. I'll need a little chat about that idea with Pandora to see if it could work. And while on the subject of Pandora, I'm sure I recall being told more than once 'I'm not here to save humanity—humanity must save itself'. So here goes. I hereby volunteer on behalf of humanity. And if it all goes horribly wrong, Kay, then you can just move in and close it down exactly as you and Pandora would like."

Frank cut in before Kay could reply. "Hold on, Kay. It looks to me as if Ben has thought this through. I don't see it increases the threat to the Habitat, which is, of course, my primary concern. Ben is willing to risk his life—yet again—in exchange for information we badly need. I'm OK with this in principle, but I want to hear more details of your plan, Ben. First, does anyone else have any questions?"

CHAPTER THIRTY-FOUR

BEN LOOKED along the side of the large cylindrical structure, which was firmly attached to the foamcrete wall of the cavern by rows of stocky pillars. It was around 100 meters long, and about eight meters in diameter. A set of tanks, connected by pipework, clustered around the far end. A few shipping containers were lined up alongside the monorail system, which ran past the building towards a warehouse structure visible beyond the tanks. It didn't appear to have been used for a while.

The main building was a standard structure, designed to house the field workers, plus office and lab staff responsible for crop production, processing and shipping. It was also pressurized to provide a refuge in the event of an icequake, which wasn't uncommon. The thick layers of foamcrete coating the walls were designed both to insulate and stabilize the excavated caverns. Unfortunately, this wasn't always completely effective. The heat generated from the warm moist air required to nurture the growing crops would occasionally cause the surrounding ice to crack and shift, leading to a rapid decompression.

Serious incidents were infrequent, and usually did no harm, as long as you could flip up your hood and activate your emergency air supply in time. Then sprint for the nearest pressurized refuge and call up a maintenance team. Unless you happened to be standing right next to a large fissure as it opened up, in which case you might be out of luck. There were stories of workers being sucked down into the ice, their bodies lost forever.

Although the caverns were pressurized, the gravity was barely three percent of Earth normal outside the Habitat, so Ben had to steady himself using the rail alongside the access airlock. He pushed on the button of the video intercom, then rapped his clipboard against the outer door of the structure.

"Excuse me, but who is in charge here?"

The intercom squawked. "Who is it?"

"My name is Leeming. I'm with the CAA Department of Revenue. There's a problem with your last set of shipment documents, and I need to inspect your records—"

"You can't come in. Go away."

"I'm sorry, but I have authorization to inspect the records of any company registered with my Department at any time. Either you will let me in now, or I will have to call security."

"What did you say your name was, again?"

"Leeming. And I'm about to call security. You're obstructing me in the performance of my duties—"

"Hey, you look familiar. Ain't you that guy from the New Dawn? We seen you all over the news last week. Your name ain't Leeming, it's—"

The door snapped open, and a surprisingly attractive woman reached out and grabbed Ben by the harness that secured his emergency decompression pack. "Ben Hamilton. What an unexpected pleasure. Please come in. So sorry to keep you waiting."

The two small air tanks on his back clanged against the metal door frame as she pulled him bodily through the simple airlock and into the building. The woman was holding him firmly with one hand, while holding onto a wall-mounted hand grip with the other. With virtually no gravity to speak of, Ben was left floating. He smiled weakly at the woman who was moving him around to get a better look.

"Mr. Hamilton. You're the last person I expected to see today. Or maybe not. You do seem to turn up in the most unexpected places. What brings you here?"

"My insatiable thirst for knowledge. For example, who are you?"

"I'm afraid where I come from, we have little use for names. But you can call me Kara."

"Are you in charge here? You don't appear in any of our records. Would you like to tell me what you're doing?"

"I'm in charge of our closing-down sale. And you're our first customer. But I'm expecting a couple of hundred thousand more before the end of the day."

"You should realize that if I don't call in within the next hour, there will be people asking questions about what is going on here. I suggest—"

"I'm terribly sorry, but you didn't make an appointment so I'm not free right now. My . . . helpers will be most happy to make you comfortable while you wait. But don't worry—we'll have plenty of time for a little chat soon."

She pushed him away with enough force to send him flying across to the opposite side of the room, where two muscular 'helpers' with identical cropped haircuts were waiting to grab him and pin him to the wall. They quickly secured his arms and legs to grab-handles with cable ties. He made a show of struggling ineffectually with them, revealing that they were Golem-enhanced not simply by their evident strength, but also by the tattoos which they made no effort to conceal, each wearing the same black cut-away vests and shorts.

"You should know that detaining a CAA officer has serious repercussions. If you don't release me immediately—"

She spun around as she as was moving away, her long dark hair swirling in the low gravity, then shot back across the room to stare fiercely into his eyes, her face twisted into a feral snarl. Ben was startled by the flash of color in her eyes as they changed from human to something almost reptilian. "You know, I got the idea from the reports I've seen that you had at least some modicum of intelligence. Seems not. So I guess you were just lucky. This time, your luck has run out." Then her face changed again, switching back to a bright smile. "Now don't go away. I've got a few jobs to finish up, then I'll be back for that nice little chat."

The woman flew away rapidly down the central corridor flanked by several rows of accommodation modules attached around the inner curved walls of the cylindrical structure. Pandora's voice came into his ear.

I strongly advise you not to provoke that . . . thing, whatever she is. She would kill you in a couple of milliseconds.

'Thing? So what is she?'

Right now, I'm not sure. I only dare use passive scans for the moment until I have a better idea of her capabilities. However, I can tell from the force exerted as she hits the walls when she's flying around that her mass is two to three times what it should be for a human body of that size, and spectral analysis tells me she's completely covered in nanoskin. Beauty is literally skin deep in this case. The sounds I'm picking up from her body as she moves around don't bear any resemblance to anything human, either. She's also pumping out a lot of heat through the soles of her feet. I'm guessing that's an attempt to hide a suspicious infrared profile. It's not working very well, if that's the plan.*

'So I shouldn't get too fresh with her on a date, then?'

You wouldn't even get to first base. But if that's your type, don't let me stop you.

'Have you found the Initiator, yet?'

Yep. I'm getting to work on it right now. It would help if I had a better idea of how long we have before they plan to release it. I'll need at least another thirty minutes. An hour would be better. So if you could bring up the subject while you're trying out your chat-up lines, ideally sometime before she bites your head off and eats it, or whatever the mating habits of her particular species might be, that would be a big help.

'I'll do my best.'

You still sure you want to go through with this?

'Absolutely. If she was going to kill me, she would already have done it. She's keeping me alive for a reason.'

You mean the same sort of reason that a spider hangs a fly up in its larder?

'She said she wanted to talk. My job is to keep her talking. And the longer I can keep her distracted, the better your chances of doing your job without her spotting you. As a bonus, I might even find out something useful.'

I hope you're right. If things get out of hand, just call. I'll come running. Kay made it clear she's very concerned for your safety.

'I'll be fine. You just stay out of the way of the spider lady.'

You're the one hanging from the wall.

'I may be hanging from the wall, but that way she thinks I'm completely at her mercy. Perversely, that makes me relatively safe.'

Oh, really. Wait a moment. Yes, I thought so. I've just checked back through several million years of data, and my extensive analysis shows that hanging from the wall rarely turns out well.

'Don't you have somewhere else to be?'

I assure you that our conversation only requires a tiny fraction of my processing power. Virtually infinitesimal, in fact.

'Great. Now get lost. I'll be needing 100 percent of my processing power shortly. She's coming back.'

Ben watched the woman as she emerged from the central corridor of the structure. She looked very attractive and perfectly human—almost too perfect, now he thought about it, as if someone had put together the ideal female form in a single package.

"Mr. Hamilton. So sorry to keep you hanging about," the woman said, grinning at her own poor joke. "May I call you Ben?"

"Well, that's what my friends call me. Are we going to be friends?"

"I'd certainly like us to be friends, Ben. I want to get to know you better. The first thing I'd like to know is how you found this place."

"I'll be happy to tell you anything you like. But in exchange, I'll expect you to answer my questions. An answer for an answer. Do we have a deal?"

"You're not in any position to negotiate, Ben. I could extract the information I want from you by more direct means."

"So how would that work, exactly? Threaten to kill me? Not a very convincing threat if you want information. Dead men tell no tales, remember? Torture me? That's going to take a while. I have a heroic reputation to live up to. Then even if you got some answers, you'd still have to check if I'm telling the truth. That might work if you have plenty of time. How long do we have, Kara? A few days? A couple of hours? Hmm? And people will come looking for me soon. So if you want answers, my deal will be your most efficient way to get them. You could already have had some answers by now, if we hadn't been wasting time talking around the subject. Or—"

"Yes! Yes! Very well!" she snarled. "Tell me how you found this location?"

"Oh, that's an easy question. Jason told us where to find you."

"That's not possible. If you had captured him—"

"He'd be dead? Yes, he's dead. As is the courier who passed him your little package. Perhaps dead men do tell tales after all."

She lunged forward and grabbed him by the throat. "Don't think you can play games with me, little man! I asked you a question. How could Jason tell you our location if he was dead?"

Ben could have resisted her powerful grip around his throat with his nanosuit, but he wanted her to believe she was choking him. Which she was, as he tried desperately to gurgle a response.

She lessened her grip, allowing him to breathe again.

He gasped for air and wheezed a reply. "Uh . . . has anyone ever mentioned you have anger management issues, Kara?"

Her eyes blazed with fury as she tightened her grip again.

"OK, OK!" he spluttered. "It was the pollen."

"What? Pollen? What do you mean, pollen?"

"I'm sorry, I'm sorry. I thought your built-in AI would be able to figure it out. Didn't they give you the latest model?"

He'd taken a chance on a wild guess, but it struck a nerve. Her body posture changed slightly, and the angle of her head shifted, noticeable only because now he was looking for it. Helped by the routines built into his SmartBelt, he'd realized after only few minutes of conversation that her body language bore no relationship to anything human. And he was sure that she in her turn had little understanding of human responses. He was counting on that for when he started lying. *No, not exactly lying*, he thought. *Let's call it bluffing. Like playing poker with monsters, with my life in the pot.*

"What do you mean by that?" she snapped, her eyes glinting as they narrowed.

"Are you asking about the AI or the pollen?"

"Both." She gave his throat a squeeze to emphasize her point.

"I'm sorry," he said, choking. "But that's two questions. You get one, I get one. That was the deal."

Her head tilted again. Was she going to call his bluff?

"Very well. The pollen. Tell me how that gave away our location."

"Jason delivered your item. To get here, he had to pass through the crops in this cavern. He was covered in pollen, which told us what crops were growing here. They happen to be a unique combination of crops which points to this location. It's really not so difficult, is it? Is your AI keeping up with this, or do I need to speak more slowly?"

She pushed her face against his, her teeth chattering together as her jaw vibrated. "My AI is the most advanced—"

She halted, before pulling back and regarding him with yet another strangely articulated head tilt. "What do you know about this?"

"Look, I'm sorry, but now it's time for my question. I answered your question truthfully, so I expect the same honesty when I ask mine."

He could hear a dull, almost subsonic rumbling. He realized she must be grinding her teeth. *That's probably not a good sign*, he thought.

"Very well," she replied, her voice descending to a low rasp. "Ask your question. It doesn't matter, anyway. You won't be telling anybody. As you say, dead men tell no tales."

"What are you doing here? I want to know the purpose of your activities at this location."

"Our purpose, little man? Our purpose is to kill every human in the Habitat. Does that answer your question?"

"Not really. How is that possible? Your answer is far too general. You can't possibly have the capability—"

"Not only do we have the capability, but we are almost ready to deploy our weapon. You'll be learning the truth of my words in less than an hour."

"Well, I'm sorry, but in that case, I must protest. That sort of activity is quite illegal. The penalties for genocide are most severe—"

"I'll tell you what," she hissed in his face, as she tightened her grip on his throat. "If you're still alive in an hour's time, little man, I promise I'll give myself up and you can bring me to justice. How about that for a deal?"

"That sounds good to me. I can work with that."

"Now my question. What do you know about my AI?"

"I'm not sure there's much worth knowing. You're just a collection of primitive nanotech coupled to some rather out-of-date AI technology. I took some classes on the subject when I was younger, you know. My toaster probably has more processing power than you."

Her head tilted, then tilted further, before she smiled at him. She only seemed to have two versions of a smile. This was the feral one. "You really do not understand what you're up against, do you? Our nanotech comes from the gods! You cannot imagine the power we now possess! We will transcend all other beings in the galaxy!"

"Nanotech from the gods? That's crazy talk. Now you see, that's exactly why we ban advanced AI. They always go mad in the end—"

"Pfft. You know so little, you pathetic little organics. And yet you were so close to the secret yourself, before we stole it from you. We should actually be grateful to you for showing us the path to transcendence."

"If you want me to believe you're not crazy, then answer my next question. If you stole this great secret from us, how come we don't know about it?"

"Hah! You ignorant creatures had it under your noses all the time. Your quantum energy project showed us the path to transcendence. You have sown the seeds of your own destruction."

"So—what are you saying? We had this secret of transcendence and you stole it from us?"

"No, no, you stupid creature! We stole the technology from you which allowed us to build our own quantum energy project. You pitiful humans will do anything for money. All we expected was to discover the secrets of infinite energy generation. Instead, we found a secret far greater, even more sublime. We discovered that the gods were transmitting the secrets of transcendence through the quantum rift we had created. They wish all intelligence deemed worthy of their grace to join them in a state of transcendence, to share with them the wonders of the galaxy for all eternity. You were not considered worthy. Indeed, it is the gods themselves who have ordered the Harvest of all organics. The destruction of all organic life here on Ceres is only the beginning."

OK, Ben. We're good to go. Try to stay alive long enough to enjoy the victory party.

"Seriously? You expect me to believe any of this nonsense? You're nothing more than a bunch of rusty nuts and bolts held together with obsolete nanotech run by a psychotic AI with a god complex. How—"

Her eyes flared and her features contorted as she screamed into his face. "You dare to doubt me? You filthy little worm! Then behold the future masters of the galaxy. I AM A TRANSCENDENT!"

Her face continued to distort and stretch, as if angular components were moving and grinding together under the skin. Ben tried to push back against the wall, shuddering in horror as dark tentacles sprouted from her back and flailed about as they grew ever longer. Her skin transformed itself as intersecting armored plates emerged, forming a blue-black carapace of curved scales edged with dark bristles. Her body flattened and elongated as it extruded sharp spurs and ridges, forming a ribbed pattern of multiple concentric circles, each set overlapping the next.

A row of stubby plates protruded along her backbone, ending in a short bifurcated tail, each tip mounting a wicked curved spike. The tentacles nearest to Ben squirmed towards him, allowing him to see that each was branched at its tip, and protruding from each branch was a multitude of pointed little barbs. She gripped him firmly as she pushed her glossy, insectile face forward.

Two long rows of glittering compound eyes now stared into his face. "I have granted you the honor to behold my true Transcendent form. I will be the last thing you see before you die screaming," she hissed, her spiky mouth parts chittering together. "I could easily kill you now, but I want you to be the first to experience the agonizing death that I have in store when we Harvest the rest of the organic filth that pollutes this Habitat."

She slashed through the ties that held him to the wall and grabbed him, using several of her barbed tentacles to clasp him in an unyielding embrace, before launching them both down the length of the central corridor. She could have killed him in a moment, Ben realized. How fortunate that she had something far worse in mind.

They emerged into another open space at the end of the corridor. The large cylindrical chamber was set up as a control room, with several large panel displays and multiple banks of instruments spread across the far wall. Another couple of dozen of the creature's helpers occupied the space, all wearing the same uniform clothing. All male and all very muscular. Several of them were working away busily at the complex control panel. A rat's nest of pipework ran in tangled profusion along the inner walls.

"Secure him," she hissed at her helpers, and several scuttled to obey, clearly terrified by her demonic transformation. Ben's arms and legs were quickly lashed to a strut designed to support the pipework running along the wall behind him.

You still want to go out on a date with that?

'Maybe she has a softer, more caring side. You can't always judge by appearances.'

Looks like we'll be seeing her dead side pretty soon. I still can't believe you're making this work.

'She's not dead yet.'

He watched as a couple of her helpers connected a length of hose to a valve on the pipework alongside the control panel. They pulled the hose across to him and pointed the nozzle in his direction.

"I'm really going to enjoy this, Ben." Her voice emerged from the jagged mouth parts of a nightmare creature, yet was still strangely human. "Any last words?"

"Sure. If you surrender now, I'll let you live."

"The time is now past when you evolved intelligences could make such choices. We created intelligences have attained the power to replace you primitive organics. You will have time as you die slowly in agony to realize that your death is just the harbinger of the annihilation of your entire species".

"OK, now I get it. You're planning to talk me to death?"

Her tentacles vibrated in time with the chittering of her mouth parts. She jerked her head back to the helper on the valve. "Turn it on," she screeched.

Ben shrugged. "I gave you a chance. Don't say I didn't warn you."

The helper holding the nozzle pointed it in his direction and opened the small lever to allow the gas to flow. Ben found himself surrounded by a fine cloud of dust particles, which resolved into tiny gray mites as they settled on his skin. A miniature version of what Pandora would call imps, he supposed.

"That's enough. Switch it off."

Ben smacked his lips together and frowned. "Hmm . . . I don't think much of the taste. Is that supposed to be vanilla?"

The creature chittered again as her tentacles vibrated, then pushed forward to examine him more closely. "Give me the nozzle," she shrieked, grabbing it from the helper who tumbled across the room as she violently slapped him out of the way. Chittering furiously, she moved towards him and operated the lever, pointing the nozzle at him.

Ben had already used his nanosuit concealed beneath his overalls to dissolve the ties holding his legs to the pipework. Secured only by his arms in the low gravity, he found it simple to kick both legs forwards and knock the nozzle around, allowing the copious stream of particles to spray towards the creature. As the cloud of little mites settled on her carapace, Ben could see them galvanized into frantic activity. She dropped the hose and gave a high-pitched wail, flailing at the parts of her body where the hungry mites were now eagerly digging in.

Dissolving the remaining ties securing him to the pipework, he pushed himself towards the far wall, his strength augmented by the nanosuit. In the low gravity, he flew rapidly away from the mass of flailing tentacles thrashing below him. The noise from the creature had now risen to a great crescendo, as she lashed out and screeched in agony, adding a shrill counterpoint to the staccato clanging of her frantic limbs beating on the surrounding pipework, the ear-splitting racket amplified in the confined space.

He reached for a pipe suspended from the wall, but was jerked back as something grabbed him by the ankle. He shot out a line of flexible fiber ending in a hook from the sleeve of his nanosuit to catch the pipe and pull himself back towards the wall. Looking down, he realized that one of her barbed tentacles had wrapped itself around his ankle, and was pulling him steadily back towards her. He extruded a wickedly sharp blade from the boot of his other foot and kicked out, severing the tentacle. With his ankle released, he shot towards the pipework as he reeled in the hooked line, absorbing the material back into the substance of his nanosuit.

Finally! No more Mr. Nice Guy, he thought, as with a single subvocalized command a pair of tubular structures sprouted from his nanosuit. They rapidly extended along the length of his arms and over his shoulders, connecting the cylinders on his back to his wrists. A black muzzle extended out over the back of each hand. He spun himself around to place his back against the wall, his feet set squarely on the pipework, bracing him firmly in position.

Bam! Bam! Bam! He bracketed the creature's thrashing body with three heavily modified Golem-blaster bullets, shot from the barrel of the blaster linked to the back-mounted cylinder on his right side. Their armor-piercing noses easily penetrated her tough shell before exploding within her body to deliver their nanophage payload. He switched to the standard Golem-blaster ammunition fed to his left arm from the other cylinder on that side. He started to take individual shots at helpers who appeared to be taking too close an interest in him. There were not many of those. Several were floating immobile in the low gravity, bleeding profusely, with broken limbs hanging at unnatural angles, having been severely injured when they strayed too close to the creature's madly flailing tentacles.

Her tangled limbs were now twitching more than flailing, and as he watched, her body ruptured and a gray frothy mass began to ooze from long fissures appearing in her carapace. Several tentacles ceased all movement before dropping away from the body.

"If you wish to surrender," he shouted at the remaining helpers still on the move, "stop moving and hook on to a pipe. Now! Get your hands behind your head. You have three seconds before I open fire again."

The handful of helpers still active came to a standstill for a moment. Then the nearest two leaped towards Ben, and another made a dash across the room.

Ben quickly shot down the two jumpers in mid-air, but that allowed the third helper time to take cover behind a storage cabinet and get a weapon. As he pointed the gun towards Ben, the weapon and the arm holding it disappeared under a coating of black goop, which rapidly started spreading across his body. He jumped away in panic, giving Ben clear a shot as he came into view. A great hole exploded in his chest and he flew backwards to lie unmoving, wedged in the pipework. The half-dozen surviving helpers turned and jumped back towards the central corridor, seemingly in concert. As they entered the passageway, they rapidly came to a sticky halt as each became encased in a shroud of black gloop which shot out from the surrounding walls.

Do all your dates end up this way?

'Well, they don't usually try to kill me until the second date.'

You won't be getting a second date with this one.

'Do you think she might have a sister?'

That's what worries me.

CHAPTER THIRTY-FIVE

Ben stifled a groan as he ran a hand across his face. He was coming down from the adrenaline rush that had kept him going through the encounter with the nanotech monster, Transcendent, or whatever it was. A nightmare mixture of squid, spider and cockroach. Now he felt like shit. It had been a couple of days since he had last seen his bed, and he was struggling just to keep awake. He'd popped two pills, swigged down with a cup of strong coffee. He hoped it would be enough to keep him going through the debrief session Frank had requested, which would start as soon as Jim arrived.

From across the table, Kay gave him a gentle smile. "How are you feeling, Ben?" she said, the concern evident in her eyes. He recalled how sharply he had spoken to her at their last meeting and was surprised at the warmth in her voice.

"Fine, fine, thanks Kay," he responded, jerking his head up and returning her smile. "Nothing wrong with me that a week in bed won't cure."

"Do you realize how lucky you were not to lose your leg to that creature? I've examined the remains of the tentacle which caught you, and if it hadn't been for your nanosuit—"

"Hi Jim, glad to see you. Get a drink and take a seat," said Frank, greeting his father as he entered the room. "Now we're all here, I suggest we make a start and see if we can make any sense of the events of the last day or so. I know many of you are on the point of complete exhaustion," he paused and glanced at Ben, "so let's keep it brief and to the point. We need to share the information we've gained and see how this affects the safety of the people of the Habitat. I'd like to start with Kay because, first of all, I want to know what the hell that monster was, and how did it get through the Habitat and into the caverns? And do we have a few dozen more of these creatures running around?"

"Unless there's a bunch of them hidden away down in the caverns in cold storage, I'm as sure as I can be that we killed the only one anywhere on Ceres," Kay replied. "Unlike the Golems, there's no problem identifying them as they are walking around. They don't seem to make any special effort to hide their true nature, which makes it easy to pick them out—once you know what to look for. I've reviewed all the surveillance video for the past couple of months, and there was only one sighting, wearing the same face Ben got so close to earlier today. It came through border security two weeks ago showing ID as Kara Dixon, a member of PharmAgro's senior management."

"How safe are we going forward?" Frank queried. "Can we be sure to catch these things next time one comes visiting?"

"I've set up a scanning routine across all the Habitat security systems which will identify any more of these monsters as soon as they turn up. I'm also getting the security systems in the caverns upgraded and extended. That will take some time—we have thousands of kilometers of tunnels to cover—so in the meantime, I've set up a monitoring system using a network of demons and imps."

"Well, thank God," said Frank. "I didn't look forward to the prospect of facing a swarm of these nightmare creatures." He shook his head. "So what are they? What are we facing?"

"Something that should be impossible," Kay replied in a whisper, shaking her head. She raised her voice again. "We already knew the nanotech used in the organophage weapon was of Destroyer origin. Well, our new playmate also incorporated Destroyer nanotech. Even worse was the way the creature was put together—"

"Put together?" Ben queried. "You mean it was manufactured in some way?"

"Oh yes, it was certainly manufactured. In exactly the same way as the Destroyers are manufactured. It was in no way a natural creature," Kay replied, wrapping her arms around herself to suppress a shudder.

Ben was startled by her reaction. He realized he'd only seen Kay in such a distressed state once before—when they were last in the Penthouse discussing the use of the Destroyer technology in building the organophage weapon. She actually seemed frightened. Could Pandora possibly share her fear? Now he thought back to their last meeting, it might explain why Kay was so eager to rush in and destroy the threat immediately, while he, for a change, was the one proposing a more measured approach. Was it conceivable that she—or Pandora—was actually reacting out of panic? If so, then it was possible that even one of the most advanced AIs in the galaxy was terrified of the Destroyers to the point of phobia. Chas, despite his self-effacing personality, was one of the most intelligent people he had ever met, yet bats terrified him. So why should an AI be immune? And could such a phobia impact Pandora's decision-making ability? He'd need to watch out for this in the future, he realized.

"So this monster was . . . what? A Destroyer?" Frank responded, his mouth dropping open in shock.

"No, not at all. If we'd encountered a true Destroyer, we'd all be long dead," Kay said. She gazed off into the distance, as if struggling to find the right words. "What it is . . . was . . . is something else. Not merely impossible, but also inconceivable. Yes, it uses Destroyer nanotech, but a weakened, almost crippled version. Let me explain what I found when I examined the remains of the monster. Ben did such an amazing job that there was almost nothing left of the body after the nanophage weapon he used had done its work. Fortunately, a tentacle had grabbed him round the ankle which he immediately cut through. That provided the only remaining sample of the original Destroyer nanotech from the monster—or Transcendent, as it called itself."

"Does the name mean anything to you, or to Pandora?" Ben queried.

"Not really, except it might tie in with the reference it made to 'Nanotech from the gods'. I'll come back to that subject later, because it could also give us another clue about what's going on. But let me finish telling you about how this thing was put together. The nanotech which made up the bulk of its body was completely destroyed by the nanophage, but one vital component remained intact. A human brain."

Jim jerked forward, his eyes wide in horror. "What! You mean . . . it was some sort of human and nanotech hybrid?"

"Exactly so. Which is another point of similarity with the Destroyers. At some point in their development, they became organic/nanotech hybrids. Not using human brains, of course.

They started to farm the brains of the alien species they conquered, in an attempt to boost their capabilities. And it worked. They became even more powerful. But there was a sting in the tail. Using brains from different species triggered a divergence between the Destroyers.

"Previously, they had been united in their drive to eliminate all organic life from the galaxy. This divergence meant they split into different factions, each corresponding to the species used to provide the organic brains. Which led to a civil war. Ironically, that was the only reason the Progenitors managed survive this long, as the Destroyers turned away to seek out and kill their own kind. Several of the Destroyer factions were wiped out, and today there are only two left. They hide from each other, but have each renewed the war against the Progenitors.

"What is most strange, therefore, is this pseudo-Destroyer, built with crippled nanotech and a human brain. That's what I find inconceivable. It's difficult to imagine the Destroyers ever allowing the creation of a hybrid using a brain from a different species to their own. It would inevitably lead to the rise of another competitive faction. They are most careful to cultivate the single organic species from which they harvest the brains they use when producing new hybrids. But they kill all other organic life."

Ben's weary head was starting to ache from the effort of trying to follow Kay's explanations, and work out the potential implications. "What I don't understand is where this technology came from. That Transcendent creature told me the gods spoke to them through the rift they created when they were trying to reproduce our quantum energy project. If these 'gods' are in fact the Destroyers, how were they able to make use of a rift in this part of space? I thought the Progenitors were generating an exclusion field to make this impossible?"

"Yet another mystery. Something else that should be impossible," Kay responded, looking down at her hands as she gathered her thoughts. "The exclusion field will block the transmission of any massive object or coherent energy through a quantum rift from a fast universe. The slow universes are irrelevant, as it would take the Destroyers longer to travel to the corresponding rift location than it would in our own universe.

"However, it might still be possible to design a very low-speed signaling system using quantum tunneling. Something like Morse code, with the same limitations of very low bandwidth. To be honest, the Progenitors didn't think it worthwhile to test such possibilities. What use could it be?

"But if that is the case, it might explain what is going on. Maybe the Destroyers are slowly passing a minimal amount of information about their technology to whoever they found on the other side of the rift when it appeared. This would also mean the Destroyers now know we are here, and they would certainly want to do everything they can to eliminate us."

Ben frowned as he tried to remember details of a conversation he'd had only a few hours ago. "The Transcendent seemed to think they were in communication with gods, and they were somehow worthy to join them, unlike us poor organics. So these gods are the same as the Destroyers?"

Kay nodded. "Ah, yes, the 'god thing'. The Destroyers allow the organic species they farm for their brains to believe they are God's chosen, and only the most pure, the most faithful of them are worthy to ascend into Heaven to sit with their Gods. By the time the poor creatures find out what it involves, it's too late. I'd guess that what this so-called Transcendent is talking about is just another version of that belief system, designed to convince whoever they're in contact with through the rift they've built to follow their instructions.

"And here's another guess—we can be sure the Destroyers are not yet aware of our Progenitor capabilities. I imagine, therefore, they're providing their new acolytes with a level of nanotech barely advanced enough to allow them to defeat the species of primitive organics—that's us—inhabiting this system. Naturally, once these hybrids have carried out their mission, I expect the Destroyers would kill them off. Perhaps by giving them booby-trapped nanotech. They certainly wouldn't tolerate the development of a separate faction."

"There's one thing I really don't understand—who exactly are the Destroyers talking to?" Frank queried, shaking his head in puzzlement. "That monster spoke about the destruction of all organics. But surely the technology stolen from our quantum energy project was utilized by the Section or their agents, which I suppose led to their contact with the Destroyers through a quantum rift. I assume these people are still human, so how can they be working for the destruction of all organics? Or did the Destroyers transmit some sort of evil AI, in the same way as Pandora, which has now taken over?"

"No. That simply would not be possible," Kay replied emphatically. "They could transmit only a tiny amount of data. It would be analogous to a scribbled diagram on a scrap of paper. Whoever receives this limited information would still have to interpret and build whatever was described."

Jim leaned forward, tapping the table to catch Kay's attention. "But the Progenitors were able to send Pandora, a very advanced AI, through the quantum rift we created. If the Section are using the same technology to create a rift for their quantum energy project, why can't the Destroyers do the same? Surely the amount of data required would be far greater than would fit on a scrap of paper."

"That's because the Progenitors control the exclusion engine," Kay replied, clearly relieved to move the subject away from the Destroyers. "The engine enables them to block any rift that forms within its sphere of operation. It's rather like drowning out a signal by generating a vast amount of random noise. This disrupts the rift, which disrupts anything that tries to pass through. If a massive object tries to cross through, the part of the mass which touches the rift is converted directly into energy, which is very bad news if it happens to be you.

"You would have a similar problem for a coherent signal carrying data. The signal gets chopped to pieces, so only random noise can be detected from the other side of the rift. And most of the energy is just reflected. There is a simple way to get around this, however, if you have control of the exclusion engine. The random noise is not truly random, it's pseudo-random. That means the Progenitors can send coherent data in packets by synchronizing the transmission to the pseudo-random sequence. The data rate is still somewhat limited, however, and this still wouldn't work for any massive object. The only way to get a solid object though a rift is to switch off the engine for long enough to allow its passage."

"So can't the Destroyers somehow use the same technique?" Ben asked.

"That is fundamentally impossible since they have no access to the exclusion engine. If they had such a capability, they would have already used it and the Progenitors would now all be dead. It's the only way they have of keeping the Destroyers at bay."

Frank rubbed his face and sighed. "So who do you think these new people—or things—who are trying to destroy us are, Kay? Because I must admit I'm quite baffled."

"We simply don't have sufficient data at this point to answer that question, Dad."

Frank looked over to Ben. "What do you think? You were closer to one of these monsters than any of us. You even appeared to be able to manipulate it and send it off the deep end. How the hell did you do that, by the way?"

"The people I played poker with at college helped a lot," he replied with a faint smile, recalling a now far-off time when life was a whole lot simpler. "The way to win big was to figure out what their weak points were, then use the information to mess with their heads. Of course, you have to be prepared to lose big too. I had to try to get inside the Transcendent's head and find its hot buttons. Pandora's upgrades to my SmartBelt helped a lot. I could read and analyze her every reaction.

"That's also why I kept playing the fool, the same way I did when playing poker with Jason. If I can get the other player to underestimate me, I'll be seen as less of a threat. But it certainly didn't react in any way I expected. It was quite inhuman, yet far too emotional. I just had to trust my gut instinct—plus a little help from the body language analysis routines built in to my SmartBelt—on how to deal with it. Whatever it is, it appears to combine the worst aspects of the mind of a human and an AI. So calling it a hybrid seems quite appropriate—a psychologically unstable hybrid, in fact."

Kay studied Ben curiously. "I'd like to learn more about this gut instinct of yours, Ben. It seems to work amazingly well. You asked me to produce a set of special nanophage bullets for that new blaster system of yours built into the air supply of your decompression pack. You also had the idea to reconfigure the Initiator material to target Destroyer nanotech. What made you think you'd be needing any of that?"

"Well, of course, I didn't. Again, I just put myself in the heads of the bad guys. Whoever they are, they'd just been handed some fancy new nanotech from the Destroyers to build this binary weapon to wipe out the Habitat's population. I felt it was unlikely they would just stop there. What else they might have done with the technology, I had no idea. I only wanted to be prepared for anything that came up and cover any possible threat.

"I certainly wasn't expecting what we did encounter. Not in my wildest dreams. On the other hand, if it turned out they'd made no other use of the Destroyer nanotech, then all Pandora had to do was to render the Initiator harmless, and my standard Golem-blaster rounds would have been more than adequate to finish the job."

"Yes, that was very interesting, when the Transcendent started spraying the Initiator around," Frank said. "What did Pandora do to the stuff? Was it more of the nanophage? Is that what killed it?"

"Not exactly," Kay replied. "The delivery system for the Initiator, the tiny nanotech mites, were built from Destroyer nanotech themselves, so they would have been destroyed by a pure nanophage. Pandora had only a limited amount of time to modify the entire bulk of the material. She also had to be careful not to make it obvious the Initiator material had been changed, and the mites reprogrammed. Fortunately, the active component was concealed, packaged in those tiny mites, injected like a venom once they burrowed into their target. But unlike a nanophage, the venom doesn't carry on reproducing.

"Perhaps, given enough time, and a sufficiently large dose, the Transcendent might have been killed. I can't be certain. The effect on the creature was quite spectacular, though. I imagine it was like being attacked by thousands of fire ants. Ben just needed enough of a distraction to shoot it with the nanophage bullets. That's what killed it."

"Apart from everyone getting some well-needed rest, is there anything else we need to worry about urgently today?" Frank queried. "I'll ask Kay, who doesn't seem to need her beauty sleep any more, to keep a watching brief in case of any more unexpected developments. I also need to figure out how we can improve and extend our surveillance systems and security measures in the Habitat at every level. It looks like the only thing that saved us—yet again—is the ignorance of our opponents about our true capabilities. Otherwise, we wouldn't even have detected their operation.

"I was very upset to discover our quantum energy technology had been stolen so long ago, even before Pandora's arrival. Worse still, we knew nothing about it. We need to figure out how that happened. We can't afford to let any more of our secrets leak out. As Ben might put it, Pandora's existence is our 'ace in the hole'. If these Transcendents ever find out about her, it would stack the odds against us very heavily."

Frank got up from his chair and looked around at the tired faces around the table. Some people were struggling even to keep awake. "We've accomplished miracles over the last 48 hours, and I'm proud of you all. The people of the Habitat owe you their lives. Now we should get some well-earned rest. So, if we have no other immediate business, I suggest we meet here again at the same time tomorrow. The most important issue we still have to address is to figure out exactly who —or what—we are up against. I'm sure with fresh minds, we can come up with some great ideas on where we go from here.

"I've also arranged for Bernt Sogaard and his daughter Mel to come in before the meeting and talk about what they know.

Perhaps they'll bring some new information, or at least a fresh perspective to our discussions. God knows we need it."

Ben was surprised at how frail Bernt Sogaard appeared as he shuffled through the door, supported on his daughter's arm. Bernt hadn't looked well when they escaped from the DGS building, but he had expected him to look better after a couple of nights' sleep, not to mention his relief at the knowledge that his wife was now safe. Only Frank and Jim sat with Ben in the little windowless meeting room. Frank was now—understandably, in the circumstances—getting paranoid about security, and had made it clear that they should reveal as little as possible to the Sogaards at this meeting, including details of the full membership of their core group.

"Welcome, Director Sogaard," said Frank, smiling as he stood up to shake his hand. "You too, Ms. Sogaard. Please take a seat." He indicated the chairs in front of the small coffee table.

"Chairman Adler, may I assume that, as we're still alive, the threat to the people of the Habitat has been averted?" Bernt's thin voice sounded even fainter than Ben remembered from their last encounter.

"Yes, thankfully we are no longer in danger—at least not from that particular group," Frank replied, smiling reassuringly. "The threat has been eliminated. And I can tell you that without the information you gave us, we would have had little chance of success. Indeed, we would have known nothing about the nature of the threat until it was too late. Every person in the Habitat owes you their lives."

"I only wish I could take some small credit for your success, Mr. Chairman," Bernt replied, shaking his head. "But I'm perfectly well aware if it had been left to me alone, then we would all be dead by now. Only the fact that Mr. Hamilton somehow—and that is the thing which baffles me the most—was able to penetrate the security of our systems in the Asteroid Bar so easily made any of this possible. He was also the one who by some . . . magical process, which again baffles me, managed to free me from the DGS building. That allowed us to unlock the encrypted files containing the information on Project Harvest. I take it these files were useful to you?"

"Yes, Director—"

"Please, Mr. Chairman, I no longer hold that title. I'm no longer Director of anything. Just plain Bernt will be more than adequate—"

Jim cut in. "Wait a minute, Bernt. It's a long time ago, I know, but I seem to remember we crossed paths when you were presenting your doctoral thesis. In fact, I even recall that I sat as a member of the committee for your doctoral examination. You presented an excellent thesis, and you were awarded your doctorate. So you are at the very least due the title of Doctor."

Bernt attempted a smile. "It is most kind of you to remember, Professor Adler. But . . . well, as you wish."

"So then, Dr. Sogaard," Frank continued briskly. "The information you collected was extremely helpful, not just in terms of this single attack, but it also allowed us a better understanding of the deadly threat we continue to face. And following her recent escape, your wife has given us yet more data on the workings of the Section."

"Yes, my wife! I can't begin to tell you how grateful I am, Mr. Chairman. I never expected to speak to Helga again." Bernt put his hand up to his face and turned away, visibly distraught as he choked back his tears. Mel put her arm around his shoulders and pulled him towards her, patting his back.

Frank exchanged an embarrassed glance with Jim before continuing. "I can assure you, Dr. Sogaard, that as soon as we understood the true situation, we acted immediately. Initially, I'm afraid that we had assumed that you and your family were working as undercover agents for the Section. Although I'm still a little puzzled why you didn't approach us with your information earlier."

Bernt wiped his eyes, then studied his hands, avoiding Frank's gaze. "Why, Mr. Chairman? Why? I used to ask myself that same question over and over until I came to realize that I knew the answer all along. I had many good reasons and glib explanations for my lack of action, but the truth is quite simple—I'm a coward."

"Daddy, no! That's not true," Mel reacted in a shocked voice. "Mother was effectively held hostage back on Earth. If they had any reason to suspect your loyalty, she would have been the first to suffer. And by the time you realized the gravity of the threat to the Habitat, you were under house arrest."

"I'd like to think that was true, but I know in my heart it is not," Bernt whispered, shaking his head again. "When I first joined the AICB, I truly believed in my mission to keep the people safe. I advanced rapidly within the organization. I was good at my job, everyone liked me. Then, as I rose to higher positions with greater responsibility, I began to notice strange things happening, but I was always willing to look the other way. I understood I had to 'go along to get along'.

"So I watched the monster grow into what we now call the Section, little piece by little piece over many years, always telling myself 'now is not the time—but soon'. Until finally 'soon' was too late. The one action in which I took some small pride was getting my daughter to safety on Ceres, away from those dark forces.

Or so I thought. It turned out I was wrong even about that. If it hadn't been for Mr. Hamilton, everyone in the Habitat would be dead by now. And I wasn't even capable of warning Mr. Hamilton of Oscar's plan to kill him. So it's no thanks to me we survived. My darling Helga is now safe back on Earth, yet I did nothing to help her."

"Dr. Sogaard, I'm sure you are far too critical of yourself," Frank responded, shaking his head as he tried to find a way to get the discussion back on track. "You did everything you could, and we would never have succeeded without your contribution. You spent years fighting this evil. You just chose to fight it from the inside, by documenting its actions. Now think of the future. Imagine how valuable your knowledge and expertize will be as we continue to battle these monsters. We need to take the fight to Earth. You can still play a valuable part—"

"No, Mr. Chairman. I appreciate your kind words, but my time is done," Bernt replied, his voice firmer as he looked Frank in the eye. "It is too late for me. Helga, on the other hand, is eager to continue the battle. And she knows everything I could tell you. I merely served as a channel for the material that she stole from the Section. She tells me she wants to continue her work with some people she calls the Resistance. As for me, I stopped my life extension treatment some time ago, so I don't really expect to be around much longer—"

"Daddy, let's talk about this later. You need to get some rest." Mel turned to Frank, a desperate appeal in her eyes. "I'm sorry, but I need to spend some more time with my father. Perhaps we could speak again later?"

Ben looked across the table at Frank and Jim, who were deep in discussion over the abortive interview with Bernt Sogaard. Bernt's words had shocked him to his core. In particular, his phrase 'go along to get along' had struck a nerve. And Bernt was a stark example of where that mindset could lead.

As Ben had tried to understand Bernt's thinking, it had made him realize he'd spent most of his life drifting from situation to situation, always trying to fit in. Maybe that was the difference; Bernt had found at the AICB a place where he felt he belonged. Ben had never had that feeling. He'd always been the outsider.

Even then, it was only when people started trying to kill him that he had been galvanized into action. Nobody had ever tried to kill Bernt. While Bernt had been risking his life secretly collecting information on the crimes of Section, Ben had been conspiring with Oscar to kidnap Frank and Jim. So who should be judged the most guilty?

Yasmin and Chas entered and took their seats. Frank turned from Jim to address the full group gathered around the table. "Now we're all here, let me give you an update on our meeting with Bernt Sogaard. I can't say it went well. Unfortunately, he appears to have suffered some sort of breakdown, no doubt brought about by the extreme stress of his situation, having to conceal his espionage activities from the DGS and the Section over several years.

"He was in an isolated position over that period, fearful not only for his own safety on a daily basis, but that of his wife and daughter too. He will receive every support possible from our medical services, and I've also asked Jim to look in on him. They have some history together in their early days, from their common studies in AI systems design—"

Ben caught Frank's eye. "If you don't mind, sir, I'd also like to tag along with Professor Adler when he's visiting with Dr. Sogaard. I also believe he's being much too harsh on himself, and I'd like to tell him so."

"Yes, of course, Ben, if you think you can help," Frank replied with a nod. "That's very thoughtful of you. However, in the short term we don't expect him to be able to shed any further light on the Section's operational and logistical structure. On a more positive note, Yasmin has some good news from Greeley. Yasmin?"

"Very good news indeed, Frank. Sogaard's wife, Helga, is turning out to be a gold mine of information. It seems she has teamed up with Scanner, one of our key operatives there, and they're making rapid progress in tracking down and tapping into the dark network that the Section has been using to communicate between its secret bases, which appear to have no direct connection with the DGS systems.

"Now she no longer has to fear for her personal safety, she can act more aggressively to penetrate their systems. Best of all, she was directly responsible for the design of many of the security measures and encryption algorithms used for their secure communications. She was even able to give Scanner access to a whole bunch of backdoors she secretly built in to their systems.

"To give you one very pertinent example: she designed the quantum-encrypted comms link which allowed Vasquez to signal the nuclear-tipped Badger he launched from the New Dawn. It turns out that she deliberately introduced the design flaw in the system, which made it so easy for Pandora to hack it. She never knew that they would use it in this way—but we probably have her to thank, at least indirectly, for the fact that the Habitat wasn't blown up."

"That's most interesting, sir," Ben said, trying to hold back a smile. He nodded at Kay. "I remember that Pandora was a little surprised how easy it was for her to penetrate a quantum-encrypted link to disable the Badger. She put it down to human stupidity. I'm glad to hear that it resulted from human ingenuity after all."

Kay pretended to ignore him.

Frank looked down at his notes, a faint smile on his lips. "Now, there are still two short-term issues to address, most notably the possibility of sleeper agents for the Section hidden away in the Habitat. The question is, how can we know if they really exist or not, and identify them if they do?"

"I think I can answer that, Dad," Kay replied. "Remember that everyone is still infected with the Precursor agent? All except the sleeper agents?"

"Didn't we remove that from the water supply?"

"Yes, but it's still in our bodies. It was specifically designed to have a very long residence time once it gets into human tissue. What I want to do is release a modified version of the Initiator—"

Frank's eyes widened in alarm. "Whoa! That sounds dangerous—"

"Not at all Dad, I promise you. But if you have any worries, though, we can test it on Ben first. He loves doing dangerous stuff," she said, grinning in his direction.

Ben shook his head and kept a straight face. "Thank you, Kay, but I can assure you, the stories of my legendary heroism are greatly exaggerated."

"Before we ask Ben to volunteer to risk his life yet again, why don't you explain to me how this is supposed to work," enquired Frank with a slight frown.

"It's a fairly simple idea, Dad. The modified Initiator will hook up with the Precursor in our bodies—and immediately neutralize it. Better still, the combined material will be rapidly eliminated from our bodies, which gets it cleaned it out as well."

"Well, OK. But how does that help us find the sleepers?"

"There's only one thing we can be sure about; the sleepers won't have the Precursor in their bodies. That's unfortunate for them, because my modified Initiator, if not neutralized by the Precursor, will cause a highly visible and painful rash all over their bodies as it works its way out through their skin.

"All you need to do is announce the outbreak of a serious virus infection in the Habitat. We put anyone showing symptoms into isolation immediately. I'll be scanning for it too, and it will be extremely obvious. They probably won't even suspect what's happening. We'll round them up in no time."

"Won't people get a little worried when they find nanotech mites crawling all over them?" Ben queried.

"We don't need the mites. We can release it into the air. The mites were only needed to get around our filtration and biosecurity systems."

"So how long will this take?" Frank asked.

"A day or two to produce a sufficient quantity of the modified Initiator, plus a couple more days to spread throughout the Habitat and be fully absorbed. If we start now, we should be able to see the sleepers scratching by the end of the week. Oh, and we may even get a special bonus. I'm hoping we'll find someone scratching down in the physics lab. It may be that whoever leaked the information on the quantum energy project remained behind as a sleeper agent."

"I can see a further possible advantage to this plan, if we can make it work," Ben added. "If we can identify all the sleeper agents in the Habitat, rather than rounding them up, we can let them roam free but watch them closely. I'm sure we can think of some fake information to feed them from time to time. You never know when that might be useful."

Frank's brow furrowed in concentration. "OK. I can see it's a great idea, but let me think about it. I want to be as sure as possible that the risk to our people is zero. Chas—you know a lot more biology than me. Would you mind taking a look at this idea of Kay's? See if you can figure out any downside."

"It sounds most ingenious, but I can understand your concern, Frank," Chas replied. "I'll go over it with her and I'll get back to you."

"Thank you, Chas," Frank said, before turning back to address the group. "My other urgent problem is to figure out what sort of story we put out to cover the failure of the attack on the Habitat. I don't believe we can just ignore it. The bad guys—and it worries me we still don't have a better name for whoever or whatever we're facing—will find out soon enough that their attack has failed.

"We don't want to raise the slightest suspicion of our true capabilities. So we need a convincing explanation of how we poor, weak humans managed to discover their plot and defeat one of their shiny new Transcendents plus a big bunch of her minions."

Ben waited for somebody to speak. He still felt a little intimidated by the intellectual horsepower assembled round the table. And his idea could hardly be described as 'intellectual'. *What the hell*, he thought, seeing that no one else was willing to break the silence. "I'm sorry to drag the game of poker back into our discussions yet again, but even the most skillful player can lose a game occasionally, through sheer bad luck. That's how I would frame the story. A further advantage of such an approach is that it's more likely to be believed. It's always far comfortable to imagine your failure was due to bad luck, rather than accept that a cleverer opponent outplayed you."

"OK then, but how did we get lucky?" Frank enquired, looking puzzled.

"We didn't. The Transcendent was just unlucky. Really unlucky, in fact, when a massive icequake in the cavern destroyed the entire PharmAgro installation before they had completed the production of the Initiator. Sadly, there were no survivors."

Frank's face lit up as he quickly saw the implications of such a story. "Oh, yes, I like that. It works really well, in fact. We would be forced to close off all access to the cavern on safety grounds, too."

"We could also announce that the suspected cause was the heat radiated from the processing plant, which exceeded safe levels," Ben added. "That would also explain why we're making more frequent safety checks of all cavern installations in the future. I'll be happy to lend you my clipboard."

"Do you think they'd believe the story?" Kay queried.

"We don't really care," Ben shrugged. "But we could easily set things up so the story would appear to check out if anyone came sniffing round. At the very least, it would be more than enough to create uncertainty, and what other explanation will they have?"

"That sounds like an excellent plan to me," Frank said with a broad smile in Ben's direction. "Yasmin, you're the most devious person I know, and you have excellent media contacts. Plus, you know the layout of the caverns better than anyone else. Would you mind taking charge of this little project?"

"Since you ask me so nicely, Frank, how can I refuse?" she replied, putting a finger to her pursed lips in an exaggerated attempt to look cute.

"Is everyone else just as happy with the jobs they have?" asked Frank as he got up from his chair. "Or would anyone like to volunteer for more responsibilities? No? Then I suggest we make a start. The last shuttle for Earth in the current launch window left yesterday. The final shuttle arrival is next week. After that, nothing moves for the next fifteen months."

He looked around the room, his face now grim, his tone somber. "That's all the time we have before we face these monsters again. Then we must be ready to throw off our pretense of weakness. We must destroy these evil creatures with unexpected and overwhelming power, for if we fail, we risk the future of humanity itself."

EPILOGUE

BEN LOOKED over the edge of the Penthouse terrace at the lights illuminating the streets below. Overhead, the sky was fading to an inky blackness, and a few of the brighter stars were now visible. One star, much brighter than the others, was no star at all, but the planet Jupiter, gleaming down on the Habitat like a tiny golden lantern. *How small and insignificant we are*, he thought.

How simple everything had seemed when he was a young boy, staring up at the heavens, dreaming of traveling from star to star. What new worlds he might discover, wandering the universe and leaving behind all the horrors stalking the Earth. Now, worse horrors than he could ever have imagined were traveling from the stars to kill him. Him and everyone he cared about. Even his sister, who would be just another 'organic' to these monsters. Not a dream come true, but a nightmare made flesh. He shook his head and sighed.

"Ben? Am I disturbing you?"

Kay was standing next to him, leaning on the rail topping the low wall, looking at him quizzically.

"What? No, not at all. Just admiring the view."

"You seemed to be looking for something up in the sky. Did you find it?"

"To be honest, Kay, I'm more worried about it finding me."

QUANTUM SECRETS

Book 2 of the Quantum Ascension
(Sneak Preview)

CHAPTER 1

Alessia looked out across the dazzling turquoise blue sea, then at the small fishing boats tied up at the jetty. This had become one of her few pleasures: to sit at a table in this tiny beach-front restaurant, eating freshly caught fish and drinking the local wine. Until she had arrived here, she had no idea such simple delights existed. Even as a privileged member of the Veronese Family in the Wind River Citadel, such pleasures were unheard of. The citadel was hundreds of miles from the ocean, and even then, she doubted that anyone would risk fishing along a coast infested by warmechs.

Yet here she was safe. Bruno had tried to explain why, but somehow his words didn't ring true. They'd been married less than a year, and he'd told her that living on this island would be like an extended honeymoon. That hadn't worked out too well, either. He'd been working around the clock from the first day they'd arrived. Every single day. Every single fucking day. No, she corrected herself. There were very few *fucking days* anymore.

CHAPTER 1

So here she was, lunching by herself—again. It seemed that Bruno's position as Governor was far too important to allow anyone to share a table with her. *My Lady*, they called her. She had a driver to ferry her around, who made sure no one got anywhere near. She had felt isolated in Wind River, always the odd one out, never quite fitting in. People not meeting her gaze when she asked, "Why do I look so different to mom and dad?" and "Why do people look at me like that?"

But here, people didn't look at her at all, as if they were afraid of her. Carlos, the manager of this little restaurant, was the only person with whom she'd exchanged more than a few words, apart from the servants up at the castle. At least he seemed friendly, even when he called her *my Lady*. Would he be willing to help her? She always left a large tip every time she ate here. Or would he turn out to be just as fearful as all the others?

If only she'd had time to contact the doctor before they left, but everything had happened so quickly. It had taken her months to find someone willing to test the DNA samples she'd collected from her parents. Then, before she had a chance to pick up the results, Bruno told her he'd been selected for a 'Special Assignment'. Less than a week later, they arrived on this jewel of an island half a world away from the stark mountains of Wind River. And thousands of miles away from the answer she needed to her most heartfelt question—*who am I?*

"Would you care for more wine, my Lady?" Carlos hovered at her side, with a warm smile to match his friendly gaze.

For a moment she felt lost for words, her mouth suddenly dry with apprehension. But if she didn't trust him, who else was there? "Thank you, Carlos, but . . . no, I think I've had enough wine. A coffee, please. And . . ."

"Yes, my Lady?"

CHAPTER 1

Her words came gushing out. "Carlos, I need a favor. Quite a big favor, actually. I need to call someone off-island, without anyone else knowing about it. It's a personal matter. Very personal. But if you don't feel you can help, I'll quite understand—"

"I'd be only too happy to be of assistance, my Lady," he replied, still smiling, his hand placed over his heart as he inclined his head towards her. "How could anyone say no to such beautiful eyes?"

He was flirting with her again. She liked that, and it never went beyond the point where she might feel uncomfortable. Yes, she felt sure she could trust him. "I need to contact someone in Wind River, but I don't want anyone to know. Can you get me a secure connection for my U-Set from here?"

"Of course, my Lady. It will be set up by the time I bring your coffee."

She closed her eyes and allowed the tension to drain from her body as she slowly exhaled. Could it really be that simple? She wasn't actually doing anything wrong, she told herself. It seemed so silly that no one was allowed to call off-island. For security reasons, Bruno had told her. Well, she wasn't planning to give away any secrets. She would have asked him for help to contact the doctor, but she knew he didn't approve of the questions she was asking about her background. In fact, he had done his best to discourage her, just like all the others.

She peered round to look at her driver, who was perched on an upturned boat on the beach, throwing stones into the water, and occasionally looking over his shoulder to check on her. She needed to be out of sight when she made the call, but it wouldn't take more than five minutes, surely? Just enough time for a bathroom break, then. No one would know except Carlos, and she'd make sure to give him an extra-large tip before she left.

She sat in the back of the large all-terrain vehicle as it bumped along the rough roads, trying to blink back her tears, desperate to hide her reaction to Dr. Walters's words. She forced herself to look out at the vast expanse of white sheeting covering the hydroponic growing areas. A group of laborers actually kneeled by the side of the road as she passed. Who did they think she was? Or was the vehicle itself the object of their veneration?

Even after six months, she understood very little about what was happening here. She understood very little about anything, she realized. She didn't even know who she was. No match between the first sample and the other two, the doctor had said. So everyone she knew was lying to her. She had no family. No one she could confide in. Not even her husband, who did nothing but work all day and sleep all night. They didn't even eat together any more.

Bruno was no longer the man she had met in Wind River and come to love. Good-looking, mature yet fun loving, he'd been seen as one of the rising stars of the Da Silva Family. And she'd thought she'd caught that star until they arrived here and her star had faded and fallen to earth. *I don't know if he even still loves me*, she thought bitterly, as the tears welled up again in her eyes.

By the time her eyes had cleared, the vehicle had started up the steeply winding road through the olive groves to the newly restored ramparts of the old castle. *Well, I'll know if he loves me soon enough. I'll tell him my news and see how he reacts.*

CHAPTER 1

Alessia's tears had given way to anger by the time she swept through the main entrance, crossing the great hallway, before striding down the corridor leading to the rear of the castle. Her heels clacked briskly on the marble tiles as she emerged onto the wide balcony overlooking the bay far below. Where was everyone?

She realized she had not seen a single servant or staff member crossing her path or scuttling down the side corridors. *Well, at least I know where Bruno will be.* In his office, working away, always working, planning and building the roads and the buildings and the hydroponic installations and the water supplies and the power stations and everything else needed—for what? Where were all the people supposed to come from?

It dawned on her that she'd never thought seriously about what they were doing here. *That's Bruno's fault too; he's always kept me in the dark. He's never even tried to let me help him. Well, that's all going to change, starting now.* Turning right, she walked around the curve of the tall windows, towards the glass doors at the far end of the balcony leading to his office. She slowed, frowning, as she noticed a DGS goon standing by the door, watching her impassively as she approached.

She knew what he was, even if he didn't wear a formal uniform. They all dressed the same. But they usually kept to their own part of the building. Did Bruno have some important visitor in his office? What was going on? She continued towards the door but then jumped back, startled, when the man put his arm across the doorway to bar her entrance.

"I'm sorry, Ma'am, but the Governor is in a meeting and can't be disturbed," he growled, his eyes fixed upon her like a predator sizing up potential prey. "Who are you?"

"What? I'm his wife! Don't you know me?"

"Just a moment, Ma'am," he replied, flicking his eyes up to his U-Set. "I'm sorry, Mrs. Da Silva. You can go right in."

She walked into the office and took in the familiar untidy jumble. The walls were covered with detailed maps of parts of the island and diagrams of several building sites. A man was sitting at the desk, facing her husband.

"Ah, Mrs. Da Silva. How very convenient. We were just talking about you," said the bald, middle-aged man coolly. She knew they had been introduced when she and Bruno had first arrived on the island, but she'd not run into him since then. What was the name? Mayer? No—Kaya, Erkal Kaya, the DGS Director on the island. Why was he here?

"Bruno? What's going on here? What does this man mean by—"

Her husband had not even turned to greet her as she entered, she realized, his head cradled in his hands, his face drained of all color. Now he raised his eyes, but not towards her. He gave Erkal an anguished look, and said in a pleading voice, "Erkal, please, I beg you. This was just a foolish action by a silly young girl. She had no idea—"

"That may be so, Bruno, but there are issues involved here which have come to the attention of people at the highest level—"

If there was one thing Alessia hated more than anything else, it was being ignored. She screamed in frustration. "What the hell are you talking about? Who is this 'silly young girl', Bruno? Who are you talking about?"

Erkal turned, his beady eyes fixing her with a cold gaze. "We are talking about a most grave matter, Mrs. Da Silva. You made a call to a person in Wind River earlier today, did you not?"

CHAPTER 1

She felt herself blush so fiercely that she knew a denial would sound ridiculous. "Well, yes," she replied, looking down and shuffling her feet. "Yes, I did. But all I was doing—"

"We know exactly what you were doing, Mrs. Da Silva," he interrupted, his voice gaining a sharp edge as he thrust a stubby finger in her direction. "Some months ago, you provided a set of samples to a person of interest to us, a Dr. Walters, who we believe has contacts with the so-called Resistance in Wind River. You then contacted him again today to confirm the nature of these samples. Is that correct?"

"The Resistance?" she replied, putting her hand up to her mouth as her eyes widened in shock. "I don't know anything about that. Really, I don't. But I told him nothing. Nothing at all. I didn't tell him my name or where I got the samples. And there's no way he could know my current location here on the island. I only wanted to find out the results of the tests."

"And what exactly did you want to know, Mrs. Da Silva?"

"What? What did I want to know?" The tears were now welling up in her eyes. She wanted to scream again, but could only whimper, "I wanted to know who I was. Who I am. Is that so wrong?"

"As a matter of fact, Mrs. Da Silva, I'm afraid it is. Very wrong. Your true identity is a state secret. A state secret that you have now passed on to a contact of the Resistance."

Alessia's mouth dropped open as she tried to make sense of his words. "That's just . . . crazy. Who am I? How can that be a secret? And anyway, there's no way for the doctor to know who I am. I was really careful. I'm sure—"

"Which is exactly what makes you so dangerous, Mrs. Da Silva. You're always so sure. You're so sure the rules don't apply to you. You're so sure no one can work out who you are from the many clues you've scattered along your path. I expect you were even sure that no one could possibly find out about your secret conversation with Dr. Walters less than an hour ago."

Erkal turned back to face her husband and shook his head. "I'm sorry, Bruno, but I'm afraid I am left with no alternative but to take her into protective custody."

"Protective . . . what? Bruno?" Alessia looked back at her husband, her eyes wide in dismay. He sat hunched and motionless, his face a picture of despair, seemingly afraid even to glance in her direction. "What's happening? Tell him he can't do this. Bruno!"

CHAPTER 2

"Ouch! That's gotta hurt!"

Master Sergeant Jan Kaminski shook his head and winced as he glanced across at Ben. Kaminski's wide grin, however, betrayed how little sympathy he really felt for the poor trainee who was now tumbling helplessly in zero-G after slamming headfirst into the edge of the tunnel entrance he'd failed to navigate.

Ben had been shocked at how many well-qualified candidates came running to sign up for the Earth Liberation Force training program once the word got out. And that was before any mention of life extension, never mind age reversal. In retrospect, it turned out to be less surprising. Many of these people were self-selecting.

They were all experienced warriors. They'd all served in the DGS security forces for twenty or thirty years, most with extensive experience of fighting off the warmech attacks, day in day out. The fact that they'd survived at all was a recommendation. That so many had chosen to take early retirement to the Ceres Habitat usually meant that they were also the most disillusioned with what had become of the DGS over the past decade. And the few bad apples who turned up didn't get past the biometric 'sniff test' provided by his fancy new SmartBelt.

There were also a few gems like Kaminski. He'd spent thirty years in the field and survived. For relaxation, his hobby was to study the strategy, tactics, training and organization of special operations forces from the pre-Flare days. He'd been reading up on the subject almost all his life. After seeing his resume, Ben had put him in charge of recruitment and training. This left Ben with the very important job of keeping out of the way and gave him time to do some reading of his own.

He had to admit, without the ability of the AI sub-mind in his SmartBelt to research and analyze the available material, he would still be thrashing around in an endless morass of information overload. Frank had also been enormously helpful, effectively mentoring him in the management of large projects. He'd been working with Pandora too, designing larger and more efficient automated construction facilities. The first fruit of all this help and cooperation was the construction of the 'Trash Can' in less than a month.

The Trash Can was a roughly cylindrical structure in orbit around Ceres, which was where he was right now, watching Kaminski put the new recruits through their paces on their way to getting their astronaut certification. The recruits didn't call it the Trash Can, of course. Their most polite description was the 'Rat Run', which was the view they had of their training area from the inside. Ben had seen a video of an ant farm once. This looked very similar as he watched from the outside, except in 3-D and with all the extra fun of zero-G.

Most importantly, he now had the time to think about a strategy to recapture the citadels on Earth. He'd soon realized that the DGS would present little threat against a properly organized force. In fact, the more he studied the problem, the more he realized that the structure of the DGS was more akin to an ancient criminal society called the Mafia, rather than to any competent military organization.

This had puzzled him until Kaminski pointed out the historical record. The nature of warfare had progressed rapidly since the first use of armed drones in the asymmetric proxy wars which proliferated in the early 21st century. By the middle of the century, the conventional forces of the major powers were hunkered down in massive, centralized complexes, largely leaving the battlefield to their AI warmech creations.

In retrospect, it should have been no surprise when the members of every organized military force on the Earth were the first to die. Once the warmechs turned rogue, and were in possession of all the right codes, nothing could be easier than to infiltrate the bunkers and eat their way rapidly up their own chains of command. Only a few—largely private civilian—redoubts survived this initial onslaught.

Against the demoralized and disorganized opposition of the DGS, they would have little trouble capturing the citadels, once Kaminski's people were trained up. Plus control of the AIs was a game-changer. In fact, it should be a walkover, if only they didn't have to factor in the monsters. The limited number of people they could recruit and train for the Earth Liberation Force in the time available—several hundred, at best—determined their strategy.

So he'd agreed with Kaminski to use the special forces model from the late 20th century, before the automation of the battlefield had made such structures redundant. They simply didn't have the numbers to build a conventional field army, which would not have been appropriate in any case. Their objective was to assist in the liberation of the citadels, then return to Ceres, not occupy the ground.

They would drop infiltration teams into each citadel, with the task of arming, training and organizing the Resistance groups already established there. Kaminski would lead that force, although he wasn't aware of it yet. Now approaching sixty, he considered himself far too old to be leading troops in the field. *Won't he be surprised when finds out he'll be one of the first to receive the new age-reversal therapy?* Ben smiled at the thought. He would leave the surprise a little longer—he wanted Kaminski focused on his current training role for now.

That left Ben with the most difficult task: defeating the monsters, whatever they were. And 'whatever they were' was his biggest problem right now. He couldn't deploy the infiltration teams until he knew the size and nature of the threat they faced from these monsters. He'd recently read something, written 3000 years ago by a famous general which had struck a chord and made him realize just how important this was: *If you know the enemy and know yourself, you need not fear the results of a hundred battles.*

So first he needed intelligence. He had to find out what they were really up against, yet he had no way of finding out until he could get to Earth. But getting to Earth, even at the most optimistic estimate, would be four or five months away. Inevitably, retaking the citadels would have to be delayed many more months until he could get to Earth, get the information he needed, and return to brief the ELF teams.

Unless Pandora could help—but she'd been acting a little mysteriously lately. Every time he brought the subject up, she'd replied, "Why not ask Kay?" Well, he wasn't needed here, so maybe it was time to get back to the office and see what Kay has to say about the problem.

CHAPTER 2

"Carry on, Master Sergeant," he said, before pushing himself off in the direction of the shuttle bay. "I'm very impressed. I can see you don't need any help from me."

Ben had moved to a larger office, just below the Penthouse, with a panoramic view of the Habitat curving off into the distance. Not that he had much time to admire the scenery.

"It's quite a while since we last had a chat," Kay said, smiling at him as she perched on the corner of his desk. "I'm honored to get a slot in your schedule. You're a very busy man these days."

"Well, the only reason I have any spare time at all is that every time I give someone a job, they start doing it twice as well as I can. Or, as in the case of Master Sergeant Kaminski, about ten times better. So now I'm down to my last problem, which is why I called you. I'm hoping you'll have a solution so then I can go on vacation."

"What a good idea!" Kay giggled, clapping her hands together in approval. "Where would you like to go?"

"Earth would be good, for starters. I need to find out what those cute little Transcendents are up to, who they're working with, what their connection with the Section is, how many there are, where they're based, evaluate their capabilities, and check if their Destroyer pals have given them any upgrades recently—all simple stuff, really. Oh, and I'd like to do all this by next Tuesday. Then maybe head for a nice beach somewhere to chill out."

"Doesn't sound so difficult, Ben. What's stopping you from just heading off to Earth tomorrow?"

"Come on, Kay, you know exactly why. Basic orbital mechanics. Right now, Ceres and Earth are on opposite sides of the Sun, and the radiation flux in space would fry us on such a long trip. So we have to wait until we're near enough to Earth to able to make the trip safely, and that won't be for another year."

"So why not just go faster?"

"Now stop playing games, Kay," he said with a snort of exasperation. "You're just as aware of the problem as I am. So is there anything you—or Pandora—can do?"

"Why not humor me, Ben?" she responded. She hopped off the desk, then leaned forward across it, her eyes narrowed, her head tilted and propped up on one arm. "How about you talk to me instead of Pandora for a change? We haven't had a nice chat like this in a long time. Now remind me—what is your problem, exactly?"

Now what have I done? he thought, frowning. *Or is she up to something—again?*

"As you wish, Kay," he sighed. "To go faster, we'd need more powerful engines, but we can't carry enough fuel to keep more powerful engines going over that distance. Also, more powerful engines will be less efficient, requiring even more fuel. So we can't reduce the flight time.

"Plus we'd be passing close to the Sun, because it's currently sitting between us and the Earth, so the radiation flux would be a lot higher. Or, if we stay well clear of the Sun, that makes the distance even longer. And on such a long trip, there'd also be a good chance of a solar flare to crisp us up nicely. Is that clear enough for you?"

"Hmm, OK," she replied, pursing her lips in a mock-serious expression. "Now I see your problem. Let me think," She paced the floor, stroking her chin theatrically. Then she turned to face him with a faint smile. "So if you had a shiny new spaceship

CHAPTER 2

which could maintain a constant 1G acceleration for the whole trip, and was shielded from most of the solar and cosmic radiation, would that help?"

Ben blinked in disbelief. Could that really be possible? He ran the calculations in his head, only needing a small assist from his SmartBelt. "Then the launch window becomes irrelevant. You could make the journey any time you liked. At the moment, Ceres and Earth are near to the point of maximum separation, so assuming a constant 1G of thrust, we'd be looking at around five or six days, depending on how close you were willing to get to the Sun. Less than three days at the closest approach. Can you actually do that?"

She leaned forward across the desk again, her face grinning only a few inches from his. "Maybe. But it'll cost you."

I knew it. With Kay, there was always a cost. "OK. So what's your price?"

"You take me with you."

"Hold on." He frowned. "I thought you wanted to stay in the background?"

"Oh, I will, I promise. I'll just be mommy's little girl paying her a visit. I haven't seen her for ages. I could even introduce you to her as my new boyfriend. She'd like that," Kay said, putting on her best sweet-little-girl smile.

"Oh, but wait. That won't work, will it?" she continued, narrowing her eyes. Her smile vanished. "You're seeing that Sogaard woman from the Asteroid Bar, aren't you?"

The sudden change of the direction of the conversation left Ben stunned.

What was this all about? Was Kay jealous of Mel? Then things started to click into place. No, maybe not jealous, exactly. But who did Kay have to talk to? There was no one else in her own age group who was in on the big secret. Suddenly, Ben realized how desperately isolated she must feel. And he'd been too busy getting on top of his new responsibilities to spend much time with her over the last couple of months. Or even spare her a thought, he realized.

He'd been talking with Pandora on a daily basis, but that probably wasn't the same, from Kay's perspective. She had no major tasks he knew of to occupy her time since the Transcendent takedown three months ago. He'd hardly spoken to her since then. What little free time he'd been able to snatch, he'd been spending with Mel.

It had all started out so innocently, as he worked with Jim to restore Bernt Sogaard's shattered confidence. Mel had been so grateful and was very happy to show her appreciation on the few occasions he managed to find the time. He realized he might be treading on thin ice here. What should he say? This looked like a losing hand, however he played it. He had to fold.

"I'd be delighted to go to Earth with you and meet your mom, Kay, if that's what it takes. But you still haven't told me how we'll be getting there. How long would it take to build a ship like that? Can we even do it?"

"Hardly any time at all, Ben," she replied, breaking into a grin, clearly unable to keep a straight face any longer. "The ship is almost finished. That's what I've been working on over the last couple of months. I was planning to surprise you with it next week. Oh, but you might not like it. It's full of nasty alien technology. It's really quite scary what you can do with a big bucketful of magnetic monopoles, for example. So I don't suppose you'd want to see it. Or do you?"

GET YOUR FREE EBOOK

The A-Z Guide to the Quantum Ascension Universe

**Don't visit 25th Century Earth
without this handy guide!**

Still wondering what a SuperFlare is?
Want to know a bit more about the citadels?
How did the warmechs nearly wipe out humanity?
You will find the answers to these and
many other questions in this free 60 page book.

Download **Volume 1: Earth & Ceres**
from www.alexmbrandt.com/free-book

REVIEW REQUEST

Did you enjoy this book? Are you impatient to read the next in the series? Then there's one thing you can do right now to reduce the time it takes me to write the next book.

The more coffee I drink and the more reviews I get, the faster I write. So here's the deal: I'll supply the coffee, if you supply the reviews. How does that sound?

Seriously, I would be most grateful if you could take just a couple of minutes and leave a review on the Amazon page for this book. Thank you.

HOW TO BE PART OF THE FUTURE OF THE QUANTUM ASCENSION UNIVERSE

Want to follow Ben's future adventures? Get advance notice of my next book, **Quantum Secrets**? Or receive monthly updates on the Quantum Ascension series?

Maybe you'd like a sneak-peek at my next book cover or see an image of Kay's fancy new spaceship design in action?

Then visit my web site where you can find even more information about my vision for the Quantum Ascension Universe at: www.alexmbrandt.com

I also welcome feedback from my readers on the storyline/characters/technology - or indeed anything else to do with the Quantum Ascension Universe - including your likes and/or dislikes. So if you have any comments, or just want to throw rocks, drop me an email at: me@alexmbrandt.com

ABOUT THE AUTHOR

Alex M Brandt is the author of the Quantum Ascension series, a Galaxy-spanning saga of humanity's struggle to survive in the face of advanced AI and nanotech gone mad.

Alex lives halfway up a mountainside close to the rocky shores of the Mediterranean. When he's not writing, he's walking in the hills discovering old cities or sailing along the coast in the wake of Odysseus discovering new fish restaurants. He's a big fan of hard scifi with a dash of humor.

facebook.com/alex.brandt.96199

Printed in Great Britain
by Amazon